PRIMAS AND PREDATORS

ROSE GRAVESTONE

Dedication

To all those who like a male lead that doesn't ask for a second chance; he takes it.

Author's Note

Hello, lovely reader! Welcome to Primas and Predators, book two of the dark and sensual Greywood Elites Series. I am so excited to bring you this book. As ever, I've poured my heart and soul into it.

Please be advised that this book has some dark and triggering content within. If any of the following don't appeal to you, this book probably won't be for you.

- Dub-con.

- Mentions of past sexual trauma, including discussions of S/A on a child.

- Alpha-hole hero.

Ian is a character with questionable morals and is something approaching a sociopath, so only proceed if you like your characters *dark* morally grey.

CONTENTS

PROLOGUE, PART ONE

Ian Vargas, age eight

Whenever I'm bored or annoyed, which is always, I head to the same place. A twenty-minute walk from my house and into the nearby forest takes me directly to a footbridge that hangs over a pretty stream. Watching the water rush and hearing the birds and other animals sing and rustle around makes me feel calm in a way nothing else does. Not completing my newest Lego fort, or pulling an epic prank on my nanny, or even striking a match and watching it burn—one of my favorite things, since Mom and Dad *hate* when I do it.

After setting up a honey-and-wool spider trap for my nanny this morning, I figure it's best for me to stay out of her way. She'll discover it soon enough, curse me in all the languages she knows, and probably quit on the spot. That's what my last nanny did, anyways. Sometimes I wonder when Mom and Dad will realize that I don't need or want a nanny; it's why I make a point of having them quit before they've been with me for more than a few months. The longest lasting one since I was five stayed for four months before I scared her off.

I scratch the back of my neck, squinting up through the trees at the bright sun. It's a pretty day out today, and the web I wove in the guest house and covered with honey will probably be extra melty. If Bri doesn't quit after that, I'll just have to up my game.

When I turn a corner of the dirt trail leading through this stretch of forest, and the footbridge comes into view, I freeze in place. The footbridge is well hidden and a spot that nobody else knows about—at least, I've never seen anybody else on it, and I've been coming here for a while to get away from people. The first time I came here two years ago, Dad *freaked*, which was hilarious. That's why it's weird to see that today the footbridge isn't empty; there's a girl sitting on it, legs hanging over the edge of the wooden boards, head in her hands and making soft noises that sound kinda like a dying animal's wail.

For a second, I think about turning around and going back home, getting a first-row seat to Bri's outrage when she gets tangled up in the sticky web I created for her, but something stops me. There's something interesting about this girl—I don't know what it is, but I'm going to find out. I don't like it when girls cry around me; the few times I've seen Mom cry, I wanted to make her tears go away. With anyone else, though, like the girls in school, I just walk away from them and let them deal with their own tears.

Right now I don't want to walk away. After all, this girl is on *my* bridge, staining it with *her* tears and I need to find out why.

I keep walking to the footbridge, my steps quiet. Once I reach the wooden boards of the bridge, they creak under my weight, giving me away. The girl gasps, head rising and turning in my direction, and I feel something weird in my chest as I get my first good look at her. Kind of like the warmth I feel when I'm hanging out with Mom—a fuzzy feeling that I like.

Her eyes are almond-shaped, her skin is golden, her hair looks like long strands of dark silk, sort of like the threads I pull from Dad's black suits when I want to annoy him. I want to see what the girl's hair feels like, but I also don't want to scare her away. That's weird; usually I like scaring people away. It gets them to leave me alone. Not now, though. Now, I kinda want to wipe away her tears and be mean to whoever made her cry.

We stare at each other in silence for a while, before the girl says, "I thought this spot would be empty." Her voice is wobbly but pretty, reminding me of the low melodies Bri sometimes hums around the house.

"It is most of the time," I tell her, nodding. I take a few steps closer to her, and I see her shoulders stiffen.

"Why are you crying?" I ask her as she reaches up to swipe at the lingering tears on her cheek.

The girl frowns. "None of your business."

Oh, I like that. The way she snapped at me. I think I like her, too, but I'm not sure yet. I *am* sure that I'm going to find out.

"I can pull a mean prank on whoever made you cry, if you want," I say, which surprises both of us. I pull pranks for my own entertainment, not anyone else's, and definitely not to help or avenge someone else. I'm not an avenger; I've heard people whisper behind my back that I'm growing into a villain.

A moment later, I stop caring about my offer to pull a prank for someone else's benefit, because it makes the girl smile. I really, *really* like that smile, but it's gone too fast. I want to see it again. I'm about to go into detail on the sort of prank I'd pull to see if that might make her smile more, when she speaks again.

"Some kids who live on the same street as me were making fun of my eyes. Said they're shaped wrong."

That irritates me as much as most people do. I walk up to her and take a seat beside her, frowning. "That's stupid. They're stupid. Your eyes are pretty. What are their names? I'll be mean to them for you."

That makes her giggle, and I like the giggle even more than I like her smile. The giggle quickly fades, though, and she looks sad again, which makes me mad. I don't know why, but I want to protect her from anyone being mean to her.

"I don't know their names," she says softly. "I just moved here a few weeks ago."

Huh. That must be why I haven't seen her before. I know all the kids in my neighborhood and the surrounding ones, I go to school with most of them. The smart ones do what I tell them to do, and I'm going to tell them that if they're mean to her, I'll be mean to them. That should stop them from making her cry again.

"Where did you move from?" I ask her, curious. I want to know more about her. If she lives close enough to walk here, we'll probably be going to the same school when it starts up again in two weeks.

"New York," the girl tells me. "We used to live in the city. I miss it. Nobody looks like me here, I don't have any friends here. I want to go back."

I don't want her to go back, because then I wouldn't see her anymore, and I don't like that thought. I want to see more of her. I wonder if she'd come back here to meet up again if I asked her to. I bet she would if I scare the idiots being mean to her into being nice.

"I'm your friend," I tell her.

That makes her tilt her head to the side as she looks me over. "We just met. We can't be friends already."

I frown. "Why not? I want to be your friend. I promise I'll be nice to you."

I don't add that she'll be the only person other than my parents I'm nice to, even though it's true. I'm not always *mean* to the kids at school, but I don't care enough to be nice either. I do care about being nice to her, though.

After a while of her just staring at me, looking confused, a smile stretches her lips again, and I feel that flutter in my chest again. "Okay," she says. "We can be friends."

"How old are you?" I ask her. If we're the same age, then she'll be in my class at school, and it'll be easier to protect her. Even if she's not, though, I'll find a way.

"Seven," she responds quietly.

I frown. "So you'll be in second grade. Do you know what school you'll go to?" I'm pretty sure we'll be in the same school, but if not, I'll need to figure out a way to scare her classmates into leaving her alone.

"White Pine elementary," she responds, scooting closer to me. "What about you?"

I smile triumphantly. "Same school, but I'm in third grade this year. I'll still make sure nobody else is mean to you, and we'll still be friends. Where do you live?" She's not in the same neighborhood as me or I'd know, but she must be close by.

"I live that way," she says, pointing to the left. "The neighborhood has a really big oak tree in the middle of it. There's a park with a playground near my house, too. It's a quick walk from there to here. Do you know it?"

I nod. "Yeah. I go to that park on weekends sometimes. What house?"

Her nose wrinkles. "The smallest one on the street. Made of old red bricks."

That's the Sampson's old house—my parents were friends with the people who lived there before her. They moved out at the start of summer, and I guess she moved in not long ago. She's not too far away from my house, I walk to the park in her neighborhood often enough with whichever nanny I have at the time. I like it more when my mom takes me, but she's usually too busy.

"I know the one you're talking about. How come you came here instead of the park closer to your house?"

She shrugs. "I was at the park, then some boys and a girl started making fun of me, so I left. I should probably go home, though, Mom won't like that I'm out alone. She says I'm too young to wander strange places."

I bump her shoulder with mine. "You're not alone, you're with me. Will she be okay with that?" Usually, I don't care what other parents think about me, but if I'm gonna spend more time with this girl her mom needs to like me.

"I don't know," the girl says. "Maybe if she meets you. What's your name?"

"Ian," I tell her. "Ian Vargas."

She sticks her hand out. "I'm April Stein."

I grin, take her hand, and shake it. "I think we're gonna be good friends, April."

PROLOGUE, PART TWO

April Stein, age ten

I get back from dance camp only a week before school starts again. My first order of business is to head to the footbridge. I was away for the last two months, training up with some famous teachers, and the girls at camp weren't allowed to have phones or make calls, so I haven't heard Ian's voice or seen his face in way too long. I sent him letters weekly, though, telling him all about camp, and he sent ones back sometimes twice a week telling me about his summer. Apparently he went on a big vacation in France and England yet he still never missed a week—his letters had the coolest stamps and cards.

In his last letter, he told me to meet him on the footbridge when I get back. It's sort of become our spot. He stuck to the promise he made me the day we met there, becoming my best friend and protecting me from the stupid bullies going to our school. I protect him, too, from the girls who want to be close to him because his parents are rich and kind of famous.

Like I expected, Ian's on the footbridge when I get there. He already has a phone while my parents won't let me get one until I'm 12, and he's sitting with his legs dangling over the edge of the bridge, scrolling through it. When he hears me coming up behind him, he stands up, pockets his phone, offers me a brilliant smile and pulls me into a hug. I hug him back tightly, having missed him like crazy over the summer.

"How was the last week of camp?" he asks me, pulling back and taking a seat on the bridge again. I join him in the position we've taken up hundreds of times, side by side, staring at the rushing stream below us.

"Really good," I tell him. "The ballet was amazing. The girl in my group who was supposed to play the lead snowflake got sick, so I ended up playing the lead snowflake since I was her understudy. It was *awesome.* Mom and Dad came to watch the performance, and Dad got me the prettiest bouquet of roses as a present. How was your trip?"

"Good. I wish you came with me, though, the other kids who came along were boring as hell. We saw a really cool old castle that I think you would've liked. Oh, I also got you something."

He reaches into his other pocket and pulls out a small figurine of a ballet dancer, wearing a little pink tutu. I smile widely as I take her from him, running my fingers over the smooth edges of her skirt.

"Thank you. I love it. Where did you get it?"

"Royal opera house in London," Ian tells me. "My parents dragged me there. I don't like ballet's unless you're in them, but it was worth the trip since I got you a mini ballerina. When you grow up, you'll probably be dancing on the best stages in the world."

My heart warms at his confidence in me. "That's the hope," I respond. "What was your favorite part of the trip? You were gone for almost as long as I was at camp."

"Writing letters to you. Picking out cool stamps and cards, thinking about which ones you'd like most," Ian says seriously. "Did you like them?"

I nod. "I kept all of them. The Eiffel Tower one was the prettiest, I want to go there some day."

"I'll take you there," Ian says resolutely. "Once we're grown up, I'll take you all over the world. Wherever you want to go."

"I want to go everywhere, see everything," I say eagerly.

My family can't afford extravagant trips like Ian's—my parents do well enough to support us and our lifestyle, but not well enough to travel the world on a whim. We go on an international trip every two years once they've saved up enough, but we travel to different states to ski every spring break as sort of a mini trip. Ian's started making his parents plan ski trips along with mine, so for two weeks every spring he and I get to ski together. That's pretty much my favorite time of the year—snow plus my favorite person. What's not to love?

"Cool. Everywhere it is," Ian says easily, like it's the simplest thing in the world.

Our friendship puzzles a lot of people around us, mainly because Ian doesn't really have friends. He has people who are scared of him and will do whatever he says, he has a lot of social power at our school, but he's mean or standoffish to almost everyone, except for me. I like that; love knowing that I'm the one person he doesn't want to scare or control, the only person aside from his family he's nice to.

Our parents have become friends because of our friendship; they come together for dinners every few weeks, and sometimes they'll even let us have sleepovers afterwards. Those are my favorite times; cuddling up with Ian and falling asleep in the safety of his arms, knowing he'll protect me from everything.

"I wish I was here so I could've come to see your ballet," Ian murmurs, frowning. "I bet you were the best on stage."

"The best in my group, maybe, but the camp had girls from ten years old to seventeen; the older girls were better because they know more. In my age, though, I think I was one of the top ones."

"When you're older you'll be the best in the world," Ian tells me.

I lean closer to him, resting my head on his shoulder. "I hope so. I have to work twice as hard as the others just because I look a little different from most of the other ballerinas. It's tiring, but worth it."

"You're prettier than all of them combined," Ian says, sounding irritated. "Anyone who disagrees is a moron."

That makes me laugh with delight. "I love you," I tell him.

He smiles at me, and as always, my belly flutters at his smile. It's beautiful and warm, like standing in the sun, and I know that smile is reserved only for me. I've never seen him give it to anyone else; for the others, he smirks. For me, he smiles.

"I love you too, Sugarplum."

The nickname practically makes me preen, because Ian knows one of my goals in dance is to get cast in The Nutcracker as the Sugar Plum Fairy. She has the most beautiful variation. I want to dance it one day.

"We need to stay best friends for life," I inform him. "I don't want to let you go. When you get married, I guess I'll have to make sure your wife likes me, so she doesn't put up too much of a fuss over our friendship."

Ian frowns. "Why are we talking about my future marriage?"

That makes me quiet for a moment. Something that's been on my mind more and more recently is how much attention Ian gets from girls. All the girls at school have crushes on him and moon over him even though he doesn't give them the time of day. That gets difficult to ignore.

"Because I don't want to lose you, ever," I finally respond. "I see how girls look at you; they're trying to close in and snatch you up. I don't want them to."

"Screw them," Ian says mildly. "I don't care about any of them, I only care about you. Don't be worried about my future wife. If anything, I'll probably marry you so I can keep you forever."

The thrill that travels through me at his words is so intense, so bright, I realize just how much I want to spend my life with Ian. He's been my closest friend since the day we met, and we do everything together. I'm the only person he'll tell about his darker activities. They used to be pranks, now they're borderline criminal acts, but I don't care. I know Ian's different from most boys, he has an *otherness* to him and total disregard that's hard to miss. I love that I'm the only person he's not distant with and mean to. I love him and am 100% on board with marrying him if that's what it takes to keep him.

"I'm okay with that."

He smiles. "I'm glad to hear that, but it wouldn't really matter if you weren't okay with that." His smile morphs into a frown. "I might have to kidnap you then, until you're on board with my plans, but I'd figure it out. Whatever it takes."

"You're sick," I tell him affectionately, because I know he is. Our schoolmates and teachers know; everyone knows there's something off about him.

"Probably," Ian agrees. "I don't think my brain works the way most others do."

"I'm pretty sure you're right," I comment. "I love you anyway. You won't have to kidnap me, I'll come with you willingly." I tack on teasingly, "So long as you take me to see the world."

"It's a deal," Ian says with a nod. "I show you the world and I get to keep you. Sounds like a fair trade."

I kiss his cheek. "It totally is. Now tell me more about your trip! Show me the pictures."

Ian pulls his phone out, clicks over to the photo app, and starts showing me *stunning* shots of historic streets, ancient castles, cute shops, fountains; pictures I know he took for my benefit. The first time he traveled after he got a phone, I was furious with him for not taking any pictures to show me. Now he always comes back with plenty.

"Your parents and you are invited over to dinner tomorrow night," Ian tells me once I'm done looking through all the photos.

I smile. "Good. I'll let them know once I'm home. Does your mom still like me?"

"My mom loves you, as you already know," Ian tells me. "She thinks you keep me sane. What's not to like?"

Even Ian's parents know there's something not quite right with him, and he's told me they appreciate my presence in his life because he's calmer when I'm around. His attention that usually goes towards destruction is focused on me instead.

"I am very likable," I agree with a nod. That's mostly true; I can make myself very likable, a tool I picked up while dealing with racist kids and adults surrounding me. Kill them with kindness. Still, I'm not a terribly nice person by nature; I'm insular and get snappy when people invade my space or get too close to me. Anyone but Ian, that is.

"You made me like you, and I don't like anyone," Ian points out. "Now, you want to stay here a bit longer or go to the park by your house? The ice cream truck's usually around this time of day." Seeing the way I perk up at the mention of ice cream, he smiles faintly. "Park it is, let's go."

***

April, age thirteen

Ian stopped sending me letters this summer. I went to camp for two months like I always do but didn't receive a single letter from him like I have every summer I was away since we met. He didn't pick up my calls or answer my texts when I came back, either. He's completely ignored me, and it feels like I'm spinning out of control without my best friend.

He's starting high school this year while I'm stuck in eighth grade, so we won't be at the same school anymore, which is already a depressing enough thought. The fact that I haven't heard a word from him for months makes a sinking feeling settle in my chest.

When I get to the footbridge, I see his familiar frame in his usual spot, and my heart clenches. When he hears me coming, he looks over his shoulder, but he doesn't smile. Doesn't stand. Doesn't hug me like he always has. He just stares at me, and I notice a new bleakness in his green eyes that I've never seen before. It makes me worried.

He doesn't say anything, letting an awkward silence linger between us. I've always felt exceptionally close to Ian, like he's the other half of me I didn't even know existed. Now, though, it feels like there's a pit the size of a universe between us, which I can't stand.

"I haven't heard from you all summer," I say gently.

"Yeah," Ian replies. "I wasn't really in the mood to talk."

That hurts like I've just been punched in my solar plexus. Ian's not a talkative guy with most people, but he always has been with me. We tell each other everything.

"Did I..." I pause to suck in a deep breath. "Did I do something wrong? Are you mad at me?"

Ian stares at me for a long moment before shaking his head. "No, April, I'm not mad at you. I'm just over you. You were a great friend, but I'm not a kid anymore, and neither are you. We're going to different schools now, there's no point in keeping our friendship alive."

His words literally knock the breath out of me, because they come from absolutely nowhere. Before we both went away for the summer—him for travel, me for camp—we hugged for at least an hour and he told me he'd miss me. Even jokingly threatened to kidnap me away from camp and take me with him. Now... now it feels like I'm staring at an entirely different person, not my best friend of six years.

"What?" I gasp. "How can you say that?"

Ian shrugs. "We weren't gonna stay friends forever," he tells me flatly. "We're from different worlds. Your family works to the bone to scrape by, while mine cruises through life."

I shake my head. "You've never cared about the fact that my parents aren't as rich as yours."

"Yeah, well, I was a stupid kid," he replies. "I'm not anymore, though. You're too small for me, too low for me."

I rub a hand over my chest, right on the spot that his words take a sledgehammer to. Ian's never once cared about money or our different lifestyles. Our parents are friends because of us, for fuck's sake. My mom and dad might both be working upper-middle class, but they pull in enough money to support us just fine. It doesn't make sense that he suddenly wants nothing to do with me just because I'm not a bazillionaire like him.

"You're lying," I say. "There's something you're not telling me. Why are you being so mean all of the sudden?"

Ian rolls his eyes. "Get over yourself, April. I'm not lying. I just don't want to be friends anymore. You don't interest me like you once did."

I curl my arms around my waist protectively, feeling like he's twisting a knife inside me. Right now, he doesn't look like the Ian I know, he looks like the Ian everybody else knows—the cruel asshole that people try to suck up to or avoid.

I've always interested Ian, just like he's always fascinated me. That can't just go away in the span of a few months...*can it?*

"I don't believe you," I say weakly, even though I am starting to believe him. His posture, his demeanor, his expression, all of it's closed off in a way that feels painfully final. Like he really is done with me.

Ian stands up, taking a few steps towards me. "Then I'll put it simply. You're pathetic, April, and I don't want anything to do with you anymore. You're too small for me, too poor for me, too *weak* for me. If you keep pushing me, I'll assume it's because you want me to push back. You should know by now that my methods of pushing back can be pretty destructive. We're done."

With that, he walks away, leaving me feeling like my heart's shattering within my chest. I watch him disappear down the path leading back into the residential area, and once he's out of sight, tears start to roll down my cheeks. Any sense of self-confidence or worth I'd accumulated through my friendship with him disappears. I'm left crying like a fool, just as I was the first time I met him. This time, though, he doesn't comfort me or threaten to be mean to whoever made me cry. This time, he's the one to make me cry.

Chapter One

Present Day

April, age eighteen

"You got fucked to high heaven last night, didn't you?" I ask Eliana, my close friend and probably the sweetest, most genuine girl attending Greywood, as she takes a spot beside me on the hardwood floor.

We're in one of the dance HQ studios, stretching in preparation for our first day back from winter break. This week's going to be particularly long because Pandora's Box—the new ballet our teacher, Mr. Sanders, choreographed—is having its first performance of spring term on Friday. We had opening night just before winter break, but only got one show in before the holidays started. Before break, Sanders was beside himself in the midst of preparations, losing his temper nearly every rehearsal and snapping at corps dancers like it was his job—I suspect the same behavior will continue for as long as the show is running.

Elia and I haven't had to be on the receiving end of his rage just yet, probably because we work our asses off to be as close to perfect as a ballerina can be. We make up two of the three leading roles in the production; a fellow dancer in our company, Sean, is the third lead. Elia's Pandora, Sean is Epimetheus, and I'm Zeus. Sanders did a lot of gender reversals in casting, just another reason why he's my favorite instructor in Greywood's elite dance program.

"Why do you have to be so crude?" Elia asks me primly, taking her pointe shoes out of her bag.

I shrug. "You're rocking the post orgasm glow. You always are, though, since agreeing to be with your boys. How are they, anyways?"

Elia's cheeks turn pink. "They're good. Being in a relationship with both of them has been a whirlwind but I'm glad I chose them."

I nod. "Orgasms on the regular must be a bonus."

She slaps my shoulder lightly, her blush deepening. "If you want to discuss adventurous sexual escapades, we should start with yours. We've been at Greywood three months, and you've gone through how many people?"

"Seven men, three women," I reply blithely. Elia knows damn well that I go through people like dancers go through water. I enjoy the thrill of having a new partner, but that thrill wears off quickly, at which point I get bored and go searching for someone more interesting. "At least I don't fuck anyone in the company; I know not to shit where I eat. Which is unfortunate, because Andrew is really hot." My eyes slide over to the talented soloist where he stands at the barre.

Elia shakes her head. "You really are a siren, you know that? Luring sailors to their doom."

I smile at her, pleased with the compliment. "Thank you. You're one to talk, though. You ensnared not one but *two* of Greywood's finest. I don't know how you managed that, but kudos to you, sis. Carson Ajax and Seth Balor are firmly obsessed and head over heels in love with you."

The three of them are sickeningly adorable together. Carson's light spirited, fun to be around, and was a total fuckboy before Elia came along. Seth, on the other hand, was an absolute psychopath until Elia tamed him. Now, I figure he saves his insanity for the bedroom.

"You also have one of Greywood's finest pursuing you," Elia points out playfully. "I saw Ian loitering around program dorms and outside of dance HQ several times before winter break, almost like he was waiting around to run into you. He was there this morning, come to think of it. Seth and Carson pulled the same shit in the beginning."

The difference between our situations is that her men worship the ground she walks on, treating her like a queen. Ian, on the other hand, did an excellent job of fucking with my life for *years*, for no reason other than being an asshole. I should've known even as a kid that our friendship wouldn't last, that eventually he'd drop me. I couldn't have anticipated the sheer force of his cruelty, though. For the three years we shared a high school, he treated me like an enemy and had all of his followers do the same.

"Don't care," I say blithely. Of course, I *do* care, but not because the idea of Ian having any interest in me makes me feel warm and fuzzy—I care because if he's going to come after me here like he did in high school, I need to plan ahead to protect myself.

Ian has an interesting way of controlling people around him, getting them to do his bidding without even having to ask. That's why, the summer before senior year, some of his high school buddies decided to continue carrying his torch of being awful to me. They took it to a whole new level that not even he broached, and I learned that the best thing is to avoid the attention of people like Ian.

A frown mars Elia's dark eyebrows. "Why do you hate him so much? What did he do to you?"

"Typical playground bully shit," I respond, which is mostly true. It was his friends and followers that took things much, *much* further. "He also sicced a bunch of his pets to torture me. I was glad when he graduated, because it meant I had a year to myself without him hanging over my head."

Elia nods. "Your high school dance team took nationals your senior year, right?"

I smile at the memory. "Yeah. I was a tough captain—Sanders' tantrums are mild compared to the way I drilled my team. It worked, though, and the fact that I got our school a very big, very shiny trophy made it difficult for people to keep me in the social outcast column."

Despite the horrendous summer beforehand, I used my senior year to redeem myself. To prove to myself and the petty idiots around me that I am not so easily broken, and that if they wanted to get on my bad side, there'd be consequences. I actually learned a great deal from Ian, whether or not he meant for me to. Though our friendship crumbled to dust, I never stopped watching and observing him, even when he did his best to ostracize and destroy me. A lot of lessons I learned from him served me well in his absence.

Elia's quiet for a few beats, before offering, "If you want, I can sic my men on Ian. Carson could fire him, and Seth is very proficient with ruining lives."

A startled laugh bursts out of me. Eliana is so sweet and kind, I sometimes forget that she has quite a spine. It's one I suspect has grown throughout her time with her boyfriends, though she's always had a quiet strength. At the start of the year, she slapped down Greywood's star dancer who was spreading horrible shit about her around social media—that was quite the sight to see.

"That's okay but thank you for the offer. I adore you for it. If Ian fucks with me, I'll fuck with him. Contrary to what he might believe, I'm quite good at screwing up lives all on my own. I'd prefer not to go to war with him since I'm not sure this school would survive it, but I will if I must."

Elia worries her bottom lip. "Whatever he did must've been bad, right? Worse than playground bully shit. There's so much hatred in your voice when you say his name, it makes me think he crossed some serious lines."

Ian crossed plenty of lines, but it's his lackies that put the nails on the coffin of my innocence. That's fine, though; I got them into the sort of trouble they'll never get out of.

"It wasn't good, but it's over now. I don't want to look back." It's bad enough that my scars still sometimes itch, as if I need any reminders of what I endured.

Elia says quietly, "You know he's coming to Friday's show, right? He'll be in the best box in the house along with Carson and Seth."

I didn't know that and I'm not particularly happy to hear it, but I'm good at avoiding people. If Ian's there for me—which I assume is the case since he doesn't know anyone else on the team—I have to consider the possibility that he intends to stir something up, maybe try to make me miserable the way he did in high school. If that's the case, he'll be in for a rude awakening. He hasn't yet learned that I'm quite good at making other people miserable, too. *I learned from the best.*

Mr. Sanders breezes into the classroom, clapping his hands together. "Alright, team. Five minutes to finish warmups, then we're jumping right into The Box variations."

Our schedule has been switched around this semester to make more room for Pandora's Box rehearsals. At the end of last semester, we had class with Sanders every day from second period onward. This semester, our entire schooldays on Monday, Wednesday, and Friday belong exclusively to Sanders.

Elia leans close to me and whispers, "I can't believe I thought he might be the killer for a while."

I wince. "Yeah, but he seemed like a more likely suspect than fucking *Moira*, who was the dance program director and seemed hoity toity as shit. Who'd have expected the old bat to have that level of crazy in her?"

In the first months of the schoolyear, campus was plagued by a killer who would grab mean girls from fine arts programs in Greywood, torture them to death, then dump their bodies somewhere on campus. A few weeks before winter break, Elia happened to stumble onto the killing ground, which was in this very building's basement. Evidently, batshit Moira had been killing for quite some time, though she hadn't moved her nefarious activities to campus until this year. Moira almost killed Elia to ensure her silence, but Elia managed to knock her out and call the police. I know for a fact that Seth wanted to end Moira's life for touching his girl, but he settled for getting her thrown into the worst prison in the state for several consecutive life sentences.

"Certainly not me," Elia murmurs back. "Hey, Carson and Seth are busy tonight—Seth needs to meet with his agent, and Carson's working late. You want to hit up that bakery in the city? They're dirt-cheap but serve the *best* coffee and pastries."

Like Elia, I'm a scholarship student, which means pinching every penny and living on discounts. I could accept money from my parents, but I'm determined to make it on my own, so the only money I spend is the money I earn teaching dance to young girls, along with the money I've saved from doing so the last several summers. That fact probably has something to do with Ian convincing the entire student body in high school that I'm a gold digger, something he still won't leave alone.

"Let's do it," I tell her. "What time are you done with your art history classes?"

In addition to the dance program, something that takes up the first half of each school day for enrolled students, Elia's decided to submit herself to an art history degree, which means she gets very little free time. Now that she's officially accepted her boys, they tend to eat up all her remaining hours.

I have a French elective I take outside of the gen ed courses that dancers are required to do online and barely have any time to myself, so I can't imagine how Elia swings it.

"Six," Elia tells me. "We can meet up at program dorms at around seven? Take the bus into the city?"

I smile. "That works."

***

A grueling six hours of dancing later, with a bonus hour and a half of French class, I head to the small park on the edge of campus to enjoy the afternoon sun and get some homework out of the way while waiting for Elia's text. The park borders a forest, with plenty of benches for students to laze on. Most of them are unoccupied, probably due to the unforgiving January coldness, so I get to study in relative solitude. I set myself up on one of the benches with a textbook and notebook in my lap, pop my headphones into my ears and turn on a classical music playlist before getting to work.

It can't be more than twenty or thirty minutes later that I feel the fine hairs on the back of my neck stand on end, just before a shadow falls over me. In my life, only one person has been able to illicit that reaction from me, which is why I know who I'll be facing even before I look up from my notebook.

As expected, Ian Vargas towers over me, staring down at me with his evergreen eyes. He's tall, standing at a solid six foot four, and has a very well-muscled frame that probably comes from years of smashing the skulls of his enemies together. It also helps that he played football throughout high school—his biceps are bigger than my calves. Everything about him screams danger, but he's not wearing the cruel expression that used to be a precursor for him ruining my day. Instead, he looks faintly interested as he watches me.

Absolutely not. I know firsthand that the only thing worse than having Ian's anger is having his interest, because it'll inevitably turn into anger, and he'll then ruin the life of his object of interest. I experienced this once when his interest in me throughout middle school turned into anger in high school; I'm not going through it again at Greywood.

He sits down on the bench beside me, his thigh brushing mine, which makes me stiffen. I briefly contemplate ignoring him in hopes of making his interest disappear, but that's exactly what I've been doing in the weeks since finding out he goes to Greywood, and it obviously hasn't done me much good. Before winter break, I continuously ran into him in all the campus spots I frequented—the café, the library, even outside my dorms or dance headquarters. I'd hoped he'd gotten bored and would go back to leaving me alone after the school break, but apparently not.

I pull my earbuds out of my ear, then fix him with my most uninterested stare. "What do you want?"

CHAPTER TWO

Instead of answering, Ian leans over to look at my notebook. "French, huh? Solid choice of language, very useful. Especially if you're still planning to travel around Europe. You still have those dreams, Sugarplum?"

I slam my notebook and textbook shut, ignoring the fact that his use of the endearment sends a small shiver of pleasure down my spine. If Ian sought me out, it's probably because he wants to fuck with me, which I will not tolerate. Not anymore, not here. Greywood's mine as much as it's his—I have considerable social power among the fine arts students, and Elia reminded me of her offer to sic her boys on Ian before we parted ways.

"If you're here to try to ruin my day—"

"Nah, I'm over that," Ian says, waving a hand. "High school was a juvenile time, I've grown up."

I very much doubt he's grown out of his life-ruining phase, and I don't believe that he's here without a nefarious reason. Ian hasn't sought me out for any purpose but to screw me over since we were best friends as kids. Since our days of friendship are long gone, dead and buried six feet under cold dirt, I believe it's a safe bet to assume that he isn't here to discuss my dreams of traveling.

"Have you," I say flatly and disbelievingly. "Good for you. If you don't mind, there are half a dozen other benches you can choose from—go sit on one of them. I'm busy."

"I can see that," Ian replies with a nod. "I can help you practice if you want. I'm still fairly fluent in French."

"I don't want that," I respond, frowning. "Seriously, what are you doing here?"

He shrugs. "I was walking by, happened to notice you here all alone. You looked like you could use some company."

That's absolute bullshit, and we both know it.

"I prefer to be alone, as you should be aware. So if you don't mind," I make a shooing gesture with my hands.

A slow smirk spreads on his lips. "Getting rid of me isn't so easy, April, you should know that."

"You're the one who got rid of me when I was thirteen," I snap. "Then, because that wasn't enough, you had to mess with my life in high school. What the hell are you doing here, Ian?"

He looks pleased at my response, which reminds me that Ian is someone who lives for reactions. The louder and angrier I get with him, the more it feeds into his need for chaos, which means it's in my best interest to just walk away.

"That was then, this is now," he says, as if that explains everything.

I bark out a cruel laugh, then shove my textbook and notebook into my backpack. "Right. That totally makes sense. Fuck off."

I stand up, ready to leave him in the dust, only to pause when he snatches my backpack from my hands and looks over the frayed fabric. "Why are you carrying around such a tattered bag? Your family might not be rich, but they should have plenty of money to get you decent school supplies."

I growl with irritation, snatching my backpack away from him and swinging it over my shoulder. "I pay for my own shit. Getting called a gold digger enough times has an interesting effect on a person, even when they've never once tried to be with someone just for money."

That appears to surprise Ian. "I don't *actually* think you're a gold digger. You're above that. I was just fucking with you when I said that."

"Which time?" I shoot back. "The weekly insults in high school or when you called me a gold digger in front of my best friend and her boyfriend?" Last semester, he called me that in front of Eliana and Carson which infuriated me.

"All of the above," Ian responds, standing up. It takes a pointed effort not to step back from him, because everything about him is too much. His muscles, his height, his presence alone. There was a time when I liked those things about him because they protected me. That time is long gone.

"You should really learn to ignore the bullshit people spew about you. It's just that; bullshit," he advises.

His suggestion irritates me beyond belief, because he is the person who's spewed the most bullshit about me. He has no right to give me any advice or tell me how I should ignore the words of others. The fact that he's even here right now is galling. It goes to show that he hasn't done *any* maturing since high school. If he did, he would have the grace to leave me alone.

"Thanks for the life lesson," I quip. "If you could kindly fuck off, I'd greatly appreciate it."

"Why?" Ian asks, sounding genuinely curious. "We can be friends again."

That statement is so absurd, I don't know what to do with it. After that day on the footbridge when he told me he was done with me, I tried repeatedly to reach out and rekindle our friendship. All I got for my effort was repeated humiliation until I knew better.

I shake my head, reaching up to run a hand through my hair, wondering if this is some sort of very weird dream.

"I don't want that. I don't want anything to do with you. I may have once, then you showed me how wrong I was. Good on you, Ian. If you have any decency, you'll leave me alone."

"You don't want to be friends?" he asks, amusement dripping from every word.

Hoping to put him off, I laugh in his face, which is an appropriate response considering our history. "The day I need a friend like you, I'll shit one out."

Ian's expression transforms with a smile, one that speaks of his growing investment in our interaction. His smiles are so rare, I forgot just how beautiful they are. His entire face transforms in a way that makes him painfully handsome and impossible to ignore.

"You used to be so sweet, Sugarplum, so nice. What happened?"

I say honestly, "I was never nice, Ian, I was just nice to *you*."

That appears to take him aback. He stares at me for a long moment before uttering a quiet, "Huh."

I nod. "Yeah. As lovely as this conversation has been, I'd rather jump off a cliff than continue it. Have a horrible day, Ian, I'll pray that a random bolt of lightning strikes you down and saves your future victims."

I turn to walk away, only to be reminded exactly why it's a bad idea to turn my back on a predator when Ian's arm bands around my waist, halting me.

I always knew Ian was different, intense, predatory, but there was a time when he used those qualities to protect me rather than hurt me. Even when he started using his power against me, to cut me down, I was still hopeful that someday he'd get past whatever rancor he felt and we'd go back to our friendship. Then, he shattered any hope of it.

"I was going to let you go, Sugarplum, so I wouldn't taint or infect you. But then you had to come back into my life. You had to choose Greywood of all places. That was your mistake. I'm not letting you go a second time."

Taint or infect me? It almost sounds as if he thought he was doing me a favor by deliberately targeting me in high school. Despite my intuition screaming at me to get away from him, there's a small, long-dead part of me that enjoys his heat at my back. It's the child in me, I realize, the girl who adored and trusted Ian completely.

Reminding myself that he killed that girl, and his friends sealed the grave, I throw an elbow back into his gut. Or try to, at least. It doesn't work; he predicts my move and counters it by gathering my wrists in his free hand and pinning them against my lower back.

"I like the meanness in you. I miss the sweetness, though. Will you be sweet for me again, April?"

I snarl, "No way in hell. You had your chance; you threw it away. I would've stuck with you for anything, Ian. You want sweet, for someone to fawn over you? Go to a strip club. I hear they always have a girl named Candy around."

He dips his head down so it's hovering right by my ear, and his warm breath on my neck stirs something in me that I'm startled to realize is arousal. Oh, *fuck* no. Not with him. Literally anyone *but* him.

"I don't want anyone else. I want you. You had your chance to get away from me, instead you came back. That's your fault, not mine."

What the hell?

"I see your insanity has only grown since high school," I quip. "If you think I chose to come here for you, you're dead wrong. If I knew you were here, I would've gone to Juilliard."

"It might not have been a deliberate decision, but you were brought to me—whether it was fate or chance, I don't fucking care. I'm *owed* you. I'll have you."

"Over my dead body. That's the only way you'll have me, if you kill me. Let me go, or—"

"Or what, April? What will you do to me? What *can* you do to me? Nothing. I'm richer than you, better connected, more powerful."

Enough of this shit. He can't steamroll me anymore; I'm not as naïve and pliable as I once was. I abruptly headbutt him *hard*, hard enough for him to curse and for his grip on me to loosen. I use the chance to slip away and turn around to face him head on. A trail of blood runs from his nose—he swipes at it with his fingers, then looks down at the red staining his skin, as if he can't quite believe it.

"Go find someone else to fuck or fuck with, Ian. You keep coming after me, I'll assume you want to go to war. And money or not, connections or not, I will *decimate* you if we find ourselves on the opposite side of a battlefield."

Ian's eyes flick back to mine, and the darkness combined with interest swirling there makes me nervous.

"Run, Sugarplum," he rumbles. "Run as much as you want. I don't mind the chase, not when my prize is so delicious."

I scoff. "You should've thought of that before you made me watch another girl give you a blowjob. Or before you branded me a social outcast and had all your bitches target me. Or the time when I came to you, heart in fucking hand, to ask what I did wrong and how we could go back to what we were, and you laughed in my face. You had opportunity after opportunity to walk back your mistakes; I threw you chance after chance like the idiotic little girl I was. I'm not that girl anymore."

I have the scars to prove it. I still remember when the scars on my back came to be, and the memory alone makes me shudder. Those marks gave me two options; break or toughen up. I chose the strong path.

In a way, I have Ian to thank for my strength, though not because he helped me. He and his lackies did their level best to ruin me, yet I was the one left standing at the end of it. With a few new scars and skin made of steel, I survived and got strong.

I point a shaky finger at him. "Find someone else to terrorize; I'm no longer an option."

"I'm not here to terrorize or hurt you," he tells me, his tone serious. "That doesn't interest me. I'm here for you, period. You were mine once, I guarantee you'll be mine again."

Obviously, he's not going to listen to reason, which means it's time to end this conversation. It was stupid of me to react to him as much as I did, I know that'll only throw more fuel on him. Done with this interaction and done with him, I take off in the direction of program dorms in a sprint. Usually I don't shy away from my problems, and I'm not a runner; Ian is the one entity in my life that I will run from, because I know full well he is capable of bringing about my destruction *again.*

Chapter Three

A week of laborious training and hectic evening rehearsals leads up to a phenomenally successful performance. The standing ovation we get at the end of Pandora's box on Friday night, while the cast is taking their bows, lasts for well over five minutes. The lights glaring onto the stage dim, allowing a small glimpse into the theatre, which is filled to the brim with people—every seat in both the balcony and main auditorium is taken, and there are even people *standing* beside aisles, clapping and cheering.

After I've collected my flowers from Mr. Sanders and taken my bows with Elia and Sean, the rest of the corps dancers gracefully run onto stage behind us, also taking bows. Elia holds my hand through all of it, beaming at me and the crowd, tears gathered in her eyes from the sheer adoration she's receiving from the masses. I'm a little humbled at the turnout and sound of cheers, as well, though I'm not one to get teary over such things.

The curtain falls down, momentarily plunging us into darkness. Then, the stage lights come on. Elia practically leaps at me, engulfing me in a hug, squeezing me with surprising strength for such a small dancer. "You were fucking *incredible!*" She squeals in my ear. "God, I've never heard cheers that loud. Not even on opening night."

As soon as I release her, before I can return congratulations, she's swept into Sean's arms and they share an embrace, while Andrew squeezes my shoulder with a warm smile. All the dancers cry and laugh and hug each other for several minutes, until members of stage crew ask us to go backstage to dressing rooms so they can start cleaning up.

Since Elia and I are both technically leads, we have shared use of the female star's dressing room, which is a nice change from the tiny dressing room meant to squeeze in a dozen corps dancers. We talk about all of our variations, the responses from the crowd, and the sheer exhilaration of such a successful performance as we change out of costumes and into street clothes. I pull on jeans and a blouse while Elia opts for leggings and a huge cashmere sweater that I'm pretty sure belongs to either Carson or Seth, then we make our way to the lobby to greet the audience.

The building is old as dirt, one of the oldest in the city, but it's been renovated in recent years. Refurbished pillars hold up a high dome ceiling in the lobby. Slivers of stained-glass weave through the brick of the dome, glimmering from the moonlight outside. Old fashioned lamps that once ran on kerosene lend a glowing, restful ambiance to the room, despite the crowd and many conversations. I pad my way across the floor, exchanging smiles with other cast members, then startle when Sanders stops me and Elia dead in our tracks.

Our teacher says, "You were both incredible. If the turnouts continue like this, Pandora's Box will be going on tour this summer, and I expect my two leading ladies to continue in their roles. *Excellent* work, girls, you've made a retired ballerina proud."

He offers both of us a brilliant smile before getting pulled into a conversation with some patrons.

Elia says, "Wow. I didn't think he was capable of such high praise."

Her words are cut off when Carson pushes through the crowd and sweeps her into a hug, murmuring in her ear. Seth isn't far behind him, and as soon as Carson's released her, he pulls her into his own tight embrace. He doesn't let her go when they're done, keeping a possessive arm wrapped around her waist.

He tips his chin at me. "Stein. I didn't know you were that good; well done."

I snort. "Thanks, Balor." Then, because I don't want to intrude on their cutesy moment, I give them a nod before disappearing into the crowd. I'm segued multiple times by patrons passing on congratulations, but I stop cold when I catch a familiar glimpse of stern, wrinkled features, dark brown hair, and the icy grey eyes of a man waiting by the doorway.

My heart speeds to a race as I crane my neck to get a better look at him, ensuring I'm not hallucinating, and see a glimpse of my mom's regal features and black hair pulled back into her usual, elegant twist. She and Dad are murmuring to each other at the edge of the crowd, scanning the crowd around them, probably looking for me. I push through the remaining people separating me from my parents; as soon as they see me, both of their eyes light up.

I throw my arms around Mom first. She's a few inches shorter than me, though I got most of my genes aside from height from her—we share similar facial features, dark hair, almond eyes, and golden skin.

"I didn't know you were coming," I murmur in her ear, feeling my heart burst with joy. I stayed at Greywood for winter break, which was the first time I was separated from them for holidays. I wanted to be here so I could make use of the dance studios and keep an eye on Eliana as she continued to recover. They were saddened, but they understood, and I didn't think I'd see them until spring break.

Mom pulls back, taking my face in her hands and smiling softly at me. "You danced beautifully, my love. You should be proud."

Dad pulls me into one of his crushing bear-hugs next. He says in his thick Russian accent, "We wanted to surprise you, but you should know better than to think we'd miss watching you dance. We couldn't make it opening night, but we certainly can now, especially since you didn't spend the break with us." He squeezes me even tighter. "You gave a very good performance, April. Greywood has served you well."

The praise might sound faint to most others, but I know that coming from my soviet-bred, very Russian father, his words are high accolades. When I pull back from him, he palms the back of my neck and gives me a nod. "You've brought me and your mother much pride."

I kiss his cheek, feeling my eyes prickle and burn. I'm not much of a crier but hearing those words from my father, who generally believes that praise is for the weak and the dead, means a great deal. I say, "Thank you, Papa," my voice faintly choked.

He releases me, just in time for Mom to make a faint noise of surprise. "You didn't tell us Ian would be here tonight, darling," she says.

That causes me to stiffen, which my dad catches with his sharp eyes. The man misses little—he comes from a world that made him very observant.

I knew Ian would be here thanks to Elia's tip earlier in the week, but I hoped I'd be able to avoid him. Now, there is no chance in hell I'll get away without notice, because my parents know Ian from our childhood friendship and my mom is fond of him. I didn't bother telling either of them how our friendship fell apart, though my dad had his suspicions—ones he never voiced aloud.

I tense up even more when I glance over my shoulder and see Ian cutting a path through the crowd toward me. I can't avoid him now without making a scene, and a scene in front of my parents is the last thing I want. If they weren't here, I might be fine with publicly blowing Ian off, but I'm not interested in alarming either of them.

To my absolute shock, when Ian comes to a stop beside me, the motherfucker *slides an arm around my waist* the same way Seth did with Elia, as if we're *together.* Dad tracks the motion with furrowed brows, before turning a not altogether friendly gaze on Ian. My mom, however, seems delighted as she smiles at him.

"What are you doing?" I ask between gritted teeth.

Ian offers me a charming, charismatic smile that looks entirely out of place on him. Then, his smile turns sheepish as he looks at my parents. "Oh, sweetheart, you haven't told them yet, have you?"

"Told us what?" Mom asks, excitement brightening her amber eyes.

"What is it, precisely, that we do not know?" Dad echoes, narrowing his eyes at me.

Ian gives a small laugh. "My apologies, I didn't know April was keeping the news to herself. We're dating."

Sheer horror turns my stomach into a sinking pit as I take in his words and realize the play he's making here. By advertising to my parents that we're *dating* when we most certainly are not, he's putting me in a very precarious position. I could say that there's no way in hell I'd ever date him, which would raise questions I don't want to answer. I could tell my parents that he's joking, which would also raise questions and doubt.

"Oh, that's wonderful!" My mom says, clapping her hands together with delight.

"It's certainly something," Dad mutters, turning a scathing glare to Ian. "How long have you been…together?" He forces out the last word like it leaves a sour taste on his tongue. Which, I imagine, it does. Dad doesn't like to envision me with boys; he spent a decent amount of my life scaring any potential suitors away.

"About three months now," Ian lies. I've only known he was at Greywood since mid-October, when I had the misfortune to run into him, and it seems he's using that very timeline for his false dating claims.

"Why didn't you tell us, love?" Mom asks me, amusement glittering in her eyes. "You know we've always liked Ian."

"You've always liked Ian," Dad corrects.

Mom lightly slaps his chest in admonishment, before giving Ian a bright smile. "Don't mind him, he's just protective of his little girl. Ian, why don't you join us for dinner? We have a table reserved at the best sushi restaurant in the city."

I say, "He's busy," at the same time that Ian tightens his grip on me and says, "I'd love to, thank you."

When Dad's gaze hardens, I understand I need to backtrack or risk creating a mess I won't feel like cleaning up later.

I tell Ian, "You said you had homework to do."

Dad frowns. "Your boyfriend wasn't planning on taking you out to a congratulatory dinner after the biggest ballet of your life had its second performance? Did he also neglect you on opening night?"

"He's not my boyfriend." I can't stop the words from slipping out, and I see the moment suspicion shadows my father's eyes.

Ian says with a light laugh, "April's making me work for everything, refuses to put a label on us." He pauses. "I finished my homework early so that I could take her out."

I'm frozen with a mixture of horror and rage at his fucking *audacity* to pull a stunt like this, to trap me with him in front of my goddamn parents.

Mom's eyes sparkle with mirth. "I made her father work for everything, as well. How else would a woman know if a man is serious about her?"

"I'm very serious about your daughter," Ian assures my parents. "If you'd like the night to yourselves, since you haven't seen each other in some time, I don't mind."

"Don't be ridiculous!" Mom says. "We'll be happy for you to join us."

Ian turns to me with a smile that says *checkmate*. "I can drive you if you want, Sugarplum."

"That's probably a good idea, our rental is quite cramped," Mom says. "I'll text April the address of the restaurant so she can navigate."

Dad puts a hand on my arm, pulling me away from Ian and into another hug. Quietly and in his native tongue, Russian, he asks in my ear, "Is there something I need to know? Are you okay?"

I could tell him that this whole situation is absolute bullshit, that I can't stand the thought of Ian and haven't been able to for years, but I know that'll create a stir. My father is a man of action, and he still has some connections in the old-country; if he wants to makes someone disappear, he can. His business might be clean and legal, but I know he has some friends who work in the shadows.

"I'm okay," I reply, also in Russian. I might not want to be in the same room as Ian, but I'm not cruel enough to want him dead.

Dad pulls back with a nod of understanding, then takes Mom's hand. "We'll see you two there, then. Reservation's in twenty minutes." Mom kisses me on the cheek, then pulls Ian into a brief hug before following Dad out of the theatre.

As soon as they're gone, I turn to Ian. "I'll tell them you got sick or something. Go home."

Ian arches an eyebrow. "Didn't you hear? We're dating. I figure meeting the parents is part of that repertoire," he tells me. "Well, technically I've already met your parents, but not in this capacity."

I glance around the lobby, noting that the crowd has begun to dwindle, before focusing back on Ian.

"We are not dating. We are not together. I made it very clear that I want nothing to do with you."

"You wanted nothing to do with the version of me you knew in high school," Ian corrects. "That wasn't really me, April. I pushed you away because I thought I had good reason to, and I'll admit things got taken a little far at times. But you know the real me; you were his best friend for six years."

He calls three years of sheer misery *pushing me away?* Because he thought he had *good reason to?* Even if that's the case, even if Ian thought he was doing the best thing in the world by being a total asshole to me, it doesn't change anything. It doesn't make me feel better, and it doesn't make me see him in a different light. My memories of our friendship are like a distant dream, whereas my memory of the way he treated me for years is a very vivid nightmare.

I let out a long breath. Maybe if I approach this from an angle of rationality rather than anger, he might actually listen to me.

"You hurt me, very, *very* badly. Your friends and lackies hurt me even worse—I'll wear their scars for the rest of my life." The latter statement slips out without my permission, and Ian's eyes sharpen on me. I quickly backtrack, "Emotional scars." *Ha. If only.* "I am not a masochist, Ian, I do not like pain. I'll endure it for the sake of dance, but ballet is the only thing I will hurt myself for. You are a representation of some of the greatest pain I've felt. Seeing you, even being near you, *hurts me*. If you want to hurt me, continue on as you have. If you have any regard for me, though, you'll walk away."

"I have a great deal of regard for you," he says, frowning slightly. "I meant to hurt you in the past, to keep you away from me."

"You succeeded," I tell him plainly.

I don't know what reasons he might've had or if something happened to him the summer before high school that changed him. Frankly, I don't care. It took a lot of effort for me to stop caring about him, but I managed, so his experiences and hardships no longer concern me, only my own do. The fact of the matter is that a great deal of my hardships originated from him. I won't submit myself to that again.

"I don't want to hurt you now," he says, disregarding my statement entirely.

My irritation grows. He doesn't seem to grasp the concept that, first of all, I don't trust him, and second of all, even if I did trust him, I would not risk an iota of emotional investment in him ever again.

"Then what the fuck *do* you want?" I hiss.

"You," he replies simply.

I growl. "Have I not made it patently clear that I am not an option? If I haven't, let me remedy that; I am not an option for you. Do I need to fuck someone else in front of you to get that point across?"

His eyes darken. "If you want that person to live, I wouldn't recommend it."

"You did that exact thing to me!" I exclaim, my voice growing louder. "How do you not get that there is no possibility of anything between us? You're the one who made sure of that, Ian."

He sighs as if I'm being unreasonable, glancing down at the watch on his wrist. "Come on, we don't want to be late. I don't want to make a bad impression. We can talk more in my car."

"I don't want to talk to you," I tell him.

He already knows that, though; Ian's problem was never that he lacked perceptiveness, it's that he doesn't care enough about other people to take their thoughts or feelings into account. He works on his own schedule with his own plans and will readily steamroll anyone who tries to get in his path.

Ian shrugs. "Then we don't have to talk. This conversation is just going around in circles, anyway. We can listen to music instead. You still like Tchaikovsky?"

"This conversation *is* going around in circles, and yet you continuously miss the point," I say. "Tonight was supposed to be a good night. I haven't asked you for anything in a long time, if ever, but I am asking you now not to ruin tonight. I had an excellent debut, and I'm seeing my parents for the first time since I left home. You had three years to make my life hell, you do not get to pull the same shit in college. I won't fucking allow it."

Ian strokes a hand up and down my arm in a poor imitation of a soothing gesture. "I won't ruin anything, I promise. You were stunning on stage, by the way. I wanted to tell you, but you interrupted me with all your protests. I can honestly say I've never seen anyone dance that beautifully, and I've seen ballets all around the world. You're going to be a star, I'm sure of it."

"Thanks, but I don't want your compliments. You are making my evening worse by being here; please leave. I'll make an excuse on your behalf, order myself an Uber to the restaurant."

Ian shakes his head. "The only person ruining your evening is yourself. I have been nothing but pleasant and cordial, and you insist on sticking to your old hatred of me like it's the hottest fashion. It won't get you anywhere, April. Hating me won't stop me from coming for you, it'll only serve to make you miserable while I do. I don't want you miserable, believe it or not I'd prefer it if you were happy."

He truly must be insane to try to blame my current unhappiness on *me*. I was perfectly content until I found out he was at Greywood; even then, I continued being content so long as he wasn't anywhere near me.

"What's your endgame here, Ian? What do you want from me? If it's sex, I'll fuck you if that's what it takes to get you to leave me alone. I've been known to be charitable from time to time."

That makes him chuckle. "I'm not looking for a pity fuck, April, though I'll have you in my bed eventually. What I want from you is the same thing I wanted the day we met on the bridge; you."

Chapter Four

"Then why the fuck did you *throw me away?*" I demand.

This about-face from him makes absolutely no sense, which bothers me as much as his presence in my life does. He made it perfectly clear just how much he couldn't stand me only two years ago, and now he's doing *this*? How the *hell* am I supposed to respond to that?

"I did what I did because I believed, for a time, that I could never have anything more with you. Some shit happened to make me feel that way; I'll tell you about it someday, but not today."

Despite my better sense, the old part of me that thought Ian was the moon and stars stirs at his words, and a brief flicker of concern passes through me. There have been times when I wondered exactly what prompted his hostility towards me, but it all came back to his words when he told me that I was beneath him, pathetic, and ended our friendship on the bridge where it began. It wouldn't surprise me if something happened to him that changed him, but that doesn't explain his treatment of me, nor does it make me resent him any less.

My phone buzzes in my pocket, I pull it out to see my mom having texted that they're at the restaurant, waiting for us. Ian takes it from my hand, reads the message, then returns it to me with a smirk. "We should get going. We can hash our shit out later."

"We won't," I assure him. I might not be able to get out of tonight, but I can damn well ensure that I don't get caught in a situation like this again. I can do everything in my power to avoid Ian—avoiding people is something I became very proficient with during my high school years. I'll get through tonight with gritted teeth, then devote myself to staying the hell out of Ian's way.

He smiles faintly, as if I've amused him, before taking my hand and leading me towards the exit of the theatre. I stare at his hand engulfing mine, too swept up in memories to pull it away as quickly as I should. He's grown up quite a bit since we were in elementary and middle school, but his hand always dwarfed mine when he held it, and he used to hold it all the time. I forgot until now just how often we used to touch—whenever we were together, going somewhere, he'd lead me by my hand. When we were sitting together, either at the bridge or our school's playground or in one of our houses', he'd have an arm around me and my head would always rest either on his shoulder or chest.

He opens the theatre door for me, and I snatch my hand away, shaking off old memories. Ian is not the boy he once was. He's a man now, filled with as much destructiveness as he always was, but now I know what it's like to have that destructive energy pointed at me. I don't want to deal with that again. I can't. Not now, not when the work I do at Greywood will either make or break my career.

"I almost forgot you already speak two languages," Ian remarks randomly as he puts a hand at the small of my back and steers me towards the parking lot. "Russian and Japanese, right?"

"You already know the answer to that," I respond flatly.

He chuckles. "I do. Your parents only spoke to you in their native tongues until you were five and started school, at which point you also learned English. Even then, you only spoke with them in their languages at home until you hit middle school."

I'm mildly surprised that Ian remembers such details, but I shouldn't be. He's always been observant, an information-gatherer by nature, because Ian understands better than most that information is the most valuable form of currency. That's something I might've admired about him, if I had any goodwill left for him.

Ian stops in front of a dark red BMW, the color of blood, which seems terribly appropriate for him. He opens the passenger's side door to me, and I briefly turn my eyes heavenward, praying that this will be over quickly. All I have to do is grit my teeth through the dinner, then return back to dorms and figure out an effective plan on how to stay out of Ian's way. That might include almost never leaving my dorms outside of class and work time. I don't like the idea of hiding away like a coward, but I do like the idea of not giving Ian another opportunity to hurt me. He's already proven to be much too good at it.

"C'mon, Sugarplum," Ian says, giving me a nudge. "Get your ass in the car. We're already late."

"Will you stop calling me that?" I snap.

He arches an eyebrow. "Why? You used to love that endearment."

"Yeah, well I used to love you. Circumstances change," I snap back.

For a brief moment, I could swear that something like pain flashes across Ian's expression, or it could be remorse. I know better than to read into it; Ian's impervious to pain, and he's too much of a goddamn psychopath to feel remorse.

Then, his face returns to its usual impassive mask, and he stares at me coolly. "You must not have loved me very much for the love to dissipate so wholly."

He pushes me into the car none too gently, and once I'm in, slams the door shut. I watch as he stalks around to the driver's side and slips in. He aggressively clicks on his seatbelt before starting up the car, all the while I watch him with what might be nerves swirling in my stomach. If I didn't know better, I'd think my statement hurt Ian, and his anger right now is caused by pain. I do know better, though, so I can only assume his pride is injured.

"I loved you more than the whole world," I tell him, my voice quiet. "I didn't stop loving you for quite some time after you decided to make me the target of your hatred. I held onto my love with everything in me. Eventually, though, I realized that loving you came at the cost of constant personal pain. My love for you made me stop respecting myself, which is why I finally let it dwindle and die."

Ian's jaw clenches, but he doesn't reply as he shifts the gear into drive and pulls out of the parking lot. Once we're on the road, he turns on the speakers, and I startle as Chopin floats through the car. It came on automatically, which means he was listening to it on the drive to the theatre.

I was the one to introduce Ian to Chopin, Tchaikovsky, Bach, all the great composers of eras past whom I love. I'd listen to them as I danced when I was younger; I still do now. I remember once complaining to Ian that I didn't have anyone to play piano accompaniment when I was practicing on my own. He surprised me by *learning to play the piano* specifically for me, which gave him an opening to be around me when I practiced. Previously, I hadn't allowed him in the same room when I danced because he was a constant distraction; with him at the piano, I couldn't refuse him. There was a time when he did a great deal to be close to me. Thinking of it makes me feel faintly sad, because I was once *so* sure we were meant to be best friends forever. I was ready to marry him if it meant keeping him, and it's so beyond unfair that he ripped that away from me, only to now come back into my life, demanding a place for himself in it.

"Do you still play piano?" The question slips out without much forethought, and I internally curse myself for showing interest. That's counterproductive for both of us.

He nods. "I do. Never stopped. I have a gorgeous baby grand in my apartment." He pauses. "If you want to come over, I can play accompaniment while you rehearse. Like we used to."

My heart clenches as I look away from him and out the window, trying to stave off memories of the hundreds of hours we spent together doing just that. When we were friends, Ian did not like being away from me. He was extremely possessive and wanted us to spend all our time together, which delighted me. He took interest in my interests, learned things just for me, did everything in his power to be around me at all times.

"I'll take your silence as a yes," Ian says when I don't respond. My eyes flutter shut and I shake my head.

He really doesn't know how to take no for an answer; he never has. When he wants something, his only setting is full steam ahead. I once admired that quality, liked that he knew how to get what he wanted under any circumstances, especially since back then the main thing he wanted was me.

"Stop scratching at old scars," I murmur. "It's just making me sad."

"That's not the intention," Ian says, sounding irritated. "You don't have to be sad. I don't want you upset or angry."

"It feels like that's exactly what you want," I respond, my voice sounding exhausted and hollowed out.

Tonight was supposed to be a victory, and having my parents surprise me by showing up was an extra bonus that should've thrilled me. Having them take me out to sushi, my favorite food, and spending time with them *would've* thrilled me, if Ian wasn't around. Now I understand I'll spend the evening remembering what we could've had, and there's no way to be happy while thinking of that. He's serving me a reminder of something I once desperately wanted, but choosing him now would be turning my back on myself—I did that for him before, I won't again. Never.

The scars on my shoulder blade and lower back start to itch uncomfortably, giving me an extra reminder why it's in my best interest to keep away from him. I fucking *hate* that my skin was actually, permanently scarred—if it wasn't, maybe I could forgive and forget. Probably not, I'm one hell of a grudge holder, but there could be a slim chance. With the scars, there's no chance. No matter how a part of me yearns to reclaim what we once had.

"How can I prove to you I'm not here to hurt or screw with you?" Ian asks after a long stretch of silence, his voice gritty.

That just makes me more miserable, and the itch on my back intensifies until I reach back and scratch at the old wounds, feeling them prickle beneath my nails.

"A time machine," I tell him. "You knew me better than anyone. You know I don't change my mind when I've decided on something. I stick to my convictions, the few that I have."

"And your convictions about me are?" Ian prods.

"That you were almost the end of me once, and I'll never let that happen again," I reply.

"What do you mean by that?" Ian questions, his brows drawing together as he glances at me.

I don't feel like expanding on the fact that his treatment of me nearly cost me my life on one especially dark night. That's none of his business, and something I ended up taking care of on my own, with a little help from Dad. The way I know my dad was involved in some dark shit in his youth is because he knew exactly how to take care of me when I came home, soaked with my own blood, a mess both physically and emotionally. He ended up taking me to the hospital. I never told Dad exactly what happened, though, no matter how many times he asked. I haven't told anyone, and I don't intend to. That experience will come with me to the grave.

I shake my head. "Just that you were a good life lesson for me; if something seems too good to be true, it absolutely is. All that glitters is not gold."

Ian pulls the car into the parking lot of an upscale looking restaurant, and I belatedly realize I didn't give him the address, which means he must've come here before. I doubt it was alone, so he probably took some date with him to wine and dine before fucking. Something ugly curls in my stomach, and it takes me a few beats to realize it's jealousy. *Goddammit.* He's not worth jealousy; there's nothing to be jealous of. It's certainly not like I would've ever come here with him willingly.

"I'm not gold, Sugarplum, and I've never pretended to be. If anything, I'm obsidian; dark, jagged, hard. You know that, though. You know me better than anyone."

"I don't know you at all," I whisper. I did once, but not anymore. Ian is a complete stranger to me, one who I do not trust in the least.

"That's bullshit," Ian snaps, pulling into a parking spot and shutting off the car. "You do know me best. You always have." He takes my hand in his, tightening his grip when I try to pull it away.

There's no point arguing with him; I can see that. Doing so would waste both of our energy, and I need every ounce of it to get through dinner with him and my parents without throwing a tantrum.

"We should go," I say softly. "We're already late. If you could try to avoid pissing off my father, I'd appreciate it. He already has his suspicions about you, I don't feel like seeing what happens if those suspicions are confirmed. I don't want him to ask questions I won't feel like answering. Odds are, things will get bloody."

"So you *do* still care about me, if you don't want to set your father on me," Ian says, victory in his tone.

"I care about my father and his sanity. I care about not having to answer the questions I know he'll raise. Let's just...get through tonight. Then I go back to avoiding you like the plague you are, and you can go back to whatever psychopathic activities keep you company."

His hand tightens around mine, his eyes blazing with intensity. "This isn't the end, April. Don't make the mistake of thinking it is. It's just the beginning."

If it's the beginning, then it's a beginning to *my* end. But he's not listening to reason, so there's no point in trying to convince him. I've already tried, he either didn't believe me or didn't want to believe me, which means it's on me to put a stop to whatever he's trying to pull.

CHAPTER FIVE

I open my car door, and Ian releases my hand with a sigh as I step out, then follows suit. After he locks the car and pockets the fob, we start walking across the parking lot and towards the glittering entrance of the restaurant.

The building is made up of rustic looking wooden logs, with fairy lights pinned to the exterior. Ian opens a polished dark wood door for me before ushering me inside. Once in, he wraps an arm around my waist; when I try to remove it, he murmurs, "Don't want to make your parents suspicious, right? Just go with it."

For tonight, it looks like I'll have to. Ian walks us up to the hostess stand, giving the young blonde waiting there a charming smile.

She smiles back brightly, a faint blush staining her cheeks. "Good evening, Mr. Vargas. I have your table for two ready to go—"

"Change of plans," Ian says mildly. "I'm here for the Stein reservations."

I realize that Ian *did* intend to take me out after the performance, even went as far as to make in-person reservations in advance to prepare. If he thought I'd actually agree to go anywhere alone with him, his arrogance is more jarring than I assumed. I wouldn't have, not even for what's said to be the best sushi in the state.

The hostess nods. "Of course. The Steins are already seated. Please, follow me."

She leaves the stand and starts leading us through the bustling seating area. We pass a sushi bar, with a glass display case showing off many different types of fish. Behind it, chefs are at work making rolls, and a few customers sit at the counter to watch. The atmosphere of the restaurant is pleasant, with an interior made up of polished red wood, pretty lights dangling from the ceiling, and soothing classical music playing from hidden speakers, underscored by the quiet chatter of patrons.

The hostess leads us towards the back of the restaurant, where I see my parents. They both stand to embrace me again and Mom smiles brightly at Ian as he pulls out my chair for me. Once I'm seated, he sits beside me, and I mentally prepare myself for a shitty night to come.

I'm surprised to find that conversation flows easily with the four of us. Ian really turns on the charm, and it works wonders with my mother. He even manages to pull a reluctant smile or two from my father as we eat, talk, and laugh. The sushi is as delicious as I expected it to be, and despite myself, I enjoy the evening. I was dreading this catastrophe in the making but it isn't catastrophic at all; instead, it's very pleasant.

As we're waiting for dessert, Dad asks Ian, "What are your intentions with my daughter?"

I tense, while Ian stares Dad right in the eye as he says, "To make her happy."

I have to suppress a snort of disbelief, while Dad tilts his head to the side, appraising Ian with a critical eye and faint expression of distaste, all jovialness wiped from his demeanor.

"You weren't dedicated to her happiness in high school. In fact, I suspect a great deal of her sadness in those years came from you. What's changed?"

I can't hide my wince. My father's spot on with his assessment; I just hadn't known he was paying such close attention to my emotional state. I should've, the man sees everything.

"Leave it alone, Dad," I mutter.

Dad spares me a brief glance. "No, *milaya*, I won't. Not when it comes to you."

His use of the Russian endearment warms me as it always has, but it doesn't make my anxiety ease. If Ian says the wrong thing right now, I'll have to defend him for the sake of keeping peace, which is the very last thing I want to do.

"I didn't believe I deserved your daughter in high school, which is why we grew apart," Ian explains, returning Dad's direct stare.

I can tell his honesty pleases my father, but that's not enough to make him stop.

"And you suddenly believe you do deserve her?" Dad questions, arching a bushy eyebrow.

"No," Ian responds, shaking his head. "She's far too good for me. If men only went after what they deserved, most of us would be single and depressed."

Mom clears her throat, placing a hand on my father's arm. "Come now, you weren't exactly deserving of me when you began pursuing me."

"I changed for you," Dad tells her. "To become worthy of you." He looks back to Ian with a challenging expression. "Are you willing to do the same?"

Ian nods. "I am. I've already begun to, and I don't intend to stop until I'm good enough for April."

I really can't take much more of this; the dinner suddenly can't end fast enough. Ian sounds so damn sincere, which just turns my anger from a simmer to a boil. He wouldn't have had to change if he hadn't sealed the coffin on any relationship between us; I loved him for exactly who and what he was.

Thankfully, Dad lets the topic lie, switching around to discussing spring break plans. Since I missed winter break, my parents are even more set on wanting to continue on with our skiing tradition for spring break. All throughout high school, we continued doing spring breaks with the Vargas's, and Ian used the opportunity to ratchet up his torment of me to level one hundred. I didn't get a moment's peace on those so-called vacations, and by junior year, I'd come to dread the trips.

Which is why, when Mom eagerly suggests that we rekindle the tradition, I burst out, "That's not necessary. I'm sure the Vargas's have plans of their own, like last year."

Dad's eyes narrow on me, while Ian puts a hand on my thigh under the table and squeezes, silently telling me to back off. His demand is not one I'll heed; he's ruined too many things for me. Our skiing trip last year without the Vargas's was nothing less than bliss. It reminded me of my love for the slopes and the freedom and beauty found in the mountains during wintertime. I don't want to lose that again.

"We don't," Ian assures my parents. "My mother actually brought up that very same suggestion recently, I think it sounds like a lovely idea."

Mom starts chirping about potential destinations and excitedly forming plans, which Ian gladly encourages. I stare at my teacup silently, understanding that no amount of protest from me will change anything.

Ian will always do what he wants to do regardless of other people's sentiments. If he wants to find a way to constantly accost and harass me, I'll need to seriously up my game to prevent that. That'll probably entail staying in my dorm room or in heavily populated areas where I can't be caught alone.

Once dinner is over, I exchange hugs and kisses with my parents, who are leaving on the earliest flight tomorrow morning. Dad needs to get back to Connecticut in time for a business meeting in the afternoon. It warms me that they made a trip out here for a single night, just to be able to attend Pandora's Box and watch me dance.

The four of us walk to the parking lot together. Before my parents leave, Dad swings by his car to bring back a small gift he and Mom got me, a beautiful pair of aquamarine teardrop earrings. I thank them, hug both of them again, then watch as they drive off.

"You're still close to your parents," Ian observes once they're gone.

"Of course I am," I reply. "They made me, raised me, shaped me, and have always supported me. I'll never not be close with them."

I walk back to his car with him, rolling my eyes when he opens the passenger door for me again. He doesn't slam it shut this time, which I suppose means his mood's improved. I'm so tired from the performance and the emotional strain of dinner, my eyes try to close of their own volition as he drives. I don't let myself doze off, though, I know better to relax in the presence of a predator.

"So, my place or yours?" Ian asks.

"You really don't grasp the concept of being denied, do you?" I mumble in response. "Take me to program dorms, please."

"You got it." Ian pauses. "That is, if you agree to another date."

I frown. "What do you mean, *another* date? Tonight wasn't a date, it was a farce. A good one, well played on both of our ends, but that's it."

Ian nods. "Alright, then, my place it is."

I groan. "No. I'll repeat it again in case you didn't understand the first time: *abso-fucking-lutely not.* End of story."

"I don't mind some resistance, but you might want to ease up on it," Ian remarks calmly. "When you fight and run, it awakens the hunt and chase instinct in me. I'm not the nicest hunter, as you know."

I let my head fall against the cool window, sighing. "I'm beyond tired, I need to sleep. Take me back to dorms. I'm not present enough to have this argument with you again."

"Remember what I told you when you were ten and I was eleven?" Ian asks.

I frown, feeling like there's slush in my head instead of a brain. "No, but I'm sure you're about to tell me."

"We were talking about marriage," Ian reminds me. "You'd said that you needed to be friends with my future wife so you and I could stay best friends, and I told you that if anything I'd marry you so I could keep you. I also said that, if you didn't agree with those sentiments, I'd probably kidnap you until you changed your mind. That's still on the table."

"You really are a twisted fucker," I murmur. "That's your problem, not mine. Try to kidnap me, I'll call the damn police on you."

"And say what?" Ian asks. "I don't have a history of going out of my way to accost or abduct people. There are plenty of old hookups who can attest to the fact that I don't care enough to chase after girls; it's usually the other way around. My parents will throw money at the problem to make it disappear, and you'll end up raising those questions with your parents that you said you wanted to avoid."

God, the man is really tiring, and I'm not in the right mental state to spar with him right now. The path of least resistance might be in my best interest at the moment, so I say, "I'll agree to a date if that's what it takes."

Of course, I have no intention of actually fulfilling my agreement, but Ian doesn't need to know that. He's told me plenty of lies; chiefly, that he'd always be my best friend and protect me. Turnabout's fair play.

A pleased smirk curls his lips. "Lovely. Are you free tomorrow?"

Nope. In the morning I'm giving lessons at one of the dance studios in this city, where I teach the young girls the basics of ballet and help train them up. Then, later, I have a coffee date with Eliana, and tomorrow evening I'm right back to rehearsals. There's another performance Sunday night—Pandora's Box will be running with two shows weekly, every Friday and Sunday, until spring break. There's the potential for a few more performances to get tossed into the mix, depending on the demand for tickets, so I will be swamped with school, rehearsal, teaching, and performances for the foreseeable future.

Instead of saying that, I reply, "Sure. What time?"

Ian's eyes narrow and he gives me a glance from the corner of his eyes, his gaze filled with suspicion. He probably thinks I'm folding far too easily after putting up one hell of a fight, so I add on, "I'm tired of going around in circles. If a date is what you need to understand there will never be anything between us, that's fine by me. I'll waste a few hours on you if it buys me solitude going forward."

That seems to appease Ian, and he lets out a dark chuckle. "Quite the contrary, Sugarplum, it's *I* who will prove to *you* that things very much can and will work out between us. Be ready at noon, I'll pick you up at dorms."

I nod. "'Kay." At noon I'll be at the studio, earning some much-needed money, which he'll discover when he shows up to dorms and finds out I'm not on campus. I wonder how long it'll take him to realize I stood him up. If the universe has any sense of humor, he'll get stuck waiting for me the way I waited for him for *years* before giving up.

Chapter Six

Ian

After I reluctantly drop April off at dormitories, I end up driving around aimlessly for a while instead of heading directly back to my apartment, thinking. I know I painted myself into a corner with the way I treated April in high school; at the time, that was my intent. Destroy any possibility of there ever being an us. Though she'll probably never understand it, I did what I did to protect her from me.

I was spinning out of control at that point, so naturally, I took things too far a few times. Back then, I saw that as a good thing, saw it as a permanent solution to keep her away from me. To stop myself from truly tainting her.

I never stopped obsessing over her, though. Never stopped thinking about her. There hasn't been a day that's gone by since I first met her where she wasn't on my mind, especially in the times when I treated her like someone I despised. Even after I graduated and sealed my fate of never having her, I thought of her constantly.

I was intent on never seeing her again, yet I couldn't stop thinking about where she was and what she was doing. I often wondered if the world of dance had truly noticed and uplifted her the way she deserved. It was a daily struggle to stop myself from stalking her social media or getting a private investigator to follow her around and keep me updated on her activities, since I was too far away to stalk her myself.

I promised myself I wouldn't for her sake, so I didn't. I tried to forget, though it didn't work. Then, by chance, I happened to cross paths with her *here.* At my school, where she'll be for the next four years. That felt like a sign from the universe that I was never meant to give her up, and I was done fighting myself when it came to her. I've always wanted her, and now I no longer care about the possibility of tainting her; I know she's too strong for that. Even if she weren't, I'm not sure I'd care. I'm too desperate.

The problem now is to figure out how to get out of the corner I'm in and find a path forward. While I didn't expect for things to be easy, I also didn't anticipate the force of April's vitriol. I never stopped loving her, though my love came through in twisted forms for a while; it was like a punch to the gut when, earlier tonight, she made it clear she'd stopped loving me.

I can see my primary issue to contend with is the fact that she doesn't trust me. I've never lied to her about my goals, not even in the worst points of our history—I was very clear in high school that I would tear her down, and I stuck to it. It was the best way to keep her away from me and my problems. Now, she seems to be under the impression that I'm trying to play some sort of game with her, and the only way to prove her wrong is consistency.

Joining dinner with her parents tonight was a bit much, I can see that, but it was the only way to ensure I'd get time with her going forward. Spring break is now a sealed deal, I'm sure my mom will be thrilled to rekindle our tradition of doing school holidays with the Stein's.

My thoughts flick back to April's angrily-spoken words earlier, when she mentioned scars. The way she quickly amended to emotional scars makes me think there's something more to the story; I have a niggling feeling that there was someone who truly hurt her. If I'm right, then whoever hurt her is going to meet a painful end, but I don't expect to get a name out of her. Even before I look for a name, I need confirmation of what happened.

Cricking my neck, I pull out my phone and dial the one contact I have who can find out anything about anyone: Seth Balor. I wouldn't call us friends, we're much too alike to have anything more than suspicion for each other, but he's a reliable contact.

He picks up after several rings, hissing, "This better be fucking important, Vargas. You're interrupting my celebration."

Just like I'd never ignore a call from someone like him, because if he asked me for something he'd be in my debt, I understand he won't ignore a call from me for the same reason.

"I'll be quick," I say mildly. "Word on the street is that you're exceptionally good at putting together dossiers on people. Is that true?"

There's a pause, and I hear a feminine voice in the background calling out softly, followed by Seth's muffled voice telling her to go back to the bedroom, that he'll be there in a moment. I roll my eyes, knowing he's talking to the girl he's in some strange, three-way relationship with; Eliana Pierce, who also happens to be April's best friend at Greywood. If Eliana was a man, I'd consider her competition, but as she's a woman and one already claimed by two others, I don't see her as a threat.

Seth comes back on the line. "You've heard correctly. I'm proficient when it comes to gathering information on people, and what I can't find, my PI absolutely can. I'll venture a guess that you're looking for a dossier on April Stein?"

"Yes," I respond. "There are some holes in her past I'm looking to shed light on."

Seth's quiet for a moment. "Elia likes April a great deal. If April were upset, it would make my woman upset, and that is not something I'll tolerate. I'll ask this once, and if your answer is not truthful, I'll treat you like an enemy and ruin you; do you intend to hurt April?"

Seth's possibly as much of a dark motherfucker as I am, though he's more controlled. I've known him for nearly two years now, and in that time, I've never seen him truly care for anyone or thing until Eliana came into his life. The way he cares for her is fierce, intense, all-consuming, and ridiculously protective. I know that if I step a toe out of line or take any action that ends up upsetting Eliana, he'd do his best to decimate me. His best, from what I've heard, is very effective.

"I don't intend to hurt April," I reply. "I did at one time, but that time is past."

Seth scoffs. "You're as destructive as I am, though not quite as meticulous. If you've hurt Stein in the past, what makes you think that damage can be undone?"

"Sheer force of will," I snap. "Will you get me the information or not?"

Another, longer pause. Finally, Seth says, "Fine. I'll do what I do. You owe me a favor for this, one that'll be called in at a time of my choosing. If anything you do blows back on Elia, I will come for you, and I guarantee you'll wish you were dead long before I'm done." With that, he hangs up.

I think I could like Seth very much under different circumstances. I drive back to my apartment, which happens to be in the same building as Seth and Carson's places, albeit on a different floor. It's the only suitable apartment complex in the area, so I'm not surprised those with enough money choose to stay here. I think, if April had accepted her parent's help, they could've readily rented or bought a place for her here.

They might not be on the same level of wealth as my family, but they're certainly not poor; her father is a very savvy and excellent businessman with a talent for growing companies. I don't like the idea that April refuses to accept help from them because of my taunts about her being a gold digger. I assumed she knew I didn't mean it, there's nothing pointing to her being someone who tries to seduce others in return for their resources. Even during our friendship when we were young, she got embarrassed when I would get her gifts or buy her meals—nothing about the girl comes across as a social climber looking for money.

That makes me wonder just what other things she might've taken to heart, and a twinge of regret tightens my chest. April always seemed so tough during high school, so impervious to the shit I threw at her, I'd escalate massively simply to get a reaction out of her. I didn't consider the fact that all of my hits landed, but she was too proud to let that show.

It certainly looks like I have my work cut out for me, but I finally have a clear vision of the future, which I've been missing ever since the summer before my freshman year. Whatever future there might be for me, April will be a part of it. She was always meant to be mine—I might've lost sight of that for a while, but I see the endgame now. I'll do whatever it takes to make my goal a reality.

***

I'm awake early the next morning, making preparations for my up-coming date. I know that April's intent is for it to be the first and last, which is why I need to make a strong case for us being together. I remember her likes and interests clear as day—not just ones she told me about when we were young, but interests I saw develop during high school. Contrary to what she and everyone else might believe, I never stopped watching her. I may not know her as well as I once did, but not for lack of observation.

April enjoys anything cultural or artful, loves the outdoors, and I remember how much she used to enjoy trying new restaurants and foods. She's adventurous and afraid of very little, so I cater the after-noon plans to her tastes.

When 12pm comes around and I show up to program dorms to collect April, she doesn't come out. I wait for five minutes, then ten, then fucking twenty. I can't go in since my student ID card isn't coded to get into dorms, and I don't have her phone number, so I can't even call her to ask where the hell she is.

It's a stroke of fortune when I see Carson and Eliana walking up to dorms, hand in hand, looking sickeningly in love. Eliana blinks a few times upon seeing me loitering on the front steps before her eyes shutter with suspicion. Makes sense, especially if April's told Eliana any of the shit I did to her in high school. If they really are good friends, then it wouldn't surprise me if Eliana hates me on principle. Well, perhaps not *hates*, I don't know that the girl is capable of hatred, but I'm certain she dislikes me.

Eliana pauses on the bottom step, staring at me jadedly, while Car-son offers me his signature bright smile. This is a man who kills with charm and kindness as much as cut-throat business strategies.

"Hey, Ian," Carson greets. "What are you doing here?"

"Waiting on April," I say through gritted teeth. I've been standing here like an idiot for nearly half an hour, and I am not pleased at being left to wait. "We were supposed to go out today."

Eliana frowns. "April agreed to go out with you?"

Agreed might be a loose term, she was actually coerced, but I nod nonetheless.

"She has work at her dance studio in the city the first half of the day on Saturdays—don't you know that?" Eliana asks, her frown deepening.

Carson squeezes her shoulder. "I think April might've kept that from him on purpose, Princess."

Eliana stiffens, and her cheeks pinken as a guilty look springs into her eyes. "Oh, shit. I'm a terrible friend."

Carson laughs under his breath. "Looks like the Dark Prince has been fooled."

I clench my fists by my side, inhaling a deep breath. I hadn't even considered the possibility that April lied last night. She's never lied to me before. Then again, it seems she's changed a great deal from the girl I used to know, so I should've assumed she had every intention of ghosting me like I'm a lovesick fourteen-year-old she wants to get off her back.

Unbelievable.

I clear my throat. "Which studio?"

Eliana's eyes narrow. "I'm not telling you that. She won't tell me what you did to her, which means it was *really* bad. I'm not throwing my friend under the bus."

I shrug, pull out my phone, and conduct a quick google search on dance studios in the city. There are only a few, and clicking on the staff section of the websites reveals that April's a ballet instructor at a youth studio.

"Pirouette Pioneer Studio for Youth," I say aloud. Then, I look back to Eliana, who now appears a mixture of worried for her friend and pissed off. "What time does she get off?"

Eliana shakes her head, refusing to answer. "I don't know what you want with her or from her, but I do know she'd be at peace if you left her alone."

"Would you have been at peace if Carson or Seth left you alone?" I query.

"Carson and Seth didn't make a point of making my life hell in high school," she snaps. "I had my drawbacks, sure, but they were possible to get past with enough determination."

Carson grins down at Eliana. "We were both very determined to have you, Little E." He looks to me and pointedly says, "We also treated her like a princess, which certainly didn't hurt things. You, on the other hand, sound like you have some redeeming to do."

He's not wrong, but I can't redeem myself to April if I can't get time with her, and I'm starting to understand that's her strategy. It's a strategy I watched her form during her junior year of high school, while I was a senior. Freshman and sophomore year, she still tried to reach out to me. By the time she hit junior year, though, she'd given up on that and settled for avoiding me, along with everyone else at our school, most of whom followed my example and were cruel to her. I should've figured that would spill over to present times; I should've anticipated that she'd say whatever it took to get me to go away, without intending to follow through on her promises.

It might be time to take a closer look at the kidnapping option. As soon as I have the thought, I discard it. I'd prefer not to go that route just yet since it won't be the most pleasant, but it'll remain in my mind as a last resort.

I start walking down the stairs, prepared to surprise April at her studio and take her with me whether she wants to go or not, but pause when Eliana's small hand lands on my arm, turning to look at her. She's staring at me with a surprisingly steady gaze. Most people find it difficult to hold eye contact with me for long periods, with April having been the sole exception to that in my life. I guess spending time with Seth must've toughened up Eliana.

"Do you care about her?" she asks me.

"More than I've ever cared about anyone else," I reply sincerely. The issue is, April doesn't believe that, and I've given her good reason not to. I truly have fucked myself over with her.

"Will you be good to her? I don't mean being nice, I mean will you worship her the way she deserves to be worshipped?"

"As soon as she'll let me." That might take a while, but I'm willing to wait. If seeing her at Greywood reminded me of anything, it's that it was always supposed to be me and April.

"What if she never wants you?" Eliana asks.

My stomach churns at the idea, and I shake my head. "She will." I'll make sure of it.

"But what if she doesn't? Will you go back to doing whatever it is you did to make her hate you in the first place?"

"No," I snap. "I won't. If she doesn't want me, I'll settle for scaring off whoever she does want and waiting."

Carson cracks a smile. "I can see why you and Seth get along."

Eliana shakes her head, but her expression is resigned.

"If you hurt her, I'll sic Seth on you," she informs me.

That's almost amusing, but also a similar threat to the one Seth made last night and not an empty one. He will absolutely come for me if I do anything that makes Eliana sad, such as make April sad. It's good that the last thing I want to do at this point is hurt April; quite the contrary, I'm rather determined to show her the ways I can *help* her. I have a sneaking suspicion that she won't be terribly amenable to accepting anything from me, which is yet another barrier to get past.

"Fair enough. Are you going to tell me when she's off?"

"Nope," Eliana responds. "I'm too loyal for that. You figure out your shit on your own, that is if you can manage that. If not, well, I'm sure April will be happier and more peaceful for it."

With that, she trots up the steps, and I start to understand exactly what about her must've ensnared both Carson and Seth; she might seem tiny and sweet, but she has a spine of steel, and doesn't let people push her around.

With renewed vigor and no small dose of irritation at the fact that April successfully ghosted me, I return to my car and pull up directions to the studio where she works. Perhaps it's time to give her a very unambiguous lesson as to why lying to me is not in either of our best interests.

Chapter Seven

April

Working with young dancers is one of my favorite ways to spend my free time. I'd be giving lessons at this studio even if the faculty hadn't offered me a paid position; seeing the young girls and boys discover their love for ballet reminds me keenly of how I found my own love for ballet.

For me, it all started with a phenomenal teacher back when I lived in New York City. My parents signed me up for all sorts of activities when I was young to see what interested me; it became clear quite quickly that, while I enjoyed sports, I fell in love with ballet. That's largely credited to my first ballet master, a stern old woman who was like a drill sergeant during class, and so passionate about her art it was impossible for me not to come to adore ballet. She was pitiless during class, but afterwards she'd often speak with the girls taking her class; talk to us about the beauty of storytelling through dance.

I want to do the same thing for other youngsters. Offer them the same glimpse into the beauty of ballet to see if they're as entranced by it as I was and still am to this day. Which is why I get up at the crack of dawn every Saturday, take the bus into the city, and spend six hours giving lessons.

Elia was supposed to join me in teaching, but then she got swept up by her men who ate up what limited free time she had. I don't mind doing it alone; seeing the exhilaration on my students' faces as they progress is so uplifting.

There's a young girl in one of my classes, Maribel, who always likes to stay late to ask me questions and go over what she's learned. The girl is eight years old, very flexible, and has great potential; she's also terribly talkative during class, which would be enough to get her expelled from most ballet schools. Throughout the time I've been her instructor, she's gotten better at keeping silent until class is over, which is promising.

Today, she stays extra late after our lesson, and I help her with an arabesque, which she's been struggling to perfect. Maribel has dark brown hair and big blue eyes that I'm sure will break many hearts when she grows up, paired with a determination that I admire. When we're done with our mini post-session lesson, she starts telling me all about her school and how she's the best dancer in her grade, much to my amusement. Her mom waits by the wall of mirrors, scrolling on her phone, not paying much attention or seeming to care that her daughter loves ballet enough to stick around for help after class.

When I hear the door to the room creak open as Maribel's telling me about a not-so-nice girl in her school, I assume it's one of the other instructors coming to request the studio space for another class. Which is why I'm shocked to catch sight of none other than *Ian*, wearing a very displeased expression that borders on feral.

Maribel turns her blue eyes to him, then says quietly, "Woah. Who's that?"

"A friend of mine. Don't worry, he doesn't bite."

Ian has always been imposing in stature and appearance, but more poignant is the intense energy that constantly shrouds him. Dancers are far more mindful of energies rather than words, because dance is all about feeling. Even little Maribel can sense the danger coming from Ian, which is admittedly a little extra today.

Maribel's mom drops her phone, then stares at Ian with wide, covetous eyes, nearly drooling at the sight of him. Yeah, he tends to have that effect on the female population; there is absolutely no denying that the man is gorgeous. His beauty just serves to hide the poison hidden beneath the surface.

"Well, *hello there*," Maribel's mother greets, reaching up with her free hand to fluff her hair. "Who are you?"

"Uninterested," Ian tells her flatly, not bothering to display any false charm. That makes the older woman gape, which then turns into a scoff as she gathers the bag sitting at her feet, beckons to Maribel, and hurries out of the room, all the while glaring at Ian.

Ian takes a step towards me. "You lied to me last night. That wasn't very nice."

I shrug. "Oops. You weren't taking no for an answer, and I got tired of repeating myself."

"Is that who you are now? A liar?" he questions pleasantly.

Total. Fucking. Asshole. "Not generally, no. I far prefer truth to lie, but when somebody doesn't accept the truth, lying becomes the only option. You weren't backing off, you actually threatened to *kidnap* me, so I said what I needed to say to go home."

Ian takes another step closer, and I have to fight the instinctual urge to step back. "I guess I'll have to be more vigilant in the future." He glances down at his watch, then sighs. "We're too late to attend the first thing I had planned today, but the second and third are still on schedule. Let's go."

I stare at him for a moment, impressed with his ability to disregard reality.

"Did standing you up not send the message that I'm not interested in going out with you?" I ask testily. "If not, let me remedy that; I am not interested in going out with you."

"I've gathered that," he responds mildly, nodding. Then, his tone hardens to non-negotiable. "You're still going out with me today. You told me you would last night, and I'm holding you to your word. Whether it be by free will or force, you are getting in my car. Make no mistake, Stein, I have zero problem hoisting you over my shoulder and taking you with me, though I think you might enjoy yourself more if you come of your own volition."

I'm stunned silent for several moments as I stare at him. For years, *years*, I tried to mend the bridge between me and Ian. *I* invited *him* to lunches and dinners, hoping we could talk things out and be friends again. Every single time, he humiliated my efforts, making me feel pathetic and inadequate for having the gall to try to be friends with him.

"Do you have any idea how ironic you're being right now?" I finally ask. "I tried with you, Ian, for quite some time before giving up. In response, you gave me excellent reasons to stay as far away from you as possible. Now, that's exactly what I'm doing; literally respecting your wishes. Do you recognize how warped it is that you're choosing *this* as the time to pursue me? When I've realized that you're too detrimental for me to waste time on?"

"I was an asshole to you for what I thought were good reasons back then. I never lied to you about my intentions, April. Not when we were friends, not during high school. I was always very clear with you as to what I planned on doing. Because of that, you should be able to trust me when I say that I am not here to hurt you or screw with you. In fact, I think I could enhance your life for the better."

Enhance my life for the better? Does he not realize how goddamn insulting that is? It insinuates that my life isn't good enough as it is, which I firmly disagree with. There are difficulties, sure, but everyone has difficulties. I'm lucky to be able to work through mine.

"And exactly how do you intend to enhance my life?" I ask flatly. "Several weeks ago you were still calling me a gold digger. What's suddenly changed?"

Ian shrugs. "I realize that I wasn't noble enough to keep away from you and that trying was pointless. I also suspect that, unlike most, you can handle me. I mean, truly handle me. You're tough as nails, April. The household you were raised in probably contributed to that, as did your negative high school experience."

"An experience that was negative because of you!" I snap, shaking my head. "No, Ian, you don't get to do this. I won't fucking accept it. You've nearly killed me once before, there is no way I'll be stupid enough to give you another chance. You will *never* have the power to hurt me again, *ever*."

Ian closes the distance between us in several long strides, slips an arm around my waist, and hauls me right against his chest, which just infuriates me even more. The fact that he presumes to have the right to touch me is so mind boggling I can't comprehend where he gets his gall. It must come from a lifetime of having more wealth than sense.

I push at his chest in an attempt to make him back off, which yields absolutely no results—he doesn't even sway. I shove harder, anger levels steadily rising. Feeling his skin on mine brings back memories of the times when cuddling with him was my favorite thing to do, which only upsets me more. I struggle against his grip with all of my might, eventually escalating from shoves to trying to kick at him, claw him, do anything to get him to release me. All my efforts are fruitless; he simply stares down at me with a look that's one part amused, one part interested, one part something that I might call regretful if I didn't know better.

"Calm down," he tells me.

"When, in the history of the world, has telling a woman to calm down actually calmed her the fuck down? Let go of me!"

He shakes his head, tightening his hold on me. I try to bring my knee up to smash his balls into his spine, but he anticipates the move and simply shifts his hips to block it. Then, he lifts me in his arms, leaving my feet dangling above the floor, kicking at air. He walks me backward into the nearest wall before setting me down, leaning his full weight against me to trap me in place. My arms get pinned to my sides, all the while I growl and struggle and throw expletive after expletive at him, growing progressively more furious.

After a few minutes, I start to tire, and my struggles slowly turn from vehement and feral to meager and weak. My eyes burn under the realization that there is nothing I can do to stop or slow this man from taking what he wants from me, doing what he wants with me—he's bigger and stronger, not to mention more powerful and better connected. In a straight fight between us, he'll always win.

"I hate you *so much*," I finally say, before giving up my fight entirely. I'm only draining my strength, which I'll need for rehearsal tonight. Ian's already a tap on my emotional energy, inciting intense anger that exhausts me all on its own; if I let him drain my physical energy, too, my dancing could suffer. I can't allow that.

His penetrating stare becomes too much to bear, so I squeeze my eyes shut to avoid looking at it or him. He's unfairly gorgeous and big and being this close to him just reminds me of how much I used to love our closeness, which is a painful thought.

"Look at me," Ian says, his tone placid and calm in the face of my tantrum.

I shake my head. "Go away."

"I won't," he replies. "I'm content to stand here like this all day, Sugarplum. I've missed feeling you against me. I've missed *you*."

"Shut up," I croak back weakly, feeling the burn in my eyes threaten to turn into tears. I will not let him see me cry; he's not worth crying over.

"I don't think I will. You want to know what I've missed most about you? About us?" he presses.

"No, I really don't, because you tossed me aside like trash." A few years ago I would've killed to be held by him just like this. I needed it back then, desperately. Now that I no longer need or want it is when he chooses to give it.

"Talking to you. Being around you. I could always be real with you, Sugarplum, which is the greatest gift someone like me can get. With everyone else, I have to wear a mask. With you, I could always be myself without fear of judgement. You're the one person who didn't judge me."

"That time is past. Now, I'm judging the fuck out of you for the way you act."

"You're a pretty liar," he responds. "Not a very good one, but a pretty one. Now that you've blown off some steam, are you ready to go?"

That makes my eyes snap open with renewed indignation. "Seriously? You're still on that?"

Ian releases one of my arms to reach up and tuck a loose strand of hair behind my ear. The gesture is heartbreakingly gentle and intimate, and it makes my breath hitch. He used to do that all the time, and I always loved it. Despite myself, there's still a part of me that enjoys it, which only makes me more upset with both of us.

"I know you don't trust me right now. I intend to do what it takes to change that. I really don't want you miserable, April, I want to make you happy. I know that I can if you give me the opportunity to."

I lean my head back against the wall, feeling sadness take root in my very soul.

"That's the thing about you, Ian. I know you could, theoretically, make me happy if I gave you the chance. I also know that giving you that chance will only afford you greater power to make me sad."

"How can I make you trust that I won't hurt you again? Not intentionally, at least. I'm a difficult person but I guarantee that it will never again be my goal to hurt you or push you away. I don't want that. I want *you*. I want to take you out today and remind you how good we are together," he says, his tone gentle but filled with conviction.

"We *were* good together. There's no guarantee that we still will be. I'm not the same girl you found crying on the bridge, just like you aren't the same boy who I thought hung the moon. Even if I did agree to go out with you and by some miracle enjoyed myself, it wouldn't change anything. I can't be with you, because that would mean betraying myself. It would be betraying my self-worth and self-respect, which isn't something I can do. Not again."

Ian's silent for a long moment, before releasing a sigh. "Fine."

I take that to mean he's finally received my message and realized that the best thing for both of us is to back off. A sharp pang of sadness travels through me, reminding me exactly why I stay away from Ian. Even now, when I'm positive I'm done with him, the idea of him finally leaving me alone after pursuing me all week hurts. Which means that, after all this time, he still has some power over me.

He steps back; a chill rushes down my spine. It only lasts a second before he bends down, presses his shoulder against my midsection, grips the back of my legs, and *actually* throws me over his shoulder. I thought he was kidding or exaggerating earlier when he threatened to do just that; this is a solid reminder that Ian doesn't bluff.

I'm frozen with shock as he turns and starts striding out of the room, but then my senses return to me. I shriek, "*What in the actual fuck?*"

I wriggle around in his hold, planting my palms on his muscular back and kicking my legs, trying to get him to let me go. His response is to tighten his grip around my legs. I'm only wearing a leotard and leggings with a small wrap skirt, and the material of the thin skirt rides up, exposing more of my body than I'm comfortable with.

"Where's your dance bag?" he asks me. "I remember you always used to have one; it was a little pink duffle with regular clothes, shoes, band aids, and a bunch of other ballerina shit. You'll need to change before we head out."

"No!" I exclaim, a touch surprised that he recalls such a thing, though the overwhelming emotion is indignance. "Put me the hell down! Are you completely demented?"

"According to some," Ian replies calmly. "You made it clear that your own methods of self-protection and self-preservation prevent you from agreeing to go out with me. I understand that, so I'm no longer asking you to come with me, I'm informing you that you're coming with me. The longer you argue, the more tempted I'll be to take it out on your ass. Where's your bag, April?"

Tempted to take it out on my ass? I can only imagine he might mean something sexual like spanking, which should *not* send heat curling through my stomach, but it does. I've had plenty of fun sex in my day; as Eliana rightly pointed out, I enjoy my fair share of both men and women, so I've tried quite a few things. I've never let anyone else spank me, though, and there have been requests in the past. A career in dance generally makes for a nice ass, which many people have admired. None of them have managed to make me feel the way Ian just did, with a mere offhanded threat.

Abort mission. I know Ian has the capacity to turn me on, which is something that's both startling and infuriating. I felt it in the park last week with him; his heat along my back as he held me against him made something uncomfortable stir in my belly. Now, his heat and scent are surrounding me entirely, enveloping me, and I feel that very same stirring, except this time it's much stronger. That makes me more compliant than I should be, because he needs to put me down *now.* This is too much for my hormones to take.

"My bag's in the locker room," I say, my tone somewhat breathy. "Put me down, I'll go grab it."

Ian chuckles. "I don't think I will put you down. I like carrying you. You're so soft, so light, so *delicious.*"

My stomach clenches at the rumbly way he says the last word. If he holds me like this much longer, there's a possibility that I'll leave a wet spot on his shoulder once he puts me down, and I can't handle that. I know I hate him, I'm so fucking *angry* with him for breaking us, but my body doesn't seem to be getting the memo.

"You can't carry me through the halls, it'll draw attention. You also can't go into the girl's locker room. I'm serious; put me down, Ian."

He lets out a long, irritated-sounding sigh before shifting his hold on me, causing me to slide down his body until my feet are touching the floor. I feel every ridge and dip of his muscular chest and abdomen as I go, which I'm sure is intentional. He must know the effect he has on the female population, and for all my strengths, even I'm not immune to just how hot he is. He looks like a dark god as he stares down at me, his arm still hooked around my waist, eyes glittering with amusement, interest, and *so much* desire.

I can see that I won't be getting out of spending time with Ian; for a reason that's beyond me, he's filled with determination. My best course of action here is, once again, the path of least resistance. Maybe if I irritate him enough he'll cut the date short and leave me alone. As soon as I have the thought, I discard it, because any reactions I give him will only fuel him further. Silence might be my better bet.

Confucius said 'silence is a true friend who never betrays'. That infamous quote was tailor-made for situations like these.

Ian finally releases my waist in favor of taking my hand. He says, "Lead the way."

I frown. "I just told you; you can't go in the girl's locker room."

He nods. "I remember. I'll wait for you outside. You take too long, I'm coming in."

Sighing dejectedly, I turn and walk out of the studio space, heading to the end of the brightly lit hall and into the locker room. I make quick work of changing while wondering how I'm going to make it through the rest of the day. Ian's like an earthquake; magnificent, dangerous, deadly, impossible to evade. Something that rattles everyone and everything around him, tumbles structures and people alike.

When I pull off my leotard, my cheeks burn to see that I did, in fact, leave a damp spot that actually made it through my panties. *Jesus.* I pull on a new pair, silently promising this one won't get soiled, use the restroom, then steel myself and head back out into the hall.

Ian leans against the wall, scrolling through his phone while waiting for me. I let out a long sigh, grabbing his attention.

"Let's get this over with."

Ian quirks a smile. "Yes, let's get started."

CHAPTER EIGHT

I'm surprised to see that our first stop is a museum in a neighboring city that's about a forty-minute drive from the studio. I don't talk to Ian during the ride, merely listen to the Rachmaninoff floating softly through the speakers. I can feel Ian's eyes flit to me periodically as if he wants to say something, but I give my full attention to the notebook on my lap, reading over notes for my History of Dance class. I have a quiz coming up that I should be studying for, though I don't get much work done; I can't seem to process blocks of text with Ian this close.

I only divert my attention from attempting to read to shoot Elia a text, canceling our coffee date.

Ian pays for our tickets when we get to the museum, something that dismays me because I suspect he'll hold that fact over my head for some time. He may have told me he doesn't truly think I'm a gold digger, but that doesn't stop me from remembering the countless times I was called one in high school, both by him and by his friends.

That was the main insult used the night I got my scars. Sometimes, I swear I can still hear the hissed words in my ear, *gold digging bitch, at least you're getting the attention you've been begging for.* They're words I've heard in my dreams many times, and occasionally I'm unfortunate enough to recall them in my waking hours.

"They have a good deal of work from the ancients here," Ian says, pulling me from my thoughts. "You still like ancient history and civilization?"

I nod. I've always had a reverence for ancient civilizations; Rome, Greece, Egypt, China... the cultures were so rich, with such astonishingly advanced art and architecture it makes me wonder if the ancients knew something that was lost to history.

Ian takes my hand as he leads me up a set of stone stairs that lets out on the second floor, which is dedicated to art from some of the oldest civilizations. For a moment it's almost endearing that Ian remembered how much I love ancient art. On the tail of that near-endearment comes the reminder that Ian is as manipulative as they come, and this is just one of his attempts to try to earn his way back into my good graces.

"Where to first?" Ian asks me, examining a map of the five wings. I glance at it too, seeing that each wing is dedicated to a different region in an ancient time period.

"The Greek wing," I respond.

"Right. You always loved the Greek pantheon. That, and the history of Egyptian pharaohs."

I frown at him as we walk to the rightmost wing, crossing my arms over my chest. He arches an eyebrow. "What, you thought I forgot? I haven't forgotten anything about you, April."

Which is goddamn unfortunate for me. It makes it harder to hate him when he says things like that, in the soft, affectionate tone that used to be reserved only for me. When he spoke to other people, everything about him changed—voice, expression, posture. With me, though, he was always gentler, kinder, more genuine and present, as if I brought out a different side to him.

I'm distracted from my musings when we enter a hall with white stone walls, matching flooring, and a high ceiling made up of windows that filter natural sunlight and illuminate the gorgeous statues displayed on plinths all around us.

Most of the statues are partial pieces; to the left of me is a muscular torso of a man carved from marble. The golden plaque on the plinth informs me that this is the torso of Apollo, excavated from ancient ruins. I step closer to it, admiring the intricately carved abdomen.

"How do they know this statue is of Apollo?" Ian asks.

"Most likely from the location where it was excavated," I respond, too caught up in the beauty of this hall to muster any ire towards Ian. "It was probably pulled from one of his temples in Delphi. Unlike all the surrounding areas, Delphi wasn't a city-state, it was a town of its own centered on worship. People traveled from all over Greece to worship there."

"Oh?" Ian questions.

I nod. "Apollo was a major deity, one of the Olympians, god of music, poetry, and the sun. Legend has it that Achilles—the ancient Greek warrior and demigod—offended Apollo, so Apollo guided the arrow that Paris shot at Achilles to the demigod's one vulnerable spot; his heel."

"So your fascination with ancient Greece has only grown through the years," Ian observes. When I turn to look at him, there's a fond smile on his lips as he stares at me, not sparing any attention for the many statues and bas-relief pieces on display.

There's a lot here that he could and should be focusing on, but instead, he's choosing to watch me. That makes me feel warm in a way I don't like—I don't want any warm or fuzzy sentiments towards him.

It took me a long time to build up the necessary shields between us to keep me safe, and I can see he's trying to tear them down.

Instead of responding, I trail to the next statue, which is a partial of Aphrodite. It's missing her legs from the knees down, and half her face is gone, but there's still plenty to admire. "The standards of what women need to look like to be seen as attractive have changed so much," I say softly, staring up at the goddess. "Aphrodite has thick thighs, thick arms, and a rounded stomach—she was an idol of beauty and fertility for a very long time. Throughout much of history, a bigger woman was considered appealing. It was a sign of nobility and wealth. The lower classes starved."

"That so?" Ian asks.

I nod. "It wasn't until the 19th century that skinny became synonymous with pretty. Before then, it varied from culture to culture, but having a flat stomach was not a requirement to be considered gorgeous."

"Interesting," Ian murmurs, putting a hand on the small of my back as I wander over to a bas-relief carving hung on the leftmost wall. It showcases a noble family from one of the great Greek houses. Ian walks a little to the left to read the label, then makes a humming noise. "Greeks didn't have last names, did they?"

I shake my head. "Not technically, no. The Greek name structure was the individual's name, followed by a patronymic name, and sometimes the place they or their family originated from was added at the end. Game of Thrones probably pulled their name structure from ancient Greece."

A half-smile spreads on Ian's lips. "You're a GOT fan?"

I shrug. "There's lots of sex, violence, bloodshed, and conflict. What's not to like?"

That pulls a full belly laugh from him, one so light and amused that I have to trap my bottom lip between my teeth to avoid smiling at him. He's making it increasingly difficult to hate him, which is why I turn away from him and continue wandering the hall, doing my best to ignore him.

He doesn't make it easy, though. As we walk through the different wings of ancient civilizations, he quizzes me on my knowledge and asks questions perfectly suited to what I've dedicated many hours to learning. I didn't intend to speak to him at all, but we end up talking nearly nonstop for the three hours we explore the exhibits and displays. Once we're done, he heads to the bathroom on the first floor, while I wait for him out in the hallway, realizing with no small dose of horror that there's a part of me that still likes Ian. Most of me hates him for what he's done and how he's acted towards me, but there's a small part that's charmed by him. Today, I got a reminder of how easy conversation used to be between us, even got glimpses of his own knowledgeability and intelligence, all of which is an aphrodisiac to me.

Needing to find a way to lessen his appeal, I start sifting through memories of the worst things he's done to me. Not things that were done by his lackies because they figured they could get away with anything, but him specifically. That takes me down a rabbit hole of a deeply unpleasant memory lane, and the specific moment my mind lands on is the last time I tried to reach out to Ian and give him a shot.

***

April, age sixteen, Junior Year

"Honey," Mom calls out.

I look up from my place at my study desk, where I have notebooks, textbooks, and loose pieces of paper along with flashcards strewn before me. In the last years, this desk has become sort of a safe space for me; I can study in peace, as my parents don't disturb me when I'm seated here, and since it's in my room, I can also be miserable in peace. High school has not been kind to me, which is attributed entirely to my former best friend.

I understand now that I should've left Ian alone after he told me our friendship was over years ago. I couldn't bring myself to, though. I had to try to reconcile, try to find out what could have possibly gone wrong. It's hard for me to believe that it's all about money; after all, his parents have become close friends with my parents, and the Vargas's don't look down on the Steins. Quite the contrary, Mr. Vargas has accepted business advice from my father on many occasions, and they're even considering starting a venture together at some point. Since Ian's parents don't look down on my parents, it made no sense to me that Ian was suddenly looking down on me because of the deficit between our wealth.

"Honey?" Mom repeats, gently knocking on my door. I shake my head to pull myself out of my thoughts and force a smile as I look at her. She stands in my doorway wearing a checkered pajama set, appropriate for 9pm on a Friday evening since she likes to go to bed early. Dad's the night owl in our family, just like me.

"What's up, Mom?" I question, meeting her warm eyes.

I notice she's holding up a card in her hand, one with my name written on it in blocky letters. That's strange; it might be Christmas season, but I'm not really one to get cards. Ian's done everything in his power to make me a social outcast at school, so the only friends I have are ones either in the dance school I attend four times a week, or the ones I read about in my books. I already exchanged holiday cards with the girls in ballet, so getting another one now is random and slightly suspicious.

"It's a party invitation," Mom tells me, walking into my room and setting the card down on the edge of my desk. I frown as I look at it—this might be my third year in high school, but I have never once been invited to a party.

I pick up the card, flipping it over and seeing that Mom's right, but this isn't just any party invitation, it's an invite to a party at Ian's house. He hosts them pretty regularly, at least once a month, and they're considered extremely exclusive and difficult to get into. They're always invite-only. Despite my better judgement, a thrill of excitement travels through me. Ian was openly hostile to me throughout freshman and sophomore year, and this year, I decided to try to give him some space, see if that could let him cool off from whatever it is that made him hate me. Maybe it worked. Maybe we can finally fix what's broken between us.

I know I should already hate Ian for the way he's treated me, but I don't think I'm capable of hating him. Anyone else, yes, but not him. I love him too much; I've loved him since the day he told me my eyes were pretty and offered to pull mean pranks on the people who had said otherwise. We were inseparable for years, and he's the only person I've ever felt truly connected to, which is probably why I can't let go of him.

A small niggle at the back of my mind points out how unusual this is. That if Ian wanted me at his party, he might've delivered the invite himself, so maybe this card came from a different source. My hope overrides my common sense, though, hope that I might somehow get my best friend back, who I've felt so bleak without.

"Are you going to go?" Mom asks, a gleam of excitement in her eyes.

I shrug, trying to play it casual when I'm anything but. "Sure. Why not? I'm pretty much done with homework, anyways."

She reaches a hand out to stroke my hair. "Of course you are, sweetheart. Keep up the work and you'll be valedictorian next year."

That's my goal. I want to make it into college without having my parents pave the path; not only do I want to go to an excellent school, but I want to go on a full ride scholarship as well, which means maintaining an above-perfect GPA. My school accepts weighted GPA's for AP classes, and I'm already enrolled in four this year. If I do another few next year and ace all of them, I could be looking at a GPA as high as 4.8. As long as I do well on my SAT and ACT, that should be enough to get me a scholarship to my colleges of choice.

I start shutting the textbooks and notebooks in front of me, piling the flashcards together and organizing everything before standing up.

"You and Ian have seemed...distant, lately," Mom murmurs, watching as I walk over to my closet and start sifting through outfit options. "He hasn't joined us for dinner in years."

I force a laugh. "He's been busy, Mom. He's captain of the football team this year and does a bunch of other extracurriculars. I'm surprised he has time to throw any parties."

"I'm surprised he's never invited you to any of the one's we both know he hosts," Mom says, frowning. Her motherly senses are probably tingling, letting her know that something's off. If I don't quickly find a way to cover for Ian, she might start pressing for answers.

"His parties can get to be a bit much," I blurt out, thankful I'm facing my clothes instead of her. If she saw my face, she'd know that I'm bullshitting. "He knows I'm not a big people person, so most of the time he doesn't bother to offer. I guess since this is his last winter party of high school, he thinks an invite is worth a shot."

"Hmm," Mom hums, not sounding like she believes me. To distract her, I pull two hangers off the rail in front of me, each holding a dress that's party-appropriate and flattering. I turn around to face her.

"Red or blue?" I ask.

Mom's eyes flick over both dresses before she says, "Red. If you really want to knock everyone dead, you'll put on some lipstick to match. Careful so your dad doesn't see, though; you know how he feels about makeup."

I chuckle. Dad is under the impression that I am still his baby girl, therefore I shouldn't know what heels, makeup, or any grown-up things are. If he knew the way Ian's been acting toward me, Ian might already be in the hospital. Or he could've just disappeared off the face of the earth—there's a good reason I keep my parents out of the loop.

"I'll go distract him in the bedroom," Mom offers.

I wrinkle my nose. "Ew."

She laughs. "Not like that, sweetheart. You know his favorite show runs tonight, I'll make him watch it in there while we cuddle, let him know you're out for the night. Don't have more than one drink, and make sure it's something sealed. Be home by midnight." With that, she gives me a wave goodbye, and leaves me to get ready.

Half an hour later, dressed and armed with more hope than I've felt in years, I climb the grand marble steps leading to Ian's house. He has the biggest home in the neighborhood, which is saying a lot because all the houses in his neighborhood are huge. The Vargas mansion sits at the very end of the cul-de-sac with a large driveway leading up to it. Marble pillars prop a stone roof over the front porch, and I can see through the large windows that the party is already in full swing, with strobe lights and dancing and teenagers grinding on each other. The front door is cracked open, so I let myself in.

I'm instantly treated to glares from my more condescending classmates gathered in the grand foyer, but I ignore them. I'm only interested in one person here tonight; I don't care that said person is the reason I receive so many dirty looks.

I'm familiar with Ian's house, so I make my way to the left of the foyer and into the living room, scanning the space for signs of the host. He's not there, so I head to the game room, and that's where I catch a break. Ian's leaned over the pool table with a cue in his hand, a shot lined up. He's surrounded by about half a dozen boys and three girls—one of them being Tabitha Riley, the girl who's led the campaign of hatred against me. She also happens to be Ian's on-again, off-again girlfriend, which means I'd despise her even if she wasn't such an utter bitch to me.

Actually, I don't know if girlfriend is the right word; Ian doesn't really do girlfriends from what I've heard. More like fuckbuddy.

Ian takes his shot, sinks a ball, then repeats the gesture four times, walking around the table and pocketing shot after shot. The fifth time, he misses, then straightens and passes off the cue. He doesn't look pleased or amused; in fact, he kind of looks bored, even at his own party. That's when he notices me standing in the entrance, and his expression of boredom disappears. Confusion briefly flickers through his eyes as he looks me up and down, taking in my dress, curled hair, and heels. Then, much to my disappointment, a sneer curls his lips.

"Stein," he hisses. "Isn't it past your bedtime? What are you doing here?"

I blink several times, staring at him. I'm here because I got an invitation, and I'm here to try to talk to him and finally put whatever shit's been going on between us in the past, but he seems to be under the impression that I should be anywhere but here, which returns my earlier suspicion that the invitation didn't come from him.

Feeling my cheeks burn as deep embarrassment sweeps over me, I clear my throat. "I got an invitation."

Tabitha pushes off the wall she's leaned against next to her bitchy friends, and gives a loud, animated laugh. "Oh my god, you actually bought that? How desperate could you possibly be?"

My throat feels like it's full of gravel and my eyes burn as I watch her saunter over to Ian in her miniscule black dress, her blonde hair bouncing over her shoulders and blue eyes glittering with a twisted sort of amusement. She puts a manicured hand flat on Ian's chest, and says, "I slipped her the invite, baby. Wanted to see if she was as pathetic as the rumors said."

I'm so used to hearing bullshit from her and her league of skinny idiots, I ignore her, even though the sight of her touching Ian feels like a knife being stabbed into my stomach.

I say, "Ian, can we talk?"

Tabitha barks a laugh. "As if he'd want to talk to a yellow-skinned nerd like you." She turns to look at one of the snickering girls still leaned against the wall, and says, "You owe me thirty bucks, I told you she'd come."

"Ian," I repeat, clenching my fists by my side. I'm already here, might as well do what I came here to do. "Please."

Ian rolls his eyes in an exaggerated fashion. "Will you never fucking learn? You're really making yourself into a damn joke, April. It's kind of pitiful."

Tabitha laughs again at that, trailing her red nails up and down his chest, tossing me a cruel smirk over her shoulder while my soul feels like it's withering away inside of me.

"At least my IQ isn't comparable to that of a flea, like the bimbo on your arm," I snap.

It takes Tabitha a few beats too long to get my joke, which just reaffirms my point. She gasps, while Ian chuckles. "I don't need her for her IQ, that's useless to me." He trains his gaze, glittering with cruelty, on Tabitha. "In fact, her brain doesn't matter. It's her other skills that interest me, such as the things she can do with her mouth."

Tabitha's cheeks redden as a few snickers sound in the room. Ian looks back to me and says, "So, unless you're here to suck my cock, get out."

I grimace. "I'd prefer not to catch ten STD's, but thanks."

Ian shrugs. "Fine by me." He looks at Tabitha again. "Why don't you show her how it's done, Tab?"

Oh, hell no. He wouldn't do that right here and now. He might excel at low blows, but that isn't just a low blow. It isn't just cruel, it's fucking disgusting. He can't actually mean to get a blowjob in front of me just to drive me away; even Ian isn't that stupid. A moment later, though, I realize just how wrong I am when a red-cheeked, obviously embarrassed Tabitha sinks to her knees, right here, in front of everyone, and her hands move to undo Ian's pants. She must really be a goner for him, even though he treats her like a casual commodity.

I don't bother wasting the breath to point out she's the one being utterly pathetic right now, putting on a public show just to be a bitch to me—she's literally devaluing herself for all to see. Even so, I don't think Ian will actually go through with it, which is why I cross my arms over my chest. Ian holds eye contact with me as Tabitha pulls down his pants and palms his length through his boxers. He keeps looking at me as she slips her hand inside and starts to rub him off, keeps staring as she pulls his boxers down and he takes a fistful of her hair, guiding her open mouth onto his cock.

That's when the message really, truly sinks in; he'll do whatever it takes to make me feel shitty and inadequate, including getting sucked off by the girl who's unbelievably cruel to me at school directly in front of me. There's no shot he won't take, no line he won't cross, all because I'm supposedly beneath him. The yellow-skinned, narrow-eyed nerd. The nobody who he made the mistake of befriending.

I blink several times as my eyes start to sting again with oncoming tears, but I don't let them fall. I don't drop my gaze to watch the show, either. I feel hollow, like somebody scooped my insides out with a rusty spoon, leaving nothing but a fractured heart. It was my mistake to trust the invitation, to come here tonight, to think there was any hope of fixing whatever's broken between Ian and me, because it isn't just broken; it's nonexistent. There's nothing but hostility between us, and there hasn't been for years. It's my naivety and ignorance that drove my hope, and now I see just how wrong I was for it.

I'm done being stupid. I'm done opening myself up only to get trampled on and hurt. Ian and Tabitha can do whatever the fuck they want, wherever they want; I don't care anymore. I can't care anymore, it's too painful. It's time for me to let go of my fantasy of being Ian's friend, maybe even girlfriend—there's no hope. Even if there were, I realize in this moment he's not the boy I knew. Who he is now isn't someone who I want to befriend or associate with, no matter our history; the person he's become is absolutely disgusting.

One of the guys closest to me, Chad, is standing with his friend Braxton, both of whom are leering at the free show they're getting. Chad turns to wink at me with a salacious smile, before asking, "Wanna join in on the fun, gold digger?"

I turn on my heel and speedwalk out of the house, hearing Ian's laughter echo behind me.

CHAPTER NINE

Crawling out of the vivid memories of that horrible night, I blink several times, surprised that moisture still gathers in my eyes at the remembrance of just how low Ian went to push me away. The night of the party, I cried over Ian for the very last time. Then, I screwed my head on straight, and threw all of my focus into academics. Even the horrible summer following my junior year only made me more determined to excel in school and dance, mainly because it was a great way to avoid everything else. I aced every AP course I took, got one of the highest scores in the state on both my SAT and ACT, then subsequently received full-ride scholarship offers to every school I applied to, including Juilliard and Greywood.

Prioritizing the important things in my life, studies and dance, was my saving grace. Without them, I don't know if I would have crawled out of the hole of darkness I found myself in. Which is why I have to ask myself exactly what the fuck I'm doing here. *Here,* in this museum, with Ian. Waiting for him outside the bathroom like a puppy ready to follow him anywhere.

I shake my head, then turn around and head for the entrance of the museum, pulling out my phone and clicking over to the Uber app. It's expensive to get a ride from here all the way back to campus, but I'd rather blow half the money in my checking account than rely on Ian. I *know* he's unreliable.

I know better than to be here with him; I know better than to let myself enjoy my time with him. I also know it's only a matter of time before he gets out of the bathroom and comes looking for me, which means I have a short window to get the hell out of here without having to make a scene. Unfortunately, the nearest Uber willing to take me back to Greywood is 20 minutes away. I order it, then look around the courtyard outside the museum, wondering if there's a spot for me to hide away in. If Ian can't find me, he'll probably assume I ditched him.

Just then, though, I hear Ian's voice behind me, calling my name. I briefly contemplate making a run for it, but that would just be weak. I ran from him at the party, I'm not running again now.

Ian trots down the museum steps, stops beside me, and slings an arm over my shoulder. Too worked up from my most recent walk down memory lane, I step back and hiss, "Don't touch me."

He blinks, looking genuinely confused for a moment, before rolling his eyes. "Not this again."

"I'm not kidding right now," I snap. "You basically forced me into this date; now, it's over, and it won't be happening again."

His eyes narrow as he stares at me, probably growing irritated with my sudden about-face, considering the fact that we did just spend nearly three hours exploring the museum and talking. What he doesn't know is that I can still see Tabitha's condescending smirk, hear Ian's cruel words, and *feel* all the ugliness from two years ago.

"What happened between the time I left to go to the bathroom and now?" he demands.

"Common sense," I deadpan, checking my phone. My ride is fifteen minutes away; longer than I'd prefer, but I can wait.

"That's bullshit," Ian snaps. "You enjoyed this. I know you did. What the hell is going on?"

I glare at him. "I pulled on one of dozens—shit, probably *hundreds*—of memories of how proficient you were in keeping me away from you and realized that a few hours of looking at and discussing old art isn't going to erase our history."

Instead of doing what any other sane man would do, such as having the decency to *go away*, Ian grabs my arm in a lightning quick move and pulls me into him, hauling me flat against his chest and wrapping both arms around my waist to hold me close.

"If you don't let me go, I will scream," I growl lowly.

He gives a cruel, short laugh. "No, you won't. You don't want to attract that kind of attention—after all, we look like we're in a lovers embrace right now. There are eyewitnesses and footage from museum cameras to attest that we spent the last hours talking and smiling together. You scream, I'll pull the mental-breakdown card, and you're the one who'll end up looking like a fool."

I realize he's right, which makes me so angry, I want to spit in his face. That'll only give credence to his insanity claims against me, though, so I grit my teeth and inhale a deep breath, trying to calm the rage coursing through my veins. All I have to do is get back to dorms; Ian can't reach me there. I should've refused to come with him to the museum, found some way to wriggle out of it. More, I shouldn't have said a peep to him or let him touch me—I was just so swept up in art, I momentarily forgot the importance of keeping him away.

I can't scream at him, I can't throw any sort of public tantrum, but what I can do is give him a dose of reality. "Remember the winter holiday party at your house?" I ask him, my tone terse. "I was just recalling it. You know, the one where your arm candy at the time, fucking *Tabitha*, thought it would be funny to fake an invite and place bets on whether or not I would fall for it? I did, because I was stupid and hopeful. Even when I realized you didn't invite me, I wanted to stay, because I thought maybe I could get a second to talk to you. Do you remember what you did?"

He blinks, the irritation in his eyes temporarily dimming. There's no regret in his expression, though. No indicator that he understands how utterly fucked up what he did back then, a mere two years ago, was. No apology; *nothing*.

"I do," I tell him. "Sometimes that scene replays in my dreams, like my subconscious is trying to remind me of all the reasons I have to despise you. There are many. I never wanted that, you did, and you succeeded."

"I took it too far," he finally admits, lowly. "I was half drunk and in a bad place. You were in the wrong place at the wrong time."

"I was in the wrong place at the wrong time for *three years*, Ian. Plenty of time to teach me that the best thing I can do for myself when it comes to you is *stay away*."

My phone buzzes, and I pry my eyes away from Ian and look down at it, only to see that my driver has canceled the ride and the app is searching for another one nearby. It's like the cosmos itself is against me right now. Ian glances down at my phone, then snatches it in one of his hands while still using the other to hold me firmly to him. I glance around, seeing that the crowd of passersby around us heading in and out of the museum are paying us no attention.

Ian snorts. "Really, April? You ordered a fucking Uber? Can you even afford that?"

"Fuck you!" I exclaim, trying to break his hold.

He slips my phone into his pocket, preventing me from taking it back, then stares down at me with his glittering green eyes.

"I'm not saying that as an insult. Although I don't think it's particularly smart for you to refuse to accept help, I respect your ambition and drive to get by yourself. God knows too few people with the option for help actually choose to forge their own paths."

I glare at him. "I don't want your respect."

He shrugs. "Doesn't change the fact that you're one of the few people in this world who has it."

"I genuinely despise you," I tell him lowly.

"Can't say I entirely blame you, since that was the end goal of how I acted towards you during our time in high school. I'm working on changing that. You're not making it easy for me."

His tone is a mixture of frustration and grudging respect, as if he's irritated that I'm not giving him an inch, but he also admires that.

"You're not going to be able to change that," I assure him flatly. "I won't allow you to. I've already told you this far too many times; you had your chance. Many chances. You proved to me that I was wrong to give them to you, so you are not getting another one, *ever*. You're only wasting both of our time. I have rehearsal in a few hours, and you have whatever it is you do that brings you joy—skinning kittens, probably."

He lets out a puff of laughter. "That's too macabre for me, April. I might not have the best morals, but I'm not *that* dark. You have rehearsal at seven, it's three right now. I wanted to take you to a restaurant that I think you'd like, but now that I see you're a flight risk, maybe I should take you back to my place instead. Order in."

"Do you not hear yourself?" I demand. "You're patently insane and seem to be willfully oblivious to the fact that I don't want anything to do with you."

"That's where you're wrong," he replies, his tone soft. "I know you don't *want* to have anything to do with me, but I also know you're interested. You hate yourself for it, but some part of you likes me. That's good for me; if no part of you liked me anymore, kidnapping might be my only remaining option. As is, I'm trying other methods first." He strokes his hand up and down my back in a gesture that's meant to be soothing, but falls short considering the circumstances. "You need to understand the fact that I'm not going to back down or go away. You were always going to be mine. I lost sight of that for a while, but I can see it clearly now. You're drowning in memories of the bad times, which I can't fault you for, but you're also disregarding the years of good times we had. You know we were good together, April. You know what it's like to have me on your side; I can be very helpful. Your greatest supporter, most valuable friend."

"We were children," I remind him. "Things are very different now."

He tilts his head to the side. "The only difference now is that there'll be sex tossed into the mix. I promise you I'm a very satisfactory lover. Well, not to most, but I will be to you."

I gape at him. "You actually think I'll let you touch me? I offered once, in exchange for you to go away, and you refused. That's the only way I'll agree to it."

"Is that why I could feel your need back in the studio?" he questions mildly, making my cheeks burn with embarrassment. "I would've taken care of you if you'd asked. I still can."

I growl, "*No.*"

There isn't even the faintest stirring of arousal within me right now; the memory of Tabitha getting on her knees for him all in a ploy to screw with me is too fresh in my mind.

He sighs. "Your loss, you'll come around eventually. I'm starting to think the best course of action with you might be taking a path that's a little more forward. When I picked you up at the studio, you nearly melted. Even now, your body has gone soft from a few minutes of me stroking your spine, and we're in the middle of a rather unpleasant argument. It knows it wants me, even if your head hasn't caught up just yet."

I realize with mortification that he's right. At some point during this back and forth, I've gone from tense as a board to leaning against him, even while glaring at him and wishing him dead. That prompts me to stiffen and shove at his chest, though I know from experience that it isn't enough to make a difference.

"We're burning daylight. Here's the deal, Sugarplum; we're going to my car."

"I am *not* going anywhere near your home!" I snap. I can't stand it, but he's right; something about him turns me upside down. The signals in my brain stop passing through to my body, which means I can't trust myself around him. Being wherever he lives, sleeps, eats, where his scent and energy is probably embedded everywhere, doesn't seem like a good idea.

"Then will you be a good girl and let me take you out to eat?"

If it's between being with him in public, where I at least have options, and being with him in private, where I'd be entirely at his mercy, I choose public. After several long moments, I give a single, angry nod.

CHAPTER TEN

I an lets out a dark chuckle. "I don't think I've ever had to convince or lightly threaten a woman to let me take her out. Most of the time, I'm the one fending off date offers from mere hookups."

"You're welcome to take any of those hookups out in my place," I grumble. "They're obviously willing and happy to spend time with you. I, on the other hand, want nothing to do with you."

He leans his head down until his lips are hovering right above mine and we're staring into each other's eyes at a startlingly intimate proximity. I shrink back, suddenly feeling very intimidated and not altogether safe, which makes Ian smile softly. He slides one hand up my back to cup the nape of my neck, which makes my eyes widen. *Is he going to kiss me?* Here and now? After the not-very-pleasant conversation we just had? More... if he does, how the hell am I going to stop him?

My dreams of him over the last years have been mostly negative, reminders of all the shit he's done to me or been the root cause of by making me the most hated person in our school, but I'm ashamed to admit that there have been a few others that weren't of such a dark nature. They were ones I often had after an unsatisfactory experience with my flavor of the week, where my mind conjured up Ian taking care of me in the way another lover failed to. Each time I woke from those dreams, I was wet between my thighs and burning up with shame, because I know I shouldn't be attracted to him. I'm *not* attracted to him—certainly not his personality—but his physical appearance is a thing of beauty, very hard to ignore.

Even more difficult now, with his lips quirked as he stares down at me, seeming amused by my discomfort and panic.

When his eyes drop down to my lips and brighten with interest, I whisper, "If you kiss me right now, I will bite your lip off."

"I don't think you will. I think part of you wants me to kiss you, but the other part's fighting it."

His observational skills are infuriating but also right. I *don't* want him to kiss me, I don't even want to be here with him, but there's a tiny part of me that disagrees and would like to climb this man like a tree. It's the part that isn't sensible enough to understand exactly why I can never be with Ian; a part driven by need and hormones. While I like to think I'm a reasonably strong woman capable of keeping my head on straight, that other side of me is making it difficult to stick to my convictions.

Fuck that. If Ian thinks I'm prey that can be trapped or cornered, I'd be happy to prove him wrong. Thus far, he's been in control of all of our interactions, because I've been focusing on getting away from him rather than outmaneuvering him. I can see that, at least for now, getting away isn't an option. What I can do is take back control and give him a little taste of his own medicine.

Before I can think too much on my idea or talk myself out of it, I rise on my toes and fuse my lips to his, giving him a taste of exactly what he's been craving and I've been denying. I feel him stiffen in surprise, which only lasts a moment before passion replaces the shock and he tries to overtake our kiss, push his tongue into my mouth to get a taste of me. Instead of allowing that, I tilt my head and bite down on his bottom lip *hard,* hard enough to break skin and draw blood. His head jerks back with shock and hopefully pain, and he stares down at me with a look of surprise. Then, his eyes darken. He leans down again, running his bloodied lip along mine, before growling, "Lick it off. You break it, you fucking buy it, April."

I bare my teeth at him, trying to reach up with my hand to wipe his blood off, but he shifts his body to prevent it. His eyes flare with a mixture of anger and interest as he stares down at me and repeats, "Lick. It. Off."

Startled by his tone and intensity, I comply, finding the metallic taste of his blood weirdly erotic. Most likely because I know I drew it from him, *I* made him hurt, which is a powerful feeling.

He nods, slowly. "Good. I don't mind it rough, Sugarplum, in fact that's exactly how I prefer it. You should know, the next time you bite me, I'll bite back." His voice lowers to a growl. "Just so we're clear, I bite harder."

I believe that wholeheartedly. I can picture Ian being a goddamn animal when it comes to sex; biting, scratching, clawing, taking what he wants to take without any regard for whether the other person likes that or not.

"Open your mouth," he tells me, still growling. "You got a taste of me, now it's my turn."

Understanding that I started a very dangerous game which won't end until he's gotten what he wants, I figure the best way to get this over with is to comply. If I fight, he'll fight back, and he's bigger and stronger and more capable than me, so I'd only be wasting my energy. His lip's still bleeding, so when I hesitantly part my lips and he falls on them like a rabid animal, I get both the taste of him and his blood. His tongue plunges into my mouth, so aggressive and hungry it's startling. The hand that isn't cupping the back of my neck moves down to my ass, plastering me even more firmly against him, as if he can't get close enough. While the kiss is almost scary in its intensity, I also can't deny that it's hot. It reminds me of the single-minded focus Ian used to display when we were kids, spending time together; he made me feel like I was the center of his universe. That's what it feels like now, too, and the attention is a little dizzying.

When he pulls away, it's to lean his forehead against mine with a murmured *fuck*. I'm breathing heavily, nearly panting, trying to get my senses back, feeling a whole lot more docile than I was before the kiss, and I'm quite sure that was Ian's exact intention. To turn me pliant and mindless, which is exactly what it did.

"I'm going to fucking devour you," Ian murmurs. His chest rises and falls with harsh breaths, as if our kiss rattled him as much as it did me.

"I won't give you the chance," I breathe back, half-heartedly. Right now it's difficult to stick to my hatred of him; I'm ridiculously turned on. My nipples are hard and there's a warmth in my core that's impossible to ignore. As much as I despise Ian, my body really doesn't. In fact, it's primed and ready for him, which is utter bullshit.

Ian chuckles. "I wasn't asking, Sugarplum. Your mouth's a liar; I think I'll take my cues from your body, which is far more compliant."

"You are such a twisted fucker," I say, shaking my head. "Do you not get how bad that sounds? You're pretty much telling me that you don't care about my consent."

That appears to clear the last of the kissing-fog that overcame both of us from him, and he looks down at me with an expression that's one part smug, one part condescending. It makes my blood heat with irritation.

"I am a twisted fucker, but even I care about consent. The thing is, I know that you'll won't verbally give it to me—not anytime soon, anyway, no matter how much you might want to. I'll take my consent from your body, which will give me all the cues I need."

The problem with that is my body will give him all the consent he could possibly want, because despite my better judgement, I'm attracted to him. If I could stop myself from wanting him physically, I would. But I don't; I can't.

"That's not fair," I say lowly. "You're being obscenely unfair. Do you want me to hate you even more?"

Ian blinks slowly before shaking his head. "No, April, I do not want you to hate me. I want you, plain and simple. You'll come around eventually."

For some reason, a deep sadness sweeps over me at those words. Probably as a tribute of sorts to the time where I didn't need to come around, I was ready for Ian and wanted to be his best friend. There were moments when I even wanted more; I'd grown to be attracted to him despite the way he treated me. I wanted whatever I could have with him. If he could've had whatever epiphany's suddenly taken hold of him back then, we might've been together and happy for years by now. But he didn't, and I can't betray myself by giving into him.

"I'm so fucking mad at you," I tell him. "We were good together, even—no *especially*—as friends. So damn good. You robbed me of that, and now you're trying to force your way back into my life, which only makes me angrier."

Ian exhales a deep breath. "I can't say I'm sorry for everything, especially since there was a good reason I pushed you away, but I can say I am sorry for the pain I caused you. And for breaking us. If it's any consolation, I really, *really* regret that now."

"You didn't then," I point out. "You had no regret or regard, just a single-minded drive to destroy me, which you damn near succeeded in." I feel my temper rising again, anger replacing sadness, which is a welcomed change. "Do you have any idea the shit that happened to me because of you? Because you decided to brand me the punching bag of the school? People listened to you like you were their god. They saw the way you treated me, and took it as permission to do whatever they wanted to me."

Ian's eyes narrow as he listens to me, and I can practically hear the gears in his mind whirring, trying to figure out what I'm alluding to. I won't give him more than I already have, though. He doesn't deserve it. He can keep on wondering, the same way I wondered for years what it was that made him hate me.

"What do you mean?" he asks.

"Doesn't matter anymore," I murmur offhandedly. I got over it, got past it and moved on with my life, coming out stronger in the end. "To avoid getting kidnapped, I'll go to lunch with you. If you could drop me off at dorms after that, I'd appreciate it, because no matter how much you've exhausted me, I still have fucking rehearsal tonight."

I expect Ian to push for more information, but thankfully, he doesn't. Instead, he ushers me to his car, casting me continuous glances from the corner of his eye.

CHAPTER ELEVEN

Ian

Lunch is uneventful. April, evidently committed to ignoring me, speaks a total of three sentences to me throughout it. I can tell she likes the restaurant I picked out, a place that specializes in all different kinds of ramen noodles. Not the packaged, shitty, dollar kind of ramen I've seen April eating a few times around campus, the gourmet kind made with good ingredients, creative and delicious. She orders the black truffle ramen; I watch her inhale it like she hasn't eaten in a century, which makes me wonder if living off the wages she earns gives her enough money to properly feed herself. Greywood has a meal plan for program students, but the food in the cafeteria is barely edible.

I don't ask, though. I've pushed her more than enough for the day. Besides, I have my own ways of getting information about her. Once we're done, I drive her back to campus as I promised I would. I don't like the idea of separating from her at the fuck all; now that I've officially decided she's mine, I want her moved in with me already. I want all of her free time to belong to me, even though I'm well aware I don't deserve it.

I remember the times when our families joined together for skiing trips during spring break; my favorite part of those trips was sneaking into April's room after our parents had gone to bed. We'd raid the minibar, occasionally order dessert from room service, then talk and laugh late into the night. Sometimes we'd put on a movie—April always loved her Disney movies—and she'd curl up against me, watching until she passed out. I'd watch her until I fell asleep, too. Waking up to her first thing in the morning was always my favorite thing, especially since her body would curl around me in the night. Most mornings she'd wake up half on top of me.

I remember the sleepy smile she'd give me, the way she'd pat my chest and kiss my cheek before sending me back to my room so we could get ready. There was nothing romantic or sexual about it, we were too young for that, but the connection I felt with her was soul deep. She understood me in a way nobody else ever had, accepted every dark corner of my personality, and still loved me. She kept loving me even after we'd fallen apart, right up until the party she mentioned earlier.

The way she spoke about it... I can tell that it was a turning point for her. I suspect that the party was the moment she'd made the decision to be done with me. After that, she stopped all of her efforts entirely. Stopped trying to get a few minutes to talk to me. Stopped acknowledging me or even looking in my direction when we crossed paths in the school halls. It's like I'd become utterly invisible to her, which only made me crave her attention more. Of course, I couldn't get positive attention from her—I needed to keep an emotional distance between us—so I settled for poking at her until she'd react whenever I got the chance. Even while I was committed to staying away from her, I'd have rather had her hate than nothing at all.

When I pull my car up to the dorms parking lot after lunch, with her in the passenger seat scrolling through her phone, I can't stop myself from saying, "I want to see you again tomorrow."

She gives a ladylike snort. "Then come to the performance. Feel free to bring along rich friends of yours and encourage them to donate; we need the funds if we're going on tour this summer."

I file that tidbit of information away for later use, though she knows coming to her show wasn't what I meant when I said I wanted to see her. I've already reserved tickets for every performance in the best box seat in the house; I've always loved watching her dance. She comes alive when she dances, and she does it so passionately and so beautifully it's easy to see why she got cast as a lead. I have no doubt she'll make it big in the industry.

"I mean before that. Or after."

April reaches for the doorhandle, so I engage the child lock mechanism that can only be unlocked from the driver's seat.

"Jesus, Ian, I don't have time for this. I don't want to see you again; today was more than enough to last for the rest of my life."

I don't believe her. I believe that she wishes she didn't want to see me again, but I watched her very carefully in the museum. For a few hours, she forgot about hating me, and in that time I saw a great deal of hope because she actually enjoyed herself. She liked talking to me, answering my questions about art. She relaxed, and I know that if I can get her to lower her guard again, we might actually make some progress. The downside is, she immediately berated herself for lowering her guard—I need to find a way to put an end to that.

"Okay, then. I guess you're leaving the when and where up to me—I'll figure it out myself," I tell her.

She rolls her eyes, and even that juvenile gesture is hot as fuck coming from her. "I have homework to do, today and tomorrow. Not to mention shit-tons of practice so I can stay on top of my game. I don't have time for you, and you know that even if I did, I wouldn't allocate it to you."

Seeing that we're not getting anywhere today, I pull her phone out of my pocket, where it's stayed since I first took it outside the museum, then quickly add my name and number to her contacts list and send myself a text. I hand it back to her and disengage the child lock. I've pushed her plenty enough for one day, and I'll be seeing her tomorrow anyways. I know that she has a busy schedule; I also know she has down time aside from studying and dance, which I'll be taking full advantage of. No use in pushing that point now, though.

"Have a good day, Sugarplum," I say as she practically leaps out of the car, swinging her dance duffel over her shoulder.

"Get fucked, asshole," she mutters, before slamming the door shut and jogging to program dorms, as if she can't get away from me fast enough.

Another twinge of regret tightens my chest, followed by an even deeper conviction that I *will* get us through the shit clouding our past and into the future. I know now better than ever that there is no future for me without April in it. She's the only woman I'd want to spend my life with, travel the world with, have kids with. Even if she hates herself for it and pretends to judge me, she's still the one person who gets me in a way nobody else ever has.

I drive home, feeling a heaviness settle over me as I do. I don't like leaving my girl, especially now that I've gotten a little taste of her. Not nearly enough to sate me, but enough to get me thoroughly hooked.

After parking my car, I let myself into my apartment, glancing around the interior. It's mostly bare; I'm not really one for decorating.

The entryway has a small black table for my keys and wallet, along with a coat closet. Beyond that, the living room has a single dark grey sofa in front of a wooden coffee table, both of which sit before a large flatscreen TV that hangs above a console table.

I have all the basics; a bookshelf, a study desk, even a small balcony, but the place lacks any true character.

I remember April's room from her house in Connecticut; it was bursting with personality and posters, as was her entire house. Her mother's a successful interior decorator who contracts with some very famous people—my mom hired her to decorate one of our country houses a few years back—and I wonder how April would spruce up my apartment, which I have every intention of making into *our* apartment at the earliest opportunity. I can imagine myself walking through furniture and decoration stores with her, maybe even a few art galleries. She's always had a knack for design, probably coming from her mother; my girl would make the barren space far more interesting, with art and lamps and tables and the works.

My phone starts ringing as I'm heading to the kitchen to pour myself a whiskey. Seeing that it's Seth calling, I pick up, putting my phone on speaker and setting it on the counter while I grab a bottle of the good stuff from one of my cupboards, along with a glass.

"What do you have for me?" I ask without greeting. Neither Seth nor I are people who like wasting time on useless things like pleasantries or small talk. There's no point in a *hello, how are you* when we both know that neither of us could give less of a fuck.

"A lot," Seth responds flatly. "Check your email for the completed dossier. Everything from grades in high school to current schedule, current grades, and the courses she's planning on picking up. Lots of useless doctors' records and the works, mostly menial shit. There are a few items that are of more interest, if you want a bullet point version instead of wading through all the menial bullshit yourself."

"I would," I reply, taking my glass into the living room and sinking onto the couch. I grab my laptop off the coffee table, set down my glass and open it, clicking over to my email.

As promised, there's an email from Seth with several attachments.

I listen as Seth prattles off a list of notable achievements, academic and dance awards, though my curiosity is truly piqued when he mentions a hospital report that was made by a concerned doctor when April was seventeen.

"Stein got admitted with a stab wound below her shoulder blade, relatively shallow, didn't hit anything major, along with a cut on her lower back. The attending doctor stitched her up and filed a police report, as they're required to for suspected abuse when it pertains to minors, but Stein refused to give an explanation or press charges, so the case never went anywhere. Her father was the one who brought her in and he insisted on a rape kit; there was evidence of physical assault and attempted sexual assault, but it looks like attempt is as far as the perpetrators got. My guess from what I've seen is that Stein fought them off, got stabbed for the effort, then ran away."

My blood fucking *boils* at his words, and I feel an itch break out under my skin, one that demands that I find whoever hurt April and kill them slowly and *very* painfully. Her words from earlier today come back to me, when she indicated that bad shit happened to her because other students in high school saw her as a punching bag. I'd assumed it was linked to what she'd mentioned about scars last night, but I didn't think it could be anything like this.

The regretful feeling from earlier returns, except this time it's not a twinge; it's a tidal wave. The idea that I had *any* connection with her being hurt like *that*… no wonder she doesn't want anything to do with me.

"I appreciate the info, Seth," I say through gritted teeth. "I owe you one."

"Yes, you do," Seth responds. "You'll hear from me when I'm ready to call in my favor. In the meantime, if I see Elia sad because April's upset, I will come for you." The line goes dead.

I drop my phone beside me, pick up my glass, and down the contents before letting out a low groan. Whatever happened to April that landed her in the hospital, she isn't ruled by it; it seems the experience made her stronger, got her to develop steel armor, which makes me proud but also presents a *huge* barrier.

My best working theory is that some fucks at our old school really did take the way I treated her as permission to up the ante and pull something criminal with her, which *infuriates* me. I might've engaged in some garden-variety bullying and I didn't discourage others from doing the same, but I also did not give anyone the go-ahead to escalate to something like full-blown assault. I certainly wouldn't have condoned it; had I known about it back then, I would have hunted down the idiots who had the gumption to touch her and made them regret ever being born.

I could ask April about it, but I don't think she'd be particularly amenable to telling me what exactly happened and who hurt her. In fact, odds are it'd probably make her try to pull away from me even more, which I can't have. I don't *think* that she associates that experience directly with me or she'd have already yelled at me about it, but it seems she sees me as a link in the chain of events that led to it, which I am. If I could go back to my high school self now, I'd beat the shit out of myself and tell the younger, dumber, less clear-sighted version of me to get his head out of his ass and do better. I can't, though. All I can do is look forward.

I need to find out who hurt April and end them, but that'll come in time. I know she's attracted to me, at least on a physical level, which means I'll get her naked eventually. Hopefully sooner rather than later. Then, I can ask about her scars in an organic manner, without having to reveal that I had an in-depth dossier about her compiled for my benefit. Maybe, with enough prodding and after some time, I'll get a name out of her; then I can get to avenging her.

For now, though, it seems best to leave the topic alone. If her father was the one who took her to the hospital, he might have a better idea of what happened than I do. Then again, if he knew more than me, whoever had the gall to touch his daughter would've probably disappeared, which would've made the news in my home city. That man might keep his nose clean when it comes to business, but there are plenty of rumors that he has some old-world connections.

Along with the many dark thoughts swirling in my head, there's also a great deal of admiration for April. I was horrible to her for years, and it looks like someone or possibly several people were even worse, yet she doesn't act like a victim at all. In fact, she seems untouchable, like nothing can phase or harm her. At this point, I can imagine very little actually could get to her. I know from personal experience that once you've survived certain things, it either breaks you or gives you the confidence to know you can survive anything.

Right now, my best course of action is to attempt some wooing. I'm not exactly proficient with it as I've never had need to seduce or woo a woman before, but I'm a fast learner. Besides, I remember plenty about April, including her likes and dislikes. For example, I know she has a fondness for sparkly objects, unique knickknacks, and rare flowers.

I call a flower shop and put in an order for her that costs a pretty penny, one that'll be delivered to her tomorrow night before her performance. Maybe that'll make her slightly more willing to go out with me after; even if it doesn't, though, it won't change my plans.

A better man might've decided to back off after hearing what Seth dug up; as for me, I only intend to work harder. I'll make April mine, find out who had the audacity to touch her and kill them, then give April the happily ever after she should've had with me long ago.

Chapter Twelve

April

I stay in my dorm room until rehearsal, then head back to dorms directly afterwards, not willing to risk another run in with Ian. I stay there for most of the day on Sunday as well, doing homework and catching up on some reading until it's time to head to the theatre in the city to prepare for the show. Curtain's up at seven p.m., so my ass needs to be there no later than five. The two hours between arrival and showtime are usually dedicated to warmups, costume, and makeup.

At around six thirty, as I'm applying finishing touches to my silver and blue Zeus-themed makeup, side by side with Elia who's also painting her face, knocking sounds on the dressing room door.

"It's probably Carson or Seth here to steal a quickie before the show," I tell Elia, rolling my eyes playfully.

She frowns at me. "I have a no-sex rule within six hours of performances, and two hours of rehearsals. My men don't grasp the concept of taking it easy, and I can't be freshly sore on stage or I won't dance my best."

I bark out a laugh, amused at her openness and her logic. To be fair, I've seen the occasional bruise on her limbs in the shape of fingerprints, so I can't blame her for setting some guidelines. If I had two obsessed men constantly wanting to fuck during show season, I'd probably have some rules, as well.

As is, I only have one psychopathic man who seems absolutely set on making me his despite my continuous protests, and I won't be letting him close enough to fuck me. As pathetic as it is, I learned yesterday that I can't totally trust my self-control around Ian. Something about him still calls to me, at least in a physical sense. If we didn't have the history that we do, I'd have already ridden him like a bull. Possibly more than once.

"It might be one of them looking for a kiss, though," Elia says, setting down her lipstick. She pulls on her wrap skirt before walking to the door and swinging it open.

In the mirror, I see a teenage delivery boy holding an absolutely *gorgeous* bouquet of flowers in a pretty crystal-ridged vase. Not typical flowers like red roses or pink tulips, but an eclectic bouquet made up of several different species, the colors ranging from dark red to black.

"Delivery for April Stein," the boy announces, popping his chewing gum.

Elia lets out a light gasp, while I drop my mascara on the counter and spin around, frowning. I slowly walk up to the delivery boy, accepting the bouquet that he thrusts into my hands. A white card sits in the middle of a beautiful arrangement of roses such a dark color they could be mistaken for black, black violas, black irises, black pansies, and dark red tulips.

I look back to the delivery boy, saying awkwardly, "I'm sorry, I don't have my wallet to give you a tip."

He waves a bored hand, popping his gum again. "Tip was included with the payment. Enjoy the bouquet." He strolls back down the hall; I kick the door shut behind him, not sure what to make of this situation.

I set the bouquet down on the counter before picking up the card. It has my name written on it in pretty cursive, and when I flip it over, I see a note.

Sugarplum,

I hope these brighten your evening. I'd wish you luck, but we both know you don't need it; you'll be the best on stage.

I'll meet you in the lobby after your performance to take you to dinner.
Ian.

I knew the bouquet was from him as soon as I heard the delivery boy announce it was for me; there's nobody else I know who would go out of their way to send me something like this. My instinctive reaction to set the bouquet on fire and shatter the vase is mitigated by the fact that the arrangement was obviously made with care, and it has some rarer species of flowers—it's too pretty and unique to destroy, no matter who it came from.

I don't miss the fact that Ian doesn't *invite* me to dinner, he *informs* me he'll be taking me to dinner, which means I'll be slipping out of the back exit to avoid him. I'll leave the bouquet here; I like it too much to throw it away, but I can't carry it with me back to dorms.

Elia walks up beside me, running her fingers over the petals of a few flowers, her eyes sparkling.

"These are from Ian?" she asks.

I let out a grunt in response. "Dude doesn't know how to take no for an answer."

Elia looks contemplative at that, her brows furrowing. "Is it the good type of not taking no for an answer? I mean, not ignoring consent, that's never good, but persistence and perseverance? If Carson or Seth had listened to my first dozen or so rejections, I wouldn't be where I am now. I'm really, *really* happy with them."

"That's because you lucked out," I tell her bluntly. "Ian is... not a good person by any stretch of the imagination. He also dedicated great deals of time and personal effort towards making three years of my high school experience utterly awful, so I know what it's like to be on his bad side."

"Did he hurt you?" Elia asks, putting a gentle hand on my arm. "Do you need help with him?"

"He never physically hurt me, I was too far beneath him for that," I murmur. "He just made me fair game for all the entitled assholes I went to school with."

"And now it looks like he's trying to make up for that," Elia responds, looking at the flowers again. "You know, I crossed paths with him yesterday. He was waiting for you outside of program dorms when I showed up to grab some things from my room. He seemed very intent on getting a date with you, and I assume he succeeded. Now, flowers." She plucks the card from my hand. "Along with another date. How was it yesterday?"

"It would've been good if I hadn't been so violently opposed to him, with good reason. The high school shit wouldn't bother me on its own, it bothers me because I was best friends with Ian for years before that. One day, he dropped me like I was nothing. So, honestly, I'm just not interested in going out with him."

"You still sound angry with him," Elia points out, setting the card down and walking back to her side of the counter. "If you were indifferent or apathetic it would be one thing, but anger means there are still some feelings there.”

“Oh, plenty of feelings,” I reply sarcastically. “Resentment, hatred, vexation, outrage.”

She arches an eyebrow at me, picking up her eyeliner. “You know what they say about hate and love. Thin line.”

“Sometimes it’s a chasm the size of a universe,” I shoot back. “Don’t confuse your situation with mine, Elia. Carson and Seth literally worship the ground you walk on—which is especially impressive in Seth’s case, nobody thought he was capable of worship. Ian threw bullets, knives, and beartraps at me for years. Flowers aren’t going to change that.”

Elia frowns a little, but then shrugs and returns to applying her makeup. I follow suit. Fifteen minutes later, my phone buzzes with a text from Ian.

Ian: Did you get the flowers?

I frown at it, contemplating if I should respond with something along the lines of go fuck yourself, but that’d only be giving him attention when my best bet is to ignore him. A few minutes pass before he texts again.

Ian: I know you did. Do you like them? I chose the arrangement with your tastes in mind.

I can’t help myself after that one, I’m too irritated with the fact that he chose perfectly.

April: You don’t know anything about me.

His reply is almost instant.

Ian: Wrong. I know a great deal about you, and I'm planning on getting to know everything before long.

I roll my eyes at that but don't text again, instead focusing on getting into my costume. Just as one of the stage crew members calls for us to take our places for the first act, Ian texts again.

Ian: Meet me in the lobby after the show.

A small laugh escapes me. If he actually thinks that I'm going to comply with any of his wishes, he really doesn't know me at all.

"Ready?" Elia whispers to me as we walk to the right wing of the stage, preparing for the first variation.

I smile at her. "Always."

The show goes off beautifully, just as it did the other night. Every cast member is committed to making Pandora's Box as close to perfect as it can possibly get, and we do a damn good job of it. My solos go well, and as always I love being on stage. Love the feeling of stage lights bathing me, love the elation that comes with executing beautiful variations. Sanders's choreography is masterful, as is the music from the accompanying orchestra. The show comes together so seamlessly, so beautifully, that it almost brings tears to my eyes.

During intermission, Elia and I hole up back in the star's dressing room, both wearing puffer jackets to keep ourselves warm and ready to continue dancing. I take a few minutes to add some super glue to the soles of my pointe shoes, a little trick I've learned to keep them usable for a few more days. Pointe shoes are the most expensive items in ballet; thankfully, Greywood gives excellent discounts to its students so that we can buy professional-grade shoes for a fraction of the market price, but still having to drop fifteen dollars every week to every other week becomes a bit tedious for someone on my budget.

The second half of the show goes as well as the first, and when the time for bows comes, the roar from the crowd is positively deafening. I beam at the attention and praise—this is the best part of performing, hearing the appreciation from the audience. Nothing can supersede it.

Backstage, I change back into civilian clothes and share a long hug with Elia, who has a tendency to tear up after shows. The girl is too sweet and kind for this world, although I've also seen just how tough she can be in the face of adversity. Still, I'm glad she has someone like Seth protecting her—the dude might be a psychopath, but I've seen his commitment to shielding Elia. His meanness protects her kindness, and he's never mean to *her*.

There was a moment when I *almost* resented Elia for having both Seth and Carson adore her, but especially Seth. He's a similar breed to Ian, the cardinal difference being that he's never used a single ounce of his darkness against Elia. He's used it to care for her and guard her, while Ian turned every bit of his darkness against me for years.

After wiping away her makeup and tears, Elia heads out to the lobby to greet the crowd and find her boys, while I gather my dance supplies in my bag and head through the maze of the theatre hallways towards the emergency back exit. I'm exhausted from the excitement of the show, albeit also elated, and absolutely starving, which means I have a date with a cup of noodles as soon as I get back to dorms.

It's late, but Sanders has kindly arranged for a shuttle bus to arrive after performances to take the students back to campus; it should be at the nearest bus stop in a few minutes. I push out of the back exit and am instantly hit by the frigid cold air which reminds me that I need to save up to buy myself a proper jacket. While my dad's genes have given me the ability to deal with cold quite well, I certainly don't *enjoy* it.

That cold is quickly dispersed; as soon as the emergency exit door closes behind me, a hot body appears from the shadows of the alleyway and presses me up against the door. Memories of the last time I got cornered in an alleyway claw their way to the forefront of my mind, blurring my vision and kicking my survival instincts into gear. Before I can completely lose my mind, though, a familiar scent of ocean air and dark masculinity envelopes me, telling me that I haven't been cornered by some random perpetrator. My vision clears, and I look up into the green eyes of my once tormentor and the current bane of my existence.

I let my head fall against the metal with a sigh, rolling my eyes heavenward. "You've gotta be fucking kidding me."

Chapter Thirteen

Ian lets out an amused laugh, tucking a stray strand of hair behind my ear before stepping back, giving me some much-needed space. "Can you really be surprised, April? I knew telling you to go to the lobby would have the exact opposite effect."

"You put a whole new meaning to unwanted suitors," I mutter, hefting my bag higher on my shoulder. "I'm too tired to argue with you tonight, we can do this another time."

Ian smiles calmly. "Good, I don't want to argue with you, either. Let's get going, I have reservations waiting for us."

He knows that's not what I meant; he's twisting my words to his advantage. I try to screw my head on straight and think about the easiest way to get out of this situation. If our last encounters have reminded me of anything, it's that Ian is relentless when pursuing something that he wants. I tried my very best to wriggle out of spending time with him yesterday, and the only result that yielded was personal frustration and tiring myself out. I'm the sort of person that takes lessons from past experiences; my experience yesterday taught me that once Ian has me in his view, trying to get away won't do anything but tire and frustrate me.

"You really don't grasp the meaning of the word no, do you?" I ask him.

He shrugs. "With most, I don't care enough to press. *I'm* the one who usually utters the rejection. You're not most, though, in fact you're quite singular. I'll persist until your *no's* turn into *yes's*."

"And if they never do?" I prod.

He gives me a half-smile. "They will."

"You sound really confident for someone who should have the good sense to leave me alone," I tell him.

"That's the thing, April, I don't have much sense when it comes to you. Only desire and need. You have it, too, though you probably won't admit that anytime soon."

I might have a touch of misplaced desire where he's concerned, but I know it's wrong, and I'm avidly working to subvert it. Having him in front of me is not making that easier; I might have horrible memories to keep me in check, but six feet plus of sheer masculine hotness is difficult to ignore.

"If I told you that I want to go back to dorms and sleep, would you let me?" I ask him.

He inclines his head. "Of course. I'll take you there after dinner."

I let out a heavy sigh. I don't want to go anywhere with Ian right now, but he *did* choose a good restaurant yesterday, and I'm not really looking forward to the dinner in a cup I was planning on. If I have to suffer his presence, at least it'll come with the bonus of food. As soon as I have the thought, though, it's followed by the deep shame I felt each time he called me a gold digger; something that still fucks with me.

"For someone who managed to convince thousands of our high school peers that I'm desperate to fuck for money, you really seem eager to spend yours on me," I snip.

I mean for my tone to be crude and insulting, but instead it comes out somewhat *hurt*, which I hate. I don't want to be hurt over Ian's treatment of me, I want to be either mad or disconnected. That's what I was for years, now he's walked back into my life for just a few days and it's battering at my anger, revealing the pain beneath.

"April," Ian says, his tone stern. "I don't think you're a gold digger. I never did. That was an insult I used to keep you at arm's length, which I shouldn't have done. I can see that now. I didn't then, but I do now. I need you to get past that, because I have every intention of spoiling the fuck out of you."

Of all the things he's said, that's what really gets my back up. "I am not yours to spoil," I snap. "You don't get to do that. The only person who will spoil me is myself."

Ian gives a cruel laugh. "How? With what funds? You're flat broke because you won't accept help from your parents out of some misplaced pride. At best, ballerinas will pull in 100k to 150k a year, but most make about as much as a kid flipping burgers."

I bare my teeth at the insult. Of course to someone like Ian, who has a nine-figure trust fund and the world at his fingertips, a dancer's wages must be a joke. To me, it's not the wages that matter so much as the experience. Principal ballerina's and soloists travel the world on their company's dime—they eat at the finest restaurants, tour the best museums, experience *so much* culture and beauty.

Besides, I intend to go into choreography or teaching after I'm done on stage. I know that ballerinas maybe get a good fifteen to twenty, in rare cases thirty, years in before their careers are over, and I'm not stupid enough to ignore that eventuality. In fact, I have every intention to prepare for it. That's why I'll be picking up more classes outside of dance and gen ed next term and will continue to do so throughout my time here; I want to be ready for when I retire from dance and need another profession to go into.

I don't tell Ian any of that, though, because he doesn't deserve an explanation. Instead, I say, "If I'm such a broke, low prospect, why are you wasting your time on me? Why are you making me waste my time on *you*?"

A frown furrows Ian's brows. "I didn't say you were a low prospect, I just pointed out that you're broke. That won't always be the case; when we marry, you'll have half of what I have, so finances won't be an issue. As for your comment on you not being mine to spoil, that's where we very much disagree. You are mine to spoil, Sugarplum, whether you accept it or not."

My jaw drops at his casual mention of us getting *married*, as though it's a matter of *when* and not *if*. The fact that he thinks I would ever agree to marry him while I need to be coerced to go out on dates with him is so ludicrous it's almost hilarious. A startled laugh escapes me, and once it's out, I can't make it stop—I laugh and laugh, the sound reminiscent of a cackling witch. I never realized Ian was this funny.

Once I've calmed, I wipe a tear away from the corner of my eye before saying, "I would jump off of a bridge and dive to a watery death before agreeing to marry you. I don't want your money, I don't want you, I don't want anything to do with you. Not that you care about my desires, because if you did, you'd have fucked off when I first told you to."

"I care very much about your desires," Ian tells me. "More than I care about anyone else's, aside from my own." He steps into my personal space again, crowding me against the steel door, reminding me just how small I am in comparison to him. "As for marriage, you're the only girl I would ever marry. I think you'll come to agree down the line, so we can table that discussion for later. But if not, I guess I'll become a spinster."

"Fuck this noise," I mutter, pushing at his chest. "Get out of my way, I'm going home."

Ian sighs. "Not this again."

Yes, this again. I was almost willing to let go of the fight for one night and go with the flow, mainly because I was too tired to battle, but he has an uncanny way of putting me in a fighting mood.

I hear the honk of the shuttle bus in the distance, which means I need to get out of the alley and to the corner of the street by the theatre if I want to get back to dorms. I try to maneuver my way around Ian, get to the bus, but he doesn't give me an inch; just like yesterday, my struggles against him amount to nothing but my frustration and his faint amusement.

"You don't have to fight me," he says. "Stop putting us on opposite sides. I want to be on the same team. I didn't mean to offend you, April. Like I've told you, I respect your drive, but you must know you need support. You can't take on the world alone. If you took it on with me, you'd get much farther much faster. I want to help you."

"I don't need your fucking help!" I half-shout, losing what calm I still have.

I'm too goddamn tired to deal with him right now. Not just from the performance tonight, but also from our time yesterday; he has a way of causing lingering exhaustion. Being around him is too much on my emotions—I'm not generally an emotional person, not anymore, but he has a knack for bringing out old sides of me. Sides I prefer to keep buried in the past, along with him.

"Shh," he attempts to soothe me.

I weakly hit his chest, fuming. That's how I always feel around him; weak. Which is why it's no great surprise when I feel tears of anger, pain, and past woes start to gather in my eyes. That only makes me angrier, which makes more tears gather until they start spilling over. I squeeze my eyes shut to try to stop them, leaning my head back against the cold steel of the door, breathing harshly and trying to calm myself.

"Don't cry," Ian murmurs.

I jerk my head to the side when I feel his fingers on my cheek, brushing away my tears, which prompts him into taking my chin in one hand to hold my head in place, and use the other to wipe my tears.

To my great consternation, the tears only fall harder at his gentleness, because I've missed the tender side of him that hid from me throughout high school, and I *hate* myself for missing it. I hate him for showing it to me now when it's too late, when accepting him would be betraying myself.

Maybe I should transfer schools. After all, if I'd gone to Juilliard, I wouldn't have had the misfortune of running into Ian.

"Look at me," Ian says, using a gentle voice one might when trying to calm a stray animal.

I shake my head. I don't want to look at him right now; I didn't want to ever look at him again, but that decision was taken out of my hands. If there's such a thing as fate, that bitch must absolutely *despise* me. She's taunting me with what I once wanted desperately but know I can't have.

Ian lets out a deep breath, then pulls me forward into his chest, wrapping his arms around me. That's when the tears *really* start to fall, accompanied by sobs. He used to hold me like this all the time, and I treasured those moments. I held onto those memories for as long as I could, until he gave me no choice but to let go of them and him.

As I cry, words come tumbling out of my mouth, barely coherent and mumbled into his chest through soul-wrecking sobs. "Why would you break us?" *Hiccup.* "We were *so* good together." *Sob.* "I was so damn good to you, and you were just as good to me, but then you demolished it like a wrecking ball." *Wail.* "And now, *now* you have the audacity to come back and try to worm your way back through defenses *you made me build.*" *Sob, hiccup, sob.* "You must want to kill me."

"I don't want to kill you," Ian murmurs into my hair, pressing a kiss to the crown of my head that just makes me cry harder. "I'm sorry for what I did, for acting like such a shit for so long. If I could go back and beat some sense into myself, I would."

"But you *can't.*" *Wail.* "It's done. I tried not to give up on you with eve—" *Sob.* "—everything in me."

"Tell me how to fix it and I will," he whispers.

I shake my head against his chest because there *is* no fixing it, and that's what sucks so much. He was too cruel for too long; he pushed over a row of dominoes that led to the worst times of my life. What I hate most about this moment is just how much I like his warmth and his touch, the reminder of the way I used to rely on his strength when I couldn't find my own.

"I can't let you go, April. Even if I wanted to, I couldn't. I tried; I really did, and then you came back and made that impossible."

"I'll go away again if that's what it takes," I mumble, feeling the strength drain from me. "If I need to transfer schools, I will."

His hold on me tightens and I feel his body tense around me. "Don't do that. I'll just follow you. Wherever you go, Sugarplum, I'll follow you. You won't be able to outrun me because I'll follow you to the ends of the earth, but you're breaking my heart right now. Tell me what to do."

"You don't have a heart," I say, sadly.

Even as the words escape me, I'm not so sure of them. If I look back at high school, he certainly didn't seem to have a heart, but he did have one before that. A heart only I ever heard or felt but knew existed. Something happened to him that must've buried his heart under mountains of armor, but I know it was there, and right now I feel it. Not just hear it battering under his chest but *feel* it in the way he holds me.

"I do, April, and it's yours. It's always been yours. All you have to do is take it. Trust me just a little."

"I won't sacrifice my self-respect for you again," I mumble.

"Then don't think about it that way." He pulls back just enough to give him room to peer down at me. "It doesn't have to be me or you. It *isn't* me or you. It can be *us*."

I blink several times, my vision blurred from my tears, though I can still see his clear green orbs staring down at me. They're filled with an earnestness that sends pain coursing through my chest, because whether or not he wants to be, he is breaking my heart right now, all over again. Presenting me with a decision where my hopes and dreams point towards him, but my common sense tells me to protect myself. I can't have him and protect myself; that's not how it works. Not even if, in this moment of vulnerability, I recognize just how much I want him.

As much as seeing me brought back a whole lot for him, seeing him has also brought back a whole lot for me. At the forefront is anger and resentment hiding a deep-seated pain, but beneath that is a desire I've been trying to ignore. A desire for him that I buried deep and thought I snuffed out entirely. I'm realizing that I never managed to do away with it, it just got covered by all the shit between us, and I grew comfortable with that. Hating him and being angry with him is safe.

"You're a cruel bastard," I tell him.

He leans down to rest his forehead against mine. "I am, but you'll never be on the receiving end of my cruelty again. *Never again*, April. I've never lied to you, so tell me you trust that at least."

It's true that Ian has never outright lied to me. After the day on the bridge when he abruptly ended our friendship, he spent my last year of middle school and his first year of high school ignoring me. Then, when I started high school and tried to approach him, he straight up told me that I should stay away from him because he'd hurt me. I didn't listen, so he hurt me repeatedly. It took me years to smarten up. Just because I've never caught him in a lie to me, though, doesn't mean he's not lying to himself.

"I can't have you," I say, more to myself than to him. Even if I trust his words, I'd be a damn fool to heed them. He might think that he'll never hurt me *now*, so his words may be true at present, but... "You also promised me you'd always protect me."

Ian lets out a long sigh that I feel against my cheeks. "I did think I was protecting you, Sugarplum. You've always been my weakness. I thought amputating that weakness would protect us both, and I was wrong."

I don't know what to make of his words. Part of me is tempted to ask what happened to make him feel like pushing me away in the meanest possible manner was protecting both of us, but I also don't want to know. If I know, he might have an easier time getting past my defenses. He's already trying to chip away at them.

"Tell me you missed me, April," he murmurs. "Tell me you've missed me as much as I've missed you."

I'm silent for a long moment, fighting back fresh tears. I really *have* missed him. The version of him I used to know, anyways. He's showing me hints of it again, and I hate him for it because I have missed that terribly, I just haven't allowed myself to see that until now.

"I miss what we used to be," I finally admit, quietly.

Ian lets out another sigh, but this one sounds more like a breath of relief. "Then let's be that again, except better. Give me a chance."

"Give you the power to break me again, you mean," I reply, my voice wobbly.

"No," Ian disagrees, shaking his head. "Give me the chance to fix us. You've always been my favorite person in the world, you know. Even when I was determined for that not to be the case, you were. You still are."

"You used to be my favorite person, too," I say sadly.

"Then let me be that again," Ian pushes, tilting his head to the side and leaning down to ghost his lips over mine. "I'll protect you from everything, even myself. I'll help you be the best you can be. I'll make sure everyone sees you shine the way I know you can. I'll be the person you can trust and fall back on. Be mine, and I'll give you the whole world."

"I can't," I murmur. Not now. Not when I'm still so mad at him. But... "If you want me, you'll have to earn me."

"Then give me a chance to earn you," he replies, brushing his lips against mine again and again until I practically melt in his hold. I'm strong, but I don't know if I'm strong enough to resist him like this.

"Fight for it," I whisper. "Fight for me."

I feel his smile against my lips. "That, I can do."

CHAPTER FOURTEEN

Ian kisses me. It's a kiss that starts out gently, persuasively, slowly. It's soft and sweet and all the things that nobody sane would ever associate with Ian, so tender it's heart wrenching. He runs his tongue across my bottom lip, then pulls it into his mouth and nibbles on it. I part my lips hesitantly to allow him entry; instead of feasting on my mouth like I suspect he wants to, he takes it slow. The kiss is terribly seductive because it's all the tenderness and gentleness I've missed from him, and it makes me soften beneath him.

I wind my arms around his shoulders, which invigorates him. The kiss deepens, moving from sweet to intense in the span of a millisecond. One of his hands tangles in my hair while the other drops further down to clutch my ass and plaster me against him. He sucks on my tongue, groaning when I return the favor. When I bite his lip again he chuckles and pulls away, gazing down at me.

"You're still a fiery thing, aren't you?"

"Always," I confirm. "At least I didn't make you bleed this time."

"I've missed that too, you know. I've missed everything, April. Every single damn thing."

I shut my eyes, shaking my head. "Stop being so...*nice*. It isn't you. It feels wrong."

He rests his forehead against mine, as if needing as much physical contact as he can get. Holding me isn't enough, it seems like Ian needs as much connection as possible. It's such a vivid reminder of what we once were, it makes my heart ache all over again.

"You were the one person I wanted to be nice to," Ian tells me. "Other than my mom, maybe, it was always you. I liked making you smile. Loved making you laugh. I liked when you'd get a little mean, too."

"There's not much niceness left in me," I murmur, frowning.

I was never a truly *nice* person at heart, not like Eliana, but I wasn't outwardly standoffish or bitchy until I learned that coldness was the best method of self-protection. I used to act nicer, make friends more easily, until making friends stopped being important to me. Spending years without a single friend has a way of changing a person. Being nice didn't really matter anymore, because no amount of niceness could get people to like me in high school, so I stopped trying and stopped caring. I became very comfortable in my own company, able to spend long stretches of time alone and in silence without getting lonely.

"I don't think that's true," Ian retorts. "You still have a sweet side. You've just stopped manufacturing it for the benefit of others, which is a good thing. There's no need to be fake to get people to like you, Sugarplum, because most people don't matter."

He's right. A lot of the parts of myself that were chipped away at through my high school experience were ingenuine parts. There were a few that were very much genuine and got demolished, but not the majority. Still, I resent that I lost much of myself because of him.

"I resent you very deeply," I inform him. If he really wants to fight for me, which I'm not even sure I want but know I can't stop him from trying to do, it's probably for the best if he knows just how he's affected me and what he'll be up against. "I don't think that resentment will ever go away."

"It will," Ian says, with a level of confidence that just rankles me. "I know you resent me, and I can't exactly blame you for that. I'd resent me in your shoes. You need to learn to trust me again, rely on me, and know that I'll come through for you. I will, April. Every time, I'll come through for you. You don't have to believe that now, only time will show, but you'll come to see the truth."

"I don't even want to trust you," I respond. I'm testing him right now; throwing up all the barriers he will face if he pursues me, seeing if they'll deter him. They'd deter any sane man, but Ian's never really been sane. "I'll be actively working against trusting you. I don't think you know what you're getting yourself into with me; I am not the girl from the bridge. I'm not the same girl you were friends with. I'm not as accepting or sweet, I'm pretty fucking jaded."

"That's fine," Ian replies. "I'm a jaded person, as well. I don't need you to be all in from the get-go, I anticipate a lot of legwork on my end for each and every step we'll take, but we will get there. I know we will. It was always meant to be us, April."

"Your confidence irritates me. It makes me wonder if you've actually considered all the variables before starting in this pursuit."

Part of me is worried that he's trying to dive in head first here, perhaps due to hormones and attraction. If that's the case, he'll have an easy time walking away, which I will be waiting for. I'm not going to give him an inch, not easily. He will have to fight me for every step. If that isn't enough to make him leave, then maybe I'll start to believe he actually intends to stay. Until then, though, I can't invest in him emotionally.

"I'm a thinker and planner, Sugarplum, you know this. I've considered the variables quite thoroughly. I don't expect any fast progress. I don't expect you to let me in easily. I also know I'll simply keep coming for you, being there, until you do. If that takes a month, great. A year, great. A fucking decade, great. I'm not going anywhere. Rage at me all you want, push me away all you want, it won't work. I didn't make the decision to come after you lightly—I spent six weeks vacillating before realizing there was never another option."

"I will purposely make things difficult for you," I press, trying to get him to see just how serious I am. "I'll intentionally do shit to piss you off. I will not be loyal to you until you've earned my loyalty, which also means you shouldn't expect monogamy."

That's finally the straw that gets him to tense and frown. He's been surprisingly accepting of the curveballs I'm throwing at him, which is why I don't believe he's properly thought this through, but the moment I mention that I won't be committed or monogamous is finally the moment that penetrates through his steel confidence.

"You will be monogamous," he informs me, his voice taking on a flat quality that invites no questions and brooks no argument.

I raise my eyebrows. "No, Ian, I definitely won't. There's no way I'm fucking you any time in the near future, and I do have needs to get taken care of, which means I will be with other people. I had to watch you with other girls for long enough, you'll end up finding out exactly how much that sucks."

Ian clasps my waist with one hand, while reaching the other up to cup my chin and stroke his thumb over my cheek. His expression is more thoughtful than irritated, which makes me wary.

Finally, he says, "We don't have to fuck for me to take care of you. I'm more than willing to get you off."

I gawk at that. I don't think he's getting my message clearly. "You do not get to touch me sexually any time soon. You will have to earn that."

He shrugs. "That's fine, but nobody else will touch you, either. It's me or no one. You've already earned yourself a reputation around campus as quite the player—rumor has it you pick up new people to have fun with, then get bored and drop them shortly before searching for someone new. That tells me you do have a set of needs that will require taking care of, but I'm telling you right now, if I see or hear about you with another man *or* woman, I will treat them like an enemy. You know what happens when I treat someone like an enemy. It isn't pretty."

That makes me tense. "I do know," I snap. "I was on the receiving end of that treatment for years."

Ian chuckles. "No, Sugarplum, you weren't. If you were my enemy, I would've fully destroyed you long ago. I treated you like someone I didn't want to be near, I did my best to keep you away from me and make you hate me, but you never found out what it's like to be my enemy, and you never will. Most of the people I've considered enemies are no longer capable of doing anything but sitting in a wheelchair."

I push at him again. "Are you saying you'll kill anyone I fuck? Men *and* women?"

He makes a face, shaking his head. "Kill? No. Campus is too small a pool, and I don't hurt women. Ruin and incapacitate? Absolutely. Any woman will find her reputation destroyed and future prospects gone, and any man will no longer be able to fuck anyone. I have my methods. They aren't even always violent, but they are *very* effective."

"You're a diabolical asshole," I snap.

He smiles, as if I just gave him a compliment. "Proudly so, thank you. It makes me very efficient. Here's the bottom line; you need something, you come to me. Anyone else won't be safe."

"I won't come to you, even if I do have needs," I clip.

He stares at me for several long moments before giving me a shrug. "Fine. I can come to you instead."

"I am *not* getting you off," I growl.

He chuckles. "I wasn't asking you to. I don't mind being on the giving end, not with you." His brows furrow as he speaks, as if that surprises him. "Huh. I really don't. I actually *want* to. That's new."

I'm as surprised as he is, but also indignant. At the same time, though, there's a low stir of arousal in my gut, as if part of me is curious to see what that would look like. The rest of me, however, wouldn't let him touch me with a ten foot pole. But that little part, the devil on my shoulder that chases tail like it's her fucking job, wants to find out what it'd be like with Ian, especially if he's in a giving mood and I'm not expected to reciprocate. In cases like this, sometimes that little devil can overpower the rest of me.

"I can't say yes to that," I tell him, reminding myself as much as I'm reminding him. Even if I wanted to say yes, which to my consternation I kind of do, I couldn't betray myself like that.

My words appear to interest Ian rather than dishearten him. He leans even closer to me, gently cuffing my wrists with his hands and holding them down by my sides, immobilizing me. I test his grip, which is unyielding, and am shocked when my arousal *grows*, as if being held in place is a turn on for me.

It never has been before. I don't like being immobilized—usually, that brings on some horrible memories. It doesn't now, though. Now, it makes that stirring in my gut expand, creating heat in my nether regions. *Shit, I might actually be in trouble here.*

"What if you didn't have to?" Ian asks me, curiously. "What if I took my cues from your body? I know it well. I've spent years watching it, even when I wouldn't allow myself near you for any purpose other than cruelty."

CHAPTER FIFTEEN

Ian's words make me hesitate. If I weren't already turned on, I'd probably be fighting and yelling right now, but instead I'm feeling cautious and not entirely opposed.

"That sounds…dangerous. And like it would take a lot of trust." Trust that I just don't have in him.

Ian tilts his head to the side, watching me closely. Then, he starts speaking to me, his voice a low, enticing rumble that has no business getting me flustered the way it does.

"You start to blush a very pretty peach shade when you're just beginning to get turned on. After a bit, that peach darkens into a deeper red, which spreads from your cheeks down to your neck. You get this glazed look in your eyes that's hot as fuck, and your pupils dilate. Then, your stomach muscles visibly tighten, your nipples pebble, and when you're *really* turned on, you start rubbing your thighs together, chasing pressure and relief. Just like you are now."

I startle to realize he's right, I *am* rubbing my thighs together, because he *is* turning me on. How he knows all of my tells, I'm not sure. It could be that he's stalked me on campus and watched me with other people. Which, now that I think about it, is very possible. Ian is an observer—he's very good at reading nonverbal cues. That's something I remember from our time as friends; even at a young age, he had an uncanny ability to read people, which has obviously only grown over the years. Why that only makes him more attractive to me, I'm really not sure. What I am sure of is that I'm getting more and more turned on the longer we stand here with him giving me that predator-hunting-prey look, like he wants to devour me.

It's insane that in the span of a single conversation I've gone from fighting him to turned on by him, but Ian's always had the ability to affect me like no other. I should've anticipated this.

"I know your mouth is a liar," Ian goes on. "A very pretty liar and sometimes a good one, but I've never had issues seeing through you. I know you quite well, April, despite your protests to the contrary, which is why I know if I dipped my hand in your panties right now, I'd find you nice and wet."

"You wouldn't," I say too quickly, guilt staining the words because they are absolutely a lie. I can feel my panties growing slick with arousal. Despite myself, I want him right now, I just don't *want* to want him. It's embarrassing, so I can't bring myself to say it out loud.

Ian grins, but his smile isn't terribly genuine, it's edged with a dark sort of intrigue. "I would. I will. Here's the deal, Sugarplum; I'm going to find out if I'm right and you're wet. If you are, I'm also going to find out something I've been wondering for quite some time." He lowers his head until his mouth is right by my ear and whispers, "How you feel when you're coming around my fingers. I'm curious to find out what you taste like, I've wanted to indulge myself and eat you until you're trembling for longer than you know, but not here. You're wet, I get you off. You're not, I back off and we go to dinner."

He doesn't even give me the chance to respond; in a lightning quick move, he gathers my wrists in one of his hands and pins them over my head, then covers my mouth with his own, kissing me thoroughly. This isn't like our kiss earlier; it's far hungrier, more intense, edged with a desperation that tells me he actually does want to get me off. I've heard my fair share of rumors about Ian as well; namely, he is not a giver. That clearly isn't the case with me, though.

He deftly unbuttons and unzips my jeans one-handedly, an impressive move, then slips his hand into my panties. I feel his grin of victory against my lips when he finds exactly what he expected to find; I am wet. Embarrassingly so.

He pulls away only long enough to say, "Fucking knew it. Your ass is so mine, April."

I gasp when his fingers rub against my slit. "Wait—"

He cuts me off with another, deeper kiss, not letting me protest or get any words out, which intensifies my arousal. It shouldn't. I should be panicking right now, struggling in earnest, but I'm not, which tells me that some part of me *does* still trust Ian. At least, trusts him with my body. Apparently, nothing he or I could do will change that.

His thumb finds my clit with unnerving accuracy while he abruptly thrusts two fingers inside of me at once. The intrusion is deliciously dominant and so self-assured it's impossible not to melt in his hold a little. I moan into his lips as he scissors his fingers inside me, trapping my clit under his thumb with firm pressure while exploring the inside of my pussy like he wants to learn everything about it and me. He takes his time rubbing up against my walls leisurely until he finds a spot that makes me gasp and rise on my toes. I try to free my hands from his grip to find some sort of purchase, something to clutch onto.

He doesn't allow it, instead he tightens his hold on my wrists until it borders on painful, which only makes more wetness rush out of my channel. He plunges a third finger inside of me, stretching my pussy around them, pulling an embarrassing whine from me. He starts setting a steady rhythm of thrusting them in and out, taking care to rub up against that sensitive spot, all while kissing me to within an inch of my life.

When his thumb starts to move over my clit, using my wetness to glide around it easily, I let out a long moan, feeling my belly start to tighten as an orgasm begins to creep up on me.

"Fuck," I cry, tearing my mouth away from his. He doesn't allow the distance, chasing my lips with his, using his thumb to explore my clit and find what exactly drives me out of my mind. When he starts rubbing it up and down with the ball of his finger, I struggle against him, unable to stop myself from wriggling and instinctually trying to escape pleasure *that* intense.

I'm not used to it being this good. I'm not used to having someone who's committed to finding and exploiting every single one of my hot spots the way Ian is. This is entirely new territory for me, and I don't know how to handle it. My lovers are usually satisfying, I ensure they are, but none of them have been *this* good, and I realize that's because none of them have been Ian.

He must be enjoying this as much as I am, because I feel his cock thicken and press against my stomach, the erection jabbing me.

"There it is," he murmurs against my lips when he finds the spot on my clit that makes stars burst in my vision as he strokes it. "Only took me a few minutes to figure out the best way to navigate this pussy."

The arrogance in his tone pisses me off but the irritation only heightens my arousal, which in turn makes me more annoyed, sending me spiraling into a vicious cycle.

Ian bites down on my bottom lip, tugging it, before releasing it long enough to tell me, "Come, April."

I shake my head. I'm not sure I want to, not for him. He has me too tied up in knots, and part of me doesn't want to give him the satisfaction. I pull at his grip again, which yields no effect. Everything within me tightens; my orgasm is *right there*, and it's only my sheer force of will holding it at bay. Ian isn't having that, though. He strokes me harder and faster while upping the pace of his thrusts.

He pulls his mouth away to bite down on my neck. "Don't you dare hold back from me. Fucking come, *now*."

I don't have it in me to disobey. Even if I wanted to, I can't; he's already figured me out too well. A choked cry is torn from me, which turns into a loud, long moan that he swallows with his lips as my pussy starts to convulse around his fingers and my entire body heats and shakes with the force of my orgasm. I can't stop or slow it; all I can do is succumb to pleasure, which sweeps over me in an all-consuming wave, making my eyes fall shut and body tremble. Ian draws out my orgasm, getting every drop from me, continuing his thrusts and rubs down below, until tears spark in my eyes. I have no control over myself right now, and it's startling to me just how hot that is.

"Please, enough," I cry out, head falling against his shoulder.

Languidly, he slows the pace of his thrusts and releases my clit from under his thumb before pulling his hand out of my panties. I pant in the aftermath of my orgasm, feeling sapped and exhausted, while he only seems invigorated.

He holds the fingers that were just inside me up to my mouth and growls, "Open."

Dizzy from pleasure, I do. He stuffs his fingers into my mouth, rubbing my arousal over my tongue, letting me taste myself on him all the while he watches me with a burning gaze. He pulls away his fingers only to replace them with his mouth in an insanely erotic kiss, sucking my taste off of my tongue and groaning against my lips as if he can't get enough of it, can't get enough of me. The kiss is wildly intense and passionate, but also deep and somehow meaningful, because it leaves no doubt that Ian *really* wants me. His erection leaves no doubt of that either, hardening even more against my stomach, but he doesn't try to do anything about it— doesn't even grind against me, reaffirming his earlier words that he really doesn't mind getting me off. In fact, he seems to have liked it and found almost as much pleasure as I did.

He pulls his mouth away from mine, leaning his forehead down and resting it against my own. "*Fuck*, April. You're going to drive me more insane than I already am."

I whine in response, trying to wrap my mind around how it's possible that this conversation went from me fighting him to go home, to me crying tears of sorrow and anger in remembrance of what we once were, to him giving me one of the most explosive orgasms of my life with just his fingers.

That's Ian, though; he's always been able to twist me up in knots like nobody else. I can't seem to stick to my convictions around him, especially not when he's fighting against them. When it comes to him, I'm still weak.

"I want to drag you somewhere to taste you properly, but I think you need food and a good night's rest more than having my mouth on your pussy," he murmurs. "I'll make a meal out of you soon enough, but not tonight." He brushes another kiss over my stunned, parted lips. "C'mon, April. Let's eat."

I don't have the strength to protest, and I know even if I did, I wouldn't get my way.

"Okay," I say simply.

His brows quirk. "Okay? Just like that? Maybe getting my way with you is as simple as making you come. You seem a lot more compliant."

I frown, opening my mouth to let out a rebuke, to tell him that an orgasm doesn't equal compliance—I'm only agreeing because I know he'll just drag me if I don't come willingly.

He cuts me off before I can speak. "Good to know. Note to self made."

Then, he buttons and zips my jeans, takes my hand and leads me out of the alleyway.

Chapter Sixteen

Ian

"How about this one?" I ask April, showing her another option on my phone.

She rolls her eyes and sighs at me again, sliding my phone back across the table to me without even looking at the picture, which just amuses me.

"I've already told you, I am not going to Scotland with you for spring break, and you are not renting out a goddamn castle for us to stay in. Stop being ridiculous. It's messing with my appetite."

I cast a pointed glance at the empty plate of food sitting to the side of the half-empty plate she's currently working on. One of the things I almost forgot about April is just how big her appetite is—she's so skinny, you'd never know she eats like it's her damn job. Then again, dancing for most of the day nearly every day does take crazy amounts of energy, and she's always had a big appetite.

"I think your stomach will survive. My parents are already talking dates and times with yours for the first week of spring break, but we're free for the second," I remind her. "I intend to take advantage of the free time we'll have. We can fly straight from the Denver airport to Edinburgh."

Another eye roll from her. "I have told you for the last three nights consecutively, I am not going on a ski trip with you for the first week of spring break, *or* to Scotland for the second. I'm staying here to keep up with schoolwork and make use of the empty dance studios. Besides, as soon as the break's over, the company will start casting for whatever production's next or decide to go on with Pandora's Box and potentially expand the show, so I'll need to be at my best. I'll also have *homework* to do and *essays* to write. Don't forget that I still have several gen ed classes that I need to stay on top of."

"What I'm hearing you say is that you're fine with me making all the decisions on the Scotland trip front. I'm not sure you'll like that, so you might want to start being an active participant. Besides, you can dance anywhere, and all of your gen ed classes are online, so I'm sure you can manage to do everything you need to regardless of location."

For the last week, since the night in the alleyway, I've sought out April every day after her classes are done, including days that I'm working with Carson at his father's company building in the city. Those days I usually come for her a bit later, since my job tends to keep me in the building until six or seven at night.

A perk of attending Greywood and being accepted into one of their elite programs is that students work jobs in their chosen fields as part of the curriculum and receive credits for their work. For fine art students like April, those jobs come in the form of dance productions or art shows. For business students like me, the jobs are more along the lines of working in one of the corporations in the city.

Our courseloads and workloads take up a lot of time for both of us, but I still show up wherever April is on a daily or nightly basis. The first few nights, she tried to get me to back off and give her space; after she realized I was having none of that shit and that I always picked good places for us to eat, she resigned herself and eased up on the protests.

"You're insufferable," April sighs, before turning her attention back to her food, taking another bite of her chicken parmesan.

We're dining at a small Italian place tonight, family-owned, with a cozy atmosphere and a short, albeit delicious, menu. April's already made her way through a pasta dish, which she called an appetizer even though it came from the main course menu, and has now moved on to her protein for the evening. I like watching her eat—it's kind of erotic, mainly due to her expressions and little noises of enjoyment. They remind me of the noises she makes when I'm playing with her body, which always get me hard.

I have to grit my teeth and suffer my way through a several hour long erection every time I'm with her, then go home and fuck my fist, pretending it's her. The release is never quite satisfactory, but I can live with that. I'll have her soon enough, and I'm willing to be patient for my prize.

I was nothing short of shocked at April's responses and reactions to me the other night—after learning the tidbits of information Seth got for me, I assumed that anything sexual with her movements limited would end up being a trigger. Instead, not only did having her arms pinned turn her on, but it also made her come so hard she shook with the force of her orgasm. That told me more than anything else that April still trusts me. At least, her body does; otherwise she would've panicked. It might take some time for her mind to catch up, but I'm willing to be patient.

"We talked about a trip through Scotland and England featuring stops at the most interesting historical castles when we were kids," I tell April. "I'm trying to check that item off the bucket list."

"You're also not listening to me when I say I cannot afford something like that, and I am not going to let you pay for it *or* ask my parents to. Ease up, it isn't happening."

I feel a frown furrow my brows at her words. It seems like one of the most damaging insults I used to throw at here were comments surrounding money. The thing is, I never thought my words got to her—she didn't act like they did. She didn't really act like *any* of my hurtful words landed the way I meant for them to back when I was determined to stay away from her, which only made me escalate. I called her a lot of things that I'm not proud of but the one that really stuck was gold digger.

The first few nights I took her out, she tried to insist we split the bill; I put that sentiment to rest pretty immovably. A few hundred bucks isn't even considered pocket change for me, but it would put a dent in her bank account, especially since she's too stubborn to accept help from anyone. I flatly told April that her paying wasn't an option; she eventually backed off.

She's stopped bringing up the gold digger comments, but I can tell they're still at the forefront of her mind. Most likely because, thanks to my antics, that became a nickname of sorts that almost everyone would call her in high school. In hindsight, I can see that's something that'll be difficult to shake. She will, though; I won't allow anything else.

"Seth and Carson are planning a wildly extravagant trip with Eliana over spring break," I say casually. "She isn't bitching about the costs."

I know my comment is the wrong one to make as soon as it's out, and April pins me with a dark, unblinking stare that reminds me I still need to tread carefully with her. One thing I know about her is that she's only *truly* compliant when something suits her needs and desires—she has firm lines that won't be crossed. Dinner means good food and what I'm hoping she's starting to view as good company, so that's one thing. The times when I corner her to play with her pussy means a satisfying release, so she also allows it. If I push too far, though, she'll push back, which is something I've always liked about her.

April isn't someone who can be manipulated or maneuvered, not even by me, which is saying something. One of my greatest lures to her when we were kids is that none of my tactics ever worked with her; she'd see right through them, which gave me an opening to be genuine that I didn't really get with other people.

"Seth and Carson also have a very different history with Eliana, and while she might have been uncomfortable with the way they spoil her at first, she isn't anymore. That girl loves it even when it's a touch extravagant. I am not her. I will never be her. *We* will never be like *them*. I'm not nearly as nice, or compliant, or sweet as her. Don't assume otherwise."

Her tone is steady and flat, and the way she stares at me kind of makes me feel like she's looking into my very soul—another thing I like about her. She has a way of seeing through people, of digging under the surface and sorting out what lies beneath.

"Fair enough. My point is, I want to spoil you, I'm going to spoil you, and it'll be more comfortable for you if you get on board with it already. I'm not gonna stop, Sugarplum."

She shrugs. "You can try all you want, but it won't work, and I'm still not spending spring break with you. End of story. Move on."

With that, she once again returns her attention to her meal. I pick up my glass of red wine and take a sip, watching her over the rim. Setting it down, I say blithely, "Alright, I'll figure out the details, then."

She snorts. "M'kay. Have fun with that."

"April!"

I turn my head to look over my shoulder at the sound of Eliana's hyper voice, in time to see her break away from Carson, who's standing in the entryway of the restaurant with a mildly amused expression as he watches his girl run over to mine. He's hovering by the hostess stand at the front of the restaurant, but quickly veers away to follow after Eliana just as the petite blonde arrives at our table.

April puts down her silverware and stands in time to receive a tight embrace from her friend as if they haven't seen each other in years.

"Hey, Elia. You seem more excited than usual," April greets, amusement coloring her words.

"Oh, you haven't seen the reviews yet, have you?" Eliana asks excitedly. She pulls her phone out of her pocket, clicks something on it, then hands it to April, just as Carson arrives at our table.

I suppress a sigh—I was hoping to have April to myself tonight. I'm greedy to get as much time with her as I possibly can, and even having both of our friends intervene serves as an irritant. Still, for the sake of manners, I also stand from my seat and clap Carson's shoulder in greeting.

"Holy shit, these are *glowing*," I hear April say, sounding surprised. "I don't think I've ever gotten such high praise."

"*I know!*" Eliana squeals. "They're from some pretty tough critics, too, which makes them even better. A few more industry reviews like this and we'll be going on tour this summer for sure."

The two of them walk a few steps away, hovering by a nearby empty table to talk excitedly with each other.

"I took her out to celebrate," Carson tells me, nodding at April and Eliana. "Seth invited a few critics to the performance on Sunday, the first batch of reviews just came through tonight. Little E's over the moon with them, I figured that merited a nice celebratory dinner. Seth's out of town meeting with his art agent, so I get her to myself tonight."

"Good call," I say with a nod.

Carson grins. "Yup. While I have you here, are you okay with a bit of business talk? Since the girls are busy squealing in excitement."

Eliana calls out, "I heard that, and I am *not* squealing."

"Of course not, Princess," Carson calls back. Then, quieter, "She's totally squealing. Seth will be pissed that he missed her good mood."

"Business talk," I remind him, redirecting. "What's going on?"

Carson's lips thin and his brows briefly crease, which makes me suspect that whatever he's about to say won't be good. That shouldn't be the case; we've both been excelling in our branch. Carson's taken over marketing for his father's empire entirely, pushing to make his oil business a little more eco-friendly and less of a menace to the planet we live on, and I've been functioning well in my capacity as his second.

"My father's not altogether pleased with the moves we've been making—says it's bad for income, even though the numbers don't reflect that. He's just being a prick because he's still sore that I got my way with Elia and fucked him over in the process. So, he's sending in my uncle to oversee us for the rest of the year—pulling the last power move that he's still capable of."

Everything within me tenses at the mention of Carson's uncle. His father's brother is a piece of work, a terrible person—which is really saying something coming from me—and someone who I've been planning to deal with in a bloody way for quite some time. The reason I actually applied for a spot in the Ajax company as part of my

Greywood work credits was because I eventually wanted to work my way up the food chain and get to that motherfucker. That *he's* instead coming to *me* is at once fortunate and a roadblock.

Dennis Ajax is not my focus right now, not since I figured out I actually enjoy working with Carson and can see my position with him turning into a career. Certainly not while I'm firmly in pursuit of April. Dennis coming to town right now is a wrench in my plans, and a complication that I do not fucking need.

I inhale a deep breath, holding back a wince as painful memories prickle at my mind. Dennis has been a dead man walking for many years now, but I'm meticulous when I lay out my plans, and I'm not a big enough fish to go after him yet. Not in the way he deserves.

Despite my best efforts, a muttered *fuck* escapes me. Carson misinterprets my ire for mere irritation at additional oversight, when that's far from the case.

"Don't worry too much about it, man. Uncle Dennis doesn't have that much power in the company—he's a minority shareholder, not even a board member, and his position is more smoke and mirrors than anything else. This is just my dad being a sore as hell loser."

I clench my fists by my side, digging my fingers into my palms so hard they break skin and I feel blood well under my nails. Still, I keep my face impassive and force myself to *think* rather than *feel*. Being a hot head in the past has only cost me the one person I truly care about; I can't afford to be rageful right now, I need to be clever.

"You really don't like your dad, huh?" I ask casually.

Carson snorts, then releases a contemptuous laugh at my statement, drawing a frown of confusion from Eliana. He waves her away, before telling me, "That is putting things mildly. My dad is a leech on this world, and he will get what's coming to him eventually." Carson clenches his jaw, giving his head a hard shake. "He's done some bad shit, Ian. The sort of shit that even made Seth get worked up. That's why I effectively grounded him and confiscated a lot of his power in the company just before winter break."

That's saying a great deal, because Seth doesn't *get* worked up. Not over anything that isn't related to his art, or Eliana. I've heard rumors that Seth occasionally functions in a vigilante capacity, going after bad people who specialize in very particular crimes; ones of a sexual nature, or ones where children get hurt. In order to rile Seth, Carson's father must've taken part in one or the other. That's unsurprising, I guess the saying *birds of a feather flock together* has some truth to it.

"You gonna unleash Seth on him?" I ask Carson, still taking care to keep my tone even and relatively unbothered, as if I couldn't care less, even though his forthcoming answers will decide a great deal.

Carson shakes his head. "Not any more than I already have. But we are going to work together to make sure Dad's past catches up with him soon enough."

If Carson's willing to unleash hell on his father, it bears the question what he might do to his uncle if he found out about Dennis's nefarious activities. The way Carson speaks about him makes him sound like a non-threatening nuisance, so I doubt he knows anything significant.

"Certain crimes do merit particular responses," I hedge.

Carson's eyes narrow on me for a brief moment, reminding me that while he might look and act like a clueless former-player, Carson's way of presenting himself as mild is a strategic move. He's far smarter than appearances and his reputation dictate, and far more observant.

"Yes, they do," Carson agrees, his expression smoothing out.

So, if I find a way to go after his uncle, there is a chance I might have Carson's support. That's integral. I won't tell him anything now; first,

I need to think and plan my next steps. Once I have a plan, though, it might be in my best interest to let him in on it.

Chapter Seventeen

Ian

Eliana breaks away from April, walking up to Carson and circling her arms around his waist, leaning her body against his. Somehow, she must've sensed his tension, and is responding accordingly. Watching them together makes envy unfurl within me; I want what they have. I don't want to wait for it, but I know I'll have to. That thought serves to infuriate me with my past actions of pushing April away, which only makes me want to come for Dennis even more.

"You look tense," Eliana murmurs, nuzzling into Carson's hold as he wraps his arms around her, smiling down at her.

"Just business, Little E. Nothing to get worked up over, I'm handling it."

A frown briefly creases her brows as she looks between us. My eyes stray to April, who's standing a few feet away, pretending to be engrossed in her phone even though I know she's watching and listening like a hawk. My girl is very good at eavesdropping, something I learned when we were best friends.

"You still look tense," Eliana presses. "Can I do anything?"

"Can you sit on my face right now?" he volleys back.

She rolls her eyes. "Jesus, Carson, *no.*"

He hums. "Will you spend the night at my place?"

Eliana sighs. "As long as you don't complain in the morning when you have to drive me back to campus at five."

Carson smiles victoriously. "Then I'm good. C'mon, let's eat." He tips his chin at me in farewell, eyes lingering for just a moment too long, before turning to tell April, "Great job on stage, congrats on the reviews, and thank you for making sure my girl eats during the day when I can't be with her."

April looks up from her phone and gives him a two-fingered salute. "No problem. Keep it up with the morning coffees and we'll call it even."

Eliana frowns at Carson, then at April. "Oh my god, is *that* why you always shove a sandwich or muffin in my bag before I run from dance to my afternoon classes?"

April shrugs. "You were literally there when I agreed to spy on you in return for coffee. Granted, I never ended up passing on any information, but Carson and I both noticed your habit of forgetting to eat, so we agreed to put our heads together to rectify that."

Eliana blinks. "I don't know whether to curse at you guys for conspiring behind my back or thank both of you because your conspiring is actually sweet."

Carson leans down to press a kiss to Eliana's lips. "Then don't think about it, babe. Speaking of not eating, let's get you fed."

I watch them take a seat at a table about fifteen feet away from us, before returning my attention to April. My thoughts are too scrambled right now to give her the proper attention I prefer to when we're together. Dennis's impending arrival is going to serve as a huge curveball, and I can't deny that it'll probably make me more snappy, which won't be good when I'm *just* starting to make the most minute progress with April.

She might've stopped outright fighting me on everything, but she's still far from sure of me. I'm positive that if I wasn't dedicating so much of my free time and effort to her, she'd have pulled away already. I have to figure out how I'm going to juggle new developments at work and continue pursuing her at the same time. In the past, I wouldn't have thought it was possible, but now that I have a taste of her, I can't back off. I *won't* back off.

April notices my new tenseness—of course she does. She walks up to me, giving me a good look up and down, but doesn't ask any questions. Either she knows I'm not in an answering mood or she doesn't care. I hope it's the former, but I can't deny the possibility of the latter being true. I haven't given April much reason to care for me in the last years, in fact I gave her ample reason to *stop* caring about me, and I know a single week won't change that.

There's a part of me that still hopes some of her love for me might've survived my torment. It's not a reasonable hope, but I can't help it—if she has any childhood sentiments of affection left over for me, it'll be easier to build something. I know the grim reality is that, most likely, the only thing that was left in her after high school was hatred, or even worse, apathy.

Hatred, I can work with; it connotes passion. Passion can be molded from hate into something more positive, such as love. Apathy is a different ball game—if I truly thought she was apathetic towards me, I would have to work a whole lot harder. She isn't apathetic or disinterested; from what I've gathered, she's justifiably defensive and protective of herself. I gave her every reason to build up high walls, now I'm working at the impossible task of scaling them.

She glances at my empty plate and at her mostly empty one, then says, "For once, I'm actually full. You done?"

I grunt in affirmative. "I'll get the bill, then we can go."

She picks up her small purse which hangs off the back of her chair and digs through it before holding out a debit card to me.

I let out a sigh, not taking the card. "We've been over this. I take you out, I pay."

She grumbles, "I didn't even want to go out with you any night this week, yet I have and you've paid every single night. These aren't dates. Let's split the bill."

I frown at her. "These are absolutely dates, what gave you any other impression?"

"The fact that I've repeatedly told you we are not dating," she deadpans. "Take the fucking card, Ian."

I pluck the card from her hand, slip it right back into her purse, then turn and walk to the hostess stand. Hearing April's curses behind me, I half-smile while paying the bill, then return to her and say, "Let's go, Sugarplum."

"Stop calling me that."

"Why not? You like that nickname," I respond, feeling my lips tilt up.

"I *used* to like that nickname," she snarks. "That's in the past. We've kind of been over this."

I wrap an arm around her waist, pulling her close, loving the feel of her tucked against my side and also finding great enjoyment in sparring with her. I didn't think anything could lift my mood after hearing that Dennis Ajax is coming to town, but she's proving me wrong. It's hard to think about that asshole when I have April in front of me, wrapped in my arms, watching me with her big doe eyes that hint to both resentment and reluctant interest.

"Whenever you lie to me, it just makes me want to fuck you. Ease up on the protests, *Sugarplum,* they won't get you anywhere."

I'm not kidding; sparring with her, having her try to deny the truth, always seems to serve as a turn on. *Everything* with this girl is a turn on—she can breathe around me and I'll end up hard. It's a bit ridiculous, but I long ago resigned myself to wanting her more than I could bear. That's what drove some of my hostility in high school; I was furious that I wanted her—wanted *everything* from her—but believed I couldn't have her, so I lashed out.

I know I *can* have her now. I have every intention of making her mine. I just need to get her on board, which is a slow progress, but progress *is* being made.

"You're an asshole," she grumbles, half-heartedly attempting to pull away from me.

"Very much so," I agree with a nod.

I know she doesn't really mean her attempts to pull away; she just thinks she *should* want away from me even if she doesn't. That's a big problem between me and April; she won't just fight me, she'll fight herself if she thinks that I'm a threat to her. Fight her own desires and wishes in favor of self-protection. I'm slowly trying to show her that I am not a threat to her, that I will never be a threat to her, that if she puts her trust in me I will protect it. It's an uphill battle, though, and I'm well aware that I only have myself to blame for my predicament.

As we near the door of the restaurant, Carson calls out, "Have a good night, lovebirds. And, Ian, don't worry about Dennis—he'll be a nuisance, nothing more."

I feel my jaw clench as Carson's piece of shit uncle is once again brought up, but I don't react, only give Carson a small wave over my shoulder. I can't help but get the sense that Carson mentioned Dennis just to see my reaction—he seemed to notice that something was off when he first brought his uncle up, and he may be trying to fish for more. I don't give it to him.

Outside, I navigate April to my car, opening the passenger side door for her before getting into the driver's seat and peeling out of the parking lot.

After a few minutes of silence April asks me, "What's wrong?"

"Nothing," I snap, then internally wince. April doesn't deserve my ire, I'm just not in the best mindset—not with a headache coming on and horrible memories clouding my thoughts.

I slide her a sideways glance in time to see her brows furrow and lips part. They quickly seal and a brief frown flickers over her features before her expression smooths out.

"Okay," she says, her tone so utterly disinterested it rankles me. There was a time when April would push and push until I finally opened up, but we are no longer in those times, which this is a stark reminder of. I can see that, for a moment, she wanted to press me but then she subdued the urge, and now appears irritated with herself for asking in the first place.

I'm irritated as well; despite my snapping at her, I want her to push. I want her to *care*. I miss having her care about me—I loved the fact that she was the one person who wouldn't back down when I growled at her.

"You're not going to ask again?" I question, my tone somewhat testy.

I know being offended by her apparent disinterest is ridiculous, but I can't help myself. If I sensed she was in a bad mood, I would keep asking her until she explained.

"Nope. Whatever it is, it's your problem, not mine," she responds breezily.

My hands clench on the steering wheel. Another glance sideways reveals that she's now taken out her phone and is doing something on it—in effect, pulling away from me.

April is not the girl she once was: too caring for her own good. She's no longer terribly kind, seeking the approval of everyone around her, uncomfortable in her own skin. She's meaner now, doesn't give a shit about anyone's approval save for the people who truly matter most to her, and is more than comfortable with who she is. In fact, she's become quite the siren. She used to rely on me for my strength; now she has enough of her own that she doesn't need me. *I* need *her* far more than she needs me, which is a complication. If she were still in need of another's strength to replace her own, she might be more open to a relationship with me, but she doesn't. I don't think she needs anyone other than herself.

"You used to care about my problems. They used to be *our* problems," I growl. I know I should stop while I'm ahead, but I can't. I'm too bitter—mainly at myself—to do the smart thing, shut the fuck up, and move on.

"Yeah, well, you used to deserve my care," she replies calmly. She isn't snapping or growling or raising her voice, she genuinely sounds like she doesn't give a shit.

"And now I don't?" I demand.

She confirms, "Nope, you don't. We've kind of been over this; I spent *wayyyy* too long caring for you, and just got fucked over for my effort. Why would I do that again? I've already told you that I'm not a masochist, Ian."

"I'm not going to hurt you," I say testily. "That's what I'm trying to prove to you, but it doesn't seem to be getting me anywhere."

The patience I've been forcing myself to have simply evaporates. I want everything with her *now*, and she knows better than most that I have a habit of taking things I'm not entitled to. Considering how important she is to me, I'm going to be even more entitled and greedy.

"I once read an article that said it typically takes triple the amount of time to undo emotional damage than it takes to inflict it," April retorts blithely. "You've got something like three years of damage under your belt, you should not expect it to go away in the span of a week. I told you I'd be actively working against your efforts, Ian. I warned you pretty fucking clearly exactly what you were in for if you wanted to try to go after me. Don't start whining because I'm protecting myself in the exact way I should. If you don't like it, do both of us a favor and *choose someone else*."

"I *can't*," I roar, unable to keep quiet. "Don't you get it, April? You're a fucking *compulsion* for me. I can't stay away from you; I've never been able to. Not even in high school, when I was determined to be done with you for both of our sakes—I couldn't stop myself from bullying you, because I'd rather have your hatred than nothing at all. I'm not going to choose someone else."

That makes her fall silent again, but this time her silence seems pensive rather than disinterested.

I try to get my temper under control, battling with the shitty memories of the very events that prompted me to treat her the way I did back in high school. I recognize now what I failed to see then; If I had chosen April, come to her rather than pushed her away, we wouldn't be in this mess. If I had simply *spoken* to her instead of deciding that being done with her was best for both of us, she wouldn't have mountains of anger to get over, and I wouldn't feel like there's a chasm the size of a universe between us.

"The way you speak makes it sound like I'm precious to you," April murmurs.

"Because you are. You're *the* most precious thing to me," I grunt.

She lets out a sigh, frustration palpable. "Then why did you act like I was the shit stain on the sole of your shoe for years? That day on the bridge... I didn't want to believe that your sudden decision to be done with me was based on the wealth disparity between our families or the lives we lead. It never made a difference before; you didn't care about money. Besides, it's not like my parents were destitute and living in the slums—they've always done well enough for themselves, just not as well as your parents.

"I tried to believe it wasn't that, but all the comments you made, the way you had of making me feel so goddamn *inferior*... can you see why it's hard for me to just forget that? Why it bothers me that you pay the bill when we go out? I'm waiting for the next time you cut me off. If I let you do things for me like take me on a ridiculous international trip, that'll give you more fuel when our next falling out happens. You'll be able to call me a gold digger and actually defend that insult. I don't want to get hurt by you again, Ian. Frankly, I'd rather get fucked over by anyone other than you, because with you it's too personal. You're asking me to give you my trust, I'm telling you to earn it. The thing is, I don't even know if you can or how you can."

I inhale several consecutive deep breaths, trying to gather my scrambled thoughts. April's shielding her heart and mind from me *very* effectively right now; the only real in I have is with her body, which already trusts me. If what I have to do is exploit our physical connection while waiting for the rest to follow, I will.

"You missed the turn for the road back to campus," April says, sitting up straighter.

"I'm not taking you back to campus. I need you with me tonight," I tell her.

She's too damn good at using the hours we spend apart to put distance between us; I won't allow it, *certainly* not tonight. I'm already in a bad mood; if I have her with me, that mood might lift. One thing I've learned in the last days is that there's nothing capable of holding my attention as wholly as her body and reactions when I'm playing with her. Every inch of my focus goes to her, to the quickening rise and fall of her chest, to every one of her verbal and nonverbal responses—there isn't room for anything else. That's what I need right now. I'm pretty sure being inside her and feeling her tight pussy squeeze my cock would be even better, but even in my current state I won't push that. Watching her surrender to pleasure is enough.

"You going to tell me what has your panties in a twist?" April asks. "Since you're actually following through on that kidnapping threat."

I bark out a laugh. "If I actually kidnapped you, Sugarplum, there's a very high chance I'd never let you leave. I'd need to have a much better plan in place. You can call this an impromptu rendezvous of sorts, but it isn't a kidnapping."

I purposely don't touch on the first part of her statement, because I don't want to talk about it. Not tonight, not when things are too fresh. Tonight, I want to forget, and lose myself with her.

April hums but doesn't seem all that worried or afraid, which is good. "If I asked you to take me back to campus, would you?"

"No. I'll take you back in the morning, though, in time for classes."

She rolls her eyes, seeming somewhat exasperated. Then, her expression grows serious. "If you don't want me to push back on this, you need to give me something. You're trying to get under my armor without letting me under yours—it won't work. *If* I ever let you in again, it will be after you have let *me* in."

I guess she won't let that lie—classic April. I can see that I won't get very far with her until I've started to open myself up more. I will, eventually I intend to tell her everything, just not yet. Certainly not tonight. I understand that I can't give her nothing, though, so I try to think of something I can say that might appease her without picking at old wounds. If I hadn't gotten the news that I did from Carson I might be more open to talking about things, but right now I want away from those festering memories, not to dive back into them. I don't know if I'll be able to control the worst parts of myself if I do.

"I didn't drop our friendship because of anything to do with money," I tell her through gritted teeth. "Not because I thought you were beneath me, either, I know you're better than me in the ways that matter. That summer was... bad for me. Shit happened to me that should never happen to *anyone,* and as a result, I felt dirty and unworthy. Tonight I got a reminder of dark memories. I don't want to pick at those scabs tonight. I told you that I'd tell you everything, and I will, April, but not tonight. Tonight, I just need you in my space, by my side."

Chapter Eighteen

Ian

I can tell that my words soften her. She relaxes, leaning back, and lets out a quiet sigh of resignation. When I peek at her again, I see that she looks conflicted, but she's not protesting. It makes me wonder if she still has an empathetic core beneath her tough exterior—yet another thing I've always loved about her. I think she does still have that soft center, but it's hidden behind lots of steel armor that she had to build to survive the shithead version of me.

"I'm not having sex with you," she grumbles.

I chuckle. "I wasn't asking for sex. I just want you in my bed tonight. I want you to be the first thing I see when I wake up tomorrow, I'm pretty sure that'll improve my mood drastically. That was my favorite part of ski trips, you know."

"Stop being so sentimental, it's unlike you," she says, though there's no real rancor in her voice.

"I'm not a very sentimental person in general," I allow. "I am sentimental when it comes to you, though. Always have been, even when I didn't want you to see it."

I pull my car into the parking garage under my apartment building, park it, and open April's door for her. Just knowing that she'll be with me tonight without putting up a fight has already taken the edge off my bad mood, and I no longer feel like blowing something up just to let off steam.

She doesn't protest when I take her hand and lead her to the elevator, but she doesn't lean close to me, either. I get the sense that while she's not totally on board with this or completely trusting of my intentions, she also realizes that I need her right now and won't deprive me of that.

"Remember when my mom caught us curled up in bed when I was ten and you were eleven?" she asks. "Dad kind of wanted to castrate you, while Mom thought it was the cutest thing in the world, proclaimed us childhood sweethearts, and then jokingly started talking about our wedding with your mom."

A faint smile pulls at my lips. We had interconnected rooms during the trip she's referring to, which made it easier for me to sneak in her room after our parents had gone to sleep. It was a cold night up on the ski mountain, the heating in our hotel hall had gone out, and April was freezing, so I'd taken the blankets from my bed over to hers, wrapped us both up in them, and held her tightly until she stopped shivering and fell asleep. The next morning, it was her mom's squeal of excitement that woke us up—we'd slept straight through the morning alarm I always set to remind me to go back to my room.

Then, April's dad came into the room and started interrogating me about my presence in her bed, as if we had been up to something nefarious at that age. I calmly asked him if he'd have preferred for me to allow his daughter to get frostbite, which only pissed him off more. April's mom cooled him down.

My parents, on the other hand, were positively delighted at my closeness with April; namely because they saw that I calmed down a great deal around her. All the energy I usually focused into destruction for my own amusement instead got laser-focused on April, saving many unsuspecting people from being on the wrong end of my pranks. I remember hearing Mom and Dad quietly discussing their hope that April and I would eventually grow into a relationship and get married—they saw her as the antidote to my darkness.

When we hit high school, they suspected I had a falling out with April because my destructiveness returned three times over; Mom even asked me about April a few times. I snarled and snapped at her, which made the questions stop. I'm not proud of that time in my life—I was in a dark place, and I took it out on everyone around me. Most of all, I took it out on April.

When I called Mom earlier in the week to request that she coordinate spring break with April's parents again, she asked if I've rekindled my friendship with April. When I mentioned that April and I are more than friends, and casually dropped the fact that I have every intention of keeping April, Mom squealed so loudly that I still hear the echoes of her excitement ringing in my ear.

Dad was equally pleased with the new development, and I think that's because he believes that April is to me what my mom is to him; the person who keeps him centered. I know I inherited my darker tendencies from my father—I've seen him lose his cool in moments, watched him tear down opponents or enemies in his business world in a way that would make even a sadist cringe—and Mom's the person that keeps him sane and has an uncanny ability to calm him down.

A sense of peace settles over me as I unlock my apartment door and let April inside, shutting and bolting the door behind her. I like having her in my personal territory, it settles something inside me that demands for me to be close with April at all times. I spent years fighting that part of me; I won't anymore.

I'm reminded that April's quite the explorer when she toes off her shoes, then takes herself on a tour through my apartment. First, she wanders into the kitchen, glancing over the gleaming white tiled counters, brown cupboards, and stainless-steel fridge. She opens a few cupboards before exploring the contents of the fridge. She doesn't touch or take anything; just familiarizes herself with the space in the way she's always done when she's in a new place or environment.

I stand in the doorway of the kitchen, leaning against the crème-colored wall, content in just watching her explore. When she's done, she heads into my living room, taking in the setup. She walks over to the console table beneath my TV, picks up a few photos my mom placed there, and frowns when she sees that there are several of us together. I kept all the photos of my favorite times with her—exploring nature, skiing on freezing cold mountains, spending time together at either of our houses. There's even a picture of us taken by her mom after one of her ballet performances. April's beaming at the camera, still wearing a little bumble bee tutu, holding a bouquet of flowers I had proudly presented to her.

April doesn't comment on the photos, instead she moves on to peruse the bookshelf on the back wall of the living room, running her hands along the spines before squatting down to examine my collection of old records, and the even older record player propped up on a shelf. It's the antique record player *she* got me for my eleventh birthday.

She moves to the sliding glass door that lets out onto a small balcony, cracking it open to step outside and inhale the fresh evening air. Back inside, she peeks her head into my bedroom, giving a cursory glance over the dark wooden chest of drawers, my king-sized bed covered in a rumpled navy-blue bedspread, and the TV hanging on the wall opposite to the bed.

She walks back into the living room and plops onto the couch, casual as you please.

Standing beside her, I say, "I forgot how much of an explorer you are. You still like to find every nook and cranny of a space before settling."

April shrugs, unrepentant. "Yup. You shouldn't have brought me here if you didn't want me to nose around—it's kind of what I always do."

"I don't mind," I tell her, somewhat surprised by the truth of that statement. I really *don't* mind having her be nosy in my personal space, and she's the one person I can say that about. If anyone else conducted themselves that way in my territory, including my parents, it would irritate me, but I'm not annoyed with April in the least. It's telling that she's comfortable enough to look around.

"You want to watch something?" I ask her when she picks up the TV remote.

A small smile curls her full lips. "Yes. And, if you remember me as well as you claim to, you'll know exactly what I'll want to watch."

"A Disney movie," I say on a sigh. "Either Brave or Moana, if things have stayed the same."

Her smile widens. "Ding-ding, we have a winner."

I shake my head, dropping onto the couch next to her, close enough that our thighs are pressed together. I drape my arm on the spine of the couch behind her and say, "Fair enough. You still have all the songs memorized?"

She snorts. "Ian, I have the entire damn script memorized for most Disney movies."

"Cool. I have Disney Plus. Go for it, Sugarplum."

She casts me a somewhat surprised glance. "You really don't care that I'm about to torture you with animated films?"

I shake my head. "Nope. They make you happy and always bring a wide smile to your face—there's nothing not to like there. Knock yourself out, babe."

Her brows furrow. "You realize I'm going to sing along at the top of my lungs, right?"

"Hard to forget that tidbit. You've always had a beautiful voice, though, so go ahead."

With an expression that says, *you asked for it*, she puts on Moana. True to her word, she sings every song, and I'm reminded that I still like her singing voice. It's pretty, melodic, and still makes a warm feeling take up residence in my chest. I love seeing her so relaxed in my apartment, love the way her eyes *still* tear up at the end of the movie, just like they used to. April's still a sucker when it comes to Disney movies—a remnant of her childhood that never quite left her.

At the end of the movie, she insists on watching Brave next.

"Fine by me, on one condition," I tell her.

She raises her eyebrows. "That condition being?"

"Sit your pretty ass on my lap and let me play with you while we watch," I tell her. The only thing better than watching a movie with April is if I'm also stroking and petting April while we watch, feeling her melt on top of me like she always does.

She narrows her eyes at me. "Fine, but I expect an orgasm."

I feel my brows knit. "Only one?"

A surprised laugh bursts out of her, though I don't see why my words are surprising. Whenever I've found time to play with her, it's always been in a secluded corner where I had to be quick or risk someone discovering us—bathroom at a restaurant, my car at a rest stop or just pulled over at the side of the road, a sparsely populated spot on campus. I haven't *really* had the chance to take my time to get fully acquainted with her body, which has a lot of new delicious curves I'm eager to explore.

Her laugh cuts off when she sees in my expression that I'm dead serious. Then, she tilts her head to the side, curiosity lighting up her gaze. "You really don't care that I don't reciprocate, do you? You actually enjoy getting me off. That's weird."

"With anyone else, yeah, I'd care about getting off—in fact it'd be my only concern. You're different, though. Pleasuring you satisfies me as much as any release ever has."

She blinks. "Huh." After a moment: "Well, I'm not gonna complain about that. I happen to be a fan of orgasms."

And *I* happen to be a fan of the way she melts into an easily maneuverable puddle of relaxation when I touch her just right.

I pat my lap. "Come on, then."

When she shifts to the side, I say, "Take off your clothes first. I want easy access."

That makes her pause. She arches an imperious eyebrow at me, gives me a haughty princess-to-peasant look that never fails to make my dick twitch, and says, "You want them off, take them off."

Chapter Nineteen

Ian

With pleasure. I stand from the couch, pull April to her feet, and finger the hem of her shirt. Slowly lifting it, I get a mouthwatering view of her toned abdomen, small waist, and all that luminous golden skin I'd like to bite and mark. That's exactly what I intend to do.

"Arms up," I tell her. She lifts them above her head without protest and I tug off her shirt, tossing it aside. She's wearing a simple nude bra that I leave on for now while I get to work on her pants, revealing a matching thong. The v between her thighs taunts the hell out of me, and I'm a little enthusiastic in getting the panties off her—so much so that I rip them with one hard yank.

Dryly, April says, "You owe me a thong."

I grin. "We'll go shopping for lingerie at some point in the near future."

She gives me that haughty look again, making my cock twitch and stiffen. "Will we, now?"

I nod. "Yup." I don't add my suspicion that her tight budget only allows her the cheap, bare basics of clothes, and I want to see her draped in silks that'll mold to her golden skin like a work of art. I have plenty of erotic images in mind of her in different lingerie sets, and I have every intention of making those fantasies into a reality. I don't, however, want to offend her. I've already done that enough for a lifetime.

"You seem damn confident considering the fact that I haven't agreed," April observes.

I don't bother responding to that, since I'll wrangle agreement from her soon enough, in one way or another.

I drop back onto the couch and spin her around, getting a mouth-watering view of her full, round ass that I can't help but spank. Then my eyes wander further upward, and I feel everything in me stiffen when I see scars on her back. I knew they were there—Seth told me as much when he did research for me—but *knowing* about them versus actually seeing the faded pink scar tissue are two entirely different things.

April feels me stiffen, and I sense the moment she catches onto what I'm staring at, because she stiffens, as well, realization overcoming her. She must've been distracted enough by the movie, banter, and calm atmosphere to forget about what I'd glimpse when I saw her bare back. The muscles in her back tense, her spine snaps ramrod straight, and her breathing quickens—not with arousal, but with discomfort. It takes everything in me not to demand who the fuck put those there so I can get started on avenging her—if I leap onto that right now, it'll make her withdraw, so my best bet is going for a more casual approach.

The moment the thought crosses my mind, I instantly realize it won't work; April will get suspicious if I'm casual. She knows me too well, knows that I'm a very intense person. So, I don't make any effort to mask the anger in my voice when I say, "What the fuck?"

Unable to help myself, I stand back up again, tracing my hand over the long, jagged scar on her lower back as well as the smaller one by her shoulder blade—the place where she got fucking *stabbed*.

"Hiking accident," she says tersely, the words sounding like they come through gritted teeth. Her tone doesn't invite any questions or further prodding, so I muster up all the self-control I have and keep a leash on myself. She'll tell me eventually, and then I will fucking destroy whoever did this to her. Repeatedly. Until they wish—*beg*—for death.

I force myself to relax and let out a doubtful *huh* that transmits the fact that I don't believe her, but I also won't press her for details now. Tonight is meant for exploring and getting to know her body more intimately—I have the rest of my life to find out who did this to her and handle them.

I move my hands down to her waist, refocusing on the luscious ass that is just begging to be marked and spanked, plop down on the couch, and tug her down on top of me.

"Back to the lingerie," I start, letting her know that I won't press the issue of her scars, "we're going shopping. If you say some bullshit about money, it'll piss me off. Considering I have you naked and vulnerable, perfectly situated on my lap, I don't think you want to piss me off. That might put me in a mean mood."

I feel her relax in my hold, though not entirely. She's calmed since I made it clear that I won't push her to talk about what she doesn't want to talk about, but her muscles are still a little stiff. She seems glad about the change in topic, though.

She turns to give me a somewhat unamused glance over her shoulder. "You won't hurt me. Not really."

I nod my agreement. "You're right, I won't hurt you. Not in any way that you don't want, anyways. I am going to spoil you, however, so get used to the idea."

She gives me an eyeroll that silently transmits *what-fucking-ever*, before scooping up the TV remote and clicking over to Brave, hitting play. As the movie opens, I force myself to stop thinking about the scars and start thinking about the lovely expanse of smooth, toned golden skin and sheer beauty that I have tucked firmly against me. I almost feel like a kid on Christmas unwrapping a bunch of exciting presents, looking between the options and unsure where to start first.

After a few beats, I decide I want April relaxed before I really get down to exploring, so I lift my hands to her shoulders and start kneading them, massaging the tension from the muscles. She likes that; the low groan she lets out tells me as much. I spend the first several scenes of the movie just massaging her back and arms, forcing myself not to think about the scars and instead enjoying the feeling of her relaxing against me inch by inch. When I'm satisfied with that, I undo the clasp of her bra and shift our positions in a quick move that doesn't give her time to protest, laying her out along the couch.

She frowns at me. "I was kind of watching the movie. You're distracting me."

I raise my eyebrows at her. "So keep watching—you still have a clear view of the screen. Let's see how long your focus lasts."

She narrows her eyes at me and gives me a look that says, *challenge issued, challenge accepted.* Then, she pointedly turns her head back towards the screen. I spread her thighs and kneel between them, which makes her breath hitch, though she takes care not to give me any attention. That's fine; she can pretend not to notice all she wants, soon enough that won't be an option.

I fill my hands with her breasts, loving the way they fit in my palms. Her nipples are a pretty pinkish-brown color, stiffened into tight peaks that are too inviting for me to resist. I lean down and run my tongue along her breast, feeling the way she arches underneath me, before closing my lips around one nipple. She does her best not to react as I suck and lave and play, but a small moan escapes her when I test her stiff peak with my teeth, wanting to see if she likes a bit of erotic pain added to the pleasure, and she certainly does. I spend ample time getting better acquainted with her smooth, soft breasts, licking and nipping and sucking until she's writhing beneath me, though her head stays stubbornly turned towards the TV. It's only when I start kissing my way down her body that her attention finally switches over to me. Her amber eyes meet mine when I drag my teeth down her navel, shifting on the couch until my face is level with her pussy.

I've been dreaming, fantasizing about eating her out and tasting her straight from the source rather than just licking her arousal off my fingers after I've made her come, and now I finally have my chance. I spread her pussy with my lips, feeling satisfaction travel through me when I see that she's already glistening, her pussy practically begging for attention that I am more than happy to give. I lean down and run my tongue along her slit, feeling a low groan escape me as her nectar coats my tongue and turns me from curious to feral in the span of a millisecond.

I descend on her pussy like a starved man eating for the first time in years, loving the feeling of her fingers winding into my hair and tugging, loving the way her moans start to fill the air, overshadowing the noise from the movie. I thrust my tongue inside her, trying to get as much of her taste as I possibly can, before licking a path up to her clit and rubbing the flat of my tongue over the little bundle of nerves. She whimpers at that, squirming, making me feel like the most powerful man in the world.

I've never enjoyed eating a girl out—I've done it once or twice, mainly in an act of curiosity, and found that I don't have a particular appetite for it, not with other girls. I absolutely want to eat April, though, and the longer I do, the hungrier for her I get. Her reactions—moans, whimpers, tugging at my hair, wriggling beneath me—are all an aphrodisiac that I could easily get hooked on. Her taste—spicy with a hint of sweetness—is even more addictive, and I want as much of it as I can get.

When I suck her clit between my lips, her back arches and she lets out a loud cry. Growling, I spear two fingers inside her, feeling her pussy clench and flutter around them; the noises she's making turn desperate. I shove a third finger into her channel, curling all of them upward to find the spot that I know she likes. When I feel the telling pulses around my fingers, hinting that she's about to come, I move my mouth to her thigh and bite down *hard*, hard enough to leave a mark that should last a few days. If she tries to get with anyone else—which I wouldn't allow anyways—the guy will see *my* marks on her skin and hopefully be put off. Then, I'll find him and kill him.

A cry that's bordering on a shout escapes her, and I feel more of her arousal soak my fingers. The fact that she likes pain mixed in with pleasure is so goddamn arousing I'm pretty sure my cock is about to punch a hole right through my pants.

"Scream for me," I tell her, scraping my teeth down the center of her swollen clit before sucking it back into my mouth, and she does. She implodes around my fingers, screaming and shaking and shivering, tugging at my hair so hard it almost hurts, and grinding against my face while I thrust my fingers in and out of her, wishing they were my cock and silently promising that I will feel her clenching around it soon enough.

I draw out her orgasm for as long as I can, until she's pushing my head away, teeth chattering, panting, her cries sounding more agonized than pleasured. I'm mildly surprised to find that my heart's racing nearly as fast as hers, and I think I might've enjoyed that as much as she did. No, not think, I'm pretty damn certain I liked going down on her even more than she did, and I know that'll be added to the list of regular activities between us.

"Fucking hell, your mouth is *lethal*," she pants. I look up to see her eyes glazed and lips parted, a sex-drunk expression that makes me keen to draw another orgasm from her.

In a move that surprises me, she slips out from under me and kneels on the floor. "Sit up," she tells me. "I'm gonna return the favor."

Feeling my eyebrows raise, I do, pulling down my pants and briefs to release my cock, which is harder than a steel pipe after tasting her. April firmly grips it in her hand, and says, "Now *you'll* scream for *me*."

My eyes narrow at her. "I don't scream."

A devious smile spreads on her lips. "Maybe not, but you'll be crying out for god."

Then, she makes good on her promise.

Chapter Twenty

April

Ian doesn't let up on his pursuit of me in the week after I spend the night at his apartment. I keep expecting him to grow bored of my refusal to fully give into him, but he doesn't. He's pushy to spend as much time with me as he possibly can, rarely does an evening end without an orgasm for me, but he doesn't demand sex in return for his efforts. I can tell he's not terribly *content* with the fact that I rarely respond to his texts, never seek him out, and spend most of our time together shooting him down in subtle or not so subtle ways, but I'll give the fucker this; he's determined.

Ian isn't put off by my resistance; he seems accepting and even understanding of it, though not happy. I allow him to take me out to meals, mainly because I know protesting won't do me any good, and because I'm a fan of delicious food—he always picks good spots. I let him work over my body and make me come because I like orgasms, and he's proven to be a master at delivering them. Besides, if he weren't taking care of my needs, I would absolutely turn elsewhere, and considering his threat to ruin the life of anyone else I'm intimate with, that might be problematic.

That's as far as I let him go, though, and only because getting good food and pleasure suits me as much as it does him. I don't acquit on any other front; I maintain the fact that I am *not* spending the upcoming spring break with him, in the states or on some extravagant trip. I don't let him buy me things even though he consistently hints at it. I refuse to give us a label—I don't even agree whenever he mentions that we're dating, and the one time he brings up the boyfriend/girlfriend label, I laugh in his face. I only give him as much as it suits me to give, no more, even though it's plain to see he wants much more. He wants *everything*.

The fact of the matter is that, while I'm no longer vehemently opposed to being in his vicinity, I still don't trust him very much. I trust that he won't hurt me *now*, because he wants me, but I don't trust that he won't do another about-face in the future and go back to the cruelty that cost me so much in the past. I'm okay existing as we are now, but I won't commit to him, because that would entail envisioning a future for us. I can't do that even if a part of me wants to.

I want to dance my best years on stage, probably until I'm in my early thirties, then transition to either teaching on a professional level or directing and choreographing ballets while starting a family. I want to be a mother, and I don't see myself having children with Ian. He's never struck me as the paternal type.

I'm careful not to get too comfortable with him or too used to his presence in my life, because I don't see him being a permanent fixture in it. Eventually, he'll tire of my refusal to give into him and move on.

If I maintain emotional distance between us, him moving on won't hurt me. I will *never* give him the power to hurt me again.

I don't like how easy it's become to be around him in a casual capacity—don't like how much I actually enjoy speaking with him and debating him, so I make sure what we have is relatively meaningless. Something that I'll be ready to drop at a moment's notice. I don't make time for him unless he comes to me first, I don't seek him out, and I absolutely do not *rely* on him for anything. I can see that my resistance is starting to rankle him more and more, but that's his problem, not mine. I might've agreed to let him *try* to build something with me, but I'm not going to help him. In short, I treat him in the same way I've treated the rest of my lovers in the last months and years, like casual commodities. Treats that I might enjoy but are easy to forget.

When Ian works a late night in his office the following Thursday, I finally make time to head into the city and hit the café Elia mentioned a few weeks ago. We've both been too busy and swept up in our personal lives to actually make it to a café date—Elia has two men that are constantly vying for all of her time and attention, and Ian is currently laser-focused on me. I'm happy to finally get some time to hang out with her, though; I freaking adore this girl.

The café is a quaint little wooden shop, featuring a glass display case boasting delicious treats, and a menu drawn on a blackboard behind the front counter where a barista stands. The scents of coffee and pastries waft through the room, creating a mouthwatering aroma, and there are a few square wooden tables with accompanying chairs scattered around the shop. Elia and I each order a coffee and some fruit tarts, then settle at the corner table.

"How are classes going?" I ask her, taking a sip of my drink, wincing as it scalds the roof of my mouth.

"Really good," Elia tells me. "Midterms are coming up in a few weeks, which is stressful, but I'm well prepared. It helps that Seth has an undeniable obsession with art history, and we spend a lot of time together talking and debating topics from our classes. I expected him to drop the classes we share since he only enrolled to get close to me, but he hasn't, and he's made a great study partner." She lifts her tart and takes a bite, before moaning. "Holy shit, this is amazing, you have to try it."

I follow suit, also biting into my pastry; my eyes nearly roll into the back of my head as the flavors of fresh glazed berries, lemon cream, and perfectly cooked dough explode on my tongue. I chew and swallow, taking the top off my coffee to let it cool a bit.

"How are things going with you and Ian?" Elia asks in turn. "I've noticed he still attends every Pandora's Box performance and sends flowers most evenings. He's also been carting you off to dinners just about every single night."

I shrug, trying to keep my muscles from tensing at the mention of him. "Things are fine. I'm waiting for him to get bored, which I expect he will soon enough, since I'm not giving him what he wants. Not really."

Elia arches an eyebrow at me. "And what is it that he wants?"

"Everything," I respond simply. From what I've gathered, Ian wants all of me; wants an exclusive relationship, wants to have complete access to my mind, body, and to have a place in my heart as he once did. "Since there's not a snowball's chance in hell I'll accommodate that, he'll move on eventually."

Elia takes another bite of her pastry, looking pensive as she chews and washes it down with a sip of coffee.

"You know, I expected the same thing of Seth and Carson; I held them at bay in the beginning, waiting for them to find another object of infatuation. It didn't work."

I let out a long breath. I've tried reminding Elia that our situations are not the same; while she might've been fundamentally against dating *a* trust fund kid, let alone two, her men were committed to having her and treated her like a priceless treasure from the very beginning. There was no bad blood there. With Ian and me, there is a surplus of bad blood and proven reasons as to why we can't be together in the long run.

"Ian and I aren't a good fit, Elia," I tell her. "There's too much shitty history, and I have too many reasons not to trust him. Your boys worked themselves to the bone to prove to you again and again that you can trust them. There was a time when I trusted Ian completely, when he was my favorite person in the world, and he made a point of shitting all over that trust and breaking us. I won't make the same mistake again. Fool me once, you're the fool, fool me twice, I'm the fool—I don't intend to make a fool of myself on his account."

Elia makes a noise of irritation. "You still won't tell me what he did to you. That makes you a shitty best friend, just so you know."

I snort. "I am not a shitty best friend, and I *have* told you—typical playground bully stuff. Name calling, petty insults, that type of thing. None of it would have bothered me if I hadn't been such close friends with Ian beforehand." Hence why I refuse to let him in again.

Elia shakes her head. "I don't believe you. There's something more. You had—still sometimes have—so much anger in your voice when you speak about him. It couldn't have just been name calling and hair pulling stuff."

I let my eyes flutter shut for a brief moment. Elia is far more perceptive and clever than people give her credit for. She's just so pint-sized and innocent looking, most don't suspect she has a gaze as sharp as a hunter's and misses very little. I open my mouth, ready to give her some excuse, but then hesitate.

If there's anyone I truly feel like I can talk to and confide in, it's the girl sitting across from me. I've only known her for a few months, but that's been plenty of time for us to grow close. Something about us clicks well, and Eliana has a goodness in her—a drive to help and protect—that makes her an incredible friend.

I remember how, during the dance retreat before the start of the school year, Elia was ridiculously busy from getting cast as a lead in Greywood's recurring opening production of Sleeping Beauty. I knew she was looking for a job near campus but didn't have time to apply anywhere, so I sent out applications for her to dance studios since we both wanted to get some cash through teaching. When she found out about that, she pitched my dancing skillset to Sanders, and got me a spot in Pandora's Box before casting had even begun.

Since then we've shared everything—she confided in me about her struggles with Carson and Seth, and I was the one to first put the idea of a three way relationship in her head, which certainly paid off. She's also told me about her past problems with an eating disorder, hence why I double check after dance classes to make sure she has something to eat before she runs off to her afternoon courses. Maybe it wouldn't be the worst thing in the world to open up to her.

The only problem is, I don't have much of a habit of opening up to *anyone*. The one person in my life I was ever fully open with was Ian, and he taught me a lesson; being open and trusting only leads to pain. Elia isn't Ian, though, she's much kinder at her core.

"There was...an incident the summer before my senior year," I start slowly, folding my hands in my lap and clenching them so tightly my knuckles turn white. I hate even *thinking* about that night, let alone speaking about it, but maybe it would help to open that dark corner of my past to someone I fully believe I can trust.

Elia sets her coffee down. "If Ian hurt you, I will hurt *him*."

Chapter Twenty-One

A laugh bursts out of me. "I adore you for the offer, but it's not necessary. Ian never physically hurt me. But he did spread horrible rumors about me around high school. He also had a social status as the king of the school, so people would take their cues from him—since he was an absolute asshole to me, other classmates were even worse. Up until the incident, the only way my classmates were cruel to me was through disparaging comments, being horrible to me on social media to the point where I had to close my accounts, stuffing my locker with gross shit—the typical high school bullying stuff.

"The summer after my junior year, there were a few boys who took it a lot farther. They had just graduated alongside Ian after being on the football team with him for years, so they were the first to hear the newest bullshit he spewed about me." My lips twist and I give my head a shake. "Before leaving our city, Ian spread around the rumor that I was happy to fuck in return for money; getting called a gold digger was the usual for me, but being outright dubbed a whore and prostitute was much worse."

I pause as my heartbeat speeds up to a gallop, and my mind momentarily clouds with horrible memories that I've done my best to work past or simply suppress. Talking about the incident is digging up an old boneyard, and a lot of skeletons are deciding to make themselves known. Still, I persevere, because I've carried this information with me alone for way too long.

"Anyways, there was a night when three of the boys cornered me—I was heading home from a late trip to the grocery store, and they jumped me, pulled me into a dark alleyway. One of them had a knife, I think they just meant to use it to scare me into compliance, but I wouldn't comply with the sick shit they wanted. They were throwing dollar bills at me, laughing at me, tearing off my clothes, and I fought back. Hard. Like any dancer, I'm stronger than I look, so I managed to fend them off before things went too far and ended up getting stabbed and sliced during the struggle."

I cut off when Elia's face turns sheet-white and her lips part with abject horror. "I'm sorry. I didn't mean to ruin your mood—"

"No," Elia cuts me off, shaking her head. "If you want to talk about it, I'll listen. I'm glad you're opening up. I just fucking *hate* that you went through something like that, but I'm here for you, April."

I inhale a shaky deep breath, blinking several times to try to clear the worst of the images from my mind. "The important thing is I got away before the physical assault turned into sexual assault. Made my way home. My dad—a really, *really* Russian man, soviet born and bred—took me to the hospital and tried to pump me for information. I didn't give it. I was too scared and too out of sorts. A doctor stitched me up and did a rape kit on the insistence of my father, which didn't turn up much. I was a mess for a few weeks, but then my fear turned into burning anger. I made sure that those boys could never do to someone else what they tried to do to me in a pretty definitive way."

Elia clears her throat, takes a sip of coffee, then asks, "What did you do?"

I pause at that, mainly because I did some very illegal shit to get back at them, and it's not in my nature to expose myself to anyone. I didn't even tell my dad, and I trust him implicitly; I just learned from watching him as I grew up that certain things are best left unsaid. He's never been intentionally elusive or evasive with my mother, but there have been times when she asks a question and he tells her, as kindly as possible, that it's best if she doesn't have the answer. I understand that's because he doesn't want her implicated if his past ever catches up with him. It won't, he's too careful for that, but nonetheless he wants her to have deniability.

"Things that could get me thrown in jail if they're ever discovered," I admit lowly. I also recognize in hindsight that now I can never legally go after the boys for what they did to me—not that I ever had any intention of doing that, but now I no longer have the option. I've committed some crimes of my own.

Elia frowns. "I'd never tell anyone, April. Seth's told me about some of the things he's done when he's functioning in a vigilante capacity, and even introduced me to some individuals who have dark dealings. I know how to keep my mouth shut. You don't have to tell me, of course, I'd never force or coerce, but you also don't have to worry about anything said here ever getting out. It won't."

I look at her for a long moment, trying to gauge her sincerity. I believe that she's heard some bad stuff from Seth—whispers say he's done some dark shit in the past. If I were a betting woman, I'd wager he still does those things on occasion. Like Ian, Seth is someone who has a deep-rooted darkness in him. Darkness like that needs sating to hold at bay or it can take over entirely and consume any existing light.

Finally, I respond. "I did the same thing to those boys that a parent does when a child proves it can't treat its toys well; I took their toys away. I got my hands on the knife they used to stab me, which was covered in all of their fingerprints, along with some other DNA evidence they left behind on my clothes that could've been used to prosecute them in court and get them locked up for a long time." They did some *really* gross and fucked up shit before I managed to get away, which was horrifying, but also left concrete evidence. "The stab wound nearly killed me, almost nicked an artery and sliced straight through two veins, so they would've been charged with attempted murder along with other forms of assault—they would've spent years in prison.

"I got in touch with one of Dad's associates from the old country who has dealings in the U.S. and purchased a substance that renders men not only sterile but makes it impossible for them to get it up. It's chemical castration, something done in certain countries to rapists. It's not usually an exact science, but the man I spoke to had a perfected formula that would make the chemicals work permanently." That associate is a bit of a mad scientist—he likes to play with chemical compounds to create things that'll cause his enemies extreme pain, and during experimentation happened to create a drug that could render a man both sterile and infertile for the rest of his life. "Finally, I reached out to the boys and gave them a choice; have me go after them legally and spend their lives in prison, or never be able to use their dicks again. They tried to call my bluff at first, but I wasn't fucking bluffing, I just didn't want to get caught up in a legal battle where I'd have to recount my experience on a witness stand and prove that I was telling the truth. All of them ended up choosing the needle."

Those sick fucks will never again try to corner and rape a girl, because they can't. Those boys aren't killers; just overentitled brats who thought they could get away with anything. Teaching them that they *couldn't* get away with anything was enough of a punishment in my book.

To my great surprise, a slow smile spreads on Elia's lips, and some of the color returns to her cheeks. I'd have expected her to be horrified by what I did, albeit accepting—after all, if she can accept what Seth does for fun to blow off steam, she can probably accept some well-deserved vengeance—but I didn't expect the delight creeping across her expression.

"That's badass," she says, approval dripping from every word. "If Seth knew how hardcore you can get, he might try to recruit you as a sidekick in some of his...dealings."

I snort, even as relief overcomes me. "I don't think I'd make a very good sidekick. Besides, I get no joy out of hurting people, but I do believe in tit for tat."

Strangely, I feel somewhat lighter after confiding in Elia. I've carried around the weight of that night and all the horror that followed for years, and I hadn't realized how heavy it was until just now, as it's easing the slightest bit. I thought—still think—that I handled the situation well, all things considered. Rather than letting it break me or turn me into a victim, that experience taught me a lot, both about the world and about myself. I learned that I have an inner strength that allowed me to get the hell out of that alleyway, even stabbed and sliced and bleeding heavily. I also learned I have a knack for vengeance.

Still, it's been a heavier weight to bear than I assumed it was, probably because it became second nature to keep it to myself. And, while there's some worry in me that now that this information is out in the open I've potentially exposed myself to harm, I trust Elia. I don't think she'd betray my confidence.

Elia half-smiles. "Yeah. Seth... I love him, truly, but he can be a fucking sadist. It's scary sometimes, but I know he'd never want to hurt me." Her cheeks turn pink. "Not in a way I wouldn't enjoy, that is."

I point at her. "I knew you were kinky. It's always the innocent-looking ones."

Elia raises her eyebrows. "And you *aren't*? You have a tendency to overshare when discussing your sexual escapades, April, and so far I'm yet to hear a single vanilla thing about you."

"Vanilla is boring and unsatisfying," I say with a shrug.

"So... have you and Ian—"

"Not all the way," I tell her. "I'm not up for that. We've exchanged favors, though. Funny enough, that has been fairly vanilla." Save for Ian's propensity to hold me still while he pets and strokes me. "Probably because most things are off the table."

"Do you see him as responsible for what happened to you?" Elia questions carefully.

I wince. "Not directly, I don't think so. He would never have done something like that, nor do I think he would have condoned it, but he did tip the first domino in the chain of events that led directly to that horrible night. I don't think I would've been trapped in that alleyway if he hadn't done what he did throughout the entire time we shared a school together. So, I don't really blame him or see him as directly culpable, but he perpetuated a culture that set me up for what happened."

Elia purses her lips, looking down at her coffee, pausing to take another sip. "Do you like Ian, April? You've told me before that you guys used to be best friends, and you don't speak about him with the same open belligerence you did just a few weeks ago, but I'm also curious if you like him as a person. If, without the history of bad blood, you might be willing to give him more."

I have to think about that for several moments. On the surface, there's a hatred of Ian that stems from pain, and beneath that there's still a great deal of hurt and a profound feeling of betrayal. Pushing all that aside, I try to imagine if I would like Ian for who he is as a person if it weren't for our high school experience. It quickly becomes clear that the answer is yes; I'd very much like him.

"Yeah," I finally admit. "I would."

Elia nods. "He seems really intent on having you. The flowers, the attention, the way he acts the times I've seen you two together... I don't think he's dealing with a passing infatuation. I think he wants to keep you permanently, the way Seth decided he'd keep me."

Oh, I'm well aware that he does, but I also have no intention of allowing that.

"He probably does," I say. "Unfortunately for him, I'm not someone who forgets—I come from a long line of grudge holders. Honestly, even if that night in the alley hadn't happened, I don't think I'd be able to get over how he treated me in high school. It was just too cruel, too harsh, and something that destroyed my self-respect, Elia. Choosing him would be shirking myself. I did that once before, I will not do it again."

Elia tilts her head to the side as she studies me. "But you want him," she senses. "Even though you won't let yourself have him, you want him."

I feel myself deflate at her words, shoulders slumping, because she's right. I do want Ian. I also have too much regard for my wellbeing to set myself up for failure a second time, but that doesn't snuff out the traitorous part of me that wants to go all in with him. It's the same part that was sure we'd end up married when we were children.

"Yes," I say lowly. "Of course I do. There was a time when I was sure he hung the moon and stars; that we were meant to be. I also think something happened to him that made him turn cruel towards me; he's made a few comments connoting that he acted the way he did to keep me away, to avoid tainting me. He even mentioned that his about-face didn't come from sheer cruelty, but was the result of some bad shit that happened to him. My best guess is he had his own traumatic experience the summer before he started high school, and then made the decision to push me away. Naturally, he took it too far, because he has the sort of personality to take things too far. Now, it looks like he's recognizing that he shouldn't have done that, but it's too late."

Elia frowns at that, running her hand through her blonde hair. "Huh. So, the water's muddy on both sides, and you've both been through some stuff. Do you think there's ever a chance of him earning his way back into your good graces, or is he embarking on a pointless endeavor with you?"

I chuckle, and the noise comes out sardonic. "What I think is that it'd take a goddamn miracle for us to truly be together, Elia."

A miracle, and then some.

Chapter Twenty-Two

I'm sitting on my dorm room bed, finishing up some studying for my upcoming French test and practicing the language while trying my absolute best to keep my mind off Ian when my phone starts buzzing on my bedside stand. I check it, seeing that my parents are calling; feeling my heart warm, I answer the call.

"Mom, Papa," I greet, a smile spreading on my lips.

I speak to my parents almost every day, sometimes every other, and conversations with them always improve my mood. I grew up in a household filled with a mixture of tough love and endless warmth.

My father is very Russian, so nothing short of perfection impresses him, but he's always been my greatest supporter and close confidant—never once has he made me feel inferior for choosing dance as a career, even though he understands that ballet isn't a lifelong career. I rarely receive outright praise from him, Slavic parents aren't known for coddling their children, but he's never disparaged me. He's also the type of man who polished a shotgun while giving me his version of *the talk* in high school—where he basically told me not to trust boys my age, and that if anyone hurt me, he was armed and fully prepared to kill them. He actually cocked the gun while saying that. Which is why, when I stumbled my way home after the incident, bleeding and a mess, yet refused to give him details about what happened, he blew a gasket and nearly lost his shit.

My mom, on the other hand, is a gentler and kinder person at her core. She demands and expects academic excellence from me, as her family did from her, but she's also heavy on the praise and warmth—always sure to tell me that I'm doing a phenomenal job and that she's proud of me and so grateful to have me as a daughter. I think that's because she suffered from a lack of warmth from her own family.

Neither of my parents were terribly happy when I refused any support from them for college, but I sensed that they were both proud. My father said, *"so there's no room for doubt that you're my daughter"*, while Mom smacked his chest, cupped my cheek, and told me if I changed my mind they'd be happy to help. I haven't, which I get the sense has impressed them.

"Sweetheart," my mom's voice floats over the phone, holding a note of excitement that piques my interest. My mother's generally a happy and bright person—something that I suspect keeps my father balanced and sane—but it takes quite a bit to get her truly *excited*.

"Milaya," Dad greets, his tone also a shade brighter from his usual surliness. "How are you? How's Greywood?"

"I'm good, everything here is good," I reply, closing my notebook and capping my pen. "You two want to tell me why you sound like kids mooning over presents when the clock strikes midnight on New Years?"

There's a pause, before my dad chuckles. "Russian child through and through, complete with the knowledge that *Ded Moroz* comes at the stroke of midnight on New Years, not on Christmas Eve like the American idiots presume."

Ded Moroz, the Russian version of Santa Clause—or Saint Nicholas, as it is in the church—has always been one of my favorite parts of winter holidays. Especially when I spent the holidays on ski trips with Ian, before our falling out. The fact that my family celebrates New Years while Ian's celebrates Christmas meant double the cheer, happiness, celebration, and even presents. I'd give Ian something on Christmas as a sign of respect for his traditions, *and* on New Years because I will continue debating to the death that Russians have this one right; Americans are merely subpar copycats who mess most things up.

"Seriously, what's going on?" I ask, wanting to find out whatever has my parents sounding so unusually bright and eager. "Did your business have a sudden boom overnight, Papa?"

"Business is booming, milaya, as always. I'd allow nothing less," Dad replies.

Growing irritated with Dad's stalling, I say, "Mom?"

I hear Mom suck in a deep breath, before bursting out, "I'm pregnant! You're going to be an older sister!"

For a moment, I'm dumbstruck, sure that I've heard her wrong. I know my parents always wanted more children—two or three—but Mom experienced some health issues during her pregnancy with me that made the chances of her getting pregnant again *extremely* unlikely, something that was devastating to both of them.

It was such a painful topic that Mom didn't even tell me about it until I was eleven, at which point she and Dad had undergone a bunch of fertility treatments, none of which resulted in success. I remember hearing her cry in her bedroom and secretly wondering if I wasn't enough for them. Logically, I knew—still know—that they love me to the ends of the universe, just as I love them. But in my frazzled and already-shaky mind, thanks to Ian's torment, I felt like I wasn't satisfying or good enough.

I no longer feel that way. Perhaps it's the fact that age has imparted a touch of wisdom, or because I know beyond a doubt that my parents adore me and are proud of me, but no nerves or fear of being second-best assuage me. Instead, sheer exhilaration fills me at the prospect of Mom and Dad getting what they've wanted for as long as I can remember; another child to raise. They're both very parental souls, excellent at caretaking, and I know they always wished for a big family.

"Sweetheart?" Mom asks again, making me realize I've been sitting silently for upwards of a minute, lost in thought and my own exhilaration.

"*That is so exciting!*" I screech, beyond pleased for them, and very much looking forward to becoming an older sister. I intend to spoil the *shit* out of my little brother or sister, and protect them to death. "How far along are you? Do you know the sex yet? Tell me everything!"

"Twenty two weeks today," Mom responds, her voice slightly more subdued.

I blink several times, that tidbit of news hitting me like a sledgehammer. I recall dinner with my parents a few weeks ago; Mom didn't drink anything but tea and water, forgoing her usual order of Sake, which makes me realize that she knew she was pregnant back then—they both did—yet they didn't tell me. She also wore a flowing dress that would've hidden any existent baby bump. They might've even known before I left for Greywood; my mom's over *five months* pregnant. That makes my heart sink and brows furrow. Did they not trust me with the news?

"Why are you just telling me now?" I ask, channeling every ounce of my energy to prevent myself from snapping.

"The situation is not without its complications, my love," Mom responds. After a long pause, she says, "There have been other times. Pregnancies lost... in the earliest stages. Some as late as eighteen weeks." Her voice gets a touch choked up, and I instantly feel like the biggest asshole in the world for questioning her. Seriously, what the hell is *wrong* with me? "I wanted to wait until I was out of the most dangerous time to share the good news."

"I understand, of course," I say quickly, mentally slapping myself.

"The pregnancy will be complicated, milaya," my father tells me. "Your mother will be on bedrest for some time, starting at six months. In the meantime, she is to take things *very* easy, which means minimal traveling going forward. Unfortunately, the likelihood of us attending the spring break ski trip with the Vargas's will be very low."

"I'm sorry, sweetheart, I know you were looking forward to it," Mom says.

"Don't be!" I exclaim, a touch too loudly because this could be my way out of spending even *more* time with Ian. Quiter, I amend, "Don't be, please. Your health comes first, no questions or apologies needed. I could use the extra time to study and practice, anyways. I'm so, *so* pleased and even more excited to be an older sister."

"I told you your worries were for nothing, solnyshko," Dad says, using his favorite endearment for my mother. "Of course, April will be happy that our family is growing."

I let out a breath of laughter. "You didn't think I'd be thrilled, Mom?"

"No, of course not," Mom says quickly. "I was just a touch worried... you grew up as an only child, and only children can get a bit worked up over families suddenly expanding."

I could see how that might be the case with some, but not with me. My parents were very open with me about going through fertility treatment years ago—I grieved with them when their efforts didn't yield results. I'd been ready to be a big sister, even if it made me question my worth at a low point in my life. Now, when I have zero issues with self-respect and see myself as pretty fucking awesome, I couldn't be happier.

"Well, thank you for telling me. I am very much looking forward to welcoming a new Stein into the family. I can guarantee that I'll make sure baby Stein loves me more than either of you."

Dad chuckles. "There's that competitive spirit. Now, onto other topics... have you dropped that Ian boy yet?"

Mom scoffs, and I hear a light thwacking sound, presumably her hitting Dad's chest. "Will you ever cease treating him like an unwelcomed nuisance you want away from your daughter?"

"On the day he becomes good enough for her," Dad deadpans.

Mom sighs. "Considering you don't think there's anyone good enough for our April, that'll be never?"

"Correct, solnyshko."

I bite my lips to keep from laughing, because my parent's banter—especially when it comes to my love life—has always been endlessly amusing. I didn't have much of a love life to boast of until senior year of high school. After I whipped my school's dance team into shape, it became virtually impossible for people to continue ostracizing me; my school took champions very seriously, and I created a team of champions, so the tides that Ian had turned against me suddenly started bringing a wealth of people directly to me.

Determined to never be hurt again, I went through boys and girls like they were water—returning the favor of the disposable way I was treated for so long by consistently disposing of them. My parents noticed this, and Dad seemed to find it amusing while Mom was worried that I was unable to settle down. She's probably right on that front;

settling down takes trust, and I don't have much trust or faith when it comes to humanity.

Mom says, "I, for one, am extremely pleased about you and Ian. I always thought it was meant to be between the two of you. We had dinner with his parents the other day—they were equally overjoyed that you two are together. His mom mentioned that he plans on whisking you away for the second half of spring break, but apparently you're protesting the idea."

I roll my eyes heavenward. Since I have absolutely refused to budge with Ian on the spring break front, it appears he's decided to play sneaky by getting his parents involved, knowing that they'd get my parents involved in turn. He probably guessed that once my mom caught wind of his proposed trip, she'd think it was the most romantic thing in the world and insist I go with him, disregarding any and all protests I might give. *Fucking prick.*

"I'm going to be busy over spring break," I say tersely. "I have to keep dancing for at least four hours a day if I want to stay in shape for the dance program."

"Too busy for the trip you've been dreaming of since you were a little girl?" Mom asks, her tone incredulous.

I point out with a sigh, "I can't exactly afford something like that."

Mom says, "It didn't sound like he was asking you to pay, April. In fact, the way Meredith put it, this trip was going to be his version of an apology for your falling out during high school. *So* romantic."

"I'd still like to hear details on that falling out," Dad grumbles, sounding incredibly displeased. "You two were thick as thieves, and suddenly, you couldn't stand to be in the same room together. We stopped doing family dinners because you would always cry when we came home from them—after hours of staring at him like a lovelorn puppy and him ignoring your very existence, you were understandably upset. Then, out of the blue, you're dating. I'd love an explanation, milaya."

Mom says on a scoff, "Young boys are stupid. You, my darling, should know that better than anyone else. I recall quite well a time when I wouldn't look in your direction and for very good reason."

I stifle a smile. Every time Dad gets grumpy or snappy, Mom cuts him down to half his size by pointing out his own shortcomings, past *and* present. She might be a kind soul, but she also doesn't take shit from anyone—especially not my father. Which, I think, is part of why he loves her so much. He likes the take-no-shit brand of humans.

"Anyways, it appears Ian has grown up and screwed his head on straight now that he's pursuing April," Mom says to Dad. "After all, he could do no better than our girl."

"Obviously," Dad drawls. "He didn't seem to see that for years, however." Then, to me, "Milaya, how do you feel about his pursuit? Would you prefer him crippled and unable to court you?"

Mom gasps, "Maksimillian Steinovich!" While I laugh with delight, only cackling harder at hearing my mom use Dad's full name, which she only does when she's *really* irritated with him.

"You can't blame me for my protectiveness, solnyshko," Dad says, his voice placid. "April is far too beautiful for this world."

Mom says drily, "You should've chosen someone less beautiful to reproduce with if you didn't want a pretty daughter."

"A strategic error on my part," Dad agrees calmly. "Fortunately, she has all the viciousness of her father's blood beneath the delicate exterior, so I try not to worry too much."

My brows furrow at that. There are times when Dad says things about my viciousness or intensity that hint to him knowing more than he should, but he never elaborates, and I never ask him to. He could be referring to the vicious way I trained and drilled my dance team in high school, and not the truly vicious activities I've taken part in.

Mom says, "April, love, we have a lunch to get to, but wanted to call and share the happy news now that the most dangerous time is behind us."

"The *first* stretch of danger is out of the way," Dad says sternly. "There is still much that lies ahead, which is why you will be exceedingly careful and restful in the coming months."

A niggle of worry blooms in my chest, because I know Papa isn't the type to exaggerate danger. I also know that I was born six weeks prematurely because my mother's body simply couldn't maintain a pregnancy any longer. That was nearly two decades ago; my mom is now in her late thirties, which would make for a complicated pregnancy even without preexisting health problems. I'm not a particularly religious person, but I find myself sending a quick prayer up to whatever higher power exists, hoping and asking for everything to be well with my mother. If she's already had several miscarriages in early stages, it would destroy her if she doesn't carry to term, not to mention the heavy shadow it would cast over my family.

"Give Ian a chance to take you on a whirl around the world, April, and stay in touch with us," Mom says. "We'll keep you apprised of any and all developments with the incoming member of our family. Stay well, my love, and be safe."

"Love you both, enjoy your lunch," I tell them. "Make sure you eat plenty, Mom, since you're now eating for two."

Dad says, "I'll ensure she does. We love you, *milaya*."

After we've hung up, I'm filled with a restless energy that desperately needs an outlet. Ian texted me that he'd come find me later, but I'm too worked up to stay put, so I change into a leotard, throw a sweatsuit over it, grab my dance bag, and head out of the dorm room, making my way towards dance HQ. The several story building isn't too long of a walk, and all company members who are part of Pandora's Box have our student ID cards coded to the scanner at the front door to allow us all-hour access to studio's, since rehearsal's tend to run late into the evening. It's around 8pm now, and there aren't any scheduled rehearsals tonight, so I expect to have the space to myself.

I'm proven wrong when I get to the second floor where the largest studio spaces are and notice that lights in one of the studios are on. Wandering inside, I'm delighted to find Elia at the bar, stretching as if in preparation to squeeze in some dance time herself.

"Hey," she greets when I walk in, looking up from her split and offering me a smile. We just had coffee yesterday, so I'm surprised to see that her boys have left her alone for yet another night—they tend to be possessive of her free time.

"Hey, yourself," I greet lightly, dropping my bag by the mirror and stripping off my sweats. I pull a wrap skirt on before saying, "What are you doing here so late? Carson and Seth let you out of their sight for *two* nights in a row?"

She lets out a light laugh. "They're both at Carson's office, along with Ian, I think. Figuring out how best to deal with Carson's uncle who's now in town—there's a lot of fuckery going on there. They said they'd come for me in a bit, I figured I might get at least an hour of stretching and dancing in."

I take in the new tidbits of information, mildly interested, wondering if these developments are what's had Ian stressed recently. I noticed that his mood has been darker over the last week—though he's careful not to take it out on me, which is surprising, I've always been able to tell when something's off with him. These days, it's evident more so in the way he holds me down firmly while finger or tongue fucking me, damn near leaving bruises on my arms and wrists. Also in the way he eats at my mouth every chance he gets, and holds me tightly on his lap whenever he can, as if loathe to break contact with me. He clings to like I'm a lifeline to escape the demons in his head.

"What about you?" Elia asks. "What are you doing here so late? Your dancing is pristine, so I doubt you're here for practice."

I shrug. "Ian also told me he'd come for me in a bit, though I didn't get as many details from him, which suits me fine. I...uh...well, I received great news from my parents, though it's tinged with worry." I tell Elia about my phone call, finding it shockingly easy to confide in her after unburdening myself to her last night. I won't spread the news of my family growing any time soon; I don't want to jinx the good news and risk something bad happening, so I ask Elia to keep the knowledge to herself.

"Wow," Elia says once I'm done. "Congrats on the prospect of being a big sister—I can't wait to meet the little bean—and I'm sorry your mom's pregnancy is so complex. I won't tell anyone, naturally. I totally get why you need to let off some steam." Her lips twist as she straightens, stretching her arms over her head. "Honestly, I'm not feeling the usual ballet tonight."

I grin. "Funny, neither am I. I brought my speaker—I have a playlist I use whenever I'm stressed, it's made of indie songs with really compelling beats that always draw me in. They aren't suited to ballet, but they are suited to soulful movement. If you're down, I can put the playlist on.'

Elia's eyes brighten. "Yeah, let's do that. You cool with a pas de deux if I feel into it? I always dance best when it's with you."

"Hell yes," I agree.

I pull my speaker out of my bag, click on my playlist, close my eyes, and let the music pull me in like it always does. Movement flows from my body in accordance with the beat—twirls and dips that stem more from the bit of contemporary and pop training I have, instead of the practiced, precise movements of classical ballet.

Elia seems as into it as I am—we weave around the room, coming together and splitting apart periodically. As much as she claims that I make her dance better, she does the exact same to me; there's a synergy between us that makes us both excel. Everyone in the company, including Sanders, knows it; that's probably why we're on stage together so often in Pandora's Box. Something about us fundamentally works.

I hear the faint echo of footsteps coming down the hall, before seeing three shadowy forms appear in front of the glass door, just as the song changes to one of my favorites; Drop the Game, by Flume and Chet Faker. I find it's both a soulful and sensual song, especially since I'm already in full swing with Elia. Before Carson, Seth, and Ian enter, I give Elia a conspiratorial smile. "Want to really give them a show to remember?"

Her eyebrows raise. "What are you thinking?"

Impulsively, I say, "You gonna be weirded out if I kiss you? Platonically, of course." Eliana is absolutely gorgeous, but I've never been attracted to her as more than a friend. I am, however, attracted to the idea of finding out just how insane it'll drive the men to see us dancing together sensually.

A slow grin spreads on Elia's lips. She says, "Do it, it'll drive Seth crazy and then he'll fuck me silly," just as the boys open the glass door and file in. Seth opens his mouth to interrupt; Eliana shuts him up with one harsh glare that takes a single beat of the music. He holds his hands up in a placating gesture.

After that, they don't interrupt the dance—Seth and Carson are both too swept up in watching Elia, while Ian's eyes are firmly locked on me, his gaze feeling like a physical force crawling over my skin, turning my nipples hard and making warmth gather in my core.

I take hold of Elia's hand, and she falls right into sync with me—we lift each other, twirl, and dip, all in a seductive way that charges the air with sexual tension. Not between her and me, but there are live wires between us and our prospective suitors.

As the song reaches the chorus, an epitome of sensuality in both the music and our dancing, we naturally come together, our arms twining and our faces hovering. Surprising me, she leans close and trails her lips up my neck, her eyes flicking to Seth and Carson, before taking my hand and twirling me in a move that's more ballroom than contemporary or ballet. I pull her back by one hand, trail the other along her chest and up her neck, then use my fingers on her chin to gently guide her lips to mine, slanting them in a brief kiss that's more a brush of lips than anything else, just as the song reaches its end. I'm yanked away from her and against a hard chest in an abrupt, sharp move that leaves me breathless. I smile as I also see Seth pull Elia to him, giving her a look filled with dark sensuality, while Carson rubs his hand over his jaw and says, "Well, shit. I should crash your dance sessions more often."

Ian lowers his mouth so that his lips are right by my ear, and growls, "Trying to get me to lose what sanity remains inside me? It fucking worked, April." A soft chuckle tickles the fine hairs on my neck. "You're in trouble now." Then, he sweeps me into his arms and carries me right off.

Chapter Twenty-Three

I immediately realize I've made a mistake by taunting Ian. He's already been in a foul mood recently, and now my dance with Elia appears to have brought out the beast in him. I'm not quite sure I'm equipped to handle that.

I say, "Ian, hold on a second," trying to lower myself away from him, unwrap my legs from where they instinctually curled around his waist when he lifted me. His hands lower to grip the backs of my thighs as he makes a low noise of warning, holding me tightly to him even as he walks towards the elevator, not put off by my wriggling at all. In fact, the only reaction I feel to my protests is the way his cock hardens against me, his erection pressing right into my center and lighting my body up in a shower of sparks.

"No," he growls. "Your ass is mine now, Sugarplum. Completely. Irrevocably. You taunted me and it worked; we're sealing the deal tonight. Before the sun rises, I'm going to hear you admit you belong to me." His voice quiets to a haunting whisper that raises goosebumps of fear along my arms. "One way or another, even if I have to fuck that concession out of you."

Everything inside me stiffens as I stare at him, unable to conjure any words. The Ian I'm seeing right now is different from any Ian I've ever known. It's not my best friend, who I knew had a dark side but loved anyways for most of my childhood and far too many of my juvenile years. It's not the cruel, diabolical asshole who was determined to ruin me throughout high school. It also isn't quite the determined, dark, jagged, and devastatingly sexy man I've become acquainted with over the last weeks. *This* Ian is an absolute predator; veins and tendons on his neck straining, a crazed look in his eyes one might expect to see from a psychiatric patient, and teeth bared as he grips me to him so tightly I know he'll leave bruises on my thighs. I don't recognize this Ian, but every primal instinct within me knows that it's one I'm not equipped to tangle with.

The elevator doors pop open with a ding, startling me.

"Ian, I—"

Before I can finish the sentence, he's carried me inside, slammed me up against the elevator wall, shocking the breath out of me, and is *devouring* my lips and mouth with such fervor I don't know what to do or how to respond. He's been more intense in the last weeks, but this right here isn't intense, it's fucking *feral*.

Startled, I try to push against his chest, even as arousal blooms within me, causing heat to pool between my legs. My protests yield no effect—he only lets go once the elevator doors open again, so that he can see where he's going as he hauls me out of dance HQ and to the nearby parking lot. Even though all of my survival instincts are telling me to approach carefully, I snap, "Excuse me, caveman, but what the *fuck* are you doing?"

"Shut up, April," he growls, depositing me on the ground and tangling a harsh hand in my hair to keep me in place as he unlocks his car. "You want to know what I'm doing?" he demands. "Claiming you the way I should've the moment I saw you on campus."

He opens the passenger side door, pushes me onto the seat, then rounds the car to the driver's side in record time, getting in and engaging the child locks again, effectively trapping me. Fear and arousal mingle so thoroughly within me that I don't know which is which; while half of me is justifiably afraid of the mood Ian's in, the other half of me is undoubtedly turned on by it.

"You're kind of scaring me," I say in an unsteady voice as he rips out of the parking lot and gets on the main road, breaking just about every speeding law there is in his haste to get away from campus and presumably to his apartment. The place he's threatened to kidnap me to on more than one occasion.

He barks out a laugh. "Good. Maybe getting you to admit to being mine will be an easy task." He slams on the breaks as we pull up to a red light and turns to me. "Tell me right now you belong to me, put a label on us, and there's a solid chance I'll calm down. Maybe."

I frown. He's asking me to make concessions in return for his insanity? Abso-fucking-lutely not. Aside from the fact that I most certainly don't belong to him, I only belong to myself, I also won't credit his tantrum with giving into what he wants. If I was truly scared and not just very nervous at this new side of him, I'd be calling the police, but I don't think I'm in any physical danger, so I don't bother.

"I don't belong to you, and I'm not putting any label on us. You might as well turn this fucking car around and take me to my dorm room now, Ian, because I won't give you what you want."

The light turns green and he slams on the accelerator. "Fine. Have it your way, April. If you won't give me what I want, I'm going to take it. I'm through waiting for you to be ready; especially after seeing how cozy you are with your fellow company members."

My eyes nearly bulge out of my skull. "You're *jealous?* I like Eliana platonically—that's the only way I've ever liked her. I adore that girl, but I'm not into her. Even if I was, I don't shit where I eat."

Ian grunts. "If I didn't know for certain that Seth is going to punish her for daring to let her lips touch yours, I might view her as competition. As is, I don't, but I am not letting go of that little stunt you pulled. You brought out the beast, now you get to find out what he's like."

There's absolutely no reason his words should turn me on, rev my engines, or arouse me in any way, yet they do. An uncomfortable heat stirs in my core, and I let out a shaky breath, hating myself for the fact that I'm curious to see exactly what he'll do in response to my show. If I'm being honest with myself, I wanted to provoke him—maybe not to this extent, but enough to see what he's like when he pushes back. These days, he's always carefully measured around me, which I assume is because he's wary of pushing me away like he once did. His words and actions now aren't putting me off, even though I know they should be; instead, he's pulling me right in.

Ian gets to his apartment in record time. He keeps a firm arm around me as he leads me into his apartment, then without preamble, drags me into his bedroom and tosses me on his soft, king-sized bed. He strips off his shirt, showcasing a perfect set of mouthwatering abs, while I pant and remain in place, wondering if I should actually be running right now because the longer he stares at me with that dark, crazed look, the more my arousal is replaced by fear.

"Take off your clothes," Ian demands. "I want to see you spread out on my bed, *yesterday.*"

I inhale a sharp breath. "No. I don't think this is a good idea. You're too worked up."

"Fuck right I'm worked up," he snaps, gripping my waist and pulling me to a stand. A single tug on my wrap skirt loosens the material until it falls right off me. Then, his hands push my leotard over my shoulder, baring my sports bra. "You're temptation incarnated, and you decided to kiss someone else in front of me. You don't get to kiss anyone who isn't me, April, I thought that was clear." With a harsh tug, he pulls the leotard and my tights right off me, leaving me just in my bra and thong. "That was your mistake. Now you'll deal with repercussions of said mistake."

"I was just *dancing*," I grit out, crossing my arms over my chest. "Eliana and I are friends and nothing more—she's straight as an arrow, and I would never ruin the friendship by coming onto her. I value her too much for that, in a way I never value fuck buddies." With my latter statement, I give him a pointed look, hoping he gets the subtext; if we have sex right now, it'll put him in the column of a fuckbuddy in my mind. Once someone's in that column, they don't get out of it—I excel at compartmentalizing my life.

Ian's currently in a weird column of his own, neither friend nor fuck buddy nor romantic prospect because I don't *do* romantic prospects. Now that I really think about it, I don't think I'd mind putting him in a specific box he won't get to crawl out of. After all, there's no denying I am obscenely attracted to him. I've been holding that attraction in check, not letting myself fully have him, because I knew it would blur lines that I didn't want blurred. I realize that there's a very simple solution to my problem; fuck him, get him in the fuckbuddy box, then dust myself off and stop worrying about it. Enjoy him sexually until he gets bored of me, then move on.

I'm not someone who ties emotions in with sex—not like Eliana, who I expect can fall in love mid-orgasm. To me, sex is a physical activity with a specific purpose: getting release. Ian's already proved that he's more than versed in delivering pleasure and phenomenal release, so I wouldn't mind finding out what it's like to have him inside me, filling me, stretching me. In fact, I'm kind of craving it.

Ian takes my wrists and yanks them down before pushing me onto the bed and crawling atop me. "We're not going to be fuck buddies," he informs me, his voice hauntingly flat. "We're going to be together, *truly* together. Get the idea of being rid of me or pushing me away out of that pretty head, April, because I will not fucking allow it. Do you understand me?"

As he speaks, he tugs off his boxers, leaving him gloriously naked. My eyes wander over the hard planes of his chest, his marvelous abs, and the deliciously cut v that leads straight to his cock, which looks like it belongs on a horse instead of this giant of a man. I've jerked and sucked him the last few times we've fooled around, and the fact that I struggled to deepthroat him was enough to tell me that a ride with him would come with a side effect of pain. Good thing I like a little pain when it comes to sex; I like things raw, untamed, and uncontrolled, I like when it stings and burns a little, and I know I'll get all that and more with him.

Ian clamps his hands down on my waist and pushes me up the bed until my head reaches the pillow at the top. Then, he yanks off my panties, ripping yet *another* pair—the third or fourth at this point—and ignores my grumbling about him being expensive as he drags my bra over my head. I don't struggle like I could and would if I wanted to get away, though his jerky, harsh movements and panted breaths continue to make my nerves grow.

"You can blab all you want, but if we fuck, that means no more dates. No more accosting me. No more talk of traveling together. If you're a satisfying ride, I'll probably keep fucking you until I'm bored, but that's it, Ian."

He pins my wrists above my head with one hand while his other hand slides down my stomach and runs over my slit before thrusting three fingers inside me, shocking a curse out of me.

"Hmm, already wet, just like I knew you'd be," he rumbles. "If you really think that this is some kind of end, you truly *don't* remember anything about me. It's just the beginning, April. You don't get to shut me down or push me away—I am fucking *owed* you, and I will take you."

I blink several times, struggling to breathe as he thrusts his fingers in and out of me at a breakneck speed, making my nipples tighten even further and causing my toes to curl. "You're not owed shit—" I cut off with a gasp as his thumb moves to my clit, rubbing the sensitive bundle in the exact way he knows drives me insane. I manage to force more choked words out. "You don't—*shit*—just get to... have me because—" I break off with a moan as his thrusts and rubbing intensifies, as if in punishment for my words, which only makes me all the more determined to clarify boundaries. "Just because you've suddenly decided to want me."

"There is *nothing* sudden about it, April, I have always wanted you. I tried to hold back, I tried to let you be free of me, but I can't. I'm done trying, and I'm done waiting for you to get on board."

A long, low groan escapes me as my orgasm washes over me. My back arches as I struggle against the hand pinning my wrists, wriggling and writhing, making all sorts of noises that only seem to incense Ian further.

"I won't hurt you again, you know that. I also won't let you go again, which you also know. I thought I could be patient and wait for you to fully trust me and give yourself to me, but I see now that you're too fucking stubborn to give into me without some incentive."

He pulls his fingers out of me and my eyes fall shut as my body relaxes with only the occasional tremor running through me. Every time he makes me come, it's intense as hell, all consuming, and a huge energy drainer. Which is why I don't bother to open my eyes when his weight over me shifts, and I don't move when I hear the bedstand drawer beside my head open. Then, it shuts, and a moment later, he releases my wrists, only to replace his hold with a cool, silky material that snaps me back to myself with a gasp.

I glance up to see him knotting silk—a tie?—over my wrists. That's when my previous nerves return with a vengeance, and this time, actual fear washes over me.

Chapter Twenty-Four

"What the *fuck*?" I demand, my voice hoarse. I tug at my wrists viciously, trying to release them before he finishes whatever crazed bullshit he's onto, but that only makes him pin me with a dark gaze.

"Do not test me right now, April. I'm not in the fucking mood. Anytime you want me to stop, all you need to do is say that you belong to me. Until then, I need you in place while I use your body the way I've been dreaming of doing for fucking *years*." He arches a challenging eyebrow at me, watching as I struggle against the tight way he's bound my wrists. My struggle yields zero results—Ian's gripping the end of the silk tie, and the other end is firmly wrapped around my wrists, cinching them together and immobilizing me.

"Ian, this isn't funny. Let me the fuck go, *now*."

He shakes his head, then reaches up and attaches the end of the tie to one of the rungs on the headboard. I yank and pull and twist, wriggling and struggling in earnest, because while I've found I don't mind when he holds me down, this is entirely different territory. When *he* holds me, I usually have confidence that if I really wanted to, I could hammer his balls and get away. This, however…yeah, I can't get out of this.

"It's not supposed to be funny. It's supposed to teach you an excellent goddamn lesson on the fact that you do belong to me, until you're ready to admit it." He grips my hips, then flips me over, leaving me face down on the bed. I turn my head sideways, flexing my hands and panting, and for the first time, contemplate whether or not I should just give in and tell him what he wants, if only to get the fuck out of here. As soon as the thought crosses my mind, though, I know it won't work—he'll sense my lie, and that'll likely only make him go harder on me.

I gasp when his hand comes down on one side of my ass in a stinging slap that sends a crack resounding through the air. Outrage sparks within me at the fact that he has the fucking gall to *spank me*, only heightened when that sends even *more* arousal curling through my stomach. He doesn't stop at one slap; he rains down a series of harsh, resounding spanks on both sides of my ass, until the area grows so sensitive and sore I can barely stand it. I wriggle and struggle and curse him, promising that I will never let him touch me again and that I will rip his dick off at the first available opportunity, which only makes him chuckle and spank me harder. After what feels like an eternity and a hundred slaps, he stops, and I feel his harsh breath tickling my back as he assesses the damage.

"Nice and red, just like I always imagined," he murmurs, smoothing a cool palm over my burning flesh. "Even better than I fantasized."

"I will fucking destroy you," I say, hating the fact that my words are breathy and tinged with my arousal, which is so intense I don't know how to handle it. I've never let a partner spank me; I've spanked them on request a time or two, but never like this, and I never found it arousing—mostly amusing.

"No, you really won't. It's *me* who's about to destroy *you* with my cock. Make no mistake, April, I am about to wreck your pussy. Anytime you've had enough, you know what to say."

A whimper escapes me as he flips me over again, and the cool sheets at once feel like hell and heaven on my sore backside. I breathe deeply, squeezing my eyes shut, though they snap open when Ian's mouth closes around my nipple and he sucks so hard his cheeks hollow. Then, my whimper turns into a low moan, as I grow so wet I really can't stand it anymore. I've already come once, and that spanking served to start building a second orgasm within me. By the time Ian's done amusing himself with my breasts and his mouth travels further south, I'm so wound up, I come as soon as his lips wrap around my clit and his tongue laves over it. He thrusts his fingers back in me just in time for my channel to clench and squeeze around them as I yank at my wrists and cry out loudly, swept up by so much pleasure I think I just might black out. This scene is way more erotic than I anticipated, far more taxing, and Ian hasn't even started fucking me yet.

"You came quickly," he observes. "Spanking your ass and playing with your nipples is a good warmup for you, hmm?"

"Shut up, asshole," I croak weakly. "This won't work. You can do what you want all night and I still won't tell you what you want to hear."

Ian shrugs as he wraps my legs around his waist, lining the thick, heavy head of his cock up with my entrance. "Agree to disagree."

"Condom!" I gasp as he rubs his head up and down my slit, sliding over my already-sensitive clit again and again until I nearly come just from that. "Put on a condom."

"No. You're on birth control, we're both clean, and there's no way I'm giving up feeling you bare," Ian says harshly.

I open my mouth to ask how the hell he knows that, only for the words to get caught in my throat as he *slams* into me with such intensity my vision briefly goes black. I anticipated a sting and stretch, but as he forces his way past my swollen, sensitive walls, the pain almost overwhelms the pleasure and I grimace, closing my eyes. I feel every thick inch of him, every vein and ridge along his cock rubbing inside me, stretching me beyond what anyone else ever has, and robbing me of breath and the ability to think.

"*Fuuuuuck*," he groans lowly. He pulls out, then snaps his hips forward again, driving his cock so deep it touches places unknown to me. "Sheer fucking heaven," he rumbles, twisting his hips to grind on my clit. One hand hikes my leg high on his waist, spreading me, while the other wraps around my neck and causes my eyes to snap open and widen as I look at him. "You are mine, April. That's not a question or proposal, it's a goddamn fact. This pussy—" *thrust* "—is mine. This body—" *harder thrust* "—is mine. Your head is mine, your soul is mine and your fucking heart is going to be mine. All of you belongs to me. Doesn't it?"

As he starts fucking me with quick, powerful strokes, all while applying just enough pressure to my throat to make breathing difficult, though not impossible, I manage to croak out, "No."

His eyes blaze with anger, and his thrusts turn from harsh to straight-up rageful, intensifying the pain *and* the pleasure. This isn't any regular sex, it is a claiming, and my refusal to accept his claim only makes him go at me harder. I can barely move, can't draw in an easy breath, can't do anything but *feel*, and the sensations are so overwhelming they bring tears to my eyes. That only seems to please him as he fucks me harder, releasing my thigh in favor of twirling his fingers over my clit, making me cry out and inner muscles spasm around him. "Come for me, April. Come for the man who owns you."

I really, *really* don't want to—especially not when he put it that way. He doesn't own me, the only person who owns me is myself, but his feral thrusts, clever fingers twirling over my clit, and hand around my throat don't leave me with much of another option. I orgasm around him, squeezing his cock, just as his thrusts turn jerky and erratic. He stills inside me, throwing his head back with a roar as he also comes. I feel warmth bathe my insides as my pussy continues to convulse and clamp and flutter, unable to stop because his fingers are still working over my clit, as if he won't let me stop coming until I've given him what he wants.

I yank hard at my wrists and cry out, *"Please!"*

He releases me, but it quickly becomes clear it's not because he's done with me, it's because he needs to catch his breath for a moment. His softening cock slides out of me and his head drops down to my breasts where he pulls a nipple into his mouth, biting down on it and forcing a yelp from me. After several beats of catching his breath, he raises his head, and dark eyes lock onto mine. My vision's hazy and my strength is just about sapped after those three monumental orgasms, but his moss-green gaze tells me that he's not going to be done with me until I give him what he wants and acquit. I thought I could hold out all night, but he's too good and sex with him is too overwhelming. Amazing, but at the same time, too much for me to keep my head on straight.

"Who do you belong to?" he questions lowly.

I breathe, "Myself and ballet."

A low chuckle escapes him. He opens the drawer to his bedstand again and holds up an oval-shaped, purple silicone device that I recognize immediately, because it's *mine*. My bullet vibrator that I keep locked in my dorm room. How this motherfucker got his hands on it is beyond me, and my eyes widen with both fear and embarrassment as I watch him turn it over.

"Where did you get that?" I breathe.

"Your dorm room when I was snooping around the other day," he says calmly. "You'd be shocked how easy it is to replicate an ID badge, and the lock on your door was so pathetic a five-year-old could've picked it. This was the most interesting thing I found, lying in your underwear drawer along with your collection of thongs. I was intrigued. I figured I might put it to good use soon—now's as good a time as any. I especially like the Bluetooth feature of it, connecting to a phone app that lets someone control the intensity and change the vibration pattern."

"Wait—" I cut off, pulling at my wrists with renewed vigor when he grabs his phone and clicks around on it. A moment later, a familiar buzzing sound fills the air, and my hands clench to fists. I'm already far too sensitive from my orgasms, and I know firsthand that my bullet is an intense experience all on its own. To feel it on my pussy which is already raw and well used will be *way* too much.

"Are you mine?" Ian asks, pressing the buzzing tip of the bullet to one of my nipples, making me gasp.

No. I won't give in. I can't. It doesn't matter how many games he plays. When he trails the bullet down my body and slides it over my slit, drawing a horse cry from me, I immediately reconsider just telling him what he wants because the vibrations that are normally a lot to handle have now become impossible. I try to shut my legs, only to have him wedge his shoulders between them, keeping them apart as he moves down my body and aligns his face with my pussy, staring at the swollen flesh intently. I realize I have made a serious mistake here; he's wearing the same curious look he sometimes gets when poking and prodding my limits, which I know usually precedes him pushing really hard just to see how much I can take.

He uses one hand to spread my folds, exposing my clit entirely, then presses the tip of the vibrator right up against it, instantly drawing a scream from me as I writhe and cry and shake, unable to take it. That doesn't seem to bother him, though; in fact, it encourages him, as he starts sliding the bullet all around the most sensitive part of my body, looking for the most intense place to press it. When the tip of it presses right beneath the hood of my clit, I scream again, and he smiles darkly in response, sliding it up and down the area, not giving me reprieve.

"Are you mine?" he asks.

"*Fuck you!*" I shout, hoarsely.

He shrugs, then reaches over to his phone and clicks something, intensifying the vibrations. An all-consuming orgasm sweeps me into its grip and he thrusts three fingers into my pussy while shoving another into my *ass,* making my vision blur out as I give into pleasure entirely, feeling like I'm floating somewhere in the upper atmosphere, too overwhelmed to think clearly.

Vaguely, I hear him repeat his question. Willing to do *anything* to stop this particular brand of torture, I cry, *"Yes!"*

Instantly, the vibration stops. The fingers disappear from inside me, but my body doesn't stop convulsing for several moments, and I can't seem to stop coming, too overloaded and overstimulated to gain any semblance of control over myself. After what feels like an eternity, the convulsions within me slow, turning to an occasional tremor, and my shaky breathing starts to even out though my heart continues to race.

Faintly, I feel Ian pull at the silk knot on my wrists, releasing my hands. It's only when I feel his thumbs brushing over my wet cheeks that I realize I came so hard I actually cried—or maybe it was the emotions of trying to hold back and having him force me past that which brought out tears. Whatever the case, I'm sapped and can't seem to control myself. Which is why, when he tucks me to his side, I don't protest even though I don't usually allow any post intimacy cuddling between us—I don't really do that with anyone.

"I hate you," I murmur, my voice scratchy and weak. Despite my words, I find myself nuzzling closer. I'm so exhausted from those orgasms and Ian's intensity, darkness is quick to sweep me into his grip. As I'm falling asleep, I think I hear him say, "I love you too, April."

***

I awaken sometime later, drawn from unconsciousness by a bad dream that came in the form of a memory; the memory of the party when I was sixteen. Except, in this dream, Ian wasn't just throwing out our friendship for some bitchy girl—we were actually dating, and he deliberately broke my heart. Went out of his way to humiliate and destroy me to end it. My breaths are harsh and my heart is racing, and it quickly dawns on me why I had such a dream; I'm in *his* bed, after he just literally tortured the admission of my belonging to him out of me.

He's breathing calmly beside me, an arm slung around my waist and a leg curled over mine, pinning me in place with the weight of his body. A position that's familiar from both our sleepovers and ski trips—whenever we'd share a bed, even when he was unconscious, he'd always be curled around me, keeping me in place. I used to cuddle right up to him too—the fact that I'm currently flat on my back, arms beside me, tells me that even my subconscious is trying to protect me from getting attached to him.

I look around the darkened bedroom, shifting on the mattress slightly, wondering if it's a remote possibility for me to somehow get out of here unnoticed. Ian has me pinned pretty tightly but he's always been a deep sleeper. I remember Carson mentioning a few months ago that Ian doesn't sleep—obviously, that isn't the case when I'm around. Regardless, I don't want to stick around to find out what the morning will look like. I slept over here a while ago when Ian was in a foul mood and told me in a surly-yet-endearing way that he needed me with him. The next morning he drove me to campus after waking me up with an orgasm, but even that feels like a world away from whatever this is.

I admitted I belonged to him—after a lengthy bout of torture, perhaps, but still. And, as I'm really thinking about it, I can see that a part of me *does* still belong to him, but I don't think it's in a good way. It's the naïve girl in me who needed a protector, a girl that has no place in my current life because I don't need protecting anymore. I've become quite capable of taking care of myself. Besides that, a great deal of the pain and self-doubt within me, most of which I've either done away with or buried *really* deep, belongs to him because it stems from him. He represents a very painful time in my life, and although I can't deny he also once represented the most wonderful part of my childhood, it still feels like the bad overshadows the good. Not as much as it once did, not even as much as it did a few weeks ago, but I still resent him. I'm still mad at him. Therefore, I don't want to see what the morning will bring—I don't want to find out how our dynamics have shifted.

Despite my protests to the contrary, I've realized recently that I do still know Ian quite well. So I know that he'll take what happened tonight to be a turning point, an opening that I'm not ready for. I'm afraid of it, I'm afraid to trust him and give him the power to hurt me again because he proved to be too damn good at it. So, I slowly reach for his arm that's draped around me and lift it, settling it beside him. His breathing remains steady and deep, and his eyes don't flutter, so I start quietly detangling my legs from his. Then, pausing again to make sure he's still asleep, I scoot towards the edge of the bed, wincing at how loudly the sheets rustle in the otherwise silent room.

As I'm edging off the mattress, getting to my feet, I toss one last look over my shoulder, only to find that Ian's eyes are slowly blinking open. I freeze just as they open fully, and the sleep clears from them, before he locks his gaze on me. His eyebrows draw together and he releases a sigh that could be from exhaustion or annoyance. He reaches out to cuff a hand around my wrist faster than he should be able to considering he just woke up, and yanks me right back to him.

"Where do you think you're going?" he questions, his voice low and drowsy and coated with faint amusement.

"Bathroom," I lie.

His brows draw together in distrust, but he releases me nonetheless. "If you're not back in a few minutes, I'm coming after you."

I quickly scramble into the bathroom, snatching his shirt off the floor and pulling it on. I'd prefer to wear my own clothes, but donning his shirt is easier than getting back into my leotard. While using the toilet and washing my hands and face, I think over my options. I could try making a straight up run for it, but that wouldn't work—he'd catch me—and that'd just reek of cowardice. I could insist on sleeping on the couch for the night to try to get at least a little distance and breathing room, but he wouldn't allow that. Or, I could treat him as exactly what I want him to be; a fuck buddy, and casually declare that I'm heading back to campus for the night. Kind of like the way a one-night stand sneaks out in the middle of the night so as not to send the wrong message. He probably won't like that but I didn't want to come here in the first place, let alone stay the night.

When I emerge from the bathroom, Ian's on his back, with one arm behind his head and the sheets pooled around his waist. A glint of moonlight from the window casts a glow on his abs, and I'm not proud of the way my eyes linger on them. When he catches me staring, an amused smile curls his lips before he says, "Get your ass back in bed, April, it's late."

Chapter Twenty-Five

I clear my throat. "Yeah, no, I'm actually going to head back to campus for the night. I have class early in the morning."

Ian lets out a long sigh, flicking his gaze to the ceiling with a shake of his head, before he shoots up out of bed as quickly as a serpent, crosses to me in three strides, and hoists me up into his arms.

I let out a soft gasp as my legs wrap around his waist, clutching his shoulders and staring at him. Then, my momentary surprise turns to ire. "Do you not understand the concept of personal space—"

"Do *you* not understand the fact that you're officially mine now? You're sleeping here tonight, April, I thought that was obvious. You'll be sleeping here a lot more often, sharing my bed, where you belong." As he walks me back to the bed, he mutters, "I also thought I did a good job of fucking you to sleep to avoid this shit, but obviously not. Guess I'll have to go again, not that I mind."

I balk at him as he sets me down on the center of the mattress, then spreads my legs and cups my pussy in his hand. "What—no—you can't just fuck me into compliance!"

He chuckles. "I disagree. In fact, it seems that coming until you're too limp to protest is the best way to get you nice and agreeable."

"That's not how relationships work—" I cut off as he thrusts three fingers inside me, all in one go, shocking the breath out of me and making my back arch. My goddamn traitorous body responds to him in all the right ways, even while my mind is reeling.

"Glad you agree we're in a relationship. Now, ease up on the protests and stop squirming, I've got some work to do on this pussy. *My* pussy."

Is he goddamn serious? He's acting as though my *coerced* admittance to us being in some fucked up version of a relationship gives him a full on green-light to do whatever he wants with my body. Ian's always been a bit spoiled, but now he's taking that to a whole new level, as if our sex gives him rights to me that he most certainly doesn't have.

"You can't just do whatever you want to me!" I growl, shoving at his chest hard enough to make him falter, sway, and release me.

A slow, insidious smile spreads on Ian's lips, and his eyes light up with the prospect of a challenge. He brackets his hands on either side of my hips, and says, "That's where you're wrong, Sugarplum." He runs his hands up my body, dragging my borrowed shirt up to bare my breasts, raising my arms and pulling it over my head, ignoring my protests and leaving me naked. "This body is mine to do whatever I want with," he says, enunciating every syllable as he skims his hands up and down my sides. "This pussy is mine to use however and whenever I please," he goes on, cupping me again. "Whether it's in the middle of the day and I find a nice, dark corner for us somewhere, or at night with you in my bed—*especially* at night. I'll touch it, stroke it, pet it, fuck it as often as I want, and the fact that you love when I play with you only makes it better."

"Does free will have *no* meaning whatsoever to you?" I snap, though my words have a breathy edge as he grinds the heel of his palm over my clit.

"Depends on the situation. You have plenty of free will—you can choose to accept this, accept *us* and get the most out of having me in your life. That includes many benefits. Not the least of which are regular orgasms. Or you can push against me even though we both know you don't really want to, and I'll push back harder. I would restrain myself if you didn't like it when I confiscate your free will—maybe. In any case, we don't need to find out, because you fucking *love* giving up control. Don't you?"

I shake my head, gritting my teeth against the moan that tries to escape as he plays with my aching flesh, hating the fact that he is right. I *do* like the lack of control—at least when it comes to him and anything sexual, which just makes me want to run away from us all the more because that shouldn't be the case, and I don't want to become as fucked in the head as he is. I don't like that there's something liberating about just lying back and taking whatever he dishes out, of enjoying it when he pins me, even ties me up, of liking the edge of panic that sometimes accompanies the pleasure.

I wouldn't say that I'm a control freak, per se. I don't try to control people around me unless I'm in a position that requires it, such as dance captain of my high school team back in senior year. The only person I'm controlling of is myself; I organize every minute of my day, keep myself on a rigorous schedule, drill my body to keep it in peak condition, and constantly plan for the future, all the while still warding off the inner demons that like to plague my nightmares far too often. I *need* to maintain that control and yet when Ian forces me to do away with it, I find myself breathing an internal sigh of relief.

That doesn't mean that I want to be with him for anything beyond sex, or that I trust him with more than just my body. Even if I wanted to, I'm not sure I have that capacity for trust anymore; I'm too jaded, especially when it comes to him, and if I'm being honest with myself, I'm absolutely terrified of letting him in only to have him stomp all over me again.

The night when I was assaulted in the alleyway was horrible and left me with an unpleasant dose of trauma and nightmares that terrorize me far too often, but I have more frequent nightmares about the times when Ian was cruel to me than I do of the boys who attempted to brutalize me, and that's because I once trusted and adored Ian. I never had any regard or trust for those dickless imbeciles. The fact that the way he treated me, never laying a cruel hand on me, has a greater impact than being assaulted tells me that he did more damage than they did. I won't risk him doing that damage again.

"Don't you?" Ian repeats, the words harsher, wrapping a hand around my neck to rest at the base of my throat.

I grit out, "Maybe, but it has nothing to do with you. You're just the right cock at the right time."

My words are meant to hold him at a distance, at least emotionally, because physically doesn't seem to be an option anymore. I can see they *infuriate* him. Ian grips my throat tightly, releases my pussy in favor of grabbing my thigh and hiking my leg up around his waist, then slams the full length of his cock into me. I wrap my hands around the wrist that's holding my neck tightly, restricting my breathing, and try to stop my eyes from rolling into the back of my head as tingles explode over my skin and my pussy contracts around him. I'm wet, but the intrusion still stings, and the mix of pain and pleasure is too much to bear.

"You're a liar, April," he says through gritted teeth. "You lie to me, you lie to the world, you lie to yourself. I don't give a shit about the last two, but you don't get to lie to me." *Thrust.* "You can try, but it won't work, and it'll only piss me off. You do not want to piss me off. I've tried to be nice and understanding, to take things slow, but that's not what you need, is it?" I can't make any noise to respond, and that seems to suit him just fine. He continues slamming his cock in and out of me while speaking in that harsh, angry tone. I prefer the angry version of him to the sappy, sentimental one. I know how to handle his anger but I don't know how to handle gentleness from him, so I'd rather provoke the anger.

"What you need is to be taken and owned. You won't let me past those sky-high walls protecting you, so that means I'll just need to smash my way through them. I told you earlier, and I fucking meant it—every inch of you, every molecule, belongs to me. If I need to break you to have you again, that's exactly what I'll do."

Despite myself, his back-breaking thrusts, angry expression, blazing eyes, and sheer intensity start to scratch at me, and for some reason that's entirely beyond me, I feel tears stinging at the back of my eyes. Not the same ones from earlier, when the pleasure was literally too much for me to handle. These are tears of some strange, wobbly emotion that I don't fully understand. Maybe it's because I know Ian is goddamn relentless, and if he wants to break through to me, he eventually will. Maybe it's the fact that deep down, somewhere in a box that I locked and covered with chains, there's a part of me that does still care about him and is still hurting because of him, even though our conflict ended when he left years ago.

He doesn't deserve my emotions. I'm already beyond embarrassed by that time I cried into his chest in the alleyway after a performance; I'm not down with a repeat of that. I dig my fingernails into the tendon of his wrist hard enough to make him release my neck, inhale a gasping breath and demand, "Switch positions."

He blinks, and his thrusts stutter to a halt as he studies me. "To?"

He doesn't sound like he's in disagreement, merely curious and confused, which I can work with. Looking at his face right now is too much. Sex should remain a physical activity with no emotions entwined, especially with him; I don't want to change that up.

"Hands and knees," I say, thinking of the first thing that'll stop me from looking directly at him. I don't mind the rough sex—even if I should feel somewhat violated, I don't. He's pushing all of my hot buttons, even the ones I didn't know I had or simply refused to acknowledge because they require submission, and I'm not a submissive person. The intensity isn't the real problem; the fact that he's getting me emotional yet *again* is the problem, and I want it solved before he continues.

Ian's eyebrows draw together as he frowns, searching my expression until it feels like he's trying to look through me and see to the core of me, which only makes my traitorous eyes sting more. Nevertheless, I blank my facial expression and arch an imperious brow at him, as if I'm bored while waiting for his response.

"Or knees and elbows," I add, my tone nonchalant. "We already did missionary tonight, and it's getting redundant. Redundant is boring."

Ian's eyes narrow and realization crosses his expression before it smooths out. His lips quirk. "I don't think you're asking because you're bored, I think you're asking because I'm getting to you and you don't want to look at me. You don't want me to get through to you."

I force an eyeroll. "Don't flatter yourself."

He shrugs, small smile still tipping his lips up, and releases my thigh before sliding his hands around my back and lifting me up, keeping himself firmly seated inside me while he rearranges us. I end up on his lap, our chests pressed together, closer than ever. His hands flutter over my sides before gripping my waist and starting to move me up and down on his length, all the while staring deeply into my eyes.

I clutch his shoulders and tighten my abs, stilling his movements. "What are you doing?"

He gives another, lazier shrug, though his eyes are two burning emeralds as they stare into mine. "You wanted to switch positions, I'm obliging you."

I dig my fingernails into his shoulder, shaking my head. "This isn't what I meant. I said—"

"I know what you said," he cuts me off. "And I believe I know why you said it. To hold me at a distance. Isn't that right?"

"No," I snap.

"No," he repeats, a touch mockingly. "Then you won't mind this, will you?"

I squeeze my eyes shut, gritting my teeth and hardening my resolve. I can look at him without breaking, I *can*. As long as he continues being his normal, asshole self, I should be fine. I open my eyes again and pin him with a hard look. "Fuck me hard so I don't have to think about your irritating face."

Ian lifts an eyebrow. "Fuck you like I hate you, you mean? You'd like that, wouldn't you, April? That way, you could hold me at bay easier. But I don't hate you. I might fuck you like I do sometimes and only because we both love it, but not this time. This time, I'm going to fuck you like I love you, because I do."

I push at his shoulders. "No."

He runs a hand up and down my back, as if gentling a wounded animal, his touch too soft and too kind for me to stand.

"Yes. You don't get to choose. In bed, you take what I have to give—you should be able to admit that trusting me here works out for you. Right now, I want to make love to you, and I'm going to."

"No," I repeat, my voice a growl. "*I* don't want to make love to *you*. I can't stand it, so either fuck me—*really* fuck me—or let me go home."

Ian presses his thumb to my lips, sealing them. "Shh, you're strong. The strongest person I know, which makes it almost comical that you don't want soft. But you can take it." He replaces his thumb with his lips before I can respond, and the kiss is too gentle yet somehow still full of passion. His tongue isn't demanding or invasive this time. It probes around my mouth, gliding against mine as he starts sliding me up and down his length again, *too* slowly, too sweetly, in time with his soft, slow thrusts upward. I feel his heartbeat hammering against my chest, matching the rhythm of my own, and contrary to what he seems to believe I *can't* take it. It's too much. The hate-fucks I can handle, the angry sex I can handle and revel in, but this territory is too far out of my comfort zone, which he can read. That's why he keeps his rhythm soft and slow, even as he hits spots inside me that make stars burst behind my eyes.

I pull my lips away from his, turning my head to the side, and demand hoarsely, "Stop it."

He shakes his head. "No. I want in you, every part of you, not just your body. Let me in a little, Sugarplum."

I squeeze my eyes shut, shaking my head. "I won't."

"You will," he disagrees. "You're my strong girl, but you still have a soft core beneath all that hardness. I'll worm my way back in there. You've lived inside my heart ever since we were children, it's only fair that I live in yours, too."

He winds one hand into my hair, all the while still continuing his lazy thrusts that hit deeper than anyone else ever has, turning my head back to his and fusing our lips together again. "You're mine," he murmurs against my lips. "You were always meant to be mine. Let it happen, stop fighting it."

My chest tightens and burns as the tears sting my eyes again, this time with a vengeance that makes it impossible to hold back. I squeeze them tighter, as if that'll prevent the tears from escaping, but it doesn't. Ian somehow senses that and pulls his lips away from mine long enough to say, "That's it, break for me."

I fucking hate myself for it, but I do. The dam splits, the tears fall, and it feels like my heart's shattering all over again. I can muster my way through a lot, but not this version of him that's so foreign yet heartbreakingly familiar. I cry as he holds and fucks me, murmuring sweet reassurances into my ear and promising that I'm safe with him. I cry even as I fall apart around him, coming hard and setting off his own orgasm, and I cry as he lays us back down on the mattress, holding me tightly. All the while, I despise myself for being so weak, and despise him even more for making me into this weak, pathetic version of myself that I can't stand, that I thought I'd carved out years ago.

Most of all, I cry because his ploy of trying to work his way back into my heart just might succeed, and I know I won't survive that a second time.

Chapter Twenty-Six

Ian

The next morning, April's unusually quiet and subdued. Her eyes are red rimmed and a little puffy, and her demeanor is drawn inwards, which I really don't like. I don't push her, though; I pushed her plenty last night, and that's enough for now. The atmosphere is quiet and somewhat dull as we eat a quick breakfast before I drive her back to campus. She doesn't even protest when I pull her in for a kiss before she gets out of the car, which worries me rather than encouraging me. What worries me more is the way she kisses me back sadly, the way it almost feels like a goodbye before she slips away from me and heads into the program dorms to get ready for her school day.

I have a long day of work ahead of me, which I'm not looking forward to. I don't want to leave April in whatever state she's in, but I also won't neglect my business duties—I'll come for her later, like I always do.

My drive to the corporate office, the newest building in the city that's a shining monstrosity made of steel and windows, is both boring and filled with tension. The tension mainly stems from the fact that Carson's uncle, Dennis Ajax, is now in town. He hasn't had the balls to show his face in the offices yet, probably because he knows that Carson outranks him in every way and won't hesitate to smack Dennis down if he oversteps. Carson's father might've sent Dennis in just because he's an asshole and pissed about his slipping control in the company, but he didn't afford Dennis any great deals of power, which just proves the asshole point—and the fact that he doesn't trust his own brother.

He shouldn't. I'm sure that, by now, Dennis knows that I work here and that I'm functioning in a capacity as Carson's second—it's quite possible he's avoiding crossing paths with me, which is a good call on his part. I was here late last night with Carson and Seth, talking strategy about Dennis. While the dynamic duo want to find a way to run Dennis out of town, I have every intention of getting revenge on that motherfucker. Doing it at the same time as I'm figuring out how to scale the walls that April's erected around her heart is just an additional damn complication, but nothing I can't handle.

After our planning session last night, Carson decided to put Seth on payroll for the company as an IT expert. It's a temporary position, though that's only known by the three of us. The way Carson sees it, Seth is better than anyone at reading and digging up dirt on people, and he's also one hell of an intimidating guy, which should keep Dennis in line. They don't yet know that I'm brewing my own plan for Dennis and I don't plan on telling them until that plan is fully formed.

The lobby has marble flooring, cracked marble walls, and a high ceiling that hosts no less than three chandeliers. Across from the receptionist's desk is a collection of designer leather sofas. Pretentious even for a high-end corporate office building, but that's how Carson's father rolls; he's sickeningly wealthy and flaunts that unapologetically, albeit in a manner that lacks any semblance of taste.

I run into Carson and Seth as I'm making my way across the lobby floor. Carson smiles at me in greeting, while Seth flicks a quick glance over me before turning his attention to the other people in the lobby and scanning the area, dismissing me. I don't blame him; I'm often the same way with fellow predators. I assess them, determine whether or not they're a threat to me, and if they aren't, move forward. I've already made clear that I'm not a threat to Seth, just as he's made clear he's not a threat to me unless I upset April and it gets back to Eliana. His protectiveness of that girl, or his Little Muse as he likes to call her, really knows no bounds; he sees it as his duty to keep her happy and satisfied. I've personally seen him decimate anything and anyone who gets in the way of that.

"Ian," Carson greets, handing me a steaming cup of coffee.

"Carson," I respond with a nod, accepting the cup. Traditionally, assistants should be fetching our coffee, but Carson likes to do things his own way. That's probably why he's so well-liked around these parts. "What's on the agenda today?"

As we get in the elevator and head to the top floor, Carson gives me the rundown of today's tasks, most of which include daily operating procedures and trivial matters related to company growth, growth of this branch in particular.

Once at our floor, we split off, each heading to our respective offices. Mine is located just a few doors down from Carson's, with a mahogany desk, oak bookshelf, and back wall that's made up of windows, giving a view of the city below and mountains in the distance.

I spend a few hours working, blowing through the tasks at hand today. When lunch rolls around, I have a strange, nagging urge to seek out Seth. He's the most similar person to me in vicinity, and I can imagine that he might've had to overcome some barriers when pursuing Eliana. Not the same ones I'm facing since I've already hurt April, but I know from past conversations that his girl was very wary of him in the beginning, and he had to put in a lot of work to get her past that.

"What do you want?" he asks monotonously when I enter his office, which is a totally barren space aside from a black wooden desk set up with three computer monitors and a keyboard.

Although it galls some part of me to say it, I force out the word, "Advice."

One of Seth's eyebrows twitches, an indication of his surprise and interest. He turns his attention from his computer screen and towards me, tilting his head to the side.

"Advice with April?" he guesses.

I make a dinging sound. "Correct, give the stone man a cigar."

"I'm not entirely made of stone, only mostly," he quips. "Let me guess...whatever it is that you did to April is coming around to bite you in the ass. From what I've seen of that girl, she's smart, sharp as a tack, and has ironclad defenses protecting her—ones she might've created partly because of you. You want to find a way past them, and she's making it impossible."

I shouldn't be surprised by Seth's gift of inference, the way he reads people and situations, but I'm still startled with how he hits the nail right on the head. We're similar in that aspect, being able to read people well; it's how I knew that April only wanted to switch positions to face away from me last night because she was getting emotional, which is exactly why I stared deep into her eyes and pressed us chest to chest while I fucked her, trying to scale the walls around her heart. I'd say it worked, considering the way she broke and cried—something I know for a fact that she doesn't do often.

April's not a crier, she thinks crying is a weakness, which could be a result of my former torment or simply the fact that she grew up with a very stern father who wouldn't know emotion if it bit him in the ass. The first time I met her on the bridge was one of the few times I've ever seen her cry, and for years she showed me every part of herself openly. She prefers to get revenge instead of crying—always has. It's the deviousness in her, a part she hides well but I know is present nonetheless.

"Yep," I tell Seth with a nod. Then, I take the opportunity to prove he's not the only person here good at reading people. "I imagine you had some similar issues with Eliana, minus the murky past. I'd be willing to bet she saw you for who you were, saw your abnormalities the first time you two met, and probably tried to run far away because of them. You didn't let her, because you got fixated on her—a fixation that quickly grew into an obsession, one that makes you tolerate a three-way relationship. You got around her walls. How?"

"Simple," he says, looking me right in the eye with a dead gaze. He's not surprised by my insight, and he doesn't seem to care about it all that much, either. I think the only thing he cares about is Eliana. "Proved to her that, while I am absolutely a monster, that monstrousness would be used to protect her, never to hurt her. I showed her that all of my parts, including the evil ones, are devoted to her. Pushed out of my own comfort zone to keep her happy, kept an open dialogue with her at all times. In short, I opened myself to her and let her see *everything*. After that, she came to the realization that she was safe with me on her own."

I could do all that and more. I'm trying to do it, but April refuses to see anything positive in me, anything good that she could have with me—other than sex. I never thought I'd crave emotional intimacy with a woman; for a time, I hated emotions altogether and did away with them. Now, my emotions are still somewhat muted, but there's no denying that they exist. *Especially* when it comes to April.

"What would you do in my situation?" I ask through clenched teeth. "If you'd already proverbially shot yourself in the foot and were trying to backtrack."

Seth lets out a short, unamused laugh. "I wouldn't ever put myself in your situation. I know a good thing, something worth coveting and keeping, when I see it. It was my luck that the girl I happened to become obsessed with also happened to be a lot more accepting of my darkness than I'd anticipated, so long as it never got turned on her or innocents. She's only willing to bear the brunt of that darkness in the bedroom. Even then, when I get to be too much—which I do, I can't help myself—Carson's there to soothe the hurt. There's balance."

"So your point is that my situation is hopeless?" I ask lowly, clenching my fists because I refuse to accept that. April is it for me, she always has been, even when I couldn't see it.

"No," Seth says after a long moment, shaking his head. "You suit with April even more than I suit with Eliana; I need Carson to complete the dynamic, but you and that dancer... you fit meticulously in a way I might've been jealous of if I hadn't already figured out how to best fit with Eliana. So, things aren't hopeless, but you will have to play the long game. She's going to test you and pull away from you, fight you, possibly throw tantrums aimed at you, and you're going to have to keep steady through all of it. From what I've observed, whether or not April realizes it, she's already been testing you; so far, you've passed. Keep passing. Keep being there. Keep the pressure on, keep proving to her what you believe to be true—that you two are it for each other—but don't push too far. If you do, which might be inevitable, you fix what you fucked up immediately. Don't let her walk away and get the chance to push you away, swallow your pride and apologize. And, for fuck's sake, tell her whatever it is that made you act like an absolute prick to her. That shit doesn't come out of the blue, and women are more understanding when they have the facts. Now get out of my office; I have shit to do."

I turn and head towards the door, lost in thought as I wander back to my office. Which is why I'm not as vigilant as usual, and I find myself coming face to face with Dennis Ajax. *Fuck.*

Dennis has a face that's been injected with Botox too many times, making him look disturbingly fake. He's older now, well into his fifties, but it's clear he's done everything in his power to cosmetically enhance himself—probably in a ploy to make himself attractive. It doesn't work, though, he looks like a poor imitation of a Ken doll that was thrown in a trashcan and then fished back out by some unfortunate orphan. His blonde hair is obviously dyed, there are crow's feet around his eyes despite the rest of his face being *too* smooth, and—Jesus Christ—I think he might've even gotten lip injections. He looks like a Real Housewives reject, and his pathetic attempt at youthfulness satisfies me, because it indicates that he's even more miserable than he used to be.

The moment he sees me, he stops in his tracks, lowering the phone he was staring at and straightening to his full height, which is still a good collection of inches shorter than me. I stop as well and take my time giving him a patronizing up and down.

He clears his throat, a tad nervously. Possibly because he understands it is very well within my power to ruin his fucking life, and I have every intention of doing so. Slowly. Carefully. Not like a kid throwing shit at a wall, but like a mastermind playing a game of chess where their opponent won't even know how fucked they are until they're check-mated.

"Ian," he greets lowly.

"Dennis," I return, flatly. "You should really speak to your plastic surgeon; you look like you belong in the Atlantic with the other piles of trash. The years have not been kind to you."

Something that might be fear or anger, perhaps an enticing mix of both, sparks in Dennis's eyes as his shoulders stiffen. Through tense lips, he says, "Careful how you speak to me, *boy*."

Boy. Hearing that word from his lips sends me back nearly a decade, to the last time he called me that word. *You're such a pretty boy, aren't you?*

I suppress the shiver of revulsion that threatens to run down my spine and keep everything about my posture and expression carefully blank as I take a few steps towards Dennis.

"You have no power here," I tell him, my words barely above a murmur. "None. You're more useless than the paintings on the walls or the sofas decorating the lobby. You can't do anything to me but rest assured that *I* will do *many* things to you. Step very carefully, Dennis, because your time is coming." I allow my upper lip to curl faintly, showcasing my disgust as I give him another condescending once-over. "If you had any brain cells, you'd get out of town immediately. Since I suspect you don't, though, I will ensure you get the most out of your stay here, however long it might last."

"Y—you can't *threaten* me!" he splutters, splotches of red forming on his face.

A small, cruel smile tips up the corners of my lips. "Who are you going to run and tattle to, Dennis? Especially when you know that as soon as you tell your story, I'll tell mine. And in this day and age, who do you think will be believed? The old fuck who can't even hold down a solid position in his own brother's company and already has two lawsuits swept under the rug, or the prodigal young man who's rising fast in the business world?" I pause for a beat, enjoying the way dejection seeps into his expression, allowing him to realize that he *really* can't win. Not with me—not this time around. "Keep your head down and stay the fuck out of my way, and maybe I won't be tempted to destroy you entirely."

With that, I turn and stride down the hall, barely noticing as I cross paths with Carson. My thoughts are only on one person, the single being in this world that I want to turn to right now: April Stein.

***

Regrettably, I have to spend another five hours in the office, though the time is made slightly more bearable with how quick Dennis is to scurry away after our encounter. Something that probably shouldn't bring me as much satisfaction as it does, but then again, considering he's the definition of a truly heinous, pathetic excuse of a human being, I don't feel too bad.

On my way out of the office, I bid Carson a good night, and then find myself confined to an elevator with Seth, who's also leaving a bit early. Doubtless to find Eliana and drink up as much of her attention as he can before Carson's done for the night.

"You figured out where your girl's scars came from yet?" Seth asks, snapping me out of my thoughts and making me frown.

"No," I respond. "I figure she'll tell me when she's ready."

Seth snorts. "I doubt it. Stein's as insular as a person gets, she won't tell anyone anything unless she feels she has to, or unless she really trusts them—neither of which apply to you, and neither of which will ever apply to you unless you push hard." After a pause, he goes on, "Apparently, she told *my* girl about them, though, because not too long ago Elia came to me in tears. She wouldn't give any details, but she did say that April told her about some shitty parts of her life, and my Muse cried for the better part of three hours because of it. It takes a lot to get Elia to cry, even though she's a creature of empathy—a very foreign fucking concept to people like us—so whatever Stein's shit is, it's very bad."

I take several moments to mull over his words, feeling my hands clench into fists at my sides. I've felt the scars on April's back several times—last night, while she slept after our first round, I spent about an hour tracing over the raised scar tissue, glaring at the marks on her skin because the only marks she should wear are ones of *my* making, and those would never be jagged scars. Just a few love-bites, some deeper than others. I've wanted to ask her about them again, but I've been caught up with other matters recently, and I really didn't think she was ready to talk about it. If she told Eliana, it means that she *can* talk about whatever happened, just not with me.

That pisses me off. I want to be the person she trusts most in this world—I can admit that I'm jealous of her closeness with Eliana. Those two are best friends and thick as thieves. *I* used to be April's best friend and the person who knew everything about her. I miss that a lot, and I don't like the feeling that I'm in competition for April's attention, especially when it's with a small slip of a girl who's already been claimed by two others.

I know it's unfair, but I feel like April should've told me her story before anyone else—an irrational feeling, but one that I can't shake because I want to crawl into her skin and consume her, I want to know her better than she knows herself. In some ways, I do, but there are parts of her she keeps closed off from me, and the fact that getting through those walls is proving difficult irritates me. Both at the actions of my past self and at April for having such strong damn defenses.

"You gonna tell her about whatever it is that happened to make you turn on her?" Seth questions.

I slide him a sideways glance as the elevator opens and we step out of it. We stop in front of a small waiting area in the lobby, because this conversation isn't over yet. I'm not sure how I feel about this conversation being had period, but it is, and it seems that Seth knows more about me than he's letting on.

"Yes," I finally say.

I know it's time to open up to April, see if that gets me any closer to her or brings down her barriers just enough for me to get past them even a little. I might as well get it out of the way tonight; after all, Dennis isn't going anywhere, and I can't keep putting off talking to him simply because I don't want to dredge up memories. But they're already dredged up; it'd be better to talk about them now when they're already front and center, rather than digging them up later.

Seth nods. "Good. If you want my advice—"

"Something I'm starting to regret asking for," I mumble.

He goes on as if I hadn't spoken. "—make sure she returns the favor. A quid pro quo, if you will; you tell her something, she tells you something."

I let out a faint scoff. "She'd never go for it."

"Then fight for it," Seth replies with a shrug.

I arch an eyebrow at him. "How would you suggest pulling information out of someone who excels at stonewalling you?"

"Torture," he deadpans, and I know for a fact that he's not even kidding. Before I can tell him that there's no way in fucking hell I'd ever hurt April, he clarifies, "Not physical torture—at least not the painful kind. When my Muse needs her tongue loosened, a little pleasurable pain goes a long way. She wasn't a terribly sexual creature before I came along; your girl is, so that might work even better with her if you know what buttons to press."

I eye Seth with a newfound interest. He really is a pathological motherfucker, but I can see bright as day that he holds himself to harsh standards, especially when it comes to Eliana. I'm mildly surprised he's being so open with me; I assume that's because we're getting as close to friendship as is possible for people like us.

"You get shit done," I observe, my tone faintly approving.

He shrugs. "When you know how to get what you want, it becomes easy. Being part of the population that feels no guilt using underhanded methods, getting what we want is that much simpler. I'll remind you again, though, if you hurt your girl and it hurts *my* girl, you'll be on my shitlist for the rest of your numbered days."

With that, he strolls off, whistling the tune from Kill Bill. I shake my head, feeling a smirk quirk my lips briefly before they tilt downwards. I'll need to open myself up to April tonight, in a way I never have because I never had something this deep to talk about. Whether she wants to return the favor willingly or not, she will. It's time we get as deep under each other's skin as we should've been all along.

CHAPTER TWENTY-SEVEN

April

After my History of Dance class, I head to the park on the edge of campus to get some studying done, armed with a backpack that holds my textbooks and notebooks. On my way, I get a call from Mom, which brings a smile to my lips. I've been talking to her every day, sometimes twice a day, because I'm as worried about her pregnancy as my severely overprotective father is.

I slow my pace as I pick up the call and greet, "Mom. How are you? How's my little sister doing?" She just found out that we'll be welcoming another girl into the family; lucky for us, if I do say so myself. After all, I think I turned out pretty great.

"I'm doing well, as is your sister," Mom says, her voice warm with affection. "Everything's stable so far, thankfully—as uncomplicated as it could possibly be, though your father's still barely giving me any breathing space. He's even insisted I cut down on my work hours; can you believe that?"

"Yes," I say with total seriousness, because I'm in complete agreement with Papa on that front. Mom's always been a hard worker, putting in long hours that have made her successful in the world of interior modeling and decorating. While her work ethic has always been a good thing, her stress could be detrimental to her pregnancy, which is not a point I'd be happy about. I'm glad my father's putting his foot down even though it'll drive Mom up the wall; she needs to take it easy.

With a little huff, she says, "You and your father are like two peas in a pod. You might look more like me, but you got most of your personality from him."

I feel a smile creep onto my lips as I take a seat on a park bench, zipping up my sweater and setting my backpack down beside me. I'm proud to share my father's qualities and traits; I've learned a great deal from him.

"Thank you," I say.

"Wasn't a compliment," Mom responds with a chuckle. In the background, I hear Papa call out, *I heard that, and it* was *a compliment, solnyshko.*

"What he said," I agree.

I can practically hear Mom roll her eyes at that, but she doesn't comment any further. Instead, she asks, "How's school?"

I tell her a bit about the ins and outs of campus life, the success of Pandora's Box, and my upcoming exams in my non-physical classes. Every day in the dance program is an exam of its own, but in my language, history, and gen ed courses I have midterms coming up, which are a bit daunting. I'm studying every chance I get—every spare moment of time I have that Ian doesn't eat up—and I feel pretty confident.

"You've always been excellent with school," Mom says fondly. She adds, "That quality came from me, lucky for you. Now, tell me, how are things with Ian?"

Just like that, my mood shifts from upbeat to something else. Not the anger or disdain I'd become accustomed to feeling when hearing his name or thinking about him, something that's sadder in nature, because it's depressing how he's getting to me and how I've now cried twice in his presence. In any other scenario I'd push away anyone I cried in front of and try to forget about them and the situation. I don't really cry often, let alone with other human beings, so that's never been a necessity, but I know pushing away Ian or brushing him aside isn't viable. He won't allow it. He won't back off, slow down, or let me go. While that might perversely reassure some part of me, it frightens the rest of me.

Since I don't want to outline all those details to Mom, I say, "He's still keeping strong and trying to get me to stick with him. I applaud his effort, though sometimes I wish he'd ease up a bit. He's goddamn relentless."

Mom sounds irritatingly pleased when she says, "Good. That's how you know he's serious. Have you agreed to his spring break trip yet?"

"No, and I have no plans to," I respond. Ian still hasn't given up his hope that I'll eventually agree to the trip, and he's casually mentioned that he'd have no problem straight up kidnapping me, to which I sweetly responded that he'd require my compliance to get through airport security and customs, so kidnapping isn't a viable option.

"Hmm," Mom says, not really sounding like she believes me. "Anyways, I was just calling to check up on my favorite girl. I'll let you get back to studying; talk tomorrow?"

"Tomorrow," I agree.

After exchanging goodbyes and love you's, I hang up, turn on my homework playlist, and pull my dance history textbook out of my bag. I flip it open to the study section and get my notebook and pen positioned beside it, ready to go through the practice questions. My professor hinted that a lot of our exam questions would be similar to the study questions in the textbook, and I've already made my way through nearly two thirds of them.

I work until it gets dark outside; then, since I'm right by a lamp post, I work some more, until I've only got a few practice questions left. That's when I feel the familiar effect of all the hair on my arms and legs standing on end, the reaction I get whenever there's a certain predator in near vicinity. I glance over my shoulder and my eyes clash with Ian's emerald ones.

All at once, several reactions pass through me; embarrassment at how I broke down last night, especially since it was during *sex* of all things, irritation at him not being able to give me even a touch of space, and even some admiration for his effort. At the same time, my body lights up the way it's learned to when he's around. He's trained it meticulously by always dedicating ample time to my pleasure and release whenever we're together, and I can't help but wonder if that's one of his tactics of getting under my skin.

I pull out one headphone and call out, "I have two more questions to get through; you'll have to wait for my attention."

Rounding the bench and plopping down beside me, he frowns. "Wait for your attention? I don't like the sound of that. You know how greedy I am when it comes to wanting—*needing*—your attention, Sugarplum."

I don't bother to hide my eyeroll. "I wasn't asking you to wait, I was informing you of the wait. Besides, you already eat up way too much of my time. You can set aside the spoiled brat inside you for a few minutes and let me finish my work."

Ian's brows lift at that. "I recall you agreeing to be mine last night quite clearly. One of the most erotic moments of my life, I might add."

I pin him with an unamused glare. "You literally tortured me into that agreement, so it doesn't count. I'm still extremely ticked off with you for last night, so I'd really advise that you don't push me." With that, I pop my headphone back in and refocus on my textbook and notebook. The final questions only take me about fifteen minutes, and after checking them against the textbook's answers, I give a satisfied nod. I should be just fine on my upcoming test.

After packing up my backpack, I put away my AirPods and look over at Ian, who's staring at me with his usual piercing gaze, as if he wants to commit every detail of me to his memory.

I ask, "What will it be tonight?"

This is our usual routine; one I've grown used to. He finds me either at dorms, here in the park, or greets me at dance HQ, and promptly carts me off to dinner somewhere. Initially, I fought that tooth and claw until realizing that fighting the little things was only wasting energy that I could be dedicating to other things.

"Reservations at a Thai fusion place in about..." he pauses to check his watch, "twenty minutes. Then back to my apartment."

His latter statement makes me tense up. My track record at Ian's apartment isn't great. I'm not sure I want to go back there and see whatever I'll be in for tonight.

Before I can protest, Ian says, "We need to talk. I have some things I want to tell you. I promise I'll make the night worth your while, then I'll drive you back to campus tomorrow."

The way he says *we need to talk* piques my interest, because it's filled with hidden meaning. I ask slowly, "Talk about what?"

He pauses, and I watch his Adam's apple bob as he swallows hard. "The thing that tore the rift between us—or, more accurately, prompted me to tear the rift."

Well, that came straight out of left field. Ian's promised on more than one occasion that he'd eventually tell me exactly what made him turn on me the way he did, but he hasn't made good on that promise, and I haven't pushed because I wasn't so sure I wanted to know. I'm still not entirely sure, but seeing as he's set on his course of keeping me … I deserve to know.

"Okay," I finally respond. "If you tie me up again, though, I'll cut your fucking balls off."

His lips quirk. "But you're so pretty when you're bound and at my mercy."

"You have no mercy," I mutter. And yet, my body heats up in memory of the first portion of last night—before I broke down and cried like a child. Being bound by him was scary, but in hindsight it was also liberating. He didn't hurt me—not really. He brought me so much pleasure, made me come so many times and in so many ways that I cried tears from the sheer overwhelming sensation and made concessions I'd been determined not to, but it also taught me that I might actually like bondage under the right circumstances. I've certainly never come that hard or for that long.

"Not when it comes to working over your body," he admits shamelessly. "I like wringing every last drop I can from you; you can't blame me for that."

I roll my eyes, standing and swinging my bag over my shoulder. "Whatever."

Dinner is low-key and surprisingly enjoyable. My mood's still somewhat funky because I can't stop internally berating myself for the fact that there's still a small part of me that cares for Ian.

Ian's relatively quiet throughout our meal—while his attention still remains focused on me, there's also something about it that's turned inwards. He doesn't bring up Scotland or try to nag at my defenses the way he usually does; instead, he's lost in his thoughts.

Once we get back to his place, he goes right to the couch, and pulls me down on his lap. He slides one hand along my back, holding me to him, and uses the other to undo my ponytail and then stroke a hand through my hair. Leaning against the spine of the couch, he starts to speak.

"You know I traveled every summer with an array of wealthy family friends while in middle and high school," he tells me. "After meeting you, most of those trips were irritating, because I spent the majority of my time thinking about how much you'd like the different sights, foods, and settings, wishing you were there with me. Constantly planning on taking my own trips with you as soon as we were old enough."

I nod, a faint sense of melancholy overcoming me at remembrances of a better past between us. A state of friendship I'm not quite sure we can ever return to.

CHAPTER TWENTY-EIGHT

I an inhales a deep breath. "What you don't know is that, summer before ninth grade, I happened to be traveling with the Ajax's, Carson's family. Our fathers were in a joint business venture at the time, they wanted space to talk, but didn't want to miss out on a summer vacation, so they planned the trip together with us kids and their wives. Carson's uncle, Dennis, was also there for the trip. He was... not a good man. I got the sense that something was off with him immediately, but I was too young to really put my finger on it. Carson seemed to like Dennis more than he liked his father, but that wasn't saying much as he hated his father even then, justifiably so. Anyways, we traveled together for two weeks that summer—the Ajax's and the Vargas'. All the adults and kids had dinner together every night, then my father and Carson's would go off somewhere to talk business over a nightcap while our moms would take us back to our hotel rooms."

I get a heavy feeling in my chest as he talks, a sense of dread that's slowly building with each word because I think I might know which direction he's heading in, and it's a heartbreaking one. I'm still as a statue in his lap, stiff as stone, staring at him with wide eyes as he toys with my hair and holds me tighter and tighter the longer he speaks, as if needing to ground himself with my presence. Slowly, I wind my arms around his neck, silently letting him know I'm here.

"Dennis spent a lot of time looking at me during those dinners. When we were all together during the day, he'd ask me questions and talk to me—I wasn't really a talkative kid, as you know, at least not with anyone other than you. I blew him off and didn't pay him much attention. I just thought he was a weird old man, and while I got a bad feeling about him, I didn't know how to identify that bit of intuition for what it was; a sense of danger." He stops to inhale a breath. "On the third to last night of the trip, Carson and I snuck out of our hotel rooms late to go to the beach, mainly to be contrary because our moms had told us to stay inside. Carson went back to the hotel after about an hour, but I wanted to stay longer—it was a gorgeous night, so many stars out, and they made me think of you. Then, Dennis showed up. He was drunk—I could smell the alcohol on his breath, and he was staring at me in a way that was just wrong. He started asking me some pretty fucked up questions about if I masturbated and other sexual stuff that an old man had no business asking a young boy. I told him he was disgusting and to fuck off; he got mad, and then he got physical. The beach was empty, so no one was there when he leapt on me. I wasn't particularly strong or tall yet, and he was, so shit got bad quick. He touched my dick, then tried to make me touch his—I acted compliant, then punched him in the balls so hard it made him throw up and ran back to the hotel." He pauses, working his jaw, while I'm stunned into stillness and silence, feeling like something's cracking and fracturing in my chest. After a long moment, he goes on. "I could've told my parents; I should've, but I was scared they'd be mad that I went out after dark when I was supposed to be in my room sleeping. I was also embarrassed and ashamed of my weakness—so fucking embarrassed, April, it made me sick. So I kept it to myself. The next day, Dennis acted like nothing happened, and so did I. I just wanted to cut that memory and the feeling of... *violation* out of my mind like a cancerous tumor, but I couldn't. That sense of weakness fucking *plagued* me for the rest of the summer, and I swore to myself I'd never be weak again. I analyzed every inch of my life and tried to determine potential weaknesses; the only one I could find was you, so I cut it off."

There are tears running down my cheeks now, but I'm barely aware of them and not embarrassed by them, because my heart is breaking for that fourteen-year-old Ian who went through an experience no boy ever should, and blamed himself for it—blamed his perceived weakness—rather than the fucking monster who's actually to blame. A monster that, according to Eliana, is in town right now, working in the same building as Ian. That knowledge *kills* me and makes me want to kill Dennis.

"The thing is, I couldn't stay away from you when you were around, couldn't restrain myself, so I opted for treating you like a despised weakness rather than the treasure I *knew* you were. I was cruel to you, bullied you, let other people bully you because in my warped mind, you symbolized a similar weakness to the one that got me assaulted and I couldn't stand that." He leans in to run his nose along my neck, inhaling deeply, before resting his head against the crook of my shoulder, his lips brushing against my skin as he speaks. "I'm sorry for that, April. I know now that you've never been a weakness, you've always been my strength, but I couldn't see it then. I was in too dark of a place, and rather than letting you pull me up the way I know you would've, I treated you like shit. I hate myself for it. But when I say I never stopped caring about or loving you, I mean it. You were my lifeline even through high school, when I treated you like garbage.

Fucking with you was always the highlight of my day, because it's the only way I let myself get close to you, and even then... even when our dynamic was terrible because of me, you still managed to ground me and pull me out of my darkness if only a little, which made me resent you all the more."

A lot of things make sense now. His behavior isn't excused, and his explanation doesn't equal instant forgiveness from me because I'm still hurting after those three years when he treated me horribly, but at least I understand now, and my heart continues breaking for a young Ian who didn't deserve any of what he went through.

"I hate that you went through that," I say. "I'm sorry you were forced into such an awful situation at such a vulnerable age. I want to kill Dennis for what he did to you, and I want to kill you for not telling me and turning to me."

As ridiculous as it might be, and as much as I understand how his mind led him down the path of cutting me off, we were best friends. More than that, we were almost like platonic soulmates at that age, and I wish Ian had trusted me. I could've helped him work through his pain, pulled him out of his darkness, but instead I had to put up with his awfulness for years, thinking that he cut me off because I suddenly wasn't enough for him.

Ian's hold tightens on me, and he pulls his head away to stare into my eyes. "I very much regret not telling you now. I can see in hindsight that I should've, but you have to understand, April, I was in a bad place. I was functioning on a whole new level of fucked up, and I couldn't see things clearly. Even then, you filled up a hole inside of me; seeing you always dispelled the darkness, the chasm of emptiness in my chest. When I graduated, there was nothing but emptiness and darkness. Then, I saw you on campus a few months ago, and just like that, the hole in my chest felt like it had decreased drastically.

That's when everything clicked and I could see my mistakes clearly, could see that you were never a weakness. That's why I put all my effort into pursuing you and will continue doing so. I've always been a dark creature, and you... you are the center that exists outside of me. The conscience I don't have, the moral compass I was born without. Without you in my life, even as someone who I bullied and mistreated, all of that was missing, and I didn't even realize it was missing until suddenly it was within reach again."

I let out a long sigh. I know the purpose I once served in Ian's life; I knew there were parts of him missing early on, and I knew that I could fill those parts of him. I knew all of his darkness and fucked up tendencies, and I loved that I had the power to curb them when no one else did. I loved that about us; that we completed each other. I can even see how it still applies—just like he used to be, Ian's a lot tamer when I'm around. I've heard plenty of rumors about his penchant for anarchy around campus, the shit he's pulled and mayhem he's caused, and all of it's been subdued recently because his energy and focus has instead been fixed on me.

I know all of this, I just don't know if I'm the right person to hold him in check anymore, even if it's something that naturally happens whenever we're together. I don't know if I have it in me to tolerate him long term, because while I absolutely despise what he went through, I still resent what he put me through in turn. I deeply resent the way he broke us when I could've helped him. Not by fixing him—I've never wanted to fix Ian, I always liked him the way he was—but by being there through the bad with him.

My mind starts to wander down a path of what might happen if we do separate, if whatever we have now evaporates. He'd eventually turn to other girls, and I'd have to see him with those girls. After all the time we've spent together recently, all the reminders of how much

I do like him despite my best efforts not to, that would hurt. A lot. I don't want him to be with anyone else, and at the same time, I don't know how to be with him. When I'm not hung up on times in the past, spending hours on end with him is the easiest thing in the world, but I'm a grudge holder by nature. And, I'll always have the very real fear—*especially* now—that if something horrible happens to him once more, he might decide I'm a weakness yet again, and cut me off for good.

I reach a hand up to stroke my fingers through his hair, running my fingernails along his scalp as I think. There was a time when I didn't see a future for myself without Ian in it somewhere; in fact, for a few years, I firmly believed that our futures would be intertwined permanently, that we'd end up married and living together. Those times were some of the brightest and happiest of my life—as much as Ian says I'm his strength, he was mine, as well. I've learned to be strong without him, but I do feel stronger when I'm with him, even though his presence has a way of making me feel weak and vulnerable. Perhaps weak and vulnerable aren't the right words; more so raw and exposed, because he truly sees me. If I could trust that he'd protect me as he once did, even though I'm no longer really in need of protection, I could live with us, but I can't—not yet.

Ian leans into my touch, his eyes fluttering, and it reminds me that he's always enjoyed my touch. Even when I was a silly nine-year-old putting ribbons in his hair, finding great entertainment in it, he never minded. He said it was because my touch calmed him, and I can see that it still does.

His hands slip under my shirt, and I feel them tracing over the scar on my lower back, before one of them rises up to stroke over the scar on my shoulder blade, reminding me of their presence. I can't blame him for their existence, especially not now—he'd have never condoned what was done to me. But his treatment did give those terrible boys the impression that they could take things to the next level without ramifications. I doubt I would've ever gotten caught in that alleyway by them if I was by Ian's side, but then again, those boys might've just cornered someone else—someone who wasn't strong enough to get away from them, wounded or not.

"Tell me about these scars," he murmurs, eyes opening again.

I barely hide a grimace. "I already told you," I say, though the words come out unstable and sounding like the lie they are. I know Ian just opened himself up to me, but I don't know if that makes it entirely safe to open myself up to him.

"The hiking accident excuse is bullshit, unless you happened to fall into a bush made of knives," Ian says, flatly. "You know what happened to me. I want to know what happened to you."

I open my mouth, then shut it, then open and shut it again and again, fighting an inner war. To try to stop him from seeing my mental back and forth so clearly, from seeing more than I want him to, I lean forward to rest my cheek against his chest. The gesture isn't necessarily meant to be an affectionate one, but I think he perceives it that way because he rests his chin on the top of my head and I feel some of the tension leech out of his muscles. Despite myself, despite our whole fucked up situation, I still like being held by him. I always have. Of course, when we were kids there was nothing sexual about our touches, though Ian was always possessive. When I wouldn't reach for his hand or lean against him if we were sitting together, he'd wrap an arm around me and jerk me to him with an irate expression, almost like he was offended at the space between us. As soon as I'd relax against him or smile at him and tell him he was crazy, he'd relax—that was the only time I ever saw him relax. The rest of the time, he was tense.

Finally, I say, "I don't like talking about it."

"I don't blame you," Ian replies. "I've never told anyone what I just told you, and I hate even thinking about it, let alone saying it out loud. But I feel a good bit lighter now than I did before telling you everything. You took the burden off me. Let me do the same for you."

I already had some of my burden lifted by talking to Elia; I don't know if telling Ian will lessen the burden or have the opposite effect, putting a further damper on our relationship. There's also the possibility that Ian might shoulder the blame, which I know he doesn't have. Not really. And, despite myself, I'm still protective of him; I want to protect him from any potential feeling of responsibility. I also want to protect myself, though, and being open with him isn't conducive to self-protection.

"I don't want to talk about it," I grit out. Then, I add on more softly, "Not with you."

Telling him would open a whole can of worms; I know Ian, he'd want to get revenge on my behalf and finish what I started. The idea of him hurting people doesn't bother me as much as it should, especially when those people hurt me. What really bothers me is that I don't want him to be my avenger; I don't want him to have that role in my life. I relied on him too heavily once, I won't again—I've learned to rely on myself just fine, and that's how I prefer it. It's best to keep this part of my past quiet, just like I vowed to do on the night when I got my scars.

Ian's fingers tense over my scars, as does the rest of his body. At first, I think it's with anger at my refusal to open up to him, but then, he says, "Not with *me*. Why would that be, Sugarplum?"

CHAPTER TWENTY-NINE

I pull my head back to look at Ian, swallowing when I see that his eyes are narrowed and his lips are pursed as he stares at me. I can practically hear the gears whirring in his mind, and I don't like the feeling that he's seeing more than I want him to. I've always known that Ian is eternally perceptive. It's how he was able to plan elaborate vengeance whenever someone pissed me off or hurt me, back in the times when he considered himself my protector and avenger. He would read a person, figure out what would hurt them most, then push on their sore spots until they broke. He never even had to get physical; he was impeccable at psychologically fucking with people.

"Same reason you didn't tell me what happened for a long time," I say. "It's fucking embarrassing."

He shakes his head. "No, *I* didn't want to tell *you* anything because I didn't want you to judge me, pity me, or see me as weak. In fact, I saw you as the weakness I wanted to amputate. You not telling me something is different; you know I wouldn't judge or pity you, and you don't see me as your weakness because you were the one who succeeded in amputating me from your life, while I tried and failed to push you out of mine for years." He pauses, and one of his hands slips from out of my shirt, trailing up my side before taking my chin in his fingers. "You're holding back from me for a different reason. What is it?"

"Privacy," I snap, jerking my chin from his hold. "You *chose* to lift the veil over your past; that doesn't mean I want to do the same."

His hands curl over the nape of my neck, turning my head back towards him, making my gaze clash with his again. The look he gives me is too knowing, like he sees every part of me, including the ones I keep hidden. "Liar," he murmurs. "You told your friend, *Eliana*, about the scars, but you won't tell me after I bare my soul to you."

I frown. "How do you know I told Eliana?"

He goes on as if I hadn't spoken. "I could choose to be offended over that fact, but I don't think you're holding back because you want to offend me. I don't even think it's because you still distrust me. I think it goes deeper than that, cuts to the heart of your relentless self-reliance. It's not that you *don't* trust me, it's that you don't *want* to trust me, isn't it?"

"Of course I don't want to trust you," I reply, feeling a frown crease my brows. "Would *you* want to trust you in my shoes?"

"Hmm," Ian says. "It can't be that if you admitted to it so freely. What is it then, April? Why are you holding *this* back from me? I couldn't use your pain against you in the future—I never would. But if that's your worry then you should consider that if I planned on hurting you, I wouldn't have told you about *my* pain, thereby giving you plenty of ammunition against me. You should know that I'd go after whoever hurt you with everything in my personal arsenal and make them suffer beyond their worst imaginings for a long time before meeting their end."

Again, I stiffen at that, unable to help myself. Of course, Ian would see it as his responsibility to go after those boys, but it *isn't*. He once took pride in being my protector and avenger; then, he dropped the job, so he doesn't just get to pick it back up again. I might not want him out of my life the way I did not too long ago, but I don't want him fully in it, either—I don't know what I want when it comes to him, other than to protect myself from more pain.

Ian does a slow blink, and his eyes drop down. I follow his vision, belatedly realizing that I've sunk my nails into his skin so hard I'd be drawing blood if his shirt weren't keeping my fingers at bay. I quickly release him, snatch my arms back, and cross them over my chest.

"Ah," he says with a curt nod. "I see. You don't *want* me to avenge you. You've become this tough as nails, strong as hell girl who doesn't need anyone, haven't you? And my presence in your life threatens that. That actually explains quite a bit."

"You're wrong," I snip tensely, then shift and try to get off his lap. He doesn't allow it, tightening his hold on me, interlocking his arms around me to keep me firmly in place.

"I'm not," he replies calmly. "I'm also not a threat to your strength, April, I know you have a fuck ton of it. I won't avenge you because you're unable to do it yourself, I'll avenge you because someone hurt you, and you're mine—whether or not you're ready to admit it."

"I'm *not* yours to avenge," I snap, pushing at his chest. "I don't need you to avenge me."

"You don't," he agrees, still in that calm, assertive, steady tone that pisses me off. "In fact, you don't need me period, which irritates me to no end because *I* need *you*. I've accepted that I'll always need you more than you'll need me—but I want you to want me as much as I want you. That's a topic of discussion for another time. For now, you need to tell me what happened and who hurt you so I can make it right."

"There *is* no making it right, you goddamn idiot," I hiss. "The scars aren't going to go away, the memories aren't going to go away, and the fucking nightmares aren't going to go away—the damage is done, it's there to stay, and that's fine. I can handle it."

"But you don't have to. Not alone, anyways," Ian says. "You have me, and there's one great advantage to that; we both know I'm scarier than any nightmare you may have. I'm the bigger monster, April. The greater evil."

"You aren't making a case for yourself," I say dryly.

He shrugs. "I don't need to. You've always seen me for exactly what I was, and you loved me anyways. Now, tell me who had the gall to hurt you."

"The gall," I repeat, bitter amusement coating my words. "You want to know who had the *gall* to hurt me, aside from yourself? *Your fucking friends,* Ian. The ones who you joked about me being a gold digger with, the ones who you told tales about me spreading my legs for a couple bucks. Those made-up stories gave *them* the gall to go ahead and test your theories. Guess what? They didn't like it so much when I didn't let them have me like you told them I would. Since I was an absolute nobody, it didn't matter if they had a knife to threaten me with, did it? It *also* didn't matter that I said—*screamed*—no repeatedly, because I was just a gold digging, worthless whore. But people like them, people like *you,* don't know how to lose. I got away in the nick of time, but that escape cost me; specifically, it cost me two permanent marks that'll never go away, no matter how hard I scrub at them." I jerk back in his grip so hard it loosens, then I push his hands off me, absolutely *fuming.* With the exception of that time with Eliana, even thinking about that night makes me angry; being pushed to talk about it with *Ian*, hearing him ask who had the gall to hurt me as if that's a foreign concept to him, sends me into a rage.

"Now, you'll just have to wrack your brain and figure out who it was. You belittled me to hundreds of boys; good luck narrowing that pool down to the ones who had the *gall* to act."

I didn't intend for tonight to turn so sour; I was grateful and humbled by Ian opening up to me the way he did, especially since I know he's not an open person by nature, but he just had to fucking push me and try to pick at old wounds. It feels like every one step forward with him always equals two steps back, and right now I don't want to deal with that shit. Had he eased up, I would've stayed on his lap all night, but he didn't.

He told me something with the expectation of me returning the favor. I can see the manipulative tactic in hindsight, and it only irritates me further. I don't doubt that his story about Dennis Ajax is the truth, but I now realize he didn't offer up that information because he wanted to explain our rift, he did it so that I'd feel compelled to do the same. That's the exact asshole move I should expect from him.

He has a blank expression on his face now as he stares at me, and I recognize that look; it's the one he's always gotten when he's thinking deeply and darkly, plotting. I'm not sticking around for more of his questions or to deal with his bullshit any longer; right now, I need space and to be alone. I march to the doorway, grabbing my backpack on the way and leave the apartment, slamming the front door behind me. For once, Ian doesn't follow me, and I ignore the hollow ache that starts pulsing in my chest as I storm up to the elevator, panting and fuming, leaning into my anger so I don't instead have to experience the pain that comes with recounting the worst time of my life.

I press the elevator button once, then twice, then slam on it repeatedly like a crazy person, desperate to get the fuck out of here. I'm overwhelmed by too many emotions to name—anger, not just *at* Ian, but *for* Ian, because despite the way he pushed too far yet *again*, I hate that he went through so much pain and that I wasn't there to help him. There's plenty of anger at him as well, but it's tempered by the knowledge that he's lived through a hell of his own. Then, there's the maelstrom of helplessness, injustice, and sheer hatred that comes whenever I think of the night I got my scars; think of the fact that I was very nearly raped, all the while three boys were kicking me and holding a knife to my skin and laughing at me. While I'm a fairly strong person, I think that's enough to make anyone want to crawl out of their skin with sheer revulsion.

When the elevator finally arrives, I rush into it, and I'm quickly reminded that Ian isn't the only antisocial being living in this apartment building when I come face to face with Seth Balor. He's an intimidating figure at the best of times, well over six feet of bulging muscle and such blankness and emptiness it's unnerving. Despite his default expression of ennui or boredom, he has a presence that fills up any space he enters, making it feel stifled and suffocated. He's like a black hole of emotions, pulling everything inward. I know Seth's no threat to me for the simple fact that I'm best friends with Eliana, and he'd never do anything to hurt that girl, but I'm under no illusions that he *could* be a threat to me.

I straighten, trying to wipe my expression to match his blankness, and tip him a nod. "Balor," I greet.

"Stein," he returns, gaze briefly landing on me before flitting over the hallway just before the elevator door closes, as if he's expecting someone to come and stop me.

"You seem to be in an awful hurry," he observes, crossing his arms as he leans against the elevator wall.

"And you seem to have managed to part from Elia, even though you make a point to be glued to her whenever it's possible," I retort, my tone sharp.

He lifts a shoulder, unbothered. "I'm going out to grab a snack—Elia was craving ice cream. I don't have it in me to deny her anything."

That much I know to be true. Seth and Carson both spoil Elia rotten, which automatically puts them on my good side. Elia deserves to be treasured, worshipped, cherished, and protected at all costs. She's too kind at her core. Without someone like Seth at her side, this world would absolutely take advantage of her.

"Good," I tell him. "Keep doing that and we won't have any problems."

He arches a brow, seeming mildly amused. The look he flicks me is like a cat looking at a mouse who has the balls to threaten it. "You think you could take me, Stein?"

I shrug. "Considering that I'm the one who put the idea of a three-way relationship into *my* girl Eliana's head while she was stuck moaning and whining with fear of having to lose both of you because she couldn't choose, I'd say she trusts me. I'd never betray that trust. Take care of her, and we won't have any issues."

Seth tilts his head to the side as he studies me. "You're an unusual one, with an unusual amount of loyalty to someone I happen to love very much. Good. I hope you know that stunt you two pulled the other night, dancing together and kissing, might've put you on my shit list if I hadn't already approved of you."

I snort. "You and Ian are two peas in a pod, you know that? I'll tell you what I told him; I've never had any interest in Elia beyond friendship. She's a wonderful soul who's too kind to exist, and I want to protect her from this cruel, shitty world as much as you do. We danced and kissed to provoke our respective men—it was a purely platonic kiss. Stage-kisses happen all the time."

Seth works his jaw. "Don't I fucking know it. I want to rip the throat out of any man who touches her on stage, let alone has the audacity to press his lips to hers. Sean's lucky he doesn't have interest in the fairer sex, or he might've disappeared long before now."

I give him a pointed look. "Ease up on that. It only stresses Elia out. Her career is her life, has been the soul of her existence for a long time—don't make it stressful for her. Before you and Carson, it was all she had."

"You really do care for her," Seth says, sounding mildly interested. "Don't worry, Stein, I do everything in my power to keep my Little Muse happy and content, not stressed. We're on the same side."

The elevator arrives with a ding, and we step out. I tell him, "Good to hear. If we weren't, you'd be a fool to underestimate me."

"Oh, that much I already know. You have connections in low places, don't you, April?"

I pause mid-step, turning slowly to regard Seth, who's now leaned against the wall outside the elevator. I try to keep my expression impassive, but it's a difficult task; he should have no way of knowing I have connections in low places. In fact, nobody should know that, not even my father, who's the very person I took those connections from—albeit without telling him.

Seth lets out a low chuckle. "No need to give me that predator-stalking-prey look, Stein—I've already told you I'm no threat to you. I only recently found out that we share a mutual acquaintance, and I must say, I was rather surprised. Sergei Novikov isn't a figure many people in this country are aware even exists, let alone know on a first name basis."

I blink slowly. "What do you know about Mr. Novikov?"

Seth makes a noncommittal noise. "He's bought a few of my statues. Some paintings, as well. We have a few business dealings together on top of that. I offered for him to come see Pandora's Box during his next visit to the states; he agreed. Of course, he did research on Greywood's dance company and the cast list while scoping out the safety of attending such a performance. I was surprised when he mentioned being acquainted with you. All the more surprised that he spoke of you with a note of both fondness and respect in his voice. He didn't deign to tell me how he knows you, though, and I find myself in the rare position of curiosity." Seth takes a step forward. "How would someone like you, an American born and raised girl, come to be in contact with the most notorious Bratva boss in the world? One who owns all of Russia and most of Eurasia?"

I arch an eyebrow at him, also crossing my arms, grateful that he doesn't know details. "How would someone like you, a robotic shell of a being, come to earn Eliana's love?"

Seth lets out a puff of amused laughter. "Touche, Stein." He glances at the elevator behind him. "You're fleeing Vargas?"

"None of your business."

He shrugs. "Fair enough. You once did me a favor by encouraging Eliana to do something that seemed scary at the time yet paid off in the long run. It benefitted me and her and, unfortunately, Carson as well. I'm going to return the favor. Vargas is not a neurotypical person by any stretch of the imagination—he's similar to me in some ways. He's also very fixated on you and has every intention of keeping you. Since he's like me, he's bound to pull shit that's going to piss you off, probably on a regular basis, because you're not as forgiving or understanding as my Muse. Don't run from him—it'll only ignite his hunter's instinct."

"So, you're saying just take whatever he dishes out and be happy with it?" I question incredulously.

Seth shakes his head. "Not at all. I'm just giving you that tidbit of advice. If you need space, take it, but tell him. People like us need communication more than most, even if we don't seem like it, because we need a reason to overcome our primal instincts, most of which are on the darker side. Without communication, it's much easier to succumb to them. Do with that what you will."

He gives me one last nod before strolling across the lobby, heading towards the exit.

I contemplate his words for a few moments, wondering if I should maybe shoot Ian a cursory text. I might be pissed at him, but I also see the merit in Seth's words. I exhale a deep breath and pull my phone out of my pocket. I might be amped up, but I know I snapped at Ian when I could've been reasonable instead. As I'm typing a text to him, an elevator door opens with a ding, and Ian steps out. He stares at me, a million unspoken words in his gaze.

"April," he finally says, stepping forward and crossing the distance between us. "We're not done talking." He slowly reaches out a hand, wrapping it around my waist. I should pull away, but I don't; instead I stare up at him. It might be better to do this in person, anyways, and I know that abandoning him right now will not bode well for me in the future. He'd just hunt me down.

I sigh. "Okay. Let's talk."

CHAPTER THIRTY

We don't talk, though. I allow Ian to take me by my hand and lead me into his apartment, into his bedroom. I'm angry, and my emotions are in turmoil, but I also crave a release; both emotional and physical. If he wants to put talking on the backburner while we fuck, I'm very much amenable to that idea. I want to forget everything that's happened to him and me, and just *feel* for a little while, not think.

"Get on the bed," he tells me. "I'm going to tie you down, and then I'm going to fuck you until we both pass out." He gazes at me. "You get one chance to say no. After that, I'm going to do what I want to do, and your only option will be to take it."

My breaths shorten into pants as I stare at him. I know not to take the warning he's giving me lightly; if I say yes right now, he's going to take liberties until he's satisfied. I can see the tension cording his muscles and shoulders, the same tension that's weighing heavily on me. Right now, the best thing might really be to just... let it all go for a bit.

I nod. "Make us forget."

"As soon as you get on that bed, you no longer get a say in what I do," Ian says. His warning is spoken in the softest tone, yet falls with the weight of an executioners axe.

I don't think about his warning like I should. I'm too restless, to in need of Ian's particular brand of sex to help me forget about everything.

I strip my clothes, liking the way Ian's eyes track each one of my movements, then slowly climb onto the bed. Ian's on me in a heartbeat; he pushes me up the bed until I'm right up against the headboard and climbs over me.

His mouth descends on my neck as his hands pin my wrists above my head, kissing and licking and biting so hard I wince and arch into him.

"You shouldn't have gotten on my bed," Ian murmurs against my skin. "But you did, and now I am going to fucking *devour you*, and get everything I need. Stay still."

He pulls back. I blink up at him, then jerk as I feel cool leather snap over one of my wrists. His lips tilt up at the corners; I shrink back, startled.

"Wait—"

My protest is cut off by him wrapping another one of the leather cuffs around my free wrist and tightening it. I jerk against the cuffs, fear unfurling within me, though it's tempered by a dark sort of arousal.

"Ian, I didn't sign up for this—"

"Shh," he cuts me off, pressing his index finger to my lips. "No more talking, April. I only want one thing from you tonight, the names of the boys who hurt you. Aside from that, no talking."

I shake my head, growing more unnerved and scared by the second. Ian's unhinged right now, even more so than he was last night, and the truly terrifying thing is the absolute calmness of his demeanor. He's resolute in his actions and won't be swayed, I can see that in his eyes. When he said he'd tie me down, I figured he'd use a silk tie again, but he's actually *prepared* for this scene with the sort of restraints I can envision being used in dungeons.

He scoots down the bed. "I'd tell you to stay where you are, but it's not like you could go anywhere, is it?" He doesn't wait for my answer; merely stands from the bed and walks into his closet. He returns with two items, a long black bar that has leather cuffs attached on either end of it and a black leather bag that looks like it belongs to a serial killer.

"Ian, I think I've changed my mind," I say, watching as he drops the bag at the foot of the bed and places the bar on the mattress by my feet. "We should—" I cut off with a gasp when he grabs my ankles and uses his hold to yank me down the bed, stretching my arms taut above my head. Then, he sets to work clipping my feet into the two leather cuffs of what I realize is a *spreader bar*, something I've only ever seen in porn. My heart rate speeds to a gallop; I swallow hard as nerves, fear, and arousal mix within me and make me lightheaded.

To finish, Ian secures the bar to the bottom bedposts with clips, leaving me totally spread and immobile. I lay staring at him with a heaving chest, unsure whether it's best to surrender to him or start screaming at the top of my lungs in hopes that the police will get called.

"Just like that," he breathes. "Stunning. One more thing…" he lifts the bag onto the bed, unzips it, and pulls out a silk tie. The tie goes over my head and between my lips, preventing me from speaking, and I'm embarrassed at the heat that blooms between my legs. Finally, he climbs onto the bed, and runs his palms up my body as he settles at my side.

"Quite the predicament to be in, isn't it?" Ian asks mildly, as if we're having a conversation over coffee rather than me being tightly bound, not even able to move an inch, with him staring at my body like a child stares at its favorite toy—with glee. Except his glee is sadistic and edged with darkness, which only ratchets up the fear factor.

"It wouldn't have come to this if you'd stayed behind and talked to me," Ian goes on conversationally, circling my nipple with his finger. "Instead, you tried to flee. Bad move, April. You don't flee from hunters; you lay down and play dead or risk getting devoured. I can't say I mind all that much, though, because now I *am* going to devour you."

His bright green gaze flicks up to capture my own, and the genuine joy I see in those orbs, as if he has me exactly where he wants me, only frightens me further.

"You really do look like a doe in headlights right now—eyes wide and gleaming, chest heaving," Ian comments, leaning down to drag his tongue over the nipple he's been toying with, before running a wet trail up the column of my throat and to my bound lips. He licks along the seam of them, then takes my bottom lip into his mouth, delivering a harsh bite that cuts into my skin and makes me jerk. When he pulls back, my blood is staining his mouth, and he licks it off with what looks like ecstasy.

"You liked being tied up and tortured last night," Ian tells me. "Tonight, considering that development and the information I need from you, we're going to continue on with that theme. You're going to give me names, April, the names of those who hurt you. Since I know you won't deliver them willingly, I'm going to sincerely enjoy torturing them out of you."

His hand runs down my abs before dipping into my panties, the single item of clothing I left on while undressing. When he runs his fingers through my slit, he sucks in a breath that quickly turns into a dark chuckle. "My dirty girl likes this, doesn't she?"

I shake my head from side to side, which only makes him laugh more. "You're sopping wet already, April, and I've barely touched you. You *do* like this. Good to know. Here's the deal; I'm going to play. Every so often, I'll take your gag out and give you the opportunity to tell me what I need to know. If you don't, I keep playing until you do. And I assure you, you'll talk by the time I'm done with you. Whether that happens sooner or later is entirely up to you."

Two fingers plunge into me, making my back arch and drawing a tortured moan from my throat. I struggle against my bindings, twisting my feet and jerking at my hands, trying to test if there might be any weakness in my bindings, because I can tell the dark parts of Ian are hungry for torture. I'm not sure if I can handle that, despite the fact that I did get onto this bed after he warned me. I do *not* intend to answer the very question that I ran away from right now, I have no inclination to tell him what he wants to hear. He doesn't deserve the names. He hasn't earned the right to know every part of me, inside and out, and the fact that he's trying to *take* that right just enrages me.

Fingers sliding in and out of me, making obscene squelching noises that embarrass me, he reaches up with his free hand and tugs the tie out of my mouth.

"Tell me now, April, and I'll only play a little."

This fucking— instead of speaking and giving in, I do exactly what my anger demands; spit at him. It's a gesture of sheer indignation, rage, and pure protest. My spit lands on his chin, and his eyes register surprise. He once again releases a dark laugh, before shoving the tie back into my mouth. I don't know what I expect—maybe for him to spit at me in turn or get angry. What I don't expect is exactly what he does; pulls his fingers out of my panties, uses them to wipe at the spit on his chin, leaving a smear of my own wetness there, and then thrusts them right back into my panties, spreading my own spit over my clit and circling it. This man really is insane, and the terrifying part is that I must be too, because his ministrations make a low groan escape me. I cut it off, force myself to be silent, but that becomes more difficult as he rubs my clit like a goddamn master, pausing occasionally to thrust his fingers inside me and gather more wetness. I feel a telling tingle course through my muscles, one that only occurs when I'm getting close to coming, and I fight it with everything in me. I force myself to stay silent and squeeze my eyes shut, turning my head to the side and trying to think of anything other than how perversely erotic this is, how good his fingers feel as they tease and rub and pinch the bundle of nerves.

"You don't want to see what I'm doing to you?" Ian asks, still in that calm, stable voice that sets me on edge because I can hear the darkness it's hiding. "Fine. I can accommodate that."

Abruptly, just as I'm on the edge of an orgasm, his fingers disappear. I let out a low noise of relief, breathing harshly, and crack my eyes open in time to see him reach into the bag and pull out—*oh, shit*—a blindfold.

Being bound is one thing; being blindfolded and unable to see what he's doing, mentally prepare for it, is a whole different ballgame. It seems that everything I do right now is going to make him escalate, unless I give him what he wants. He walks around the edge of the bed and kneels beside me, holding the blindfold up to my face. When I shake my head vigorously, giving him a pleading look and trying to say *no* around the fabric in my mouth, he smiles. It's not a kind smile; it's the evil, cruel kind of smile that tells me I'm really in for it now.

"You got on the bed, April. You had your chance to say no and you didn't," he reminds me.

Despite my shaking head, he manages to slip the blindfold over my eyes and secures it around the back of my head, taking away my vision. Blackness encompasses me, and that instantaneously heightens the rest of my sensations. I hear the rustle of the bedsheets more acutely as he slips off, hear the pad of his footsteps as he walks to the bottom of the bed again, even hear the creaking of the leather cuffs around my ankles as I shift restlessly, wriggling to no avail. More noises sound as he roots around the bag again, and the mattress dips with his weight. I jerk when he lifts the front of my panties only to slip something cool and ridged into them, nestling it snugly against my clit, shifting the object around until he's satisfied.

Then, absolute silence. After a few moments of nothing I realize he's doing this on purpose, making me wait to mount my fear and uncertainty, screwing with my head and my senses. I feel a fine sheen of sweat break out along my forehead as my anxiety builds and I wonder what the hell he put in my panties and what he's going to do next.

A buzzing sounds loudly through the room; I arch with a groan as intense sensations of vibrations break out along my pussy, centering on my clit. *He slipped a fucking vibrator in my panties.* One that's held firmly against my sensitive skin by my underwear. Instantly, I start to struggle and shift, bucking my hips, trying anything it takes to dislodge the vibrator, which only makes Ian tut like one might at a child.

"None of that, April," he says in a censuring voice as he presses his palm flat on my stomach, forcing me back to the bed. "You won't get out of your bindings, you won't get away from my torture; your only option is to succumb to it until I feel like giving you another chance to tell me what I want to know. For now, enjoy the sensations." A low chuckle. "I know I'll certainly enjoy the show."

I grit my teeth, biting on the fabric of the tie, holding back any noises and clenching my muscles in an attempt to stave off the orgasm that I'm already on the cusp of. Ian's petting just a few moments ago left me hanging on the edge, now the vibrator is taking me right back to it, threatening to hurtle me off. I resist for as long as I can, which is only a few more moments before an orgasm sweeps over me, arching my back and curling my toes. I choke on my cry, fighting the tremor in my limbs, unable to contain a low whine at the overwhelming vibrations that don't stop or let up. I jerk as Ian's hands slide up my stomach to cup my breasts and his fingers set to toying with my nipples again. Then, his lips descend over my left nipple and his teeth latch onto it, biting harshly just as the vibrations along my pussy *increase* in intensity. Still, I bite down on the cry that attempts to escape, protesting with silence. The pleasure is too much; his lips, his teeth, that goddamn silicone toy buzzing insistently against my sensitized flesh, and Ian doesn't seem to be in the mood to give me any reprieve.

Another orgasm takes me in its hold, one that sets off a round of convulsions within me that make me acutely aware of just how empty my pussy is. Seeming to sense this, Ian reaches down with one hand and slams *four fingers* into me, letting out a grunt.

"Fucking Christ, you're wet, April. That's my good girl; come for me again. This time, I better hear your noises, or this is only gonna get worse."

Because he told me to make a sound, I'm all the more determined to keep silent. As a third orgasm crashes into my system, a low grunt that I swiftly cut off is pulled out of me. Ian curls the fingers inside me, rubbing up against a spot that makes me writhe on the bed even harder. He starts thrusting in and out of me, hitting that spot with each pass, and somehow the vibrations increase *yet again*. How many fucking settings does this thing have? How long will I be able to take this before I pass out?

One of his fingers pulls out of me to travel lower, rimming the bud of my ass. I'm already in the midst of a fourth orgasm when he thrusts the finger into my ass, the erotically taboo feeling joining with the sensations of him rubbing at that spot in my pussy and those ever-intensifying vibrations that finally make me cry out, *loudly*. This orgasm lasts the longest, it leaves me shaking and trembling and instinctually pulling at my wrists, trying to free my legs, anything to get away from the torture. I let out a low whine as Ian pulls his fingers out of me and turns the vibrations off.

Sagging against the bed, over sensitized and half out of my mind, I barely notice when he pulls away the gag.

"You ready to talk?" he asks softly, almost condescendingly.

I inhale a deep breath. "Fuck you, Ian. You can take your bullshit torture and go to hell—"

He puts the gag back in, cutting me off. The vibrations turn back on and I can't contain the sob of agony I let out, because despite my words this is getting to be *way* too much. I'll pass out before I give him what he wants, though; I can out stubborn a mountain. I already gave into him last night, I'm not doing the same a mere twenty-four hours later.

The mattress shifts as I tighten my muscles, clenching my pelvic floor to try to stave off the next orgasm, though I know I won't be able to for long. Dimly, I hear him going back to that fucking bag for something; a moment later I yelp and startle as a lash of *something* comes down directly on my nipple, spreading a stinging burn through my breast.

Is he using a fucking crop on me? Another lash on my other nipple, the bite of cool leather, and I'm just about certain he is. *He's cropping me like a goddamn animal*, and there is absolute shit I can do to stop him. Right now, Ian is a man on a mission. More, I can tell he likes working me over like this, making me mindless.

The vibrations increase—once, twice, three times—going to a higher setting than I could've fathomed, and Ian lashes my nipples, one and then the other, again and again. An orgasm practically *detonates* within me, I let out a scream that can probably be heard by the entire building, thrashing and begging around the gag for him to let up, but he doesn't. Doesn't even give me the chance to speak—instead *he* starts talking, all the while continuing to abuse my nipples.

"You're mine, April, we both know that much." *Slap.* "I am going to destroy the people who hurt you. I think I get why you don't want me to; you don't want me to be your protector because you don't want to rely on me or trust me that way. You want to be your own protector without letting anyone else have that roll." *Slap.* "I know you're capable of protecting and taking care of yourself." *Harder, stinging slap.* "And you should know that you'll never have to be alone in your protection again. I'll share the burden, and I'll scare off any threats because, as I've said before, I'm the more terrifying monster." *Slap, slap, slap.* "The thing is, I'm *your* monster—you own me as completely as I own you."

Despite my worn out body, the orgasms that just keep coming—I must be in the double digits by now—his words penetrate through to me, touching me in my soul, and battering at my armor until it cracks and practically disintegrates. I burst out into tears of both overwhelming pleasure and emotion, unable to help myself, feeling raw from both within and without. Instantly, Ian drops to crop and cradles my head in his palm, pulling off the blindfold. His emerald gaze blinds me as I stare into it. He lays down beside me, bringing his free hand down to my pussy and pushing his fingers back into me, into both of my holes, mastering my body completely. I cry my way through my orgasm, which somehow makes it the most intense one, alternating between sobbing and screaming at the sensations like the absolute mess I am at this moment.

When it ebbs, Ian pulls the vibrator out of my panties—*finally*—and my body shakes with aftershocks. He lays my head back on the pillow and scoots down the bed, releasing my ankles from their restraints, only to wrap my legs around him as he moves between my thighs, frees his cock from his briefs, and lazily feeds it inside of me, stretching me full.

The connection is overwhelming; I feel like our souls are entwined as much as our bodies, which makes me cry even harder. He braces one hand beside my head, uses the other to pull the gag out of my mouth and covers my lips with his, drinking from my mouth as he thrust into me slowly and so deeply. With the little strength left in my body, I lift my hips in time to his thrusts and kiss him back. It doesn't take long before I come again—a long orgasm that takes the final bits of strength from me, leaving me limp on the bed. Ian's release follows shortly afterwards, but he keeps kissing me even as his cock softens and slips out of me. He caresses my neck with his hand, making me feel treasured even after he just worked over my body and set new limits for what I can handle.

"Tell me the names," he murmurs against my lips. "Let me in. You won't regret it."

Unable to deny him at this moment, I murmur three names of three boys who nearly ruined me, then promptly pass out.

Chapter Thirty-One

Ian

After April falls asleep, I pull a sheet over her and kiss her forehead. Once I've cleaned and put away the supplies I used on her tonight, I walk into my living room, pick up my laptop, and take a seat on the couch. Instantly, I miss her warmth and being near her, just like I used to when I was a kid. A few hours or days of separation from her would send my mood into a dark spiral that would cause people to give me a wider berth than usual. Then, April would skip right into my space, and the darkness would clear back up. The beast that lives within me, aching for violence and destruction, would go silent and instead shift focus to her—while she was near me, I was at peace. Now that I've gotten a taste of that again, I can't fall back into chaos. I can't live without her once more.

I take my laptop back into the bedroom, climb onto the bed beside her and open it on my lap, setting the brightness on the lowest setting so as not to disturb her. April's in a dead sleep—I wore her out earlier, determined to finally break through her barriers and get to her. The only path open to me at that point was sex, pain and pleasure, and I think it worked. I won't know for sure until she wakes up in the morning and I get a sense for her mood, but a cautious hope unfurls within me. Maybe I've finally gotten a step closer to her instead of coming up against her steel shields.

I focus on my research for an hour or so, shooting off the names to Seth and asking if he'll dig into them for me. I remember the three boys she mentioned—Troy, Seoul, and Paxton. They were always hanger-on's to my popularity, eager to please me as everyone at that school was. Nobody wanted to get on my bad side because they understood that would mean end of life as they knew it—after all, they saw how I was to April. Now, I deeply regret pushing her away an ostracizing her, especially since it gave those dead-men-walking the impression that they could hurt my April. What happened to her is my fault. As quickly as the thought comes, it's tempered by logic; men like that, *boys* with those perversions will eventually strike—those three fucks were always bound to try that shit with a girl, but I do feel a weight of responsibility that my poor treatment and bullshit rumors might've turned them towards April.

My phone buzzes as Seth texts back that he'll get into it. Surprisingly, he doesn't mention me owing him more favors for his digging. That might mean we're approaching as much of a friendship as two men like us can have. *Huh.*

April shifts around restlessly in her sleep, letting out a low whine as the bedsheets rub across her nipples, which are probably sore—I didn't go easy on them with the crop, and the way she got off on the pain intermingled with pleasure was the single most erotic sight of my life. I pull the bedsheet down, exposing her breasts, and dark satisfaction fills me when I see that her dusky nipples are swollen and red. Her pussy's probably going to be sore in the morning, too.

I close my laptop and set it aside, then retrieve a washcloth from the bathroom and soak it in warm water before using it to clean her up, rubbing it between her thighs gently. April's eyelids flutter but she doesn't wake up, though she does sigh softly in her sleep. Because I'm not a *total* asshole and I don't want her in pain tomorrow, I grab a salve out of my bedside drawer and rub the soothing minty lotion over her nipples and her swollen pussy, trying to ignore the way my cock jumps. This time her eyes do open, and she glances at me blearily.

"What are you doing?" she murmurs in a sleepy voice, though she doesn't make any move away from me, which satisfies me.

"Making sure you won't be in pain tomorrow, Sugarplum," I respond to her simply, finishing up and capping the container before tossing it back in its drawer. When I purchased a collection of erotic toys on impulse, I also got a cream that might soothe any great hurt—I might be a monster with a predilection for pain, but I don't want to truly hurt her.

"M'kay." Her eyes slide closed again but she reaches out for me with a hand that lands on my arm and gives it a tug. "C'mon, let's sleep. It's late."

Her words thrust me more than a decade back in time—to the night we reminisced about not long ago, on a ski trip where the hotel's power went out and April nearly froze into an ice block. I always slept beside her when I could manage it, it was the only way my restless brain would shut off, but that night I was determined to find more blankets to bundle her in. Then she grabbed for me, said the same words she just uttered, and told me she'd be warm enough with me beside her.

I blink a few times, feeling my lips tug up at the memory, then slide down the bed and pull her into me. She rests her head on my shoulder like she used to and tangles her legs in mine, slinging an arm over my waist. Within moments, she's fallen back asleep, and mere minutes later I follow her.

***

When I wake up in the morning, my first instinct is to cuddle April. Before opening my eyes, I reach a hand for her, only to find the other side of the bed empty. My eyes snap open and I'm wide fucking awake in the span of a second, because *she's gone*. Abso*fucking*lutely not—I won't let her run this time. The sheets are crinkled and the spot where she slept is still warm, which means she couldn't have gotten far. I will find her, I will drag her gorgeous ass back here, and then I'm going to fuck any sentiments of leaving again right out of her brain. I leap to my feet and pull on a pair of sweatpants, not even bothering with a shirt in my haste as I grab my phone and car keys before rushing out into the living room. There, I stop short at the scent of bacon floating through the air and the sound of sizzling coming from the kitchen. Still somewhat wary that maybe April decided to start a fire before running off, I quickly stride to the entrance of the kitchen.

April's standing at the counter, scrolling through her phone while pouring orange juice into a glass. On the counter before her there's one plate piled high with bacon and another with a stack of fluffy pancakes. She's only wearing my shirt, which is long enough to reach her thighs. Her hair's wet, probably from a shower she took while I was sleeping, and she looks remarkably at home.

She gives me a cursory glance as she caps the juice and tosses it back into my fridge. Her eyes take in the car keys and phone in my hand and her eyebrows quirk, but she doesn't comment. Instead, she says,

"You're gonna need to start keeping a better stocked fridge and pantry if you want me to stay over more often. The pickings were slim. I had to make pancake batter from scratch."

I exhale a deep breath of relief, toss my keys on the counter and pocket my phone, before crossing the distance between us and pulling her into my arms, bending down to steal a kiss. Her hands slide up my shoulders and to the back of my neck. She gives it a squeeze before pulling away.

"Seriously, though, you need to provision if you want me to stick around. I won't do sleepovers if I don't find enough food in the fridge in the morning. Or if I can't find snacks for my occasional 3am munchies."

I nip her bottom lip before taking her mouth again, reminding myself that she's here and I have her. I can never get enough of this girl, and I don't think I ever will. When I've gotten a sufficient taste, I pull back to stare at her. She's so beautiful it makes my chest pang.

"I thought you tried to run off again."

She hums. "Yeah, I considered it, then I figured I might as well stay for now and raid your food supplies—it's the least I deserve after last night. I was not impressed with my findings." When I let out a low growl, she laughs. "We'll see where this goes, Vargas. I'll find out if you're okay in the long term. Consider this a test-drive. If you fuckup, though, I will castrate you and feed you your own dick."

I chuckle. "Fine by me." Then, I lift her up by the waist and set her on the countertop, pulling her shirt—*my shirt*—up to reveal her bare pussy.

"What are you doing?" she asks, her voice a little breathier.

I smile as I crouch down in front of her. "You're not the only hungry one this morning, April." After I've made her come and gotten a sufficient taste of her, I help her carry breakfast to the coffee table in front of the couch. She turns on the TV to a morning news station, while I make coffee for us, then pull her into my side as we drink and eat. Once we're done and we've cleaned up, she checks her phone and says, "Yeah, we gotta get going. I'm already late to warmups."

I plant another kiss on her plush lips, before dressing and carting her out the door, though I'm loathe to separate her even for the day.

Chapter Thirty-Two

April

"Hold on a fucking second," Elia says, holding up a hand. We sit in the campus café, surrounded by noises of coffee machines whirring and other students talking, but Elia seems most interested in my recap—the PG-13 version—of my time with Ian, and subsequent decision to give dating him a try.

"You and Ian are a thing now?" Elia asks, eyebrows raising. "Like, *officially*?"

"That does seem to be kind of out of the blue," Chloe murmurs from beside Elia, tucking her strawberry-blonde hair behind her ear. A fellow dancer in the company and someone who's become a good friend to both me and Eliana, Chloe's now a staple during our coffee dates and library study sessions.

"He's been working towards this for a while, but I recently gave in to him," I clarify. "By recently, I mean last night. The timing felt right, everything felt right, so I decided to go ahead and take the proverbial plunge."

Both Elia and Chloe are silent for several beats, mulling over the information I've just given them. Chloe looks worried and confused, while Elia seems a little brighter about my newfound relationship with Ian, though still uncertain. She knows my drawbacks in dating him better than Chloe does, so I'll need to give her a more detailed explanation of the conversation I had with Ian—or, more accurately interrogation session, though I don't intend to use those exact words—which led to me giving him names of the boys who assaulted me, and him promising vengeance on my behalf.

Although it's daunting to give up control of their fates to him, it's also somewhat liberating. I hadn't realized how much carrying around the knowledge that they're still alive, though unable to harm anyone else the way they tried to harm me, has weighed on me. Now that Ian knows, I very much doubt that those imbeciles will be alive much longer, which is more relieving than I assumed it would be. I thought I was fine with the status quo but knowing that Ian's going to take care of the problem completely is making me realize that I still felt I had unfinished business.

"How do you feel about it?" Elia asks me, meeting my eyes.

I lift a shoulder. "Cautious, but good, I think. I spent so many years at odds with Ian it feels weird to see this caring side of him, but I remember the kinder part of him well enough. When we were best friends as kids, he was very clingy and extremely protective of me. He was also kind and thoughtful in a way he's never been with anyone else." For many years, being the center of his attention morphed into something that I absolutely despised because his attention turned from caring to cruel, but I believe him when he says he won't go back to that. At least, I believe that *he* believes his words—only time will tell the rest.

"If you're for it, then I'm for it," Chloe says slowly. "But I'd be remiss if I didn't point out that Ian's as close to a psychopath as I've ever seen. He and Seth Balor are known as the campus menaces that nobody is willing to cross, because going against them would require a death wish."

"Seth isn't that bad," Elia says.

"To *you*," Chloe emphasizes, giving Elia a pointed look. "Seth is very, *very* good to you because he treasures you. He's changed for you, and he's much different with you than he is with everyone else. Notice how his eyes soften every time the two of you look at each other. Take note of how he's become a lot milder, even with others, since he started pursuing you. My point is that he put effort into changing parts of himself to suit you." Chloe's eyes turn to me and her eyebrows inch up. "Will Ian do the same for you?"

"I don't know that he'll entirely change the way he interacts with those around him for me, but he's certainly different when we're together. He always has been. For a while that meant I was the object of his affection, then that soured into hate, and now it looks like we're back to block one." I try to search for the right words to describe how Ian treats me, how he looks at me. "He treats me like I'm the most important person not just in his life, but in the world. He's attentive to a fault, observant to a fault, and, honestly, a bit obsessed."

"That's how Seth is," Elia says knowingly, nodding. "We all know that people like Seth and Ian aren't quite normal—their brains work differently from most others. I can't speak for Ian, but I know that Seth usually sees people as objects to be maneuvered—me, he sees as a human being. *His* human being that he needs to preserve, protect, and care for. The way he's explained it to me, I think he sees me as part of his life's purpose. Like taking care of me and keeping me happy is fundamentally fulfilling to him."

I'll protect you from everything, even myself. I'll help you be the best you can be. I'll make sure everyone sees you shine the way I know you can. I'll be the person you can trust and fall back on. Be mine, and I'll give you the whole world. Ian's words from weeks ago flash through my mind, prompted by Elia's musings on her own relationship with a deeply unconventional man.

I always noticed that Ian saw other people as objects to be played with, while I was a person. Through our younger years, I was a person he wanted to protect, keep, and be near all the time; then I was a person who represented his sole weakness, so he bullied and ostracized me. Now I'm no longer a weakness to him, rather a treasured person he seeks to keep once again. It's almost endearing in a twisted way. Knowing why he kept me at arm's length and turned on me helps me understand his treatment through high school, but it doesn't make the pain dissipate; it just makes me understand the cause behind his cruel words and actions. I don't know that I've entirely forgiven him, but I do think I can try to look past the bad parts of our history.

"That sounds like a nightmarish fairytale," Chloe murmurs, brows furrowing. "I mean, I certainly see the appeal of being the center of someone's world, but it also sounds like a lot to handle. I respect it as long as it works for the both of you, but I'd much rather have a nice guy who's normal. Having someone obsessed with me would be frightening."

"It's a bit overwhelming, but it's also intoxicating," I muse, thinking of the way Ian looks at me—like I'm the light in his otherwise pitch-black world, his salvation and redemption. His love is somewhat toxic and certainly a lot to bear, but it's also exhilarating.

My phone buzzes with an incoming text from Ian, asking where I am.

I quickly tap out a text informing him that I'm in the campus café. He doesn't respond, so I return to my conversation with Elia and Chloe, this time discussing some minor gossip going on around the dance company. A few minutes later, the door to the café chimes as it opens, and a dark and familiar energy fills the space. I don't need to turn to look at the entrance to know that Ian's here—I've always been able to sense his presence, have always been intensely aware of him. There's something edgy and untamed to his energy.

A moment later, a hand rubs along my bare shoulder before Ian steps into my line of sight, stopping beside the table. He's holding a gorgeous bouquet of unique flowers in his hands—a different arrangement from the one he sent to me on the night of the show a few weeks ago, but one that's no less beautiful and singular. This time the colors are pink, red, and black; a strangely pleasing mix that's at once gothic and feminine. Ian briefly flicks a gaze over Elia and Chloe, drawling a greeting, before holding out the bouquet for me. I stand from my seat, smiling as I take the arrangement.

"Thank you," I say, pressing my nose against the flowers and inhaling their lovely scent. "These are very pretty."

"As are you," Ian says, eyeing the curve of my shoulder. "You changed clothes."

"I didn't feel like wearing my clothes from yesterday, so yes, I changed when I got back to dorms," I tell him, rolling my eyes at the possessiveness stamped across my face. I'm wearing an off-the-shoulder knit sweater that exposes one of my bra straps, and Ian stares at the bared skin for several beats, eyes narrowing before flicking a dark look around the room.

"You're too beautiful," he murmurs, wrapping an arm around my waist. "I don't like how much attention that attracts."

I sigh. "Well, you'll have to get used to it, Vargas. You're the one who pursued me, leaving me with no option but to choose you, if only temporarily."

"Temporarily," Ian repeats, eyes locking with mine. "Is that so?"

"We agreed this was a test drive," I remind him.

He shakes his head. "No, *you* said that it was a test drive, I didn't dispute that for the sake of a pleasant morning. I'm in this for the long haul, April, you already know that."

"Be good and I might just join you on that ride."

"Or I can kidnap you," Ian murmurs, lowering his voice so only I can hear his words and leaning closer to nuzzle my neck. "My gorgeous captive."

Chloe stares at us with wide eyes, alarmed, while Elia's shaking her head, not seeming surprised at our interaction in the least.

"We're going on a little trip," Ian says, pulling back after scraping his teeth down my neck. "Then we'll have dinner."

"I don't remember agreeing to this plan," I reply, reminding him that ordering me around is not going to be an effective mode of communication. I won't fucking allow it.

Ian's lips quirk. "Will you accompany me tonight, Sugarplum? I have fun things planned for our time out and about."

"I suppose I can be benevolent enough to allow—" my words are cut off when Ian lowers his head to slant his lips over mine, eating the words right from my mouth and effectively shutting me up. The kiss is possessive and consuming, as much a show of dominance as it is a claim for any and all in the café to see. If his lips didn't have some sort of drugging power over me, I'd protest the very public display, but as is, all I can do is moan softly into his mouth. My breasts start to ache, nipples pulsing with pain, and my clit begins to throb.

He pulls back with a bite to my bottom lip. "Let's go, April."

"See you two later," Elia says, laughter in her voice. "Be nice to my girl, Ian."

He spares Elia a brief glance. "I'll be very good to *my* girl, Eliana. You worry about the two menaces you managed to tame."

CHAPTER THIRTY-THREE

The last thing I expected of Ian when he promised fun tonight was that he would take me to a high fashion mall. I've made it clear repeatedly that I don't want charity from him, and he's recently let up on pushing the matter, but now it seems we're back to square one.

"No," I say, crossing my arms as I stare out the car window.

"We talked about this. I don't want you buying things for me."

"Your basis was that we aren't together, and that you didn't want to give credence to my bullshit gold digger comments in the past," Ian responds, his tone even. "We both know that I do not see you as a gold digger, and we are together now. I'm going to spoil you, April. I remember that there was a time when you very much enjoyed receiving gifts from me, even when it made you uncomfortable. Now that you're mine—"

"Temporarily," I grouse.

"I have every intention of giving you the world. Starting with clothes. Ones that you don't get from a thrift store because you're too stubborn to accept help. I'll always help you. I'll always be there for you. I'll always make sure you have the best, not because what you have isn't good enough, but because you deserve nothing but the best, Sugarplum. Now, get your ass out of the car and let's head inside. I arranged for a personal shopper to meet and help us."

I shake my head again, feeling deeply uncomfortable. I'm no longer as sore over Ian's taunts about me being a gold digger as I once was, but I am still someone who prizes her independence. Letting Ian do this for me feels a bit like giving up too much of my control to him, of coming to rely on him in ways that I shouldn't.

"I don't want to lose myself," I say, deciding to go for honesty. "I like my clothes. I like working hard for what I have. Giving into you now will set me up for giving into you too much in the future."

To my surprise, Ian laughs. A low chuckle at first, which slowly morphs into loud, amused laughter that echoes through the car.

"April," he says once he's calmed, shaking his head and smiling at me fondly. "You are far too strong to ever have your will overtaken with someone else's, even mine. That's one of the things I love about you. Letting me buy some clothes for you will satisfy me on a primal level and might end up being fun. I remember how much you used to like shopping with your mom."

"That was a long time ago," I say, biting my bottom lip.

Ian lets out a long breath. "If you truly don't want to do this, tell me and we can skip it. I want to do something *for* you, not force you into it. If you feel forced, that negates the point. So tell me if you want to leave and we will. I'll be a bit disappointed and will probably fill your dorm room with flowers to make up for not being able to buy you anything here, but I won't be angry."

His words make me soften slightly, because they demonstrate that this isn't him trying to exert control, it's him trying to be a boyfriend. A rich and privileged boyfriend, but a good one, too.

"Okay," I say after a long moment. "But I'm only getting what I feel like getting, and I want to know the price so I can pay you back later."

"Yes to the first, fuck no to the second," Ian replies. "This is a gift to you, not a tab to be repaid." He stares me right in the eye, daring me to challenge him. After a few tense beats, I acquiesce.

"Fine. Any other stipulations?"

"Just one," Ian says. "When we visit the lingerie store, I'm going to choose a couple things I'll want you to wear for me..."

The mall is high-end, with many luxurious stores. A bright-eyed woman who appears to be in her mid-thirties greets Ian and I in the food court. She spends a few minutes asking me about my preferred styles and sizing me up before beginning to lead us from store to store.

I have to give her this; she has a good eye for style, and she takes my requests into consideration while shopping. She also outfits me for an entire wardrobe, not just a few items—I get everything from summer to winter clothes. Dresses, shirts, blouses, sweaters, skirts, pants, jeans, shoes... I'm embarrassed to think about the tab I run up, especially when Ian refuses to let me see the total at each store and instead just swipes his card.

The lingerie store is the last one that we visit, after we've parted ways with the personal shopper Ian hired. Ian bribes one of the employees to allow him in the dressing room with me, so that I can model borderline scandalous bra and underwear sets, nightgowns, and a few lingerie items for him. He sits on the bench beside the mirror, legs spread, hands clutching his knees so hard his knuckles turn white, watching me dress and undress with the attention of a predator preparing to pounce on its prey. I can see the outline of his erection straining against the front of his jeans, feel my mouth go dry each time he readjusts himself. At this point, I'm not uncomfortable being naked around Ian, though I still feel a bit awkward any time my back is turned towards him and I can feel his eyes on my scars.

"We're taking all of them," he says after I've tried on a strappy black set. "Two pairs."

I pause in reaching for the undergarments I came in wearing, turning to look at Ian. "Why two?"

"Because odds are I'll end up ripping all of them at least once, so you'll need backup," Ian explains, a smirk pulling at his lips. "Don't get dressed yet."

I arch an eyebrow. "Why?"

He rhythmically taps his thigh with a finger, appearing as though he wants to lunge at me and fuck me right up against the wall. "Because I said so. Come here, April." His voice lowers, morphing into a husky baritone that raises goosebumps on my naked flesh and sends a blush crawling up my chest.

"What are you going to do?"

"Come here, and you'll find out." He runs his eyes down the length of my body. "I promise you'll enjoy it."

When I don't move, equal parts intrigued and wary, Ian reaches out to snag my arm, spins me around, and pulls me right onto his lap. He curls an arm around my waist as he spreads my legs to bracket his own, leaving me wide open and shivering as cool air drifts over my pussy.

"Have you enjoyed getting dressed up for me?" he asks, his words little more than a purr. When I don't respond, he says, "Let's find out, shall we?"

Two fingers slide through my folds, and Ian lets out a low hiss. "Judging by how fucking wet you are, I think you have enjoyed this, Sugarplum. That's very good, because I certainly have, as well. We don't have much time, but I want you to come for me, April. Can you do that?"

"I—I don't want anyone else to hear," I stutter, suppressing a moan as his thumb circles my clit.

Ian smirks again. "Then I guess you'll have to promise to be nice and quiet. See, I might have asked you if you want to come, but it's not really a request. *I* want to feel you come, so I will. All you need to do is keep those moans trapped inside." He curls the fingers inside me, thrusting them in and out while continuing to work my clit with his thumb. I'm sore from everything he did to me last night, but the delicious soreness only serves to enhance the experience.

"You're so swollen down here," he says huskily. "So fucking hot, April, I might just go off in my pants. You ready to come, gorgeous girl?"

I nod emphatically, trying to reach his lips with my own. It feels insanely filthy to do this in a public place, where someone could walk in at any moment, but also deeply erotic—the idea of getting caught only pushes me closer to orgasming. Ian accepts my kiss, swallowing my moans as I start to come around his clever, knowing fingers, my body trembling, wishing it was his length inside of me instead of his fingers.

I slump over Ian as my orgasm comes to an end, my breaths coming out in sharp pants, my entire body feeling sluggish and somewhat sated yet not entirely satisfied. I need more; I need all of Ian to achieve completion. *I always have.*

Ian fists my hair, lifts my head, and brings his glistening fingers to my lips. "Open," he growls.

I obey, parting my lips, moaning when he thrusts his fingers inside, rubbing the tangy taste of my arousal over my tongue. He slips his fingers away only to replace them with his own lips, sucking my tongue into his mouth and groaning at my taste.

"Fucking incredible," he says, pulling back and wrapping his arms around me to hold me close. I let him, curling into his chest, absorbing his warmth and breathing deeply.

"I hope you know, April, tonight I'm going to fuck you until you can hardly breathe through the pleasure."

"Why?" I ask, looking into his eyes. "Why do you like making me come so much? It's not a normal thing with guys."

"Have lots of experience to draw from, do you?" Ian says, a testy edge to his voice.

At one time, I might've railed at the implied insult; now, I just roll my eyes and give him a pointed stare. "No more than you."

His lips quirk. "Fair enough, Sugarplum. To answer your question, I like making you orgasm for a wide array of reasons. First of all, it turns you into putty that's easily moldable. Second of all, satisfying you serves to satisfy me on a level I'm unused to. It makes me proud to know how well I've learned you, how readily I can make you reach a crest of pleasure. Third of all, I'll admit that I hope I can get you addicted to my touch. At the very least, I want to make sure that nobody else could compare. That way you'd have a much more difficult time leaving me."

"You're pathological," I murmur, even as a smile stretches my lips. Ian's logic is almost adorable in a twisted way; he's willing to do whatever it takes to keep me and use every method he can think of, no matter how underhanded. The predator in me can certainly respect that.

"I love you, April. I hope that's clear by now. I care about you more than anything in this world—more than myself. You're the most integral part of me, which terrifies me because I live with a moral compass and center of being that exists outside of me. I'll do anything to keep you safe and keep you with me, because I need you."

My eyes flutter closed as his words burrow into my chest and worm their way past my armor and into my heart. It's difficult for me to resist Ian most times but it's simply impossible when he shows vulnerability. When he proves that he's fundamentally human at his core, with all the hopes and fears that accompany humanity.

I lean forward, resting my forehead against his. "I love you too, Ian. I always have, even when I hated you and never wanted to see you again. That's what scares *me;* you hurt me more than anyone else has, yet I couldn't stop loving you. I tried to, really. I thought I did, but the love I've felt for you since we were children... it's always endured. It scares me that I could love you through everything and anything."

Ian tilts his head to the side, pressing another, more tender kiss to my lips, this one less of a dominating possession and more of a plea, a prayer, a silent hope.

Knocks sound on the door, followed by one of the employees asking if everything's alright in here.

"Just fine," I call back, my voice strained. "We're almost done!"

Ian chuckles as we hear the footsteps carrying the attendant away from us. "Looks like it's time for us to go, Sugarplum. In terms of dinner, I can cook, or we can eat out or order in."

"I'm craving pizza, so I don't care where we eat as long as it's on the menu."

Ian nods. "I can accommodate that." He taps my thigh. "Get up, sweetheart, it's time to feed the monster."

A few minutes later, I walk out of the dressing room with my head held high and my chin tilted up, daring anyone to comment on the fact that Ian and I spent an inordinately long time in the dressing room together. It would only take someone with two braincells to figure out exactly what we were doing in there that held us up so long, but thankfully nobody comments.

A woman at the counter rings up the clothing—Ian distracts me with a kiss so I don't see the total and ignores my subsequent grumbling "You can pay me back later," he murmurs as we walk out of the store.

"You make me sound like a whore," I say on a sigh. "I'm not trading sex for clothing."

"Not a whore, but definitely my favorite little slut," Ian says, twining his fingers with mine. Before I can respond, Ian goes entirely still, staring at something—*someone*—in the distance with the sort of glare that could turn them to ash. I follow his line of vision, my eyes coming to rest on a man who's had too much plastic surgery and looks like a poor imitation of Ken, Barbie's male counterpart. It's difficult to determine his age with the amount of Botox filling his face, but if I had to venture a guess, I'd put him somewhere in his fifties or sixties based on the wrinkle lines littering his hands.

Fake Ken notices us, pausing in his conversation with the younger boy beside him as his eyes move between me and Ian, lighting up with something dark and malevolent.

"*Fuck*," Ian mutters. "Not here—not now."

"Who is that—" I cut off halfway through my question, realization dawning. Ian told me that Carson's uncle, Dennis, the very man who ripped any semblance of childhood and youth from Ian, was in town. Instinct, along with Ian's reaction, tells me that we're staring at him right now. *Fuck, indeed.*

Chapter Thirty-Four

Dennis says something to the young man he's speaking with that causes the boy to scurry away, then smoothly makes his way towards us. Ian's grip on my hand turns painful, but I don't berate him or say anything; I'm not sure how I'm supposed to conduct myself during this interaction, but the anger that starts burning in my chest is violent and demands action. I feel an overwhelming need to stab Dennis with the nearest sharp object and watch him bleed out on the floor; I'm furious on Ian's behalf, furious at what Dennis did to my boyfriend in a time when he should've been carefree and enjoying life.

"Ian," Dennis says, coming to a stop in front of us. "Lovely to see you out in the wild. Who's this?"

"April," I answer coolly, looking at Dennis like he's a shit stain on the bottom of my shoe. "You're Carson's uncle, right? Carson's girlfriend mentioned that you were sent into town to... what was it? Right, uh, *oversee* the business here." There's a distinct mocking edge to my words, and Dennis's cheek's heat.

"Yes, I was sent to take a closer look at progress, which has been lagging," Dennis responds tensely.

"So that's why you were at the mall, talking to that boy," Ian purrs dangerously. "How old is he?"

"Legal, I assure you," Dennis growls, reaching up to tug at his tie in what I suspect is a nervous tell.

If Ian's willing to make that comment in front of me, I assume he doesn't mind if Dennis deduces that I know what he did to Ian all those years ago, so I decide to go with it.

"That comes as a surprise," I murmur, raising my eyebrows.

Dennis coughs. "I was simply offering to give him some pointers. He goes to Greywood, as well. Business major, though not part of the program. I'm considering giving him a job at the company."

"As long as you run it by Carson first, since he gets the final say for all hires," Ian says.

"Forgive my rudeness, I haven't introduced myself to your companion," Dennis says, turning a beady gaze on me. "I'm Dennis Ajax, Carson's uncle."

"I've heard plenty about you," I assure him lowly. "You're the one who loves beaches, right? Especially late at night."

Ian lets out a low snort, rubbing his thumb over mine in a silent gesture of support.

This time, Dennis's expression turns to one of anger rather than discomfort. "Well, I don't know exactly what you've heard, but I actually prefer the temperature-controlled indoors."

"Of course you do," Ian says darkly. "What can I do for you, Dennis? I'm enjoying a day with my girl."

"Enjoying it quite a bit, I can see," Dennis says, eyes dropping to the bag Ian holds, which is labeled with the name of the lingerie store. The rest of our shopping bags have already been taken to Ian's car, but this one is pretty damning. I refuse to be embarrassed in front of this motherfucker, though—I'm not the one who gets off on assaulting little boys.

"What we do in our free time is our own business, right?" Ian says, his anger palpable. "I'm sure you of all people would defend that viewpoint."

"Of course," Dennis agrees. "Lovely to see you both, I do hope you have a nice evening."

Ian's silent as we watch Dennis stroll away; silent as he leads me over to the emergency staircase, away from the monster he just faced off with. Silent as we get in his car and still silent even once we get to his apartment. I don't say anything or push him to speak; I believe he will once he's ready to, and I don't feel a need to force him.

He only speaks when he calls a local pizzeria and places an order—after that, he joins me on the couch and pulls me onto his lap, nuzzling his nose to the back of my neck, breathing me in.

"You okay?" I ask gently, unable to hold my tongue any longer.

"You defended me," he murmurs. "I could feel your anger on my behalf."

A frown knits my brows. "Of course I was angry on your behalf, Ian. Dennis is a fucking monster who deserves to burn in this world and the next. I wasn't just going to stand there silently; I wanted him to know you have support."

"And now he does," Ian says, brushing a kiss over my neck. "The flip side is that you might've unintentionally made yourself a target for him, April. That's not good. There's a chance he'll try to come after you in order to get to me."

I release a soft puff of laughter, leaning back into Ian. "He can certainly try. Like many, he'll come to find that I'm not an easy target."

"No, you aren't," Ian agrees softly. "And I'm never going to let any harm come to you. Nobody gets to hurt you. If they try, I will kill them in the most painful way I can think of."

His words should scare me, but instead they perversely endear me. I know Ian's love isn't traditional, cuddly, or sweet; it's callous, borderline cruel, and insanely possessive. His willingness to kill for me is also his form of affection, of preserving me.

"I believe you," I assure him. "I also want to string Dennis up by his balls, if he actually has any."

I feel Ian's chuckle rumble against my back, sending a shiver through me. "I'm sure you do, April, but I'll probably beat you to it."

Several minutes pass in stark silence. I can feel Ian's tension, feel his pain as though it's my own. I want to face the world on his behalf so he doesn't have to. I want to do whatever it takes to protect him, make him feel better.

"What can I do?" I ask him quietly.

"Put on one of those silly Disney movies you love so much. Sing. And stay on my lap. This is helping," Ian responds, reaching to the side to grab the TV remote from where it rests on the couch cushion.

I obey, turning on Mulan, relaxing into Ian's hold, and humming along with the movie as I always do. Our pizza arrives a few scenes into the movie; we set it up on the table in front of us. Ian feeds me slice by slice from his hands before eating himself, then returns to cuddling me like I'm the only solace to be found in a world of horror.

Once the movie's over and I'm full, Ian turns me around on his lap so I'm straddling him and pulls my shirt over my head.

"I'm going to fuck you now, April," he says. "Play with this gorgeous body until I'm satisfied. It'll be a lot. Can you handle it?"

I arch an eyebrow at him. "I'm pretty good at handling you."

"Yes, but I know you're sore," Ian says lowly. "Even with the salve I used, you've still got to be feeling what I did last night. I'm telling you right now that I won't take it easy on you. Can you take it? If not, we can cuddle and go to sleep."

I shake my head. "I can take it."

Ian's eyes glimmer with satisfaction. "Good. I want you to wear something for me. Wait here."

He picks me up from his lap as if I'm weightless and sets me on the couch beside him, then disappears into the bedroom while I hum with anticipation. I have no doubt that Ian will go hard on me tonight because of our encounter with Dennis, and I'd be lying if I said I wasn't looking forward to it. I like it when he loses control with me, even if that can feel like it's pushing me to the edge of what I can bear.

Ian returns a moment later with a strappy contraption hanging from his hand—I can't make out exactly what it is or where it goes, but it looks exceptionally kinky.

"Stand up and take off your bra," he tells me.

Throat clicking as I swallow, I follow his instructions, rising to my feet and flicking the clasp of my bra open before pulling it off. Ian's eyes darken as he stares at my breasts, approaching me slowly, drinking up every inch of me with his gaze. My nipples harden under his gaze, and I feel a flush creep over my chest.

Ian unfolds whatever he's holding, stepping forward. "Hold out your arms."

I comply, and he slips some of the straps up my arms and over my shoulders, then begins the process of fastening the contraption around me. It quickly becomes clear what it is; a harness. Circular strips of leather hug my breasts, connecting to a collar around my throat at the top, with a band below that runs along my ribs and fastens at my back. It's tight though not painful, and erotic as hell.

I make a noise of surprise when Ian pulls one of my arms behind my back and winds a loose strap from the harness over it, effectively trapping it behind me. He repeats the motion with my other arm, leaving them folded behind my back, hands clutching at my opposite biceps.

He circles me, surveying his handywork, eyes flaring with arousal and interest along with a dark sort of appreciation. "Now that," he says, stopping in front of me, "is a gorgeous fucking sight." He reaches up to run a finger along the metal ring that hangs off the front of my collar, lips quirking. "If you ever try to run from me, Sugarplum, I'm going to put you in this harness, then attach a leash here. Keep you as my pretty little pet, collared and chained."

The feminist in me screams her protest; the rest of me just about faints with the erotic picture he paints.

Ian tugs off my jeans and panties, then also undresses himself, before once again hooking a finger over the ring of my collar and pulling me onto his lap as he sinks down to the couch. One of his hands delves between my thighs, and he hums with approval when he finds just how wet I am.

"Looks like you're ready to be fucked," he murmurs. "That's good, because I'm not sure I have the patience for foreplay right now. That harness is too fucking hot. Do you like the way it feels?"

I nod, letting out a low moan as he starts to move my hips over his hard length, making the tip of his cock slide over my folds and clit again and again until my wetness starts dripping down his length, coating him.

"One of the strongest people I know likes getting tied up and fucked like a dirty little slut," Ian muses, studying my face as my brows pinch with pleasure and my breaths turn into pants. "I love that more than you'll ever know."

Finally, he starts lowering my hips over his length. He was right; I am sore from last night, but the soreness and the usual stretch of accommodating his girth adds a delicious pain to the pleasure. My nails dig into my arms as I jerk at the cuffs holding them in place, trying to grip something to find purchase but unable to. He has the upper half of me mostly immobilized, and my entire body totally subject to his mercy, of which there is none.

"Good fucking girl," he growls once I'm fully impaled on him. He cups my breasts in his hands, running his thumbs over my nipples, smiling at my wince. I'm sore there more than anywhere else on my body; probably because of how he relentlessly smacked them with a crop last night during a brutal interrogation that I never had a chance of withstanding.

He leans down to lick a path along the swell of my breast, tongue running over the straps, before drawing one of my nipples into his mouth. My back arches and my head falls at the sensation of his hot, wet mouth sucking at the stiff, sore peak; the collar doesn't allow me to go far, keeping my head upright, forcing me to watch him. His eyes are closed with abandon as his hands skim up and down my sides before gripping my waist and starting to move me up and down his length. Slowly, at first, but then with increasing speed.

The position allows for very little agency or control from me; all I can do is sit here, mostly limp, and allow him to maneuver me how he wishes. Ian's eyes open as he switches over to my other nipple, giving it equal amounts of attention, while teasing the first one by pinching it between his index finger and thumb at varying pressures. His eyes blaze at whatever he sees in my face—submission, probably, along with mounting pleasure. He hasn't touched my clit yet, though I don't even know if I'll need him to; this is erotic enough that I might just come without any additional stimulation.

Ian bites down on my nipple so hard that I let out a cry of pain, which morphs into a shriek when he pinches my other nipple, *hard*.

"Shh, you can take it," he says, releasing my nipple with a pop and leaning forward to brush a kiss against my lips, pairing the kiss with a particularly brutal thrust. "You can take all of it, can't you?"

Even though tears are prickling my eyes, I manage to nod.

"Say it," Ian demands. "Tell me you can take anything I have to give."

"I can take anything you have to give," I cry, my voice pitched low and guttural.

"That's right," Ian agrees. "And why is that, April?"

My only response is a low moan as he reaches down to roll his thumb over my clit, while continuing to control me with his other hand holding my waist, pushing me up and down his length in time to his thrusts.

Ian leans forward until his lips are right by my ear. "Because you're mine. Aren't you?"

"I am," I say on a sob, feeling my orgasm creep up on me. The harness, Ian's thrusts, the action on my clit, and Ian's words all combine and rush to my head, making me feel like I'm high while I think my body just might explode.

"Very good," Ian allows, leaning down to nuzzle my breasts. "I want you to come, April. Fall apart around me."

He sucks my nipple back into his mouth, and bites it again; my orgasm crashes into me, consuming and blinding, the pleasure washing through every limb, muscle, and nerve ending. My entire body tingles and pulses with the force of my release while my pussy clenches around Ian's length sporadically.

"*Fuck*," Ian growls, a moment before I feel the telling twitch of his length inside me as he also finds his release. All the strength seeps out of my body; I fall forward, head thudding against his gleaming chest, body relaxing, not even bothering to wriggle my bound arms, though I do wince a little as my extra sore nipples scrape against Ian's toned torso.

After a few minutes of both of us catching our breaths, I ask Ian, "Can I have my arms back now?"

He presses a kiss to my head. "I like that you're asking, but no. I didn't mean to come so soon—I'm nowhere near done with you yet, April."

CHAPTER THIRTY-FIVE

Several weeks pass as Ian and I settle into our new normal. We still spend evenings together whenever we can manage, though Ian no longer minds when we have a night or two apart during the week. My agreement to be his girlfriend makes him relax in his domineering pursuit, which allows us to fall into a comfortable routine of meeting up most nights a week, hooking up whenever and wherever we can manage, and texting several times a day to fill the gaps. My weekends are unfailingly spent at his apartment, where he spoils me with food, random gifts, gorgeous bouquets of flowers, and so many orgasms I sometimes pass out after our sex.

On the weekend that marks the start of spring break, Ian makes one last attempt to get me to agree to go to Scotland with him. I'm steadfast as ever in my refusal. Even though I'm giving us a chance and steadily becoming more comfortable in our relationship, I'm not yet willing to let him take me to a foreign country on an all-expenses-paid trip. It's too much, too soon. Since our joint family skiing vacation was cancelled in light of my mother's pregnancy, we both stay in-state for the break.

He keeps me as a virtual prisoner in his apartment, though I stay willingly. We have more sex than I ever thought was possible, cuddle, watch movies that range from Disney to rom-coms to thriller and horror movies, order in all of our meals and spend ample amounts of time just bathing in each other's presence.

I learn some new things about Ian; his favorite color has changed from black to amber, inspired by the color of my eyes. His favorite food is a burger, and his favorite drink is whiskey, especially when he drinks it off of my body. He likes to spend his free time digging into the lives of his work competitors to find blackmail to use against them. His favorite pastime, aside from sex with me, is surfing the internet for conspiracy theories.

"Why conspiracy theories?" I ask him one night as we sit on the couch and share a bowl of popcorn while The Nightmare Before Christmas plays on the TV in front of us. I feed Ian a piece of popcorn, feeling everything inside me tighten as he darts out his tongue to lick my fingers before I pull my hand away. I clear my throat. "I mean, what do you get out of them?"

"Learning about them is fun. I research random theories on the surface web, then I dig deeper to find out which ones are true and which are bullshit," Ian replies, watching as I pop a few pieces of popcorn into my mouth. "There are some that I could've sworn were real, but weren't, and some that I thought were total crap, but turned out to be true."

I feel my eyebrows furrow. "Do I even want to know how you figure out the truth? Or which theories are valid? Actually, I don't, so never mind."

Ian gives me a look of mock surprise. "What, you don't want to know if the illuminati is real?"

I shake my head. "Absolutely not. Knowing things I shouldn't could make me a person of interest on all the wrong radars, and honestly, I'd rather avoid that. You're welcome to research whatever you want, just don't get me involved with it. I'd prefer to be clueless and safe instead of knowledgeable and threatening when it comes to the eyes of the government."

Ian's smile is equal parts fond and amused. He leans forward, pressing his lips against mine in a brief kiss, and says, "My clever girl. You're right that knowing less is a good way to get the blanket safety of being a nobody in the eyes of those that matter, but if you're careful, nobody will know what *you* know, so you can still plead ignorance."

"I'd prefer not to risk it," I say, lips brushing against his with each word. "Now, shut up and let me watch the movie—Jack and Sally are a fantastic pairing, although Jack takes way too long to get his head out of his ass."

Ian pulls me close, nearly tipping over the bowl of popcorn sitting on my lap, and tucks his nose into my hair, inhaling deeply. I set the popcorn aside and wrap my arms around his torso, breathing him in, enjoying his masculine scent that carries with it a whiff of fresh ocean breeze. His warmth surrounding me staves off the chill from the cracked open balcony door, and I feel so safe, so comfortable in his presence that a memory of our childhood flashes through my mind.

***

April, age eleven

"It's too cold out!" I hiss at Ian, even while my eyes linger on the sky. The glittering stars are so gorgeous and inviting, I wish I could fly up into their embrace, get close to them, become part of the universe.

"That's why I'm going to rekindle this fire, and we're going to cuddle up for warmth," Ian responds calmly, keeping my hand firmly held in his as he leads me to the firepit our families used for smores earlier. We're all sharing a large cabin for our ski trip this year, and our parents have long since gone to sleep.

Ian and I have bedrooms on different floors, and both of our beds are too small to accommodate two people—something I suspect my father orchestrated after finding Ian in my bed last year—so I can't cuddle with Ian like I usually do when our families vacation together. Naturally, Ian's response to this is to spend a few hours outside with me, where we can stargaze in peace away from the watchful eye of my overprotective father.

Sharing a bed during vacations is our sacred hang-out; when our parents are asleep, we always join each other in one of our beds to talk into the early hours of the morning. Since we can't do that in bed tonight, we'll be doing it outside, as long as Ian actually manages to get the fire going so that I don't get too cold. I like the cold in general, but only when I'm prepared to withstand it.

To my delight, Ian successfully makes a fire not five minutes later; then he sneaks back into the cabin to grab some leftover smores supplies, and we roast marshmallows by the fire for hours, eating until I'm too stuffed to move, then sitting on a log together with his arm around my shoulders and my head burrowed into his chest.

"What do you think the meaning of life is?" I ask, feeling my eyes droop with exhaustion.

"The meaning of life itself? No clue," Ian murmurs. "The meaning of my life? You."

***

The ringing of a phone pulls me from my memory and back into the present, startling me so much I nearly jump out of my skin. Ian glances at me before leaning towards the coffee table and picking up my phone, handing it over to me.

The call is coming from my father, which is unusual, considering it's already ten pm. I click the button to answer the call, holding it up to my ear as I greet, "Hey, Papa. How are you?"

"Milaya," Dad responds, his tone tense. "There's a complication with your mother's pregnancy. We're at the hospital, and I've just been informed that there's a chance she needs to be put into induced labor for both her and the baby's sake."

His words hit me with the impact of a freight train; my entire body stiffens at the blow, just before fine tremors start to work their way through my limbs, the only outward indicator that something's wrong. There are a million questions I want to ask—more than anything, I'm desperate to speak to my mom and ensure that she's alive and well—but I can tell both from my father's tone and his explanation of the situation that Mom probably isn't available to talk on the phone right now. Not when both her life and the life of my unborn sibling hang in the balance.

"She's only twenty-eight weeks pregnant," I whisper, aghast. "Is that... will that be..."

"Enough? I don't know. Nothing's certain right now, April," Dad snaps. A moment later, he softens, saying, "I'm sorry, milaya."

"Don't be," I reply, standing from the couch, ignoring Ian's questioning look. "I'll get on the first flight home. Hopefully I'll be there in a few hours. I'll send you all the details once I get to the airport."

"No, milaya, do not interrupt your break—"

"I'll send you my flight details as soon as I get them," I repeat, more firmly. "Kiss Mom for me, please keep me updated by text. Hopefully I'll have Wi-Fi in flight, so I can keep in contact with you."

Dad lets out a long sigh—then the muted sounds of his voice speaking to someone else sound over the line, before he's back with me. "Labor is about to be induced. I need to go, I'll text you everything as it happens. I love you, milaya." He hangs up with a resounding click that sounds strangely reminiscent of a nail being hammered into a coffin.

I look at Ian, feeling my heart pound in my chest with such intensity I'm surprised it doesn't burst out like a cartoon character's. "I need to get to Connecticut, *now*. Mom's in early induced labor, Dad's freaking out—"

"Say no more," Ian interrupts, standing and pulling his phone from the pocket of his sweats. "I'll book us the first flight out. Go change and pack a duffle bag for both of us."

I hesitate. "Ian, you don't have to come with me."

He casts me a dubious glance that asks, *are you kidding me?* "Of course I'll come with you, April. Your family is important to you, so they're important to me. *Go*, get our stuff together, we can figure everything else out on the way to the airport.

I don't argue any further; I don't have the emotional bandwidth to. While I stuff clothes into a large duffle bag, Ian books a flight for us. As soon as I exit the bedroom, armed with the duffle bag and my backpack, Ian says, "I got us the red-eye. First class tickets. It takes off in just under ninety minutes, let's get our asses to the airport."

Feeling my lips wobble with my smile, I say, "Thank you."

Ian breaks every traffic rule imaginable on our way to the airport; it's a miracle that we don't get pulled over by the cops. Somehow, we make it through TSA and to the gate with half an hour to spare before our flight. There, Ian leaves me seated in front of the gate while he runs to get us food for the flight. I'm not sure I can eat anything right now, I'm too keyed up, too terrified at the thought of what Mom might be going through right now, fearing that by the time the plane lands either she or my sister might be gone, *or both*.

"Here," Ian says, plopping down in the seat beside me and dropping a plastic bag on my lap.

I blink several times, managing to temporarily clear away thoughts of the worst-case scenario in favor of focusing on his purchased goods. I open the bag and peek inside, feeling my heart clench when I see Flaming Hot Cheetos and Sour Patch kids, along with a handful of other goodies which used to be my favorite snacks to share with Ian on our shared vacations.

"You have to stop being so sweet," I say, my voice coming out choked up. "I don't know how much of this my heart can handle."

"You can handle it," Ian replies, his voice faintly amused.

Ian reaches into the bag and grabs a pair of *chopsticks* that I hadn't noticed—another blast from the past for us. I learned from my mom to always eat chips and other messy snacks with chopsticks, so that I don't get my hands dirty. I don't know where Ian even got the chopsticks—maybe from the Japanese restaurant I glimpsed while rushing towards the gate—but the gesture is profound and meaningful, because it tells me beyond a shadow of a doubt that he hasn't forgotten a single thing from our youth. He's remembered everything, right down to the way I like to eat my junk food.

Ian rips open the bag of flaming hot Cheetos, grabs one with his chopsticks, and holds the deliciously unhealthy snack up to my mouth. Although I'm not hungry, I part my lips, accepting his offering and crunching away.

"Any word from your dad?" he asks.

I shake my head. "Last I heard, he was scrubbing up to go into the birthing room—they induced labor, it's the best chance for my mom. As for my sister, it's a coin toss whether or not she'll survive."

"Everything will be okay," Ian says, sounding so certain that I wish I could bottle up his confidence and drink it like an elixir, saving myself from the current sea of *what if's* plaguing me.

I don't know what chances are that the birth will go well for both Mom and the baby, and I'm too much of a coward to google it. I wish I could pick up the phone and dial my mom; last I spoke to her was two days ago, when I told her and Dad that I was going to spend the weekend with Ian. She was excited at the news, though sad that I'd refused his offer to take me to Scotland. She has so much hope when it comes to my relationship with my childhood sweetheart, it's almost inspiring.

"How do you know?" I whisper. "I can't know that. What if... what if I never..." I break off as a sob claws its way up my throat. "What if I never talk to her again, Ian? What if I never hear her voice? What if..."

"Shh," Ian hushes, setting aside the junk food and chopsticks before picking me up by my waist and settling me on his lap. I curl up like a child, not caring that we're in the middle of a public airport as I twine my arms around his neck to hold him close.

"I knew the pregnancy was dangerous, but I didn't know it could take my *mom* from me," I whimper into his ear, trying to keep my voice down. "What will I do if she's gone? She can't *not* be okay, she's the strongest woman I know. She's wiped my tears, held me while I cried, been there through everything..."

"I know," Ian soothes, rubbing a hand up and down my back. "I know, April. You need to trust that her strength, the strength you've observed your entire life, the very same strength that shines so brightly it's even enough to impress *me*, will prevail. Your mom is so damn strong. She'll make it through this. In a few hours, we'll be on the ground in Connecticut, and you'll be able to get real-time updates. Modern medicine is so advanced, Sugarplum, it's what made *your* complicated birth possible."

His reminder of the difficulties surrounding my birth—a moment where it wasn't certain whether or not I'd live—temporarily brings me out of my turmoil and reminds me that Mom's done this before. I was born eight weeks prematurely; the way Dad tells it, I took ten years off his life, but I also added a whole lot of purpose to it. If I made it, my sister can make it, too. Granted, there's a difference between eight weeks early and *twelve* weeks early, but I have to hold out hope. I have to believe that strong genetics, or perhaps the Russian blood Dad always compliments me for having, will be enough for my little sister to pull through. I also know the strength of my mom, so I shouldn't doubt her. She's walked through fire before and come out stronger than ever, I believe she'll be able to walk through fire again.

"Boarding's starting," Ian murmurs in my ear. "Let's get going, Sugarplum. We'll be at the hospital in no time."

The plane ride is agonizing, though it's just an hour and a half—as soon as we land, Ian ushers us to the car he rented, and once again breaks every speeding law known to man in a bid to get us to the hospital. Fortunately, the traffic is practically nonexistent thanks to the late hour, but each mile we travel ratchets up my anxiety.

I snap at Ian numerous times over the most menial things, just as I did on the plane—*why is the AC so cold? Why are you breathing so loud? Could you be any more fucking annoying?* Each time, he strokes a hand over my arm, not crediting my antics with a verbal response. I know as well as he does that I'm being utterly ridiculous, but during one of the most stressful nights of my life, I can't help it.

Finally, after what seems like a lifetime instead of a few hours, we make it to the hospital. Ian swiftly parks the car in a nearly empty parking lot; together, we run towards the entrance, bursting through the glass double doors and startling the receptionist.

"Stein," I tell her, panting as I rush up to her counter. "My mom's in induced labor, my dad's there to support. Is everything okay? Where do I go?"

The receptionist blinks slowly before returning her attention to the screen, typing away at the keyboard for a moment before saying, "Sixth floor, wing B. I don't have access to status updates, but one of the nurses there should be able to read you in. Best of luck, Ms. Stein."

Chapter Thirty-Six

I forgo the elevator, instead choosing to sprint up the stairs. By the time Ian and I get to the birthing wing of the hospital, we're out of breath, jetlagged even from the short flight, and completely exhausted, but anxiety and adrenaline keep me going. As for him, I think what keeps *him* going is the need to make sure that *I'm* okay.

"Ah, Ms. Stein," the receptionist of the birthing wing greets with a nod when I give her my name. "Your father said he was expecting you. I'll page a nurse to come speak with you for details; as far as I know, the labor is going well, and both Mom and the baby's vitals are good. Have a seat in the waiting area—you can grab coffee from one of the vending machines."

I ignore the nurse's underlying suggestion that I look tired as shit; the only words that matter are *that Mom and baby's vitals are good*. I fall into one of the uncomfortable, blue-padded chairs of the waiting room, leaning close to Ian as he wraps an arm around me. We don't get to sit for more than a few minutes before a nurse wearing scrubs comes out to greet us. I leap up from my seat and hurry towards her, holding my breath while waiting for her to deliver news.

"Ms. Stein," she greets, nodding at me. "Your mom is okay, though I'm sure she's burst at least one of your dad's eardrums and bruised his hand with her grip. Unfortunately, we can't yet be sure of the state of the baby. It does appear that we're nearing the end of labor, so you should have news within the hour. Sit tight." She pauses before adding, "Your father wanted to pass on a heartfelt thank you for getting here so quickly. I'll keep you updated as best as I can between my rounds."

As she strolls away, I return to my seat and fall into it, heart racing. "Mom's okay, for now," I tell Ian. "But I don't know about the baby." I give my head a shake, inhaling a deep breath. "I haven't gotten any presents for my sister yet to celebrate her birth; I was planning to after break. I should get some, but what if she's..." I swallow the knot in my throat. "Stillborn?"

"I have an order for your sister ready to be fast tracked and delivered within two days as soon as we get news," Ian informs me. "I did some shopping while you were freaking out on the airplane. Enlisted my mom, too—by the way, my parents are ready to come here as soon as we know which way the delivery's gone."

"Thank you," I say, leaning towards Ian to give him a watery kiss. "Thank you for dealing with my insanity, for bringing me here, for being so calm... I don't think I could do this without you."

"You'll never have to do anything without me again, Sugarplum," Ian responds. "I'm here for you. I'll always be here for you, whether you want me or not. I'm yours as much as your mine, forever."

I scoot into his lap, leaning against him, taking solace in the beating of his heart as I wait to hear about the fate of both my mother and sibling. I know that things can change in a heartbeat; everything can take a turn towards the worst for Mom just as easily as it could for the baby, and that frightens me. Ian's strength is exactly what I need to stay present and grounded.

It's an hour before the same nurse returns. I leap off Ian's lap like he's on fire, rushing up to her, feeling everything inside me tense as I wait for whatever it is she has to say. Her expression is somber, which makes me think that things might not have worked out the way I'd hoped they would. My stomach drops and my chest aches as I stare at her.

"Ms. Stein..." She trails off, looking down at the clipboard she carries. Meeting my eyes, she says, "Let me be the first to congratulate you. You have a little sister. Three pounds, two ounces, ten fingers and toes. She's remarkably well-developed for such an early birth. Both she and Mom are healthy and well..." The rest of her words are drowned out by the sheer force of my relief.

A sob works its way up my throat as tears sting my eyes, and the adrenaline of the last hours that's made me feel like I'm standing on the edge of a sheer cliff, wind whipping my face and stomach plummeting with an impending fall, all leaves me in a rush. I nearly tip over at the emotional crash that follows the high of anxiety I've been kept in the grips of; Ian appears beside me just in time, wrapping an arm around my waist to steady me.

"How is she?" I manage to ask, my voice coming out wobbly and choked up with emotion. "My sister? Is she stable? Does she need to be sent to the NICU?"

The nurse shakes her head. "No. She's doing very well, is able to breathe on her own and has even begun nursing. She's definitely on the small side and might need additional help keeping her body warmth in a healthy range, so we'll keep her here for a while, but aside from that everything's better than expected. To be honest, I've heard talk that your sister seems closer to thirty or even thirty-two weeks instead of just twenty-eight. Freya's certainly a fighter."

"Freya," I repeat, a smile pulling at my lips. It seems appropriate that my little sister would be named after the Norse goddess of love, beauty, and war. Her survival alone is incredible; the fact that she doesn't need to be incubated or put on a ventilator is miraculous.

"Can I go in to see my parents and Freya?" I ask the nurse.

She nods. "Yes. Right now, we're only going to allow visitation from immediate family—you'll need to scrub up and suit up to keep any germs away from the little one. Follow me."

I look to Ian, who's lips are tilted up with a smile. "Go meet your sister," he tells me. "I'll stay here and place the orders we talked about. My parents should get here soon, as well."

"Thank you," I tell him. Since receiving the initial phone call from my dad, I've snapped at Ian more times than I can count and have behaved ridiculously thanks to my stress. He showed up for me when I needed him to, remained undeterred in the face of my mild hysteria induced by fear, and kept both a proverbial and physical arm around me throughout the very long, very dark night.

"I'll see if you and your parents can come meet her soon," I say softly.

Ian's brows knit together. "I'm not family."

"Yes," I disagree, looking him in the eye. "You are. You're my family."

Ian's eyes widen as he realizes the underlying meaning of my words—my total acceptance of him, letting go of the so-called test drive stage we're in—and a suspicious shimmer starts to shine in them. He inclines his head, Adam's apple bobbing as he swallows.

I turn and follow the nurse through the linoleum hallways lit by fluorescent overhead lights. It takes fifteen minutes for me to change into scrubs and wash my hands until they're raw and stinging, and then I'm let into Mom's private suite.

There's a TV mounted on a far wall, a window with cracked blinds and a few chairs sitting beneath it, and a hospital bed situated against the back wall. My mom lies on the bed, cradling a tiny bundle of life wrapped in blankets in her arms. She looks exhausted but jubilant as she stares at the newest member of our family, a soft smile tilting up the sides of her lips.

Dad sits beside her in a chair, one hand on her shoulder, also staring at little Freya with an expression of wonder. Both of them look up when I enter the room. Mom's eyebrows furrow as she looks me over.

"April, you're supposed to be in Vermont—what are you doing here?"

Apparently, Dad didn't bother telling her that I arrived—understandable, considering she's had one hell of a long night.

"I came as soon as Papa called," I say quietly, slowly walking over to the bed until I stand beside Mom. I peer down at Freya, who's so tiny that she almost looks like a little doll, especially with her lips parted and eyes closed.

"You didn't have to come," Mom says, frowning. "I know you wanted a peaceful spring break at school—"

"Mom," I cut her off. "I wouldn't miss this for anything. Ian's in the waiting room, too, he came with me. His parents will be here soon."

Mom and Dad exchange a glance of bewilderment, but I sense an undercurrent of pleasure.

"Well, in that case, I'd like to introduce you to your little sister, Freya Stein," Mom murmurs, proudly smiling at her baby.

"She's so beautiful," I murmur. As if she heard my praise, Freya wriggles a bit in her blankets, a faint cough escaping her before her eyes blink open and fix right on me. They're a warm amber color—the same as mine and Mom's. She blinks a few times as we stare at each other, both of us in awe. Me at this gorgeous creature that survived against the odds; her at the strange, large human staring down at her.

Her lips purse with what seems to be contemplation, before a slow, soft smile spreads on them, and everything inside me melts at the sight. The smile only lasts for a few moments before it morphs into a scowl, and then her mouth opens wide right before a loud screech escapes her.

"Someone's hungry," Papa observes. "Feed her, *solnyshko*, I'm going to go find a cup of coffee. April?"

"Will you be okay here?" I ask Mom. She's had an immeasurably difficult night, yet she looks calm and fulfilled despite the dark smudges under her eyes.

"Just fine. You two go ahead, I'd like some time alone with my newest daughter."

"Already playing favorites, I see," I say with a smile. "That's okay. I think Freya's my favorite, too."

Dad wraps his arm around my shoulders as we leave the room together. Once we're out, away from Mom's ears, I ask, "Everything's okay with Freya and Mom? No complications?"

"None whatsoever, to everyone's surprise," Papa responds. "They're both very, very strong. The birth was the most difficult part; the doctors are shocked by Freya's vitality." He shakes his head with a proud smile. "It's probably the Russian blood that protected her, just like it protected you when you were born. Now, we stay here for a few days to observe. Your mother and Freya will be discharged once the little one's grown a bit. Of course, we now have to get a whole slew of things in order—we were only halfway through decorating the nursery, hadn't even started buying clothes or toys."

"Ian enlisted his mom to help with that," I tell Dad. "We'll take care of it. Focus on Mom and Freya."

We follow overhead signs to the nearest coffee and sandwich shop, which should just be opening for the morning. Despite the early hour, activity in the hospital is already picking up; we pass several nurses, doctors, and other people in the halls, most of whom walk with purposeful strides and expressions of focus.

"So, things with Ian are serious, then," Dad says, switching gears. "They must be, with how he accompanied you here and is, apparently, helping us. That boy wouldn't help anyone unless it directly benefitted him."

"He would for me. He *is* for me. You should've seen and heard me the last few hours, Papa, I was hysterical. I yelled at him for breathing too loud, along with a whole bunch of other ridiculous things. He held me while I cried and shook with worry, took my mood swings in stride. It's been a long night for all of us, and I made his a hellish one, but he didn't blink. Didn't take anything personally. He booked us first class tickets, took care of the car rental—did everything so that we wouldn't have to and could focus on Mom and Freya."

Dad's silent for a long while after I speak. We join the cue of people waiting in line in front of a little coffee shop, which stands in a pocket of space in the large hallway.

"I see," Dad finally says. "It appears he has changed for you. It's about time."

CHAPTER THIRTY-SEVEN

I don't know that Ian will ever *change*, but he's certainly a different person when it comes to me. The rest of the world is a chessboard to him; all the people in it are pawns for him to play with.

I'm not a pawn, though. Even when I spent years thinking that I'd been reduced to a pawn for him to push around and torture, that was never the case. I was always the queen. For a while he saw me as the white queen to his black king—I was a threat to eliminate—but he's come to his senses. I'm his queen, regardless of the color, and I want to stay that way.

I've been so afraid of giving Ian my heart again and risking the possibility that he might break it, I didn't even consider the idea that he might instead dedicate himself to guarding and preserving it. The words he spoke to me a few weeks ago float across my mind: *You're the most integral part of me, which terrifies me because I live with a moral compass and center of being that exists outside of me.*

I can now see that the reverse is also true. He is the part of me that I desperately need, too. He's the strength, the conviction, the monster to protect me. I can play at being a monster myself just fine, but being monstrous in nature is Ian's strength and his burden. Together, we balance each other out; separately, we flounder.

"So, you'll stop threatening to eliminate Ian?" I ask Papa.

He slides me a disgruntled glance. "Let's not get ahead of ourselves. I'll stop *planning* to eliminate him, but threats are an excellent deterrent."

"I can see why you were once an enforcer," I murmur quietly, paying homage to his days in the old country as a mid-ranking member of the Bratva.

We place our orders with the barista before moving to the side of the large counter to wait for our cups of coffee.

"Speaking of my enforcer days, I heard from an old friend not long ago," Dad says. "I've spoken to him several times over the years, but this most recent message was quite interesting, indeed. He told me that my daughter appears to be an exceptional young woman and should she ever like a place in his ranks, he'd gladly offer it."

Dad pins me with a steady gaze while my heart breaks out into a gallop and a flush of nerves heats my skin. *Sergei fucking Novikov.* Looks like the Pakhan no longer wished to keep our previous conversations to himself. When I reached out to him for help years ago, cashing in a favor he owed Papa, he told me our dealings would be kept in strict confidence. I suppose that's no longer the case.

"Care to explain?" Dad prods.

I shake my head. "Not particularly. There was once a problem I faced; I handled that problem. That's all that there is to the matter."

"Hmm," Dad hums thoughtfully. "Should I be worried about anything, milaya?"

"Nope," I reply, which is true.

Despite Sergei's insinuation that I've had contact with him, I'm quite sure that Ian intends to take care of any loose ends I left unsevered, so Dad will never be burdened with the truth. My revenge was well executed, but it also left three people alive who ought to be dead and in hell. I suspect that they'll be moving on to their eternal pits of fire soon enough.

Thinking about those boys always used to give me hives of disgust, even after I'd ensured they'd live in misery, but not anymore. Now, I know their days on this earth are numbered, therefore I no longer have any strong sentiments towards them. I'll always be angry at the scars that mark my skin because of them, but that anger is now more of a subtle irritation than a burning fury.

"Very well," Dad accepts, stepping forward to pick up our coffees as the barista calls out our order. His upper lip curls as he hands me my vanilla latte. "You're too Americanized with that vanilla shit you like," he mutters, shaking his head. "Real Russians drink instant coffee or black tea."

"Then it's a good thing my heritage is Russian-Asian, and I was raised in this country," I remark, taking an exaggerated slurp of my coffee and releasing a noise of enjoyment.

Dad rolls his eyes. "Don't remind me that I raised you in this land of spoiled lazy idiots."

"I think I turned out pretty well," I say with a shrug.

Papa's face softens. "That you did, milaya. That you certainly did. You'll be an excellent example for Freya to look up to. Now, lead me to that boyfriend of yours—I suppose it'd only be right if I thank him for delivering you."

I bristle. "He didn't *deliver* me, he *accompanied* me and dealt with my insanity admirably." Nevertheless, I start walking in the direction of the waiting room.

"As far as I'm concerned, there's no difference," Papa replies. "Hurry up, I'd like to give him my thanks and then get back to your mother.

You should go home and get some rest, we've all had a very long night."

Ian stands from his seat when we walk into the waiting room, which has filled up with a morning rush of people. Among the newcomers are Ian's parents; the couple that raised the love of my life also stand from their seats, offering me and my dad smiles in greeting. Congratulations and hugs are exchanged all around—Ian's mom reassures my dad that she's commandeered all necessary preparations for the baby, that all he'll need to worry about is himself, Mom, and little Freya. Dad smiles amiably at Ian's parents and thanks them for coming, but glares at Ian when he thinks nobody's watching. When he shakes my boyfriend's hand, his grip is so tight I hear a few of Ian's knuckles pop.

"It appears you're still under the impression that you're good enough for my daughter," Dad mutters, eyes narrowing at Ian as they continue shaking hands for far longer than etiquette requires.

"I'll never be good enough for her," Ian disagrees, "but I'll spend every day trying to be worthy."

Dad's lips thin with irritation at Ian's clever response, but he finally releases my boyfriend's hand, which is red and strained.

Ian's mom pulls me in for a tight hug, distracting me from the exchange between her son and my father.

"I'm so glad you two finally found your way back to each other," she murmurs in my ear. Then, voice growing louder so that everyone can hear, "I always held out hope that you'd eventually become my daughter in law. I still hope it'll be sooner rather than later, and perhaps there might even be some grandchildren in my future—"

"*Mom*," Ian says, tone coated with exasperation. "We're too young."

"I had you when I was twenty-one," Ian's mom disagrees, giving me a final squeeze before she pulls away. "April's parents had her when they were even younger. There is no such thing as *too young*—"

"I wouldn't go buying baby clothes for anyone other than Freya any time soon," I advise her gently. "We've still got careers to establish and lives to figure out."

"This reunion has been lovely, but I must get back to my wife and newborn daughter," Dad says, finishing his coffee in a few gulps and tossing the paper cup into a nearby trashcan. "April, go on ahead home and get some sleep. As for the rest of you, thank you for coming, but your presences aren't needed, we have everything well in hand." Dad kisses my forehead, then strides off.

"Thank you again for coming," I tell Ian's parents. "And for helping my parents get all the supplies they need—I'm sure they'll greatly appreciate it. I'm heading home for the day—"

"I'm coming with you," Ian interjects, tone non-negotiable. "We can catch up on sleep together."

I don't bother arguing, because I don't really want to be apart from Ian. We bid his parents a goodbye, I promise his mom to join them for dinner soon, and then we part ways.

***

At home, Ian and I shower together, and then tumble into my childhood bed. I fall asleep shortly, wrapped up in the warmth and security of his arms.

It's dark outside when I wake up to the sensation of Ian fluttering gentle kisses across the curve of my shoulder.

"You slept nine hours," he murmurs.

Nine hours... shit. I shoot into an upright position, frantically looking around for my phone, worried that I could've missed an important update from Papa on the health of Mom and Freya.

"Everything's fine," Ian assures me as I flick on my bedside lamp and try to remember where I left my phone. "My parents have stayed at the hospital with yours despite your dad's insistence they aren't needed, they've confirmed that everyone's doing well. Freya's been nursing just fine, and she's slept plenty—her sleeping schedule is apparently very good considering the circumstances. Everything's okay, April."

"Thank god," I murmur, finally finding my phone and unlocking it. There are several texts from Dad, all of them affirming exactly what Ian just told me. Freya and Mom remain healthy. He expects they'll be discharged in a week or two, which is almost too incredible to believe.

I shuffle out of bed and give Dad a call, wanting to get a more current update. He picks up after three rings.

"Milaya," he greets, sounding exhausted. "Did you get some rest?"

"I did," I confirm. "It sounds like you could definitely use some, too."

"Thank you," Dad says dryly. "Always nice to hear my daughter telling me I sound terrible."

"Your words, not mine," I say. "Seriously, why don't we trade shifts? You come home and sleep for the night, I'll stay with Mom and make sure everything's okay. I'll keep you updated via texts."

"That's not necessary, April," Papa replies, though I hear the wistfulness in his tone as he turns down my offer. "I've stayed awake much longer for matters of far less importance."

I pause. "Was that in the last half-century, or back when Influenza didn't have a vaccine?"

"Very funny," he grumbles.

"Come on, Dad. I'm well rested. I'm capable of looking after Mom and dealing with hospital staff. I want some time with my baby sister, to stare at her and decide what colors will best suit her. I have a lot of shopping to do for her in the next week. I'll also need to figure out how to steal your credit card so I can get that shopping done—"

"No need to steal anything, you can use mine," Ian calls out.

"Is that the Vargas boy?" Dad growls, abruptly switching gears. *Shit.* "Milaya, did you invite a boy *into my home?*"

I clear my throat. "The very same boy who used to spend half his time here. The other half we spent at his house or out and about. Don't act like I've allowed some random stranger into our lives, Dad. I'll also remind you that the *boy* you're speaking of is the same boy that is the reason I got here in one piece."

Dad sounds as surprised by my impassioned rant as I am; he pauses for a long moment, and I can practically hear him working his jaw and considering how he should respond. If someone had told me a year ago that I'd be defending Ian to my father, I would've called them insane and probably given myself an ulcer from how hard I laughed. Now, though, I feel absolutely justified in defending my boyfriend to my father.

"Get him out of my house," Dad growls in response.

"We'll leave as soon as you agree to trade shifts with me," I tell Dad. "You know, you and Ian have a lot in common, starting with your overprotectiveness—"

"Do *not* insult me by saying I have anything in common with such vermin," Dad snaps. He switches over to Russian as he rapidly insults Ian with a colorful array of curse words that I'm glad Ian can't hear or understand.

"If you're quite done, I would really like to see baby Freya," I interrupt loudly. "If you don't ease up, I'll also mention to Mom just how mean you're being to my boyfriend. Of course, I would prefer not to stress her out, but..." I let my sentence trail off. I'd never actually tell Mom about Papa's ridiculous overprotectiveness, she has enough on her plate as is, but the threat should be enough to deter my dad.

"Low of you, milaya," Papa says, though there's a note of grudging admiration in his tone, as if he respects my cheap shot even though he's not happy to be the recipient of it. "Fine. We'll switch shifts, and you'll keep your lips sealed."

Chapter Thirty-Eight

Ian

April spends the next week trading off hospital shifts with her father so that someone's always there with her mother. I accompany her most nights, even though I always end up sitting in the waiting room. For the first week, only family members are permitted in the hospital room with Freya—both Mother and child need to recover from a very long, very difficult birth that threatened their lives.

On the seventh night, as I'm settling into my usual spot in the waiting room with my laptop on my lap and an energy drink on the floor beside me, I'm surprised to see April's father, Maksim, walk into the sterile room.

"Vargas," he says, his voice little more than an unwelcoming growl. "Come with me."

I take a moment to look him over, contemplating whether or not he might be taking me somewhere with the intent to kill me. Knowing what I do about April's father, I'd say he might *want* to kill me—and have the means to, considering the fact that he was once an enforcer in the Russian Bratva—but I don't believe he will. If there's one thing I learned about him through the course of my childhood friendship with April, it's that he is fiercely protective of his wife and daughter, and would never do anything that would hurt either of them. April's made it very clear that she loves me in the last week, so I believe I have immunity from Maksim's wrath. Besides, if he wanted me dead, I'd already be dead.

"Where are we going?" I ask, closing my laptop and zipping it up into my backpack before standing and swinging it over my shoulder.

"Out for a drive," Maksim says, eyes boring into my very soul. "It's past time that you and I have a talk."

The drive that Maksim refers to ends up being a scenic route to a construction site in a new suburb that's currently under development. If he wants to kill me, this would be the ideal place to dispose of my body. I'd be buried under layers of cement where I would never be found. Since I'm reasonably sure that I won't end up dead tonight, I figure he's taken me here to scare me.

"Let's go for a walk," Maksim says. "Leave your bag and phone in the car."

Okay, then. The possibility of me not making it back to the hospital alive is inching upward, but I'm not afraid, only mildly curious. If Maksim decides to actually come at me, I believe I'd be able to defend myself—I've done my fair share of fighting.

I follow him out of the car and onto a dirt path that winds through the construction site, leading to a long field near a man-made lake. We step onto a wooden dock that borders the lake and begin strolling the length of it.

"I won't ask what your intentions with my daughter are," he says, each of his footfalls causing the boards to creak beneath our feet.

"April's mother is quite sure you intend to marry my April, and in this, I agree with her."

"If not to interrogate me, then why did you bring me to the perfect site to dump my corpse?" I ask dryly, glancing at him from the corner of my eye.

"I didn't say you weren't here to be interrogated, I said that I wouldn't ask you about your intentions with April," Maksim says carefully, then falls silent, gazing at me as we walk.

I let the silence stretch out between us, refusing to be the first one to blink. He'll talk when he's ready, and it's best if he learns now that ominous silence won't make me nervous. I've never been a nervous person. Even being faced with a former Bratva enforcer who's very protective of his daughter won't change that.

"You're a cool one, as ever," Maksim says lowly.

"I am," I agree. "You won't kill me—it'd break April's heart—and anything that doesn't end with my permanent separation from her is something that I can handle."

"Your obsession with her when you were children galled me," he says. "But April adored you, so I allowed it. That doesn't mean that I didn't see you for what you were; it simply means I valued my daughter enough to step aside and let her have something that made her happy."

"And what, exactly, do you believe I am?" I ask him mildly.

"Then? A sociopath in the making. Now? I'd say with full certainty a sociopath, if it weren't for the love I can see you have for my April. But you're certainly something approaching one."

He's not wrong, which is why I don't bother refuting his words. I've known from a young age that I wasn't quite like the other kids around me—as soon as I was able to observe and perceive their emotions, I could see my own emotional deficit. I don't feel the way other's do, I don't care about things the way others do, and I certainly don't love like they do. While that makes me more efficient than the masses, it also makes me *deficient* in some ways.

"Being who I am makes me an ideal candidate to protect your daughter," I point out. "She'll always be my priority."

"Certainly," April's father agrees. "I don't think you'll ever intentionally hurt her—not again, anyways. No matter how much I poked and prodded, she never told me about the falling out you two had. I won't waste my time asking you because I suspect that you wouldn't admit to anything, even under torture."

"You're right," I confirm. I might feel physical pain the way others do, but it doesn't affect me like it does them—to most people, pain can be enough for them to scream and spill all their secrets. To me, pain is simply an irritant that I seek to resolve, but not one I'd break over.

"We're not here to talk about that. We're here because I have a question for you, and I'd very much like a truthful answer," Maksim says.

Curious, I incline my head. April's father stops walking, gazing out over the water. I stop as well, patiently waiting for him to reveal what's on his mind.

"Troy, Seoul, and Paxton," he says. "The names of three boys who went to school with you and April, all of whom went missing this last week. I heard through the grapevine about their disappearances—their parents are kicking up quite the fuss around town."

"Interesting," I say calmly, even though I internally grow the slightest bit wary.

Maksim is referring to the boys who hurt April the summer before her senior year. After I extracted their names from her, I began formulating a plan to permanently remove them from this world. The fact that my plan went into effect while I happened to be here is mere coincidence—I wasn't the one to take care of them, I called in a favor to have someone else do that for me. Fortunately, those three fucks were on vacation for spring break in the same place—Charleston—so I had an acquaintance ensure they didn't leave Charleston alive.

"Two years ago, April came home with a stab wound in her shoulder and a nasty slash on her lower back. I lost my mind and hounded her to find out what happened and who it was that hurt her. She told me she didn't see the faces of her assailants—I knew she was lying, of course, but I could never figure out why," Maksim says. "A few months afterwards, I got a call from an old friend in Russia, who told me that my daughter had called in one of the three favors he owed me. He also said that he didn't intend to count it as a favor, since he seemed to like my April."

Fuck. April told me not long ago that she'd reached out to the head of the largest Russian Bratva to help her punish the boys. Sugarplum didn't want to kill them, though apparently Sergei Novikov offered his services to end their lives—instead she wanted to punish them badly. Make them live a half-life, unable to ever get their dicks working again. I respect the sadism of her revenge method, respect the way she ensured they'd never again try to rape another girl, but that doesn't cover all the bases. They could still try to hurt someone again, and even if that wasn't a valid concern, I'd want them dead for the simple fact that they dared to touch what's mine. April is and always has been mine.

"Why didn't you do anything?" I ask. "You must've realized that April called in a favor with your friend to get revenge on those who hurt her."

Maksim glowers. "Because my old contact didn't give me names, only a heads up. He's notoriously honorable; his code involves never breaking the confidentiality of those he works with. If I'd known who hurt my April I would've ensured their disappearance a long time ago."

He pauses. "You're the one she told, though, and you took care of the loose ends. I respect that. I don't like you, Ian—I don't like that you were close with my daughter in the first place, and I wanted to make *you* disappear when you broke her heart—but I do respect you. Are you willing to do whatever it takes to ensure her happiness and fulfillment?"

"I am," I confirm. "Whatever she needs will be hers. Whatever she wants will be hers. Anyone who even thinks to hurt her will breathe their last breath shortly afterwards. I'm committed to your daughter. I will kill for her, give my life for her, and spend my life making sure she's happy."

I mean every single word I say. I spent years being idiotic enough to deprive myself of April because of some misguided notion that she represented weakness, when all along, she has been my strength. She gave me purpose when I was a boy, turning me away from the destructive thoughts constantly crowding my head. Being near her calmed me. Holding her completed me. She was, and still is, the center that exists outside of me. I will do anything it takes to keep her.

Even if she swore me off and decided to break up, I'd still find a way to keep her. In that case, I'd probably have to resort to kidnapping and fucking her until she changed her mind—enough orgasms work wonders on even my hard-headed April—but I'd much prefer to go the courting route. After a whole lot of legwork, along with some silent planning of contingencies, I'm finally at a place with April where I think she wants forever with me just as much as I intend to spend forever with her.

"I was a hardheaded piece of shit once upon a time, too," Maksim admits after several beats. "April's mother gave me a reason to be a better man, a better *person*, so that I'd deserve her. That is what I did. That is what I continue to do every single day to be worthy of her. My wife and my daughters are the most important things in this world to me. My family is everything and the only thing that truly matters. If you intend to make my daughter your family, I expect the same level of commitment and effort from you. Work every day to be better than you were the day before. Make her happy. Stay by her side. Love her through everything that happens—and things *will* happen, Ian. Things will go wrong, arguments will ensue, you'll both say things you don't mean in the heat of the moment because we are only human and humanity comes with many imperfections and difficulties. So long as you stay committed to her through thick and thin, I can promise I won't kill you. If I sense you slipping, if I sense your values changing, and god forbid if I ever find out you've *strayed* from my daughter..." Maksim's eyes darken. "You will wish for death long before I grant it."

I nod. "I'd expect nothing less. I get the feeling that, when I have daughters with April, I'll be the same way. That is if I ever let them date, which is questionable."

"As long as you don't have those daughters for some time, I won't have a problem with that," Maksim says, eyes warming ever so slightly. "Speaking of, I think it's time we get back to my daughters." He glances at his watch. "April usually comes around to check on you at midnight and bring you coffee, I'd like to have you back in time for that, so she doesn't get suspicious that I decided you were a problem to be rid of."

I think that if I'd said the wrong thing or pissed Maksim off too much, he might've decided that I was a problem to eliminate. He certainly took me to the perfect murder spot.

The drive back to the hospital is much more cordial; I manage to engage April's dad in a conversation about football. I also ask after the welfare of his newest daughter, and on our way into the hospital, tell him that I hope to see her soon.

"Very well," he says with a sigh as we exit the elevator and walk into the maternity ward. "My Freya is strong, just like my April, she should be able to handle your noxious presence. Follow me."

Faint surprise washes over me as Maksim leads me to scrub up and then accompanies me into the private room where his wife and two daughters are. When I step into the suite, I cast a cursory glance around. The counter beneath a row of windows is covered with bursting bouquets of flowers with vibrant colors, congratulatory cards, and stuffed animals—many of which were sent by my parents. I stop cold in the doorway when my eyes fall on April, who sits on a chair beside her mother's bed. In her arms is a bundle of pink blankets—Freya. April hums a quiet tune to her sister, staring down at her with the softest smile on her face and shining eyes. She's so caught up she doesn't even hear the door open and close—I watch with a mounting sense of wonder as she leans down to rub noses with her little sister, bottom lip quivering with emotions.

I've never really thought about having kids, beyond the cursory notion of building a family with April. I've considered knocking her up once or twice, in the dark moments when I wasn't sure whether or not she'd ever give in to me, but that would've mainly been a ploy to irrevocably bind us together. Seeing her with her sister now, the soft expression on her face and love shining in her eyes, causes the world to shift and warp around me. The idea of children with this woman is no longer a thought of how to bring us closer, but an ache that settles deep in my chest. Not now—not even a year from now—but one day I will make April the mother of my children. I want to stare at our child with the same sense of wonder and love, knowing that I made a small human with April.

Love is an emotion that often eludes me—it's more a sense of possession than affection, a wish to keep someone close and a way of seeing them as important to my being. I love three people in this world, in the sense that I know they're integral to me and will burn the world down if they're ever threatened—my father, my mother, and April. Especially April.

The sight before me feels like it fundamentally changes a part of me. A hot flash travels over my body, something that I might otherwise assume is the beginnings of a cold or bug of some sort, but I know is actually caused by seeing April with Freya and envisioning a future for me and April. Us, years from now, holding a baby of our own making. A life form that is half me, half her.

"Holy fuck," I murmur, not realizing I've spoken the words aloud until Maksim casts me a censuring glance.

My words are also enough to get April's attention; she looks up from the baby in her arms and over to her father and me with surprise, which then devolves into suspicion as she glances between us.

"I'm hoping that the two of you walking in here together means that you've worked your issues out."

"No issues, milaya," Maksim says, walking forward to join April. His wife is out cold on the bed, probably tired after a day of nursing and caring for Freya. She doesn't even stir at our voices.

"She's been sleeping?" Maksim asks, peering down at his daughters.

April nods. "She was a bit fussy earlier, even after feeding, so I sang her to sleep after Mom passed out. What are you doing here, Papa? You should be resting."

"Rest is for the weak," Maksim responds, his face softening as he watches Freya. At April's pointed stare, he chuckles quietly. "I'll head home soon. Just thought you might like some company that isn't a few days old or asleep most of the time."

"Mom deserves the rest," April says. "She's been through an ordeal. She lost a lot of blood, and—"

"You don't need to convince me, we're in agreement," Maksim says. He leans down to kiss April's head. "Call if anything happens, milaya." He steps over to his wife, also kissing her forehead. "Sleep well, solnyshko. Thank you for bringing me two daughters." With that, he breezes out of the room, glaring at me one final time for good measure. Once the door closes behind him, April gifts me with a soft, warm smile.

"Pull up a chair," she says. "Join me."

I gladly accept her invitation, dropping my backpack below the counter and dragging a chair over to April, taking a seat and leaning over her to look at her little sister. Freya is so tiny it's worrisome, except something about this child exudes the sort of strength that tells me she'll be just fine. I can tell from her energy alone that, like her sister, she's a fighter.

"She's so little," I murmur softly. "Weirdly adorable."

April frowns at me. "Nothing about her is weird. She's perfect."

"Ours will be perfect, too," I say, surprising both myself and April. Thinking the thought is one thing; actually bringing it to life with words is an entirely different thing. The look of shock April gives me is quickly replaced by warmth, and a small smile.

"Yes," she agrees. "They will be. I want at least two."

"I'll give you however many you want," I respond easily. The thought of April's belly swelling with a life I put in there... it's hotter than expected. Hotter than anything I've done with April, and I've had her in some pretty fucking hot positions.

"Here," April says, thankfully distracting me from the hard-on I'm starting to get. "Do you want to hold her?"

I swallow thickly. "I don't know how." I feel like my hands don't deserve to hold such perfection, they're dirtied with the many sins I've committed, but at the same time I very much want to hold Freya.

"Support her head," April instructs. "Keep her nice and close to your chest—she needs constant contact and warmth to maintain a healthy body temperature. Since Mom doesn't want to incubate her unless necessary, that means we're taking shifts."

More gently than I've ever done anything before, I accept Freya from April, following her instructions and letting her position my arms around her sister so that I hold her correctly. The warm feeling in my chest expands as I stare down at this miniature child, and I realize with no small amount of shock that the list of people I'd do any and everything for has just been bumped up to four. I know Freya isn't part of my family, but she's obviously important to April, and holding her I feel some sort of strange connection take place.

"Hello there, small human," I whisper. "You are weirdly—" I cut off at April's glare. "You're very cute," I amend. "Strangely so. I... I like you very much." *I want one of you with the woman watching me with endless affection in her eyes.* "I'm pretty sure I'll kill anyone who ever hurts or even thinks to hurt you." *Shit, I absolutely would.*

"Since you'll be her brother in law eventually, that's good to hear," April says, laughter in her voice. "Protect her with everything in you, just like I will."

"I will," I promise. "Always."

CHAPTER THIRTY-NINE

April

Over the next week, Freya gets strong enough to be discharged from the hospital, so she and Mom move back home. I continue taking turns with my parents for shifts with her. Dad likes the nighttime shifts since Mom hogs her during the day, but I manage to convince him to let me take over occasionally so he can sleep.

On the third morning after Freya's come home, I get a call from Eliana, who should be somewhere in Europe right about now.

As soon as I pick up, she screeches in my ear, "*Why didn't I hear from you about you having a baby sister?*"

I clear my throat. "It's been a long two weeks, Elia. Mom and Freya both nearly died during the delivery. I've been at the hospital round the clock helping with little Freya, I haven't had time to reach out to anyone, aside from Sanders to let him know I might need a replacement on stage for a week or two after break." I pause, walking to the window of my room and peering out into the morning sun. "How did you find out about Freya?"

"Ian told Carson, Carson told me," Elia responds. "I convinced them to get a ticket back to the states early, finish our trip later. I'm on a layover now, I'll be in Connecticut by evening."

I frown. "You don't have to do that, Elia. From the pictures you've texted me, it looks like you're having an amazing vacation. I don't want to interrupt."

"Too late," she chirps. "Besides, break is almost over, and I want to meet my honorary niece before getting back to Greywood. I also want to make sure that Ian's treating you well. Seth says he's under threat to, but Ian's a bit of a loose cannon."

I look over to my bed, where Ian's still sleeping. He refuses to be apart from me, much to the consternation of my father, though Dad has calmed about me spending time with Ian recently. It all seemed to change a week ago when they appeared together in the hospital room.

Right now, he's laid on his side, eyes closed, breathing deeply. His previous problems with sleep have all but disappeared—he sleeps like the dead whenever we're together, which is why I don't fight him on sharing a bed. Not that I would, anyways, since sleeping in the same bed as him means orgasms.

"Ian will always be a loose cannon, but I've managed to house train him," I say, looking back to the window. "I really hate that I cut your trip short."

"I don't. Europe can wait, but your little sister will only stay an infant for so long. I want to get in early so that I get a head start on being her favorite auntie."

"You're her only auntie," I say, amused. "Except maybe Chloe, but she doesn't know anything yet."

"She does," Elia disagrees. "I told her about fifteen minutes ago."

"Why don't you just put an advertisement in the newspaper?" I ask dryly, rolling my eyes.

"You know, now that you mention it..." Elia cuts off with a laugh when I make a noise of warning.

"How did you manage to convince your boys to share you?" I question.

"I asked really, really nicely," Elia responds. "Carson can't deny me anything, and Seth will move heaven and earth to make me happy. He refused to cut our trip short at first, so I pouted for an afternoon. It wasn't even staged, I was genuinely upset, and he relented pretty quickly."

"I'm still flabbergasted that you managed to tame Seth," I tell her. "That one is dangerous."

"Not to me," Elia says. "He's weirdly committed to making me happy. Gets *really* angry when I'm not and has a compulsive need to fix whatever's wrong. Oh, before I forget, I think my boys want to talk some business with Ian, so the visit will be multi-purposed. There's also the added bonus of Carson's mom living a few hours outside of Connecticut, so I'll get to meet her. We've spoken on the phone a lot, but we want to finally meet in person. She promised to show me all her rescue cats and dogs, I can't resist that offer."

Knowing that cutting her trip short won't be all bad, I relax. "Alright. I'll see you tonight, then. You guys already have a hotel booked and everything? I'd offer for you to stay with me, but my dad's picky about who he'll let near Freya."

"Yeah, we have a hotel suite. Seth set it up, so naturally it's the presidential one. I'll see you tonight."

We exchange love-you's, then hang up. When I look back to the bed, I see Ian's awoken. He stares at me with his emerald green eyes. "Eliana called?" he asks.

I nod. "She, Seth, and Carson are on their way. They'll be here tonight."

"Wonderful," Ian says, not sounding pleased in the least. "I like Eliana well enough, but if she tries to steal all of your time—"

"You will do absolutely nothing about it, because that will not only displease me, it'll also displease Seth," I tell him. "It's your fault for telling Carson where we are and what we're up to. He told Elia about Freya and Elia insisted they come."

"I'll take care to be more covert in the future," Ian says, sitting up. The bed sheets pool around his waist, revealing his magnificent chest and abs. Instantly, my mouth goes dry. Ian's lips tip up at the sides. "Come here, April."

"What will I get out of it?" I question, feigning nonchalance, even while dirty thoughts fog my mind.

"It's not a question of what *you'll* get, Sugarplum, it's a question of what *I'll* get. Breakfast."

Sounds good to me.

***

"Oh my *god*," Eliana whispers later in the evening.

I managed to convince Dad to let Eliana come over for dinner. His conditions were that, before leaving her hotel, she showers, scrubs her skin thoroughly clean of any travel germs, and checks her temperature to ensure she's not sick. He's been wanting to meet my best friend to approve of her since I told him about her, so he agreed easily enough.

She sits on my living room couch, cradling Freya in her arms, staring down at her like she's the most precious thing in the world.

"Holy... holy shit, April, I think I want one," she whispers.

I nod. "Freya has a way of inciting baby-fever in people. I got it. Even *Ian* got it. She's just so damn adorable. Don't let your boys hear you say that, though, or they'll set right to work trying to knock you up."

Elia smiles faintly. "They know I won't be giving them babies until I've danced as a principal on all the major stages in the world. I'm okay retiring before I hit thirty so I can do museum work, but I have some goals to reach." She pauses. "I think Seth contemplated switching out my birth control a while back so that he'd have more time with me. I refused to sleep with him for two weeks, made him watch me and Carson together without letting him join."

"I'm sure that ended well for you," I say blandly, craning my neck to check the staircase and make sure my parents are still upstairs and out of ear shot.

"I couldn't walk the day after I finally lifted the no-sex ban with him," Elia murmurs, cheeks pinkening. "God, April, can I steal Freya?"

"Unless you want to set my dad's wrath on you, I wouldn't," I advise dryly.

Eliana pouts. "But he likes me. So does your mom. They invited me to dinner and kept refilling my plate. I think that's a symbol of approval."

"It is," I agree.

Dad and Mom both come from cultures where food is a way of showing affection and love; the more they refill a guest's plate, the more they like that guest. Naturally, Dad has never filled Ian's plate and glares at Mom when she does so. "They also love the bouquet and baby-basket you brought. And the wine. Dad was *very* impressed by the vintage. He did question how you got it, given that you're still eighteen."

"Seth got it," Elia replies. "I don't drink much; I'm a dancer."

"Before it slips my mind, Dad told me earlier that he has a friend in common with Seth, so he'd like an introduction to your psychopath while he's in town."

Elia smiles, reaching down to tap Freya's nose. "Seth told me the same thing on our way here. Sergei Novikov is quite the figure."

I pause, startled. "You know Sergei Novikov?"

"I met him at Seth's art show," Elia responds. "He's a client of Seth's, and they've had, er, other dealings together. I've met his wife, Kira. She's wonderful. The story of her meet-cute with Sergei is amazing. It consists of him kidnapping her when he was in a maximum security prison and she was the forensic psychologist evaluating him pre-trial. Seth's surprised that they fell in love instead of killing each other."

I blink slowly. "Huh. I didn't know about the whole prison-abduction thing, but I have heard chatter that both of them are geniuses, and now they make the ultimate power couple." I glance at the window, my thoughts turning to other power couples, such as me and Ian.

"I wonder what our boys are up to right now," I muse.

Eliana shakes her head. "Nothing good, I'm sure."

***

Ian

"I'm not happy with you right now, Vargas," Seth says darkly, even as he drinks the four-thousand-dollar scotch held in a crystal tumbler that costs almost as much. We're in my house, seated in the parlor. My parents have gone to sleep for the night, not caring that I have company over, probably because they're familiar with Carson and his family.

"I didn't ask Eliana to cut your trip short. I also told Carson *not* to tell her about April and Freya."

Carson shrugs, unabashed. "Unless it's for her safety, I can't keep things from Elia. Have you seen the doe-eyes she makes? The way they glimmer when she bats her eyelashes?"

"I don't give a shit what your explanation is," I volley back. "Eliana's your problem, not mine."

Both men growl at that. "Elia is not a *problem*," Carson says irritably.

"She is the *solution* to a great deal of things," Seth adds on, glaring at me.

"I'm not disagreeing. I feel the same way about April." I sigh. "Look, Carson asked why I wasn't in Vermont overseeing the company; I answered. What followed is not on me."

Seth turns his glare on Carson. "You couldn't have kept your mouth shut for another three fucking days?"

"Nope," Carson replies, popping the P. "Don't pretend you could've, either. You might be a hardass to the rest of the world, but I've seen how you melt when Elia gets to work on you."

Seth's lips thin, but he doesn't refute Carson's words.

They exchange a meaningful glance, then turn to stare at me in an eerie way that tells me they know something that I don't. To mask my growing unease, I take a sip from my own tumbler, affecting an air of complete carelessness. "Everything going well in the company?" I ask.

"Splendidly," Carson replies. Then, he falls quiet, and continues staring at me. I stare right back at him, unblinking.

"Are we in a staring contest?" I question offhandedly. "If so, I can go three minutes without blinking. Can you?"

"Dennis Ajax," Seth says, and I stiffen. "I was digging for some information about him recently, some blackmail to force him out of the company. Instead of something typical like tax evasion, I found a buried report that made me want to get to work on the fuck with my sharpest knife."

"What kind of report?" I ask, keeping my tone mildly interested.

Seth leans forward, causing the leather cushion beneath him to creak. "The kind that did not go over well with me, or Carson. The kind filed by the parents of a ten-year-old boy, who say that Dennis touched their son inappropriately. The kind that means that man is the sort of pervert that deserves castration and death."

"I'd have to agree," I say. "Why isn't good old Dennis in jail?"

"Because my family has enough money to bury the perversions of all of its members," Carson replies bluntly. "The report Seth shared with me got me thinking about my memories with my uncle. Dennis gave me weird looks that set my hair on end a few times when I was younger. He never tried anything with me, though. My father would've killed him. Dad might not care about me, but he won't tolerate any slight to me, because it's also a slight to the family. My mom would've caused the scandal of a century, then put her veterinary skills to use by castrating the person who dared touch me inappropriately." He sips his scotch, watching me over the rim of his tumbler. "I got to thinking about other people Dennis might've given that look to, and I recalled something."

Everything within me tenses at the way both Ian and Seth are watching me. Carson's gaze has too much fucking sympathy for my liking, while Seth's is a piercing stare. They know. Somehow, they know. I've never told anyone but April, and she wouldn't betray me, yet they've pieced it together. For all his outward idiocy, Carson is very, *very* smart and good at putting things together. Seth has a mind that could rival Sherlock Holmes.

"Summer before ninth grade. We vacationed together so our dads could talk business," Carson says. "Dennis watched you in a way that I can see now was just *wrong*. I remember you staying on the beach late one night while I went back inside to sleep. I also remember Dennis being sick the next day. When I walked by his hotel room in the afternoon, the door was open, and I glimpsed him holding an ice pack to his crotch. I thought nothing of it at the time, but now..."

I down the liquor in my glass, then stand and walk over to the bar cart to pour myself more.

"I'm not going to say it out loud, but I need to know if what I think happened that night actually did happen, or if I'm mistaken," Carson calls after me.

"What does it matter?" I ask, turning around, knowing that my posture's more defensive than it should be. My control over myself is slipping in light of this conversation, so it can't be helped. "Who fucking cares? Apparently your pervy uncle touched some other kid, let's work off of that."

"It matters because I'm not just your boss or a fellow student at Greywood, I'm also your *friend*," Carson says.

"I don't have friends," I respond.

Seth lets out a mirthless laugh. "Hate to break it to you, but you do, Vargas. You have two of them, and they're both sitting in this room."

I feel my upper lip curl with disdain as I look at Seth. "You're lowering yourself to friendship now, Balor? Really?"

"You won't insult me, so don't try," Seth replies, his tone bored. "Yes or no, did bad shit go down the night Carson's referring to?"

I work my jaw. Drink my liquor, then refill. Take another sip, stare at the painting of my great-grandfather hanging on the wall. After several minutes of fighting an internal war with myself, I give the two men a single word. "Yes."

"*Fuck*," Carson says, shaking his head and looking at the ceiling. "God fucking dammit."

The strong reaction from him is unexpected. I'm not sure who his ire is aimed at; his uncle, or me. Before I can ask, Carson says, "Ian, man, I am so fucking—"

"*Don't*," I cut him off with a hiss, "apologize. I don't need your pity. I didn't even want either of you to know this, it's personal."

"It's not pity," Seth says in place of Carson. "It's a little something that neither of us are particularly familiar with; *empathy*. I learned it from Eliana. I expect you're probably learning it from April. There's nothing condescending about the emotion."

"Thank you for the lesson, Dr. Phil," I snap. "Why the fuck are the two of you here? What's the point of this meeting?"

"A little tip about friendship," Seth says. "When a friend extends their hand, don't bite it off. Take it."

"I need your charity even less than I need your pity," I spit.

"It's not charity, you fucking moron," Seth growls, growing tired of my attitude. "We're here because Carson cares, and I dislike the idea of someone hurting you and getting away with it. We're here to formulate a plan, not because you can't do it on your own, *but because you don't have to*. Lock up that dismal attitude, sit the fuck down, and let's talk. Keep bitching at me and I will forget that you're someone I consider a friend."

"Threats don't work on me, Seth," I remind.

"I'll rephrase. Sit down so that two of the most cunning and cruel people currently in this state can put their heads together and create a delightfully horrific punishment for someone who deserves to be punished."

"What am I, chopped liver?" Carson asks Seth, blinking.

"You're less evil than us," Seth responds. "You still have good in you. You're an *optimist*." He says the word *optimist* in the same tone some might say *HIV*.

Exhaling, I walk over to the two of them and take a seat back in my armchair. I clench my teeth, fighting against my instincts which demand that I throw these two out of my house and find a way to ensure that their mouths stay shut.

"Now," Seth says. "There are a few options open to us, but one of two paths will be taken. One, you want Dennis dead *now*. Two, you want Dennis dead *later*, after we've played with him a bit. Which one?"

On my own, I planned to simply eliminate Dennis by ending his pathetic life. I didn't want to fuck over Carson or get on Seth's bad side by screwing with Dennis Ajax, so a too-quick end was my only option. Since they both know and seem to be on board, however, I'd much prefer torturing Dennis for a good long time before granting him death.

"I want him to wish for death first," I say.

Seth nods. "Good choice."

"Agreed," Carson tacks on.

Then, we start working on the sort of plan that feeds my inner sadist.

CHAPTER FORTY

Ian

I text April to come over after Seth and Carson have left for the night and picked up Eliana from April's house. I need my girl right now, and I need her somewhere where I can hear her screams rather than having to mute the noises like I do in her house. My father had my bedroom soundproofed when I was a sophomore in high school, due to my habit of blasting music so loudly, he swears he almost went deaf. In my room I can take April however I want, for as long as I want, and that's exactly what I crave.

She rings my doorbell not ten minutes after I've sent the text. When I open the door, I'm treated to seeing her dressed in a knit sweater that has a short hem, exposing her toned stomach, and thin leggings. My parents are asleep for the night; I pull her into the house with an arm around her waist, slam the door behind her, and without preamble, toss her over my shoulder.

"Ian!" she squeals. "What the fuck?"

"Shh," I reprimand, landing a sharp slap on her ass. "Until we get to my room, be nice and quiet. Then you can scream loud enough to wake the fucking dead."

April follows my instructions and stays quiet, probably because she knows my parents are home. Once I'm in my room with the door tightly shut, I reward her for her silence by setting her on her feet, wrapping my hands around the back of her neck, and pulling her in for a long, greedy kiss.

My mood is foul after the conversation I've just had—I *hate* that there are now several people in this world who know exactly what happened that night out on the beach. It took a lot for me to tell April my secret; telling Carson and Seth as well is a step too far.

"Ian," April gasps out my name again when I finally release her lips, breathing harshly. There's a slight flush to her cheeks, one that I know will darken as I fuck her brains out.

April clutches my shoulders, looking me over, and her brows furrow. My perceptive girl can tell that something's off.

"What's wrong?" she asks. "Are you alright?"

"Had a chat with Seth and Carson," I say. "They know."

April goes very still. "*What?*"

"I don't want to talk about it," I growl. "I need to forget right now. Get on your knees."

April contemplates this for just a beat too long; growing irritated with waiting, I wrap her hair around my fist twice and tug her head back, leaning down to sink my teeth into the elegant column of her neck. She squeals; I grin against her flesh. "Get on your fucking knees, Sugarplum. I want to see your lips wrapped around my cock."

As soon as I release her, April drops to her knees right on my hardwood floor. At a different time, if I was in a better mood, I might move her to the rug by my bed or give her a pillow to kneel on, but not tonight. Tonight, I don't care about anything but fucking every hole April has until I forget about all the bad shit that's transpired in my life.

"Take off my pants," I command.

April complies, undoing the buttons and zipper, yanking down my pants and briefs. My cock springs free, and she takes it in her fist with no directions needed from me. She doesn't approach me playfully like she has before—instead she opens her mouth wide, and I feel my eyes nearly roll into the back of my head as she leans forward and swallows most of my length in one go. *Fuck.*

Pleasure blinds me from the feeling of her hot mouth wrapped around me, her tongue laving me and worshipping me. There's no sweetness to her movements—only pure vigor that drives me higher and higher. Tingles shoot up my spine barely two minutes in, warning me that if she doesn't stop I'm going to embarrass myself. I pull her off of my length before I come because I want to be buried balls-deep in her pussy when I go off. Her mouth is truly a gift of god, but being buried inside her feels like homecoming every single time, and that's what I need.

I kick off my pants and tear my shirt in half in my haste to have her. With a fist in her hair, I draw her back to her feet, then walk her backwards to the bed and throw her down. I strip off her sweater and her pants, tearing her panties. For once, April doesn't complain about my propensity for tearing her underwear—instead she eagerly strips off her bra and offers herself to me on a silver fucking platter, arching her back to present those gorgeous tits that I see in my dreams.

She scoots up on the bed, leaving her head resting on one of the pillows. I climb over her, grab her hip, and drag her beneath me, loving the startled squeal that escapes her at the gesture. Straddling her, I don't waste any time on finesse or tact; I spear two fingers inside her, growling low in my throat when I feel just how wet she is.

"You like sucking me off that much?" I question, my tone pitched low with my need. When she nods, I feel a smirk tilt my lips. "Like getting on your knees to worship me?"

"I love getting on my knees to worship you," she murmurs. "I love making you feel good. I love how you make me feel good."

"I do, don't I?" I ask her, curving my fingers up inside her, finding the spot that makes her gasp and tickling it mercilessly. "There have been many dark times in my life. I've committed many dark, fucked up sins, Sugarplum, and I'll commit many more. Having you be mine is my salvation." I pull my fingers out of her and hike her leg up on my waist, my cock aching with the need to be inside her. "You're the air that I breathe, April. The water I need to survive. The nectar of life."

A soft, choked sound escapes her, and I don't think it's from the way I slowly start sinking inside her. I think it's from my words, which turn her on more than what I'm doing to her. I think they creep inside her, burrowing under her skin, the same way she's already burrowed under mine.

"I'm addicted to you," I tell her with complete honesty as I drive myself home, loving the way she moans softly. "I'm obsessed with you. I'm so in love with you that I'm positive I've lost my mind. Or that this is a dream. If it is, I never want to wake up."

"Ian," she gasps. "Fuck me."

I grin. "What's the magic word?"

"*Now.*"

I lean down to bite her lip sharply, liking the way the metallic tang of her blood explodes on my tongue. "Try again, Sugarplum. Magic word?"

"Collywobbles."

I shake my head, amused and aroused despite myself. "I'll stay still like this all day, sweetheart, buried so deeply inside you neither of us can breathe but not giving you what you need. Not rubbing your clit the way that makes you purr or driving into you so hard you lose your breath. I could die a happy man in your pussy."

"God, you're such an asshole," she grouses. "*Please*, you jerk. Fucking please."

"Anything my girl wants."

Tonight isn't for lovemaking or slow, sweet strokes—I jackhammer into her in the way that would send most other girls running. I can see the pinch of pain in April's lovely brows from how hard I ride her, but she doesn't ask me to stop or slow. In fact, her moans and groans and whimpers all encourage me, as do her occasional, breathy words of *fuck yes* or *like that* or even *harder*. Rational thought escapes me; all thought escapes me. I forget about my foul mood, the long evening, Dennis fucking Ajax... everything disappears. My attention fixates on her the way a predator's does when they're closing in on their prey. Though April might be a predator in her own right, she'll always be *my* favorite prey to hunt.

"Tell me you're mine," I demand when I feel myself drawing closer to my orgasm, spurred on by the telling flutter of her pussy tightening around me in quick pulses. She's ready to come, too.

"I'm yours," she cries. "God—*fuck*, I'm yours."

"Goddamn right you are, April." I reach down, slotting my fingers between our tightly pressed bodies and finding the sensitive bundle of nerves on April's pussy that never fails to make her sing like a bird. A choked cry escapes her.

"Now tell me you love me and I'll let you come."

Normally, April might push back against my power games, but she must sense my need for her submission tonight because she says, "I love you, Ian, now I *have* to come."

"Give me your mouth."

She arches her neck, offering me her lips—just before I claim them, I command, "*Come.*" Feeling her clamp down around my cock, I lose myself to my own pleasure, groaning into her mouth.

It takes a long time for both of us to stop coming, but we don't stop kissing. The kiss does turn softer as my cock slides out of her and she wraps her arms tightly around me, pressing her breasts against my chest. When we finally separate, we're both breathless once again, and April's gorgeous body trembles in the aftermath of her climax.

I roll onto my side, then pull her into my chest. "You good?' I ask gruffly.

"Mmm," she agrees. "I'm gonna pass out any minute, so it's your job to wake me up by nine. And be ready to tell me what put you in that shit mood tonight."

I lean down to kiss her nose. "Deal."

***

I don't expect myself to be able to fall asleep, but somewhere in the midst of staring at April, studying the steady rise and fall of her chest, and sifting my fingers through her long, silky hair, I somehow manage to pass out cold. I wake up to rays of sunlight streaming through my bedroom window, and a yawn nearly cracks my jaw. April's body is no longer draped against mine—needing to remedy that, I reach an arm out to the side, searching for her, only to come up against cool sheets.

My cracked eyes snap fully open, as if a bucket of water has been dumped on me. I look around my bedroom and crane my neck to glance into the bathroom, narrowing my eyes to see it's open and empty. April's gone—she left without waking me up, which does *not* sit well with me.

I reach for my phone on the bedstand, picking it up with the intent to call April and tell her to get her ass back here because I have not yet had my fill of her for the morning; I'm stopped by a text from her.

> **April:** In the kitchen with your cook making pancakes xx.

I release a deep breath followed by a groan, seeing my own ridiculousness. I was ready to lose my shit simply because I fell asleep with April and woke up without her. I don't think most people understand what it is to fundamentally *need* someone the way that I need April. If anyone knew what a pussy I am when it comes to her I'd definitely get shit for it, but I've accepted my obsession with my girlfriend.

I take a five minute shower and brush my teeth in record speed, eager to get to my girl. Then, I find her exactly where she said she'd be, in the chef's-grade kitchen, chopping strawberries at the counter while my cook, Layla, fries up pancakes at the stove.

"Morning," I say, rounding the large island.

April spins away from her cutting board to greet me with a kiss and smile. "Morning."

"Layla," I greet, nodding at the woman hunched over a pan.

"Devil," My cook responds, giving me a side-glare. I did dedicate a great deal of effort to making her life difficult when I was younger, and she had to endure the absolute dick I was during the years of my estrangement from April, so I can't blame her characterization. It'll take her several decades to forgive me for that time when I put cockroaches in her stew; once she manages to get over that, she'll have to move onto the countless other shitty pranks I pulled, and she'll be long-dead before she lets go of those.

April laughs. "You call him Devil? That's fantastic. Very accurate."

"I'm less of a devil when you're around," I tell her honestly. "You ground me."

"Thank God for that," Layla says snarkily, even as she gives April a fond smile.

Layla and April have always gotten along. Layla would make April's favorite foods whenever she came over when we were kids; my cook loved that my pranks tended to calm down when April was around.

"Hope you're in the mood for chocolate chip pancakes," April says, nudging me away and returning to her strawberries. "I am *famished*."

I give her a half-smile. "I wonder why that could be."

Layla glances over her shoulder at the both of us, eyes narrowed, then promptly turns back to the stove and plates a stack of pancakes. My gaze wanders over the four additional plates also stacked with pancakes, and my eyebrows furrow.

"Jesus, are we making enough to feed a fucking army?"

"Language!" Layla snaps.

"Nope, but Eliana, Ian, and Seth are coming over this morning," April replies. "I invited them."

I blink slowly, feeling my mood dampen. I do not like anyone intruding on my time with April, our *friends* included. "What do you mean?"

"The psychopath, the reformed man whore, and the sweetest girl I've ever met are joining us," April clarifies. "I asked Layla if she'd be okay with making breakfast for us or if I should order."

"When people *ask* me for something rather than *ordering* me about, I'm willing to be accommodating," Layla sing-songs, not looking away from the stove.

I give April a dark look. "Today was supposed to be *our* day."

"You're pissy with Seth and Carson when you shouldn't be," she says. "So, after we all have breakfast together, Elia and I are going shopping at the mall. You, Seth, and Carson are going to be our couriers while talking your shit out." She beams. "Isn't that wonderful?"

"It's certainly something," I reply darkly. "You'll pay for this later, April. I wanted you to myself today."

She rolls her eyes. "You got me to yourself last night and could've had me this morning if you didn't sleep in like a lazy sap."

"Lazy sap?" I repeat, incredulous. "You—"

The doorbell ringing three times cuts me off, and I give April a look that makes it clear I plan to take out my irritation on her body later. Her cheeks brighten with a delectable flush that makes me want to bite her; instead, I settle for planting a hard kiss on her lips. "I'll get the door."

"Set the orange juice on the dining room table before you go," she says, eyes sparkling with mirth.

Grumbling under my breath, I grab the carafe of freshly squeezed orange juice, take it to the dining room, and then sulk my way over to the front door. I open it, exchanging terse greetings with Carson and Seth before directing Eliana to the dining room.

"Didn't expect to see you two so soon," I say, releasing an irritated sigh.

Seth's eyes track Eliana as she flits through the entry way and veers off to the dining room. "I don't appreciate April trying to take Eliana away from me. Keep your girl in check, Ian."

"Oh, calm the fuck down," Carson says mildly, rolling his eyes. "Elia isn't going anywhere, and she's allowed to have friends."

Seth slowly turns towards Carson. "Is she, now?"

"Yes," Carson replies. "Isolating her would be bad for her, mentally and physically. Take a deep breath. Elia loves both of us and is as attached to you as you are to her—"

"Impossible," Seth cuts in.

"—so you can trust that her having friends won't lessen her bond with you."

I tilt my head to the side as I watch this exchange, finding it mildly amusing. After all, I'm in the same boat as Seth; if I had a way to trap April somewhere and keep her entirely to myself without repercussions, I'd do just that.

Seth stares at Carson for several long moments before releasing a sigh. "I *have* recently read up about the psychological effects of isolation on the human brain. They aren't good. I'd never knowingly cause Eliana to suffer, so I suppose I'll need to live with her having friends. Only a few, though."

Carson claps Seth on the shoulder. "Whatever works for you, bud."

"Call me bud again and I will dismember you."

"Cool, bro—"

"Breakfast's ready!" April yells. "Come get it while it's hot! Don't kill each other on the way!"

Carson cracks a smile. Seth and I share a dark look. Nevertheless, I lead them to the dining room.

Breakfast is a surprisingly smooth affair; April and Eliana talk to each other about random shit like baby clothes, while I share a quieter, more serious conversation with Carson and Seth.

"How is our plan coming?" I ask Seth, watching as he cuts his pancakes into perfect cubes with near surgical precision.

"The one we made eight hours ago?" Seth inquires mildly, taking a bite. "It's fine. By the end of the week, the article we spoke of will be launched, and Dennis Ajax's life will forever change for the worst. He'll probably get arrested, though I'm sure he'll manage to make bail, at which point you can enjoy sitting back and watching his world crumble around him. I also found out, quite interestingly, that Dennis is indebted to some very dangerous people." A slow smile spreads on his lips. "Those people will come for him soon."

"Dad's hold on the company will falter even more," Carson adds in. "You'll need to step up your work hours, Ian, as will I. Seth, the offer of a permanent position for you is still on the table. You've proven to be good at what you do."

"I'm good at everything I do," Seth replies, eyes trailing to Eliana when she laughs at something April says and softening ever so slightly, in a way that could make someone mistakenly think that there's some humanity in him. Perhaps there is, but only when it comes to his single object of affection and obsession.

Carson snorts. "Right, of course you are. Ian?"

"I'll manage. If I have to put in late evenings more often, that's acceptable so long as I can take an hour or two to have dinner with April."

"That's fine," Carson says, nodding. "I have some more people I'm looking to onboard in the next few months; until they're officially hired, a lot will be left to us. We'll make it work, though."

"We will," I agree, feeling my blood start to simmer with how close I am to the one thing I've sought for so long: *revenge.*

Chapter Forty-One

April

"Do you think they're talking about the meaning of life?" Eliana asks me, her gaze fixed on the glass wall of the shoe store we're browsing. I steal a glance at Ian, Seth, and Carson—they're huddled together in the bright hallway of the mall, each weighed down by multiple shopping bags, deep in conversation with each other.

"Doubtful," I reply, running my finger over the heel of a gorgeous stiletto that I've been eyeing. "Ian and Seth talking at length can't be a good thing. Even with Carson there to temper them, they're probably planning world domination."

"Maybe," Elia says doubtfully. "I don't know that they'd actually be interested in ruling the world, though—Seth's pretty antisocial."

"So is Ian," I agree. "They'd be more likely to destroy it than try to rule it."

My phone buzzes in my pocket with a text from my dad; I feel my heart melt when I see it's a picture of Freya, wrapped up in the adorable pink onesie that came with Elia's gift basket, a teddy bear lying in her crib beside her. Her tiny fingers are wrapped around one of Dad's thumbs, and there's a thin line of drool running down her cheeks.

I turn my phone to show Elia, who also melts at the sight. "Oh my *god*, that is too cute. You need to stop showing me pictures like that, my ovaries are probably overproducing eggs in response. I might need to get on stronger birth control."

I shrug. "So have your boys bag it on top of taking the pill."

Elia snorts. "Yeah, Seth would flat out refuse, and Carson would give me that irresistible pout. I'll just have to stop thinking about how adorable Freya is and hope that I don't somehow manifest a pregnancy."

I let out a sigh. "I should be getting back. I haven't seen her today, and I'm confident that our boys have resolved whatever had Ian in a tizzy last night. He looks less... murder-y."

Elia laughs. "Sounds good. Hey, you want to get drinks on Friday, just the two of us? I'm off to see Carson's mom on Saturday morning, then I'm going to New York that evening, but we should have a girls night before I go. Might as well take advantage of being able to drink before we're back to living and breathing Pandora's Box."

"New York?" I ask, raising my eyebrows. "Are you transferring to Juilliard or something?"

"God no," Elia replies. "I'm committed to Greywood, and I'd never leave you behind. We're doing a New York trip because Seth is annoyed that we didn't get to visit a lot of museums overseas, so I pointed out that we're a few hour's drive from an epicenter of art. He booked us a room at The Plaza and plans to spend the last few days of spring break museum-hopping. He promised to take me to see a performance at the New York City Ballet, too, so I'm very much looking forward to the trip."

"In that case, getting drinks on Friday sounds good," I say with a nod.

Ian's eyes laser in on me as soon as I step out of the store; I hold up my phone to show him the picture of Freya. "I want to go see her."

"Holy *fuck*," Carson says, glimpsing the photo and stepping closer for a better look. "That is... the most adorable little human in the existence of everything. What the hell?"

"I know, right?" I agree, smiling. "I'd invite you over, but my parents took some convincing to let Ian and Elia into the house, so I don't want to push it. Maybe next time you find yourselves up here you can meet the cutest human ever. See you two later. Seth, don't be too much of a psychopath and do *not* stress my girl Elia out."

"Your opinions, though worthless to me, are noted," Seth responds flatly.

Ian snaps his head around to glare at Seth; I grab Ian by the shirt-sleeve and pull him away before he starts something he can't finish. After a few tugs, he turns away from Seth, transfers all the bags he's carrying to one arm, then takes my hand in his free one.

"What did you buy that fills up *six bags*?" he asks, sounding faintly amazed. I cast a cursory glance at the bags: four are from baby stores, and the other two are a mix of dresses, shoes, and lingerie sets I think he'll appreciate.

I smile. "Dad handed me my old AMEX card last night, after dinner. It still has all of the high school allowance money I never spent, and he added some extra cash so that I could pick up some things for Freya. Most of my haul consists of baby clothes and toys and such, but I also got a few items for myself."

"You didn't spend any of your high school allowance money?" Ian repeats, frowning. "Why?"

I shrug. "I taught dancing classes for girls on the weekends and was a counselor at my old summer camp's youth section for a while, so I had enough to get by. I wasn't big on shopping or anything. I wanted to prove some of the crueler things that were said about me wrong. Besides, I didn't really have any girlfriends to go on shopping trips with or spend money with. Most of the time when I went out it was with my mom, and she'd pay. My parents aren't as rich as yours, but they do well enough, and Dad's business has been expanding steadily in recent years."

Ian's silent for a long moment. "I'm sorry I said those things to you," he says. "I'm sorry for being such a fucking idiot. I despise myself for my stupidity."

I wave a dismissive hand. "It's in the past. You were hurt, so you lashed out at the closest person to you. I'm not happy about it, if you ever behave like that again I'll castrate you, but I'm not angry anymore. I get it now, and I can live with it. Besides, you're a good fuck and have a magical dick, so I won't let old resentment get in the way of me getting laid."

Ian lets out a soft puff of laughter as we make our way through the parking lot. "Is that why you keep me around, Stein? For the sex?"

I make a humming noise as we slow to a stop beside his rented black Lexus. "Yeah, mainly," I say, opening the trunk.

Ian releases my hand to toss the shopping bags in, then shuts the trunk and grabs my hand again. I let him usher me into the back seat of the car, interested to see where this is going.

"Well, in that case, I think I should use what I'm best at to show you just how sorry I am, shouldn't I?" he murmurs, climbing in after me and closing the door.

As much as the thought of a good fuck in the backseat of the car appeals to me... "People will see."

"The windows are tinted, and we're in a secluded corner of the parking lot," Ian says. "And even if someone does see, who fucking cares?"

"I do!" I say, even as I let him lay me down on the butter-soft leather, push up my skirt, and spread my legs. "I don't want a public indecency charge staining my record!"

"Public indecency," Ian muses. "Fortunately for you, we both have friends in high places. Nothing will stick."

"But—"

"Hush," he murmurs, pulling my panties to the side. "I'm hungry. You didn't feed me a full breakfast, so now I need a snack to tide me over."

How can I resist that? "You really do like eating me out," I muse.

"You're my favorite thing to eat, Sugarplum," Ian agrees. "A little sweet, a little spicy, fucking addictive. If I could I'd spend the rest of my life buried between your thighs."

At the first touch of his tongue, I slap my hand against the window above my head, biting my lip to keep quiet as my back arches. Ian releases a growl of approval, brushing his tongue over my clit—softly at first, then with increasing pressure. He works me over slowly, tenderly, with utmost attention to my responses and the things he's learned I enjoy, until I explode all over his tongue. He kisses me to let me taste myself on him, rights my clothes, helps me into the passenger seat despite my shaky legs, and then we're off.

Chapter Forty-Two

Friday morning arrives, and an article is released that stirs the attention of the world. Written by a seasoned reporter from a prestigious newspaper, it's the kind of article that can topple careers and lives like a house of cards. I read it as I sip my morning coffee in the kitchen, side by side with my father who's reading a broadsheet newspaper. The words of the article cause me to choke on my coffee; Dad hands me a few napkins without looking away from whatever he's reading.

"Oh my god," I murmur, wiping at my chin with the napkins and blinking at the words on my screen.

The investigative reporter pulls no punches; instead, she outlines every accusation of sexual misconduct and assault that has been brought against Dennis Ajax in the last *twenty years*. The allegations are numerous, damning, and all originate from men—some even from vulnerable young boys. Among them is a ten-year-old who had confided in his parents that Dennis had touched him where no child should be touched and forced the boy to reciprocate. Despite the many cases that have been brought against Dennis, the legal system proved indifferent.

Ian's name isn't on the list, as he never called Dennis out for his behavior publicly or gave accounts of what Dennis did to him to anyone other than me, Seth, and Carson. My heart breaks for the other boys as much as it breaks for my Ian; their experiences are horrific and inhumane.

"Fucking Christ," Dad mutters, flipping over his newspaper. From the corner of my eye, I glimpse that he's reading the same article as I am: *OIL TYCOON'S BROTHER ACCUSED OF SEXUAL MIS-CONDUCT AND ASSAULT!*

Dad tosses aside his paper just as I put my phone down, feeling sick to my stomach.

"You read it?" Dad asks, glancing over at me.

I swallow hard. "I read it. It's going to cause waves of unrest in the oil business, both in this country and abroad. The Ajax Company is significant and world-renowned."

Dad makes a humming noise of agreement. "Isn't your friend, that nice American girl, with Carson Ajax? The heir to his family business?"

I nod. "She is. Carson's friends with Ian, and Ian works at the company. This is going to send everyone and everything into a tailspin, but it'll also mean justice to those who've had to go so long without it." I shake my head, frowning. "What is *wrong* with this world, Dad? Why is everyone so horrible?"

"There's good and evil abound in this world, milaya," Dad tells me. "The unfortunate truth is that evil has a quicker and easier path to power than good, because evil people aren't bound by the same morals and principles as good people are." He shakes his head, releasing a deep breath. "I'm going to go check on your mother." He presses a kiss to my cheek on his way out of the room.

As worry overtakes me, I pick up my phone and send Ian a text.

April: You okay?

Ian: Meet at the bridge.

I let my parents know I'm heading out for the day, finish my coffee, then take off for the bridge in a brisk jog. Ian's already there, in the very spot that was once *our* spot when we were kids, sitting on the splintering wooden boards of the bridge and gazing down at the trickling stream of water beneath him. He doesn't look up when I arrive, but he doesn't need to; I know that Ian can tell I'm here. Quietly, I take a seat beside him, legs hanging off the side of the bridge.

"Hey," I say gently.

"Sugarplum," he returns soberly, swinging an arm over my shoulder and tugging me close. He turns and buries his head in my neck, I lean my body against his and let him take what he needs from me.

"I saw the article."

"I figured," he murmurs, scraping his teeth over my neck. Seeming unsatisfied with that small touch, he readjusts and bites down, drawing a hiss from me even as my nipples perversely pebble and heat travels to the space between my legs. I know Ian likes leaving marks on me, and I sense he needs that small sense of control and ownership right now more than he usually does.

It's strange, the connection that Ian and I share. He's told me that he thinks he was born without an essential piece of his soul, a piece he believes resides within me. I'm not sure if that's true, but I am sure that we both need each other for different reasons. Right now, I'll let him do what he wants with me if that'll allow him to regain some semblance of control and find even momentary peace.

Still, I whimper when he doesn't let up on his bite and instead sinks his teeth even deeper, like a hungry lion that has a gazelle caught in its enormous jaw. I almost think he wants to draw blood, but he lets up when he's just shy of it. He presses a soft kiss to the tender spot, the gentle motion at total odds with the harsh way he bit into me like I'm a hunk of meat.

"Was the article a part of the plans you've been cooking up with Seth and Carson?" I ask him. "An exposé through a third party?"

"Yup," Ian confirms. "There was talk of getting rid of Dennis right off the bat, but I don't want that. It's too fast, too easy. I want him to hurt, April. I want him to suffer in the way that's most painful. To that pompous fuck, image is everything—it's why he has more plastic in his face than there is in the Atlantic. Now, he no longer has anything resembling a good image, and the world will see him for the fucking monster he is. He'll get arrested soon enough, but not before he experiences the full force of public scrutiny. A law firm will pick up the cases against him, get him imprisoned, and then, the real suffering will begin. I'll have him killed after a few years in the shittiest prison I can put him in, but I need him to lose everything before meeting his untimely end."

"Vengeful," I remark, my tone tipped with approval.

Ian lifts a shoulder carelessly. "I pride myself in evening scores with poetic, fitting methods. It's something Seth and I have in common." He pauses, pressing his nose to my hair and inhaling deeply. "You know the thing I hate Dennis most for?" he questions idly.

"Being a perverted monster?" I supply.

A puff of laughter tickles my ear as Ian shakes his head. "No. The thing that I hate Dennis most for is that his actions were what split us up. He made me feel so weak that I became obsessed with ridding myself of weaknesses, and you, Sugarplum, were the only thing in my life that could be considered a weakness. He pushed the first domino in a chain that toppled us. Granted, if I was a little less... *dark* and fucked in the head, I'd have never turned on you, but I did. There aren't many things in my life I regret, but I regret losing those years with you more than anything." He sighs. "I should've been your first everything. Your first kiss, your first fuck, your first love... he robbed me of that."

"You might not have had the first two, but you are my first love," I tell him honestly. "Other than dance, you're the great love of my life."

"Dance, hmm? Should I be wary of the competition?" Ian growls playfully. After a moment, he says, "Thank you for coming. I didn't think that the article would hit hard, but... well, Seth didn't tell me just how many things he dug up before passing on the info to a reporter. I figured there might be a few other boys Dennis hurt, but not this many."

I lean close to brush my lips over Ian's. "Maybe you won't even be the one to get him killed. He'll have all of America and a good chunk of the world gunning for his head now."

Ian's lips tip up. "Yeah, there is that. You have plans today?"

"Drinks tonight with Eliana, but nothing besides that," I say. "You?"

"Mm, I wanted to spend the whole day *and* night with you," Ian says. "I suppose I can consider giving you up. Only for a few hours. Contingent on the fact that you make it worth my while."

"Worth your while," I echo. "Does that mean blowing you really, *really* well?"

Ian smiles, the slant of his lips wolfish. "I think you can definitely give it a shot."

***

"That's the sixth time you've checked your phone tonight, babe," I tease Eliana, raising my eyebrows playfully. "I'm starting to take it personally."

Elia sighs, setting her phone down on the table and reaching for her drink. "Sorry. I'm just texting Carson to quadruple-check that he's okay. Seth glimpsed the texts and is, of course, annoyed that I'm giving Carson more attention than him, so now I'm messaging with both of them."

I let my eyes run over the many patrons of the small bar. It's a cute little spot that I discovered online, residing in the heart of downtown, not far from the corporate sector. There's a mix of young people who look ready to party and customers who look like they came straight out of the office crowding the bar and surrounding tables. Elia and I are tucked away at a table in the corner of the bar, beside a row of windows facing the city street.

"How is everything going with the article?" I ask Elia, looking back to her.

She glances at her phone longingly, though she doesn't touch it. "Complicated. Carson's dad's board of directors is screaming for his head and demanding that he remove his brother. The old man is fighting it, but only half-heartedly. Now, Carson's intervening, using some stuff he has on his dad to make him force that sack of shit Dennis out on the street."

I feel my brows crease. "If you want to reschedule tonight, I'd totally get it."

"No!" Elia says, firmly shaking her head and reaching for her apple martini. "No, I've been looking forward to our girl's night. Carson's assured me he's okay a million times, I'm just... well, sensitive when it comes to him. And Seth is sensitive when my attention isn't perfectly split between the two of them." She shakes her head, sighing. "Have I told you how Seth reacted when he walked in on Carson finger-feeding me sushi a few weeks ago?"

"I can guess," I remark dryly. "Seth picked you up, sat you on his lap, grabbed the plate of sushi, and started feeding you himself. He probably said that it was only fair he'd also get a turn."

"Yep," Elia says with a short nod. "That about sums it up. Carson's more laid back because he knows I love him to the moon and beyond; Seth needs constant reminders of my affection, usually through physical contact."

"Ian's the same way," I admit sagely. "He gets pissed off when he isn't touching me. He gets more pissed off when he doesn't see me for a few hours, like I'm giving him some personal affront." I shake my head, sighing. "Anti-social men. Gotta love them, but dealing with them can be a lot."

Elia smiles fondly. "They're totally worth it, though." We both sip our drinks. "Did you see the email Sanders sent out?" she asks. "He only sent it to the leads of the cast, but he put out feelers for how a summer tour of Pandora's Box would be received and got *fantastic* feedback. He's started fundraising for it, and apparently, he got the base donations for a four-week tour within twenty-four hours."

I nod, smiling. "I saw it. Now we have enough funding for a six-week tour, and a few theatres in Europe expressed interest in hosting us. It looks like we're gonna have a busy summer, babe," I say. "Totally worth every minute, though. Imagine if we manage to land a spot at the Royal Opera House of London?"

I still have the ballerina figurine Ian got me from there, going there is on my bucket list, *dancing the stage* would be one of the big pillars of my career. And doing it before I hit my twenties would be *beyond* incredible.

"It would be so amazing..." Eliana trails off as her eyes lock onto the entrance and widen. Her posture immediately stiffens, and she swallows hard, face paling.

Worried, I whip my head in the same direction, only to feel a similar, visceral change overcome me at the sight of the well-dressed, heinous man that just walked through the door; Dennis fucking Ajax, in the flesh. Child molester, pervert, pond-scum that deserves to rot in jail for a good long time before he upgrades to rotting in hell.

He looks like shit; he sways and staggers a little, as if drunk. His eyes have a distinct glaze as they lock onto me, before slowly drifting over to Eliana. Those eyes darken with an unleashed rage, and I know in my very bones that he's not here for just a chat.

"Elia," I say lowly, "leave. Go out the back entrance. Call Carson and Seth."

I've seen the look that Dennis's wearing right now only one other time in my life; it's a look filled with dark malice and leaves no doubt that he's itching to cause destruction. He could have a knife hidden in the folds of his wool jacket, or something worse. I stiffen even further as he begins weaving through the patrons, his steps unsteady as he makes his way towards my table.

"Elia, *go*," I say harshly. "*Now*."

Eliana swiftly stands from her seat, but she doesn't make it more than one step before Dennis's in front of her, shielding her exit with his body. Her eyes dart around and she swallows hard. "Move away from me *right now* or I'll scream."

A cruel, callous smile pulls on Dennis's lips as he reaches into his pocket and withdraws... *fuck me*, a gun. I grab Elia's wrist and pull her back in time for Dennis to say, "I hope you do." He aims the gun and pulls the trigger.

***

Ian

I shoot off my third text in the last twenty minutes to April, growing increasingly agitated that she hasn't yet responded. I know she's on a girl's night with Elia and I forced myself to let her go, having no interest in isolating her. Still, I'm used to getting prompt responses from her, so her complete lack of attention doesn't sit well with me.

I'm seated on my living room sofa, with Seth on the opposite end of the couch. He scrolls through something on his laptop while also checking his phone every fifteen seconds. Carson's in the corner of the room, talking lowly on the phone, discussing company business with a board member.

"You know, if we put our heads together, we could probably dissolve the friendship between April and Elia," Seth comments idly. "The time they spend with each other detracts from the time they spend with us."

I let out a deep sigh. "As much as the idea appeals to me... April would be hurt if her friendship with Eliana fell apart. So would Eliana, which you should know. Leaving the status quo intact is the only way to avoid bringing either of them pain."

Seth gives me a faintly disgusted look. "When the fuck did *you* get morals?"

"I didn't," I deadpan. "But I did finally catch April, and she's always been my moral compass. Ergo, I think about things that might be inconveniencing, but are ultimately good."

"Uh, guys," Carson says, walking over to us. "We have a problem. I just got word from a contact that my uncle was seen disembarking a private jet at the local airport here. He's evaded the paparazzi for now, but a few people still spotted him. He was sighted about an hour ago."

Seth sits up straight, eyes hardening as he stares at Carson. A feeling of wrongness niggles at my gut as I glance at my phone again, sending April yet another text, this time giving her a heads up to keep a look out. My intuition tells me that something's off about this situation. It could very well be the case that Dennis flew in to appeal to Carson directly and beg to keep his place in the family company, but I think it's something more. I'm willing to bet that Dennis is looking for vengeance right now, and he might be prepared to do horrific things in order to achieve it. Indirect things that would hurt me, his former victim who's been antagonizing him for weeks.

I call April, holding the phone to my ear, counting the rings while trying to breathe deeply.

The call goes to voicemail. My heart speeds up in my chest and sweat breaks out over the back of my neck.

"*Fuck*," Seth growls, reading something on his laptop. "Fuck!"

"What?" I demand.

Seth shakes his head. "Turn on the TV, local news. This shit better be fucking wrong..."

It takes me a few seconds to get the TV clicked on and turned to the news station that reports local events going on at all hours of the day and night. My heart drops into my stomach as a cheery blonde reporter in a studio says. "In other news, there is a hostage situation underway in one of the downtown bars of Hartford. Twenty minutes ago, gunshots went off within; the premise was vacated by all but the assailant, who we believe to be Dennis Ajax, and two college students. For those of you who haven't heard, Dennis Ajax was called out in a national newspaper just this morning—"

I'm up in an instant, not needing to hear the rest as I sprint for the door. Seth and Carson are right behind me, both letting loose impressive combinations of swear words. I'm in such a rush I barely remember to grab my car keys.

"Fuck," Carson says, staring at his phone. "The bar Dennis just *shot up* is the same one where Elia and April are having their girl's night. God *fucking* dammit, *shots went off...*"

"If Eliana has a single scratch on her, I am going to torture your uncle to death," Seth says, his voice a low growl. "This will not be accepted—"

"Shut up and get in my fucking car!" I snap. "We need to get to the bar *now*."

I hop into the driver's seat; Seth gets into the passenger, silently seething, while Carson gets into the back, making several calls on his phone—presumably to Eliana—all of which go unanswered. I break every goddamn speed limit in existence during the seemingly endless drive to the bar, finally understanding how April must've felt when we were rushing to get to her mom.

Seth continues throwing out threats, his version of panic, while Carson grows increasingly hysterical with each call he places that goes to voicemail. I tune both of them out, focusing on the road, growling at the downtown traffic. Four blocks away from the bar, when I hit a jam, I growl, "*Fuck this*," double-park my car by the sidewalk, then get out and start sprinting to the bar. Seth and Carson follow behind, but I pay them no mind; my sole focus is getting to April.

Flashing red and blue lights cover the entire block around the bar, with a barricade surrounding the building that has drawn several puzzled bystanders. The local police chief stands at the barricade closest to the door, talking through a microphone, demanding that Dennis surrender himself. I push my way through the crowd until I'm next to the officer.

"I need to get into that building," I say without preamble. If I'm in there, I can protect April and find a way to overpower Dennis.

The officer blanches, cutting off mid-rant, and lowers the microphone. "Do you know what's going on in there, son? It's an active crime scene with two undergrad girls and one crazy fucker—"

"That crazy fucker happens to be my uncle," Carson says smoothly, stepping forward. "One of the girls is my girlfriend, the other is Ian's," he says, gesturing to me. "Let us in and we can help diffuse the situation, distract Dennis Ajax so he can be detained."

"I can't let you go in, I'm in the middle of a fuckin' hostage negotiation—"

Seth doesn't have the same restraint as Carson. He looks like he's about to grab the officer by his neck.

"If you don't let us go in," I tell the officer, "Dennis will kill those girls." His eyes narrow, and I continue. "He's out for revenge against me, the surest way to get it is by hurting the person I love most. The other girl is there accidentally, but she happens to be dating Dennis's nephew. Carson Ajax is set to take over the company Dennis is currently getting thrown out of. Now, if you want the deaths of those girls on your conscience, fine. But keep in mind that I will do everything in my power to make sure everyone knows you had a chance to avert this crisis and didn't act when it was most prudent. So, officer, what's it going to be? Will you be sending us in, or taking the fall when two body bags come out?"

"You insolent little—"

"Pardon me, officer," a new voice coated with a thick Russian accent interrupts, "but I believe we ought to have a quick chat."

CHAPTER FORTY-THREE

April

"You know what I find funniest?" Dennis asks, his tone borderline hysterical as he stares at a frightened Eliana. "The fact that my fucking nephew has the balls to call me out and demand my exile from the company, when he's the one in a goddamn *menage* with *you*."

After firing shots at the ceiling and scaring away all the other patrons, Dennis forced both me and Elia to retreat to the back corner of the bar, away from any windows. Now, he sits across from us at a table, alternating between pointing the gun at me and pointing it at Elia.

Outside, flashing red and blue lights alert us to the presence of the police, but Dennis either doesn't notice them or is beyond caring. I think I hear the sound of a police officer demanding that Dennis surrender himself, but I can't be sure—the bulk of my attention is going towards trying to figure out how I'm going to get Elia and me out of this clusterfuck alive.

"You're Carson's good little whore, aren't you? Spreading your legs to better your career?" Dennis taunts Elia, shoving the barrel of his gun towards her. Elia's lips part with a gasp, but she doesn't respond, seeming too stunned to speak. I need to redirect Dennis's attention before he pulls the trigger.

"She's a consenting adult, which is more than what can be said for the boys *you* assaulted, one of whom happens to be the love of my life," I say blandly.

Dennis swings the gun around to point it at me, baring his teeth. "I barely even touched Ian, and he goes and tips off a reporter about me? I *know* he's behind the article. That little fuck's been taunting me ever since I got to Vermont. Now he's gone and set all this into motion for what, revenge? To get back at me? Well, I'm gonna fucking get back at him. Him *and* my nephew. What I haven't decided is which one of you I'm going to kill first. Ian's whore or Carson's."

"If we're going by the guiltiest party, you ought to turn that gun on yourself and pull the trigger," I say calmly. "After all, Elia and I don't hurt children."

"April, stop talking," Elia whispers, horrified.

I take her hand under the table and give a quick squeeze of reassurance before releasing it. If one of us is going to get shot tonight, it will be me. I can handle a bullet so long as it doesn't land somewhere lethal; I can't say the same about Elia. She's already been through so much this year, I can't bear to see her go through more.

"Listen to your friend, *whore*, and stop talking," Dennis hisses, cocking his weapon and setting the bottom of it on the surface of the table. Hope threads through my chest as I see an opportunity unfold with his careless gesture. If I can get Dennis to push that gun forward, it'll be within reach, and I can disarm him. It's a risky move, but if I can pull it off, I'll have the gun. Then, I'll be shooting him in some *very* interesting places.

"Why? My words hitting too close to home?" I ask casually, forcing a yawn. "You know, Denny, when Ian told me about what you did to him out on that beach... all I could think was how low your self-esteem must be for you to go after a little boy." I give a short, cruel laugh, pretending not to notice as Dennis's gun slides forward half an inch. I casually brace my elbows on the table and lean my chin on my hands, cocking my head to the side as I run my eyes over his face. "I mean... could you not get anyone in your own age range to sleep with you? Or are you really *that* fucked in the head to go after a goddamn *child?*"

"You don't know what you're talking about!" Dennis bellows, throwing his hands in the air, lifting the gun off the table with the gesture. When he waves it around, I'm almost afraid it'll misfire, but it doesn't, and I force myself to be still. He's already drunk, which will foul his aim and slow his reflexes; if I can just get my hand around that goddamn gun and disarm him, this will be over.

He slams his gun back on the table, *almost* close enough for me to reach.

"You think I didn't try being normal, bitch? *I did.* It didn't fucking work. I'm not the monster that the bullshit article made me out to be, but we're all animals with instincts. The only difference between you and me is that I occasionally let mine take over. I haven't for *years,* though." He scoffs, upper lip curling, and the gun travels that final bit forward.

He opens his mouth to speak, and several things happen in quick succession. I lunge across the table, arm raised in preparation to pulverize his wrist; the door to the bar slams open with a bang; startled, Dennis pulls the trigger; my elbow crashes into his wrist, breaking bone. Searing pain explodes in my side, my hoarse cry intermixes with

Dennis's yelp of agony as the gun falls from his limp hand and clatters onto the table.

I sweep my arm across the table, pushing the gun to the floor, then give it a kick with my foot to get it away from Dennis. It slides off into a corner of the bar. With a shout, Dennis lunges for it, while a wave of dizziness overcomes me, and I become aware of wetness seeping out of my wound and staining my shirt. Elia cries out and grabs my shoulders, stabilizing me as I start to keel over sideways. She catches my weight as I crumple to the floor, my breathing harsh, heart racing, the pain in my side expanding until it becomes unbearable.

Still, I force my eyes sideways, silently praying that Dennis doesn't get to the gun. He's an inch away from it, on his knees, fumbling for it beneath a table while cradling his injured hand to his side. But the very person who burst through the door intervenes, delivering a brutal kick to Dennis's face. The miserable bastard falls over, whimpers, and moans; Ian stands over the fallen monster and presses a foot to Dennis's neck, panting, his face flushed with fury.

"April? April!" Eliana screeches. "Are you okay—I, fuck, I don't know what to do!"

"Pressure," I hiss. "Ball up your hands and press on the hole as hard as you can—" I cut off with a scream as Eliana follows my instructions, which makes Ian's head turn sharply in my direction. He looks torn between restraining Dennis and running to me.

Several more figures come through the door, though none of them are wearing police uniforms. Seth Balor, Carson Ajax, and... Jesus fuck, I must be hallucinating the third male who steps inside, dressed in a dark trench coat, his stride slow and demeanor refined. *What the hell is Sergei goddamn Novikov doing here?*

"Are you hurt?" Seth demands, rushing to Eliana. "Is any of that blood yours, Elia?"

"No!" Elia cries, tears streaming down her cheeks.

A low numbness takes up residence within me as the pain from my wound begins to fade, replaced by a strange warmth. It takes me a few beats to realize that the warmth comes from *my blood*, which is now forming a pool around me.

"I need... to get to..." I cut off with a cough. "Hospital," I force myself to finish.

"Eliana, are you *sure* none of that blood's—"

"It's not!" Elia screeches, cutting Seth off. "April protected me. *Help her!* I don't know what to do!"

Seth's jaw flexes as he turns his gaze to me, squinting at my torso. "Move your hands," he tells Elia. She follows instructions; a low moan escapes me as a fresh round of pain eats away at the numbness. Seth lifts my blouse to look at the wound. Lips thinning, he tears off a section of my shirt, balls it up, and presses down with a vigor that draws another scream from me.

"Quiet," he hisses. "You've lost a lot of blood, you'll need a transfusion. There's an ambulance waiting outside, medics should be here in a moment. I don't think the bullet hit anything—"

"*Get your hands off of my fucking woman,*" Ian hisses, dropping to his knees beside me, panicked eyes looking me over.

"I move my hands, she bleeds out," Seth says, his tone far too calm for the circumstances. "Carson, make yourself useful and get the fucking medics in here with a stretcher. The police, though..."

"Will be kept away by my team," I think I hear Sergei say. "Don't worry about them—for the time being, *I'm* the sheriff in town."

All I see is a blond blur as Carson darts out of the bar; my vision begins to darken around the edges, and my breathing becomes shallower as the taste of blood fills my mouth. Ian's hands join Seth's in pressing on my wound—that's the last straw for my consciousness, which leaves me in a rush, replaced by dark oblivion.

***

"Fuuuuuck." The word escapes me the second that I awaken from a dark sleep. A wave of pain steadily pulses over my navel, originating from the wound in my side. My lips are dry, my throat is sore, *everything* hurts. For a moment, I contemplate whether or not death might be a welcomed reprieve from this torture. A steady, irritating beep comes from behind me, beckoning me to get up so I can make it stop.

"Oh god," I mutter, wincing as I try to pry my eyes open. It's not an easy task; they seem determined to remain closed, but my determination to figure out a way to turn off that goddamn noise is much stronger.

"She's awake," I hear a voice somewhere near me say—a familiar voice that it only takes me a few moments to place as belonging to my father. I squint my blurry eyes, giving my head a shake to try to clear it, then grimace as that sends a new round of pain washing over me.

"Papa?" I question, my voice raspy and unpleasant even to my own ears. "What happened..." I trail off as my eyes lock on another figure that I only know by name and, previously, by pictures in the media. Sergei Novikov, infamous Bratva boss who I called in a favor to several years ago.

"Zdrastvuete, April," Sergei greets, taking a step away from my father. The two men are in the corner of the room, where they appear to have been in deep conversation before getting interrupted by me waking up. "Lovely work you did in the bar; stealing the gun was an impressive maneuver, even though you got a bullet for it," Sergei

compliments. His eyes glimmer with something that I might think was respect, if his expression wasn't so... flat. Not careless, but numb.

"Milaya," Dad greets, briskly crossing the room to me and taking a seat on my bed, by my legs. Even the slight dip in the hospital mattress is enough to make me wince, though I try to mask the reaction. "How are you feeling?"

"In need of *much* stronger drugs than this."

Sergei begins to chuckle. "You remind me a lot of my wife, Kira. She reacted similarly when waking up in the hospital after being abducted by some of our enemies." A smile spreads on his lips, transforming his face from handsome yet unnervingly empty to something beautiful. "She's quite curious to meet you while she's still in the states."

"Uh..." I clear my throat. "Excuse me, but what the fuck is going on here? Respectfully, Mr. Novikov, what are you doing here?" I think back to the bar, blinking several times. "What were you doing in the bar in the first place?"

"Ah," Sergei says, pocketing his hands. "That was business, fortunately it happened to cross paths with your situation, else I suspect the idiot who shot you might've gotten himself arrested. It would've been more difficult to get to him then. Dennis Ajax happened to get involved with one of my dealings, and he made the fatal mistake of crossing me." Sergei gives a casual shrug. "I was in the states for a visit, figured I might as well kill two birds with one stone, as it were. Dennis will be indisposed for the foreseeable future, he won't bother you again."

I wrinkle my nose. "I'd ask if Dennis is in police custody, but I know that's not how you manage your affairs."

Sergei laughs again. "Quite right, April, it isn't. After a chat with the police, they agreed to hand Dennis over to me and mine—he'll be dealt with in a manner befitting the organization he was stupid enough to cross." He pauses. "I'm going to make an example of him, you won't be seeing him again." Sergei tips a nod to my father. "Lovely to see you both. Maksim, do keep in touch. April, I hope you get well soon. My wife will send flowers and a basket." With that, he walks out of the room.

I slowly turn my head towards my father, puzzled. "So... you're in contact with Sergei Novikov again?"

Papa shrugs. "Sergei has plenty of above-board business dealings, and he'd like to sign on as a silent partner for one of my new ventures. We're in discussions for that."

"But I thought you swore off that life."

Dad makes a face. "I won't be an enforcer again, that's for damn sure, but Sergei is a good man, milaya. He understands the value of family. Many times, he could've caused problems for me, and instead he has helped me repeatedly. He also has a very smart wife to keep him in check." He reaches out to tuck a strand of hair behind my ear. "Enough business talk. The nurse should be coming in soon, we'll get you some morphine." He pauses. "What you did at the bar, throwing yourself in the line of fire to protect your friend... part of me wants to shake you for your stupidity, the other part deeply admires your loyalty. It's a very fine quality, and in such short supply these days."

"Oh, shit, Eliana," I say, reaching a hand to grasp his. "How is Elia? Is she hurt?" I don't remember seeing her harmed, but after getting shot I wasn't in an observant headspace.

"She's perfectly fine," Dad assures me. "Shaken and beating herself up for not protecting you, but then again, she doesn't have Russian blood in her veins. It's in our nature to take charge when situations call for it. She and her boyfriends are in the waiting room, along with that gutter-rat who's insisted on attaching himself to you—"

"His name's Ian, Papa," I say, even as humor warms my chest. "He's not a gutter rat, he's the love of my life."

Dad grimaces. "*Gospodi*, don't get started. I still hold hope that in a few years you'll realize that he's so far beneath your league it's comedic, and decide to—" He cuts off as the door swings open, and a frazzled-looking Ian steps in. His clothes are rumpled and bloodstained, there are splatters of blood on his cheek, and his eyes are wide and almost manic as they take me in.

"See? He doesn't even dress for you properly," Dad comments, frowning.

Ian doesn't respond; he hurries across the room and squats beside the bed, looking my face and body over with the utmost attention to detail, swallowing harshly. "April," he breathes. My name is both a prayer and a curse on his lips as he shakes his head. "In the future, do *not* throw yourself in front of a loaded gun, *ever*. Jesus fucking Christ, do you know how *worried* I've been? You could've *died!*"

Dad cocks his head at Ian, appearing contemplative. "Perhaps we can find some common ground, after all. Do lecture her well, boy." He stands from the bed, smoothing down the front of his jacket. "Your mother and sister are at home. Mom wanted to come, but we don't want Freya in the hospital where she can pick up an illness. I'll call and tell her you've woken up." He glares at Ian. "Take care of my daughter."

"I need you to not yell at me right now," I tell Ian once Dad's left. "I know you're mad I got hurt, I'm not exactly ecstatic about it either, but I would much rather it have been me than Elia. She's been through enough this year. I already know from experience that I can take some pain, she's sweeter and more delicate."

Ian sighs, taking the place on the bed that my dad vacated and leaning over me, carefully positioning his hands to bracket my body.

Slowly, he leans his forehead against mine. "They gave you a blood transfusion," he says gruffly. "They had to dig the bullet out of you. It's a miracle it didn't hit anything important. I nearly lost my fucking mind."

"I'm sorry," I whisper. "Truly, I wish you didn't have to see that. I wish that hadn't happened. But Dennis is permanently out of the picture, and I'll be fine." I pause. "Right? I'll be fine? I haven't actually gotten my prognosis yet."

"Yes," Ian breathes, ghosting his lips over mine. "You'll be okay. It'll take several weeks for you to recover, and you'll be off the stage for a while, but you'll be perfectly fine aside from that. Just... don't scare me like that again. I couldn't do this without you, April. Without you, I live a half-life that's utterly meaningless. Not even a half-life, more like a quarter life. You're the biggest piece of my soul, Sugarplum, if you die you take it with you. So don't."

"I'll do my best," I murmur. "I'm glad it's over and that Dennis is gone from our lives. Even more glad that Sergei took over, since that probably means that Dennis will be getting tortured for a good long while before being killed. Do you know what his dealings with Sergei were?"

"Borrowing money he couldn't repay from one of Sergei's operations in the states," Ian replies, pulling away from me and sitting upright. "Using a fake identity to try to fool Sergei, too. Bad call on Dennis's part. Sergei is not a man to be lied to or trifled with. He's dangerous in many ways. When he found out that he'd been bamboozled and discovered that the person bamboozling him was a child molester... well. Mr. Novikov is known for making bloody examples out of rapists and molesters."

I feel a smile pull on my lips. "This probably makes me a terrible person, but the thought of Dennis undergoing the brand of torture that a Bratva boss, the infamously sadistic Sergei Novikov no less, will subject him to makes me feel warm and fuzzy inside."

Ian's lips quirk. "Me too, April. Me too."

A nurse chooses that moment to walk in; she gives me painkillers via an injection, adjusts the monitor behind me so that it stops with the incessant beeping, and then slips away. She's only gone for thirty seconds when Elia walks in, accompanied by Seth. My heart clenches at seeing the dark circles under her eyes along with tear stains on her cheeks.

"Elia," I say softly. "I'm glad you're okay."

Elia lets out a small, barely audible sob, then runs over to me, totally disregarding Ian and Seth, both of whom grumble something or other at her.

"I was so scared," she says, looking desperately like she wants to hug me but not doing it because she doesn't want to hurt me. "God, I thought you were going to die in that bar. How are you feeling? Are you in pain? When I was in the hospital, there was a lot of pain, until I got morphine that made me feel fuzzy and really lovey—"

"Elia, I'm fine," I tell her. "Really. Everything's fine. I promise. Give me a hug."

Elia blinks several times and carefully leans in, gently resting her arms on my shoulders. "I'm so glad you're okay," she murmurs in my ear before pulling back. Seth promptly steps forward and pulls her away from me, into his arms. She sends him a dark look over her shoulder, which he ignores.

"You took a bullet so Elia didn't have to," he tells me. "For that, you have my gratitude. You need something, you know where to find me. I have an attractive skillset when it comes to darker dealings."

For Seth Balor, those words are as good as a declaration of unending friendship, and a confirmation of loyalty. I suppose the only way to truly earn his loyalty is to save his or Elia's life. Anything else is fairly worthless to him.

"Thank you," I tell him. "And thanks for holding pressure, even though it took Eliana begging you to get you to give me any attention while I was bleeding out."

He doesn't have the sensibility, or perhaps emotional range, to look abashed as he shrugs. "She will always be my priority."

"Seth," Elia says, frowning. "We need to work on your interpersonal skills. You can't be this mean to everyone."

"I'm not being mean, I'm being honest," he replies, looking down at her. His eyes soften a fraction of an inch as they stare at each other. "You do keep telling me the value of honesty, Little Muse, don't you? Would you prefer I lie?"

Elia sighs; Ian clears his throat. "If you can take your moment somewhere else, I think April needs to rest."

I would snark something about Ian speaking for me, but the injection of pain meds *is* making me tired. I'm ready to pass out right here and now, but I manage to keep myself awake long enough to say bye to Elia and Seth, and make Ian promise to stay here with me.

"I don't plan on leaving you alone at any point in the near future," Ian assures me. "Or ever. If I could, I'd superglue you to my side so I could always be with you."

"That's endearing in a psychotic way," I murmur affectionately. "You really are crazy, you know that?"

"Proudly," Ian replies. "Sleep, Sugarplum. I'll be here when you wake up."

EPILOGUE

April

I stay in the hospital for another week at the insistence of Ian and my father. I receive daily physical therapy to help me get safely back on my feet. Upon my return home, I'm waited on hand and foot by Ian, Dad, and even Mom, who gives me a tearful welcome. Most of her energy is being taken up by Freya, though, which is a relief because I don't like being coddled or smothered. Ian and I stay at my home for a week after spring break ends, at which point I'm given the all-clear to walk on my own and travel by plane. Upon my return to Greywood, I'm right back to PT—this time at a local hospital.

I still attend dance classes even though I can't participate much; thankfully, Sanders takes six weeks after break to make adjustments to the show, so I'm cleared for dance a week before performances start up again.

On our re-opening night, Sanders makes the *very* exciting announcement that we have enough funding for an eight-week tour over the summer, and that there will be masters from both the Bolshoi Theatre and London Royal Ballet in attendance for our performance, to scout whether or not they'd like us to dance on their stages during our tour. We're already booked for a week in NYC to dance on the stage at Lincoln Center; apparently New York City ballet is considering adapting our production for themselves, though Sanders is still on the fence about selling them rights.

Re-opening night goes phenomenally well; we have an eleven-minute standing ovation at the end of the show. Ian makes his pride very clear when he fucks me that night, staring into my eyes the entire time, telling me how much he loves me and how proud he is not only of me but of the fact that he gets to call me his.

Sergei Novikov attends a performance the following week, sending lavish gift baskets and gorgeous bouquets to both me and Elia. When the Bolshoi Theatre officially extends their invitation for us to dance on their stage for five days during our summer tour, I get the vague sense that he had some influence over the decision.

Ian insists that he'll be joining me for my summer tour, taking whatever time he can with me. I finally allow him to have a week of my time in Scotland after the UK portion of our tour, which will finish off our travels for the summer. I talk him down from renting out an entire castle for us, though he still insists on renting a country manor in the highlands and setting up a castle tour to go in tandem with the tour that Elia, Seth, and Carson plan to complete.

We sleep together on every leg of the tour, fuck every chance we get in any nook and cranny that we manage to find, as well as in our shared hotel rooms at night. I FaceTime with my parents regularly, getting to see the growth of Freya every step of the way. She gets stronger with each day, more vocal with each passing week, and seeing the love shining in my parents' eyes does something to me.

At the very end of the summer, two weeks before we return to Greywood, Ian and I sit in a lovely little restaurant in Florence. We decided to continue our travels through Europe even after Scotland; traveling with each other has been on our bucket list since we were kids, it made sense to knock some locations off our extensive travel list while we were already in Europe.

We're sharing a glass of wine after a very filling dinner during which I gorged myself on the most delicious pasta and roasted chicken I've ever had the pleasure of tasting. The restaurant is a cozy spot on the outskirts of the city, rustic and beautiful. Dark woods make up the interior, dim lightbulbs shaded by red lamps hang from the ceiling, and a candelabra sits on every table, of which there are only about a dozen. The intimate ambience of the place is completed with a violinist and pianist in the corner of the restaurant, playing classical Italian melodies.

"So," Ian says. "How are you enjoying Europe so far? Everything you'd hoped for?"

"And more," I agree. "I want to come back soon. We should retire here once we're old, or at least have a house here."

Ian gives me a strange, searching look, followed by a slow smile. "You're saying you want to retire with me?"

I give him a droll look. "Even if I didn't want to, you'd find a way to make it happen. You're unstoppable."

"When it comes to you, absolutely," he agrees. "Now say it out loud."

I suppress a smile and decide to play coy. "Say what out loud? That I love Italy? I like Scotland a lot, too. And Russia. Basically, everywhere I've been this summer is amazing—"

"*April*," Ian growls. "Be a good girl and tell me that you want to retire with me."

I let out a light laugh, sipping my wine, enjoying watching him sweat. "You're adorable when you get grumbly. Yes, Ian, I want to retire with you. I love you, I don't want to ever be apart from you." I pause. "Besides, traveling with you means getting the best treatment everywhere, staying at the best places and seeing the best sights, so I figure I might as well use you for all your worth."

Ian flicks his gaze up to the ceiling, shaking his head. "You know, Sugarplum, you never make it easy." He sighs. "That's one of the many things I love about you. As it happens, I have every intention of retiring with you, as well. I want to spend my life with you—I *will* spend my life with you, no doubt there." He inhales a deep breath, and I feel my brows furrow as an uncharacteristic nervousness flickers over his expression. Ian isn't the type to get anxious.

A flutter starts up in my chest as he slowly vacates his seat, takes two steps around the table, and then lowers to one knee in front of me. My eyes widen as I stare at him, heart pounding and everything within me tensing for what I know is about to come. I knew we'd be here eventually, but so soon...

"April Maksimilliana Steinovichna," he says, using my full Russian given name with an impressively good accent. I try to contain my gasp as he reaches into his pocket, withdrawing a velvet ring box. "Sugarplum. There aren't words to describe to you how much I love you, how much I *need* you. You're part of me—the *best* part of me. I don't want to go through life without you, I *can't* go through life without you. You complete me in ways I never thought were possible. I am so in love with you that I think I'm insane with it, sick with it, but if loving you is a fatal disease, I'd die a happy man."

A small sob escapes me. Trust Ian to use death in a proposal and still make it sound terribly romantic.

"I want you by my side. Today, tomorrow, forever. I want to build my life with you." He cracks open a box, showcasing the most gorgeous ring I've ever laid eyes on. A blood red diamond sits proudly in the center of a white-gold band, surrounded by several smaller white and black diamonds in the shape of a blossoming flower. So beautiful, so perfect for both of us.

"Marry me," he says.

I swallow thickly, trying to blink back oncoming tears. "Yes. *Fuck* yes—I mean, yeah, okay. That would be perfectly adequate, I guess—"

He cuts me off with a searing kiss.

About the Author

Rose likes to write about complex, oftentimes twisted main characters who grow stronger together on whichever journey they take. Watch out for sexy morally grey heroes and sharp, intelligent heroines within settings ranging from fantasy to academia to the underworld of organized crime.

When Rose isn't writing or listening to the whispers (or shouts) of her characters in her mind, she's drinking coffee, throwing herself at anything nature-related (especially in the winter, when there are no spiders or mosquitos to attack her), and reading.

If you'd like to connect with Rose, join her Facebook group: https://www.facebook.com/share/1AgAcE5efaztPjLq/

To stay updated on her upcoming releases, you can subscribe to her newsletter: https://dashboard.mailerlite.com/forms/892614/13013 6824777541065/share

If you'd like to browse her books and get access to VIP content such as excerpts from upcoming books or deleted scenes, visit her website: https://rosegravestone.com/

If you're interested in reading her works-in-progress (pre-edits and re-writes for publishing) she has a Patreon where she posts chapters of books she's working on: https://patreon.com/rosesreaders